small Magics

Erik Buchanan

For Colleen
Enjoy!

Erik Buchanan
World Fantasy 2012

www.dragonmoonpress.com
www.erikbuchanan.ca

Small Magics
Copyright © 2007 Erik Buchanan
Cover Art © 2010 Alex White

All rights reserved. Reproduction or utilization of this work in any form, by any means now known or hereinafter invented, including, but not limited to, xerography, photocopying and recording, and in any known storage and retrieval system, is forbidden without permission from the copyright holder.

ISBN 10 1-896944-48-5 Print Edition
ISBN 13 978-1-896944-48-7

ISBN 10 1-896944-50-7 Electronic Edition
ISBN 13 978-1-896944-50-0

Printed and bound in Canada or the United States

www.dragonmoonpress.com
www.erikbuchanan.ca

small Magics

Erik Buchanan

Dedication

For my wife Sara, who gave me the time to work.

For my dear friends and readers Chet, Kim and Katrina, who gave me their honest opinions and keen eyes.

For my daughter Maggie, who is too young yet to read.

And for Mr. Robert Currie, who 20 years ago showed me that I had a talent for the written word.

Acknowledgements

Special thanks to my editors Briana and Gabrielle, for all their fine work, for my readers Chet, Kim, and Katrina, whose keen observations and honest opinions helped make this a better book, for my wife who put up with the sight of my back as I worked at the computer too many nights to count. Also to the fine folks at Rapier Wit and Fight Directors Canada who taught me about rapier play and many other things. And above all to Gwen Gades, publisher of Dragon Moon Press, for taking the chance on this book.

Prologue

Dear Thomas,

We greatly enjoyed your last letter. It is good to know that your life at the Academy is still as interesting as ever. We wish we could hear from you more often, but we know you are doing exams and one cannot fault you for spending your time in study. Your mother and brother are well and your mother wishes me to say how pleased we are at the work you are doing, which we are. It is not every family that can boast of a son studying both the law and philosophy, let alone one that has done as well as you.

To the meat of the matter: come home! Your mother and I haven't seen you in four years and that is far too long. A summer away from your studies will do you no harm, and I should like to see you while there is still some of the boy you were left in your features. Not to mention, I should like an opportunity to show off the youngest son I've talked so much about.

If you can be here for the start of May, you'll have a chance to meet Bishop Malloy, who, between ourselves, is a pompous creature and something too proud for one of the High Father's servants. The bishop will be in Elmvale during the May festival to appoint the new priest for our parish, and will certainly be visiting our home. I have been working to secure a contract to supply all robes for the High Father's churches in our district, and expect to close the deal when he visits. I have no doubt he would like to meet an able young man like yourself.

Come home, Thomas. You can show off the skills you've gained—though not, I hasten to add, those fencing skills of which you seem so inordinately proud. I know the study of fencing is required at the Academy, but I have always held that swordplay is not the proper pastime for the son of a merchant.

But I have given my opinion on that point often enough, as you have given yours. We will debate the matter in person when you come home.

I have included enough silver for you to ride upriver in comfort, and I expect you to do so and not spend it on books.

     With love and affection,
      your Father,
      John Flarety

Chapter 1

Singing, in the distance.

Thomas smiled. He had timed his arrival almost perfectly. His friends had questioned the wisdom of setting out for home so soon after the term had ended—in truth, they had called him a fool and worse. April, they had said, was the worst time for travel. Rain, mud, and desperate brigands; that's what Thomas would have to face. And someone as small and thin as Thomas would stand no chance. The trip was certain to end in grief, they had declared between draughts of wine. Besides, what sort of an idiot would walk home when he had money for a boat?

Thomas had protested the remarks about his person—he was only slightly shorter than average, though thin was an unfortunately accurate description—and shrugged away the rest. The river may be faster, he'd said, but the walk would be far more interesting, and would give him a chance to practice his botany. There were plenty of farms to buy food from and plenty of barns to sleep in. Besides, no brigands had been reported along the river road in ten years. He would walk.

His companions had shaken their heads in drunken solemnity and continued to forecast his imminent demise.

Thomas had set out exactly as he had planned, hoping to be home for the start of the five-day May festival. There hadn't been as many barns for sleeping as Thomas had hoped, and he spent more than a few nights curled in his cloak underneath trees by the side of the road. Twice he had slept in the stone circles that dotted the landscape.

Legend had it the stone circles were part of a religion, but it was only legend. Those who built them had disappeared long before the followers of the Four Gods had come to this country, and long, long before the Four had lost their names. Now, the circles stood abandoned and overgrown, their purpose gone with their builders. Still, they made a handy windbreak, and fed Thomas's imagination as he lay against the great, grey stones, staring up at the stars.

None of the predicted brigands had appeared to accost Thomas on the road, but his friends had certainly been right about the rain and the mud. A solid week of rain in the middle of the journey had soaked Thomas through, made the roads into a quagmire and added three days to his journey.

Still, I made it, thought Thomas, listening to the singing. *Barely, but I did.*

He stopped walking and started to brush the dirt from his clothes. A moment later he gave it up as hopeless. Three weeks of travel had left his clothes ragged and dirty. His thin frame had grown thinner from the days of walking, and his black hair was a tangled mess. He should have cut it short before he left, but in his rush to leave after the term ended, he hadn't thought of it. Now, it was almost to his shoulders and completely unruly. He rubbed a hand across his face, felt the ragged edges of a very light, very scruffy beard. Fortunately he'd had the river to wash in or he was sure he'd have smelled as bad as he looked.

Thomas turned his grey eyes to the road ahead. Excitement and nerves warred within him to see which would get the upper hand. He had been fourteen when he'd left. Thomas smiled, remembering the desperate cramming he'd done to pass the Academy entrance exams, and his breathless anticipation the day before the trip.

He also remembered his mother waving and crying, his brother grinning and cheering him on, and his father beaming with pride as he drove his son to Greenwater and the river barge that would take Thomas downstream to Hawksmouth and the Royal Academy of Learning.

Four years, Thomas mused. *I wonder if it still looks the same?*

Well, one way to find out. He shifted the bag on his shoulder, adjusted his rapier and dagger on his belt, and started walking again. He grinned at the thought of what his father was going to say when he saw the blades.

The weapons were strictly functional; no filigree, no gilding, no engraving, but high quality and well made. The rapier had a plain steel bell guard to protect its wielder's hand and a long, straight, wickedly sharp blade that ended in a deadly point. The dagger's blade was thick and wide and as long as his forearm, the better to parry away attacks.

Thomas had won the rapier and a matching dagger at a fencing tournament during the winter. He had entered on a dare, using a borrowed sword and padding, and had stunned himself by emerging victorious. His friends, thrilled for him, had pitched in to buy the sword belt. He had written home immediately to tell his family about the victory.

His father's reply had been less excited than Thomas had hoped.

John Flarety had been very happy that Thomas had won the tournament. He was pleased to learn his son was studying his fencing with the same dedication as his other classes. Nonetheless, John Flarety insisted that Thomas *not* wear the blades. Such things were not appropriate for the son of a merchant. Noble fops carried swords. Soldiers carried swords. Rogues and ne'er-do-wells carried swords. Honest country folk had no need to carry swords, especially not merchants and their families.

Thomas had written back, explaining that, in the city, many honest folks carried swords, including every student who could afford one. Thomas's father disagreed entirely and the written argument had been going on ever since.

The road turned down a hill, the forest gave way suddenly, and Thomas was on the edge of the Elmvale town common. The little field was filled with makeshift booths and milling bodies celebrating the May Fair. Children ran around and between the legs of the adults, playing incomprehensible games and begging money for sweets. His mouth started to water when he spotted the pastry booth. He used to stuff himself with blueberry jam tarts, and the sight of them made him realize just how hungry he was. Lunch had been several hours before, and the stale bread and dried sausage had been far less than palatable.

Thomas left the road and crossed the common. It was buzzing with activity. He had hoped to spot his parents or his brother in the crowd, but there was no sign of them. Nearly everyone else from the village was there, though. There were men testing their skill at throwing knives or shooting arrows or wrestling—and wasn't that Liam, standing victorious in the wrestling ring? It had to be; no one else was that tall. The women were laughing at their husbands, and in some cases, showing off their own skills. Thomas stopped to watch Mary Findley put three knives dead centre into one of the targets. The sight made him smile. She'd been beating men at the knife throw as long as Thomas could remember. On the far side of the common, a small man was standing on a stage, juggling five clubs and singing a bawdy song that kept his audience bawling with laughter.

Thomas found himself grinning like an idiot. Compared to any market day in the city, the crowd was tiny. Compared to the May festival in the city, this was hardly an event at all. There were only a few hundred people here, and the entire fair took up only half the common. Thomas didn't care. There was an energy among the people here that he'd missed at the May festivals in the city. There, the festivals had been too large for any one person to take in. Here, the festival was small, intimate, and filled with the joy that comes from living through a cold country winter.

"Thomas!"

The bellow was deep and loud enough to fill the entire common. Thomas turned and saw a mountain of a man detach himself from the crowd around the juggler's stage and charge across the common. Thomas barely had time to identify the giant before he was grabbed, squeezed, and lifted off the ground.

"Thomas! I didn't think to see you before June!"

"You didn't believe I'd miss the fair, did you?" gasped Thomas between squeezes. "Now let me down, George, before you crack all my ribs."

George Gobhann, son of Lionel Gobhann, the village smith, was brown-eyed, brown-haired, and far bigger than Thomas remembered. He had always been larger than Thomas, even though they were of an age. Now, though, he stood head and shoulders taller, and was easily as big as four of him. His arms were thick and sinewy and both of Thomas's legs could have fit into one leg of George's breeches with room to spare. The chest against which Thomas was currently being crushed would certainly have over-stretched any number of normal men's shirts. George brought Thomas down with a force that rocked him to his boots and held him at arm's length. "Look at you!"

Thomas heaved in a breath. "Me? What about you?"

"You're skinny as a rake! Didn't they feed you at the Academy?"

"Not as much as they fed you. Are you a smith now?"

"As if there was ever any doubt. How did you get home?"

"Walked."

"Hawksmouth to here? No wonder you're a mess." George stood back and inspected Thomas head to foot. "What are you doing wearing a sword?"

Thomas put his hand on the hilt, turning it so George could see. "Like it? I won it at a tournament."

George shook his head in mock-disapproval. "No one wears swords, Thomas."

"No one *here* wears swords," corrected Thomas. "Everyone in the city does."

"Well, you're in the country now, and you'll look silly being the only one."

Thomas rolled his eyes. "You sound like my father." He scanned the crowd around them again. "Speaking of whom, is he here?"

"Not since this morning."

"George!" a new, female, and slightly annoyed voice called. "Who's that you have there?"

They both turned, and Thomas barely managed to keep his jaw from dropping open. "Eileen?"

The girl came closer, peering at him as she did. Her eyes widened. "Thomas?"

Thomas was stunned. The last he had seen, Eileen was a skinny, gangly twelve-year old pest who took great delight in throwing stones at him. Now though, she was a trim young woman. Her red hair, always a tangled mess before, flowed cleanly down her back and her blue eyes sparkled as she watched him taking her in. Thomas was suddenly much more aware of how much of a mess he truly was.

Eileen found her tongue first. "Well, stop staring. People will talk."

"I wasn't staring," Thomas protested.

"Oh, nay," she said, putting her hands on her hips and doing her best to look offended, "your eyes just locked onto my bodice without your brain taking any part of it."

Thomas felt a flush begin to rise, and forced it down. "Actually, I was wondering how the same family that produced such a hulking monster could create someone as lovely as you."

"Listen to you!" Eileen said, keeping her tone the same but starting to flush herself. "Is that what they taught you at that Academy? How to charm girls?"

Thomas smiled. "There are entire courses dedicated to it."

"Don't bother," said George. "The lass spends all her time up at the nunnery. I hear they're planning to keep her for their own."

"A nun?" Thomas felt a twinge of disappointment, followed immediately by a larger twinge of embarrassment. He hadn't even seen the girl in four years, he had no right to be thinking of her that way. "And you not even dressed as a novice."

"I'll not be a nun," protested Eileen. "They're just the only ones who'll teach a girl to read and write around here."

George snorted. "If she had her way, she'd run off and join you lot at the Academy."

"Thomas?" a very familiar and very nasal voice called out. "Thomas!"

The voice belonged to a long-limbed man riding a short-limbed donkey. So short, in fact, that Thomas was certain the man could touch the ground without dismounting. Thomas waved. "Gavin!"

Gavin, his long, cadaverous frame making him look like a spider riding a beetle, turned the donkey and rode towards them. He had been tutor to Thomas and his brother, Neal, from childhood, and had helped Thomas prepare for the Academy's rigorous entry exams. When Thomas had gone and Neal was finished his schooling, Gavin had stayed on to handle the family's business accounts. He was, Thomas recalled, quick and clever, polite to the point of obsequiousness, and his nose dripped incessantly.

George sighed. "So much for any fun we might have today." He looked to Thomas, "That man never approved of us."

"He doesn't dislike you," protested Thomas.

"George didn't say he disliked us," said Eileen. "He just disapproves."

"Aye, well…" Thomas could think of nothing to say to that except, "True."

"He thinks we're bad company."

"He'd be right," said Thomas, grinning. "But not to worry. He won't stay. The ass you see yonder will be taking me from the fair very soon, I expect."

George raised an eyebrow. "You're going to ride Gavin's donkey?"

Thomas's grin widened. "I was referring to the ass riding the donkey."

All three started snickering, then had to stifle it as Gavin pulled the donkey to a halt in front of them and dismounted—it was a slight reach to the ground, Thomas noted, but not much. The man, who was not young when he had started tutoring Thomas twelve years previously, creaked his way to the ground and took a long moment to straighten.

Once upright, Gavin looked down his long nose at George and Eileen, then turned and bowed to Thomas. "It is good to see you have returned, young master," he intoned with a sniff. He gave Thomas a short, meticulous examination with his eyes, then sniffed again. The slight down-turn of his mouth let Thomas know that he had been assessed and found wanting. "Indeed, your father and mother have been waiting for this day with great anticipation. I imagine they would be somewhat distraught to discover that you have chosen to remain here at the fair, rather than to come immediately home."

"And how are my parents, Gavin?" asked Thomas, hoping to distract the man.

"Sad for lack of your company, I am certain."

So much for that. "I only just arrived. George and Eileen spotted me in the crowd."

"Of course," said Gavin, raising his rather large eyebrows. "It was fortunate that I had been sent to bespeak wine for your father's guests tonight, or else I might not have spotted you."

"Fortunate indeed," agreed Thomas, doing his best to keep any sarcasm from his voice. He turned back to George and Eileen. "Would you walk with me? If you don't mind leaving the fair, that is?"

"Us?" George's tone was doubtful, and the look he gave his sister was troubled. "Nay, we should not go to your house, I think."

"Why not?" asked Thomas, surprised at the refusal. "What's happened?"

"Nothing new," said Eileen.

George nodded his agreement. "Your dad's a merchant, my dad's a smith."

"Oh, by the Four above," Thomas rolled his eyes up. "Wheel-irons again?"

"And axles and everything else they can think of," said Eileen.

"I swear they enjoy fighting about it," said Thomas.

"Aye, usually," said Eileen. "But this time it got nasty."

"Nasty? How nasty?"

"This is not a subject that should be discussed here," interrupted Gavin, "especially with Thomas so lately come home."

"Yes it should," said Thomas. "Nasty, how?"

George looked embarrassed. "Your father called ours the worst lying, thieving excuse of a blacksmith he'd ever seen."

Thomas's eyebrows went up of their own accord. "And your da didn't throw him through a wall?"

"He came close," said Eileen. "But your father stormed out before he could."

"That's not like him." Thomas remembered the various arguments Lionel had had with John Flarety over the years. They had been loud, boisterous, drawn out, and had usually ended with a handshake and a drink. This, though... "What did your father do, then?"

"Cursed your da up and down twice and swore there would be no more work done until the man apologized," said George.

"After which your da said that none of us were welcome in his home until my da came to his senses," added Eileen.

George nodded. "Exactly."

Thomas was aghast. "You must be joking."

"I am afraid they are quite right," said Gavin.

Thomas shook his head. "They've been friends for years. Whatever's gotten under my father's skin, it will pass and he'll apologize. You'll see."

"Aye, surely," said Eileen. "But until then..."

"Aye." Thomas nodded. "Well, I'll see you tomorrow then. Right?"

"Tomorrow for sure," said George. "Not even your father would miss Fire Night."

Thomas grinned. Fire Night was the culmination of the May festival. The village would build a bonfire, and all the men and women would leap over it. The legend was that each jump brought luck to the village and strength to the earth.

"Ancient superstition at its worst," sniffed Gavin. "Nothing but a chance for lechery under the cover of darkness."

Which was more or less true, Thomas had to agree, even as he rolled his eyes. The other belief was that the more couples who spent the night together in the woods and fields, the more fertile they would become. And while there was no proof of that, the lack of it did not stop anyone from participating if they had the chance. It was, Thomas's father had once said, the single most popular and practiced belief in the region.

George and Eileen were also rolling their eyes, and Gavin waited until all three of them had stopped before saying, "Now, Master Thomas, if you will go?"

"Aye, I'll go." Thomas shook hands with George, then bowed with exaggerated courtesy to Eileen. "If I can ever be of service, my lady," he said, using his best courtly manner, "do not hesitate to ask."

"Oh, she won't," promised George before Eileen could speak. "And like as not she'll ask you to haul water from the well for her."

Eileen stuck her tongue out at her brother. "You've no manners, you." She smiled at Thomas. "See you tomorrow, then."

The two walked away, and Thomas found himself watching Eileen go until Gavin sniffed noisily behind him. "Come, Master Thomas. We should not keep your father waiting."

Thomas picked up his bag and settled it over one shoulder. "No, we certainly should not."

Gavin politely offered Thomas use of the donkey, and was obviously relieved when he declined. He kept the donkey to a slow pace, which gave Thomas time to look over the village as they passed through. There had been hardly any changes in the last four years. The streets were the same deep brown earth that filled the fields, instead of the cobbles one found in the city. The houses were still mostly wattle and daub construction, with thatch for the roofs. The old tower—built on a hill overlooking the town two hundred years before to watch for raiders—was still the tallest structure in the village, and its rough, weather-worn grey stone walls still looked ready to fall down at the slightest breeze.

Despite the lack of change, the village looked prosperous. The houses were well cared-for, the roofs and doors in good repair, and all the people Thomas saw were looking healthy and happy. When they came to his father's warehouses, just outside the village, Thomas saw that two new ones had been built, bringing the total to six. Beyond that, a single path led through a strand of trees to the house.

How his father had managed to make so much money was quite beyond Thomas. John Flarety claimed to have started with one cart and built from there. The story might well have been true, though Thomas was certain there had been money in the family all along. Thomas's older brother, Neal, shared his father's zeal for mercantilism and had, since reaching maturity, helped further expand the family's business. According to his mother's proud letters, the family had gained control of the cloth trade in three surrounding counties, and was in the process of moving into others.

For Thomas, it was a mystery as to why it was all so important. Of course, given that his father's mercantile skills were paying Thomas's way through school, he was not in a position to be judgmental.

If Thomas had had any doubts about the prosperity of his family, the sight of the house, which had been built before Thomas's birth, was certainly proof enough. Half-timber, half-stucco, after the pattern of newer houses in the city, and set on a solid stone foundation, the Flarety home was easily the largest in the village. It had been kept in near-immaculate condition while Thomas had been gone, and from the looks of it, had been recently re-stuccoed and painted. The low stone fence that surrounded the yard was in perfect condition, and a new building had been added behind the house.

"What's that?" he asked, pointing.

"For the staff," said Gavin. "Your father has made many important connections in the time since you left, and has often had to entertain. Even now, your father has several important guests, and room is somewhat scarce."

Mischief got the better of Thomas. "Does this mean I'll be sleeping in the barn?"

"Certainly not!" Gavin looked appalled, and Thomas did his best to hide his smile. It wasn't good enough. Gavin's eyes narrowed, and he waved one long, skinny arm in the direction of the open front gate and sternly said, "Go home, Master Thomas."

"Yes, Gavin," said Thomas, giving his old tutor the same courtly bow he'd given Eileen. "I thank you for the escort."

The front gate—freshly painted in green, Thomas noticed—was wide open, and the stone path to the door was swept clean. Thomas was about to step through when the front door opened. A thin, rather handsome woman with a basket on her arm stepped out. She caught sight of Thomas and stopped dead.

A moment later, a man a few years Thomas's senior stepped through the door and nearly knocked her down.

The woman stared at Thomas, and Thomas grinned back. A moment later, she let out a joyous, wordless cry, dropped the basket and started running towards him. Thomas started running himself, leaving Gavin to sniff in a self-satisfied way behind him. She met Thomas half-way and enveloped him in a huge hug.

Thomas, laughing, tried to hold her with one hand and keep the hilt of his sword out of the way with the other. "Aye, Mum, it's me."

Madeleine Flarety squeezed her son tighter, and kissed him hard on the cheek. "By the Four, Thomas!" she said, scolding and laughing at the same time. "You're as thin as a twig! Did they not feed you at the Academy?"

"They did, Mum, they did!" he assured her, still laughing. "I just spent more time studying than I did eating."

"And more time carousing than either, I'll warrant," chimed in his brother, Neal, stepping up and clapping him hard on the shoulder. "I'll bet you have stories to tell!"

"A few," Thomas admitted. He held up a hand to forestall his mother's cry of disapproval. "But first I need to get myself settled and have a bath and a good meal."

"You certainly do!" She stepped back and held him at arm's length. "My word, look at you! Your hair's a tangled mess, your clothes are in tatters and…" She stopped and raised her eyes slowly to her son's. When she spoke again, her tone had changed, and not for the better. "Thomas, what are you wearing at your waist?"

Thomas prayed silently to the Four for mercy and said, "My rapier, Mother. And the dagger that goes with it."

"I read that you won them, but what in the High Father's name are you doing wearing them? Nobody wears swords, Thomas!"

"Nobody *in the country* wears swords, Mother," corrected Thomas. "Lots of people in the city wear swords."

Madeleine Flarety looked appalled. "Not merchants, surely!"

"I'm not a merchant. I'm a student."

"Your family are merchants, and we don't wear swords!"

"Mother…"

"You'll attract the worst sort of company wearing that!"

Thomas started to explain how wearing a sword could also keep the worst sort of company away, but the door opened again and Brian, the family's oldest servant and master of the household, stepped out and bowed to Thomas. "Excuse me, but your father has requested that you meet him in his study at once."

"Brian!" The man had always looked to be in his early forties, and the four years Thomas was away had not altered his appearance at all. "How are you?"

"I am well, thank you, Master Thomas," said Brian. "If you will come?"

"Such a rush!" Madeleine put a hand on Thomas's arm and drew him closer, laughing again. "Can a woman not greet her son?"

"Of course," said Brian, "but his father is insisting."

"Is he watching?" asked Thomas, stepping away from his mother and looking up at the house. He found the window to his father's study, and saw the man standing, looking down at them. Thomas waved, but got no response.

"Of course he is," said Madeleine. "And he'll keep watching until you're standing in front of him."

"Aye, that he would." Thomas went back to his mother and hugged her hard, then did the same to his brother. "I'll see you both when you get back. Time to go tell father how I'm wasting all his money."

"Now, don't start anything," warned Madeleine, shaking a finger at his face.

Thomas raised his hands in mock surrender. "I'll behave, I promise."

"You'd better," said Neal. "He's been in a foul mood for two days now."

"I heard," said Thomas. His good humour sank a bit. "George said Da had a fit over wheel-irons. What's going on?"

Madeleine sighed, and for a moment looked very tired. "I wish I knew. He's not been himself since the start of the May festival." She shook her head, sending the tired away and bringing the smile back to her face with the motion. "The sight of you should set him right," she said. "Though he won't like that sword at all."

Thomas smiled. "Now, *that*, I knew."

"Get on with you," said Madeleine, giving him a light slap on the back of the head, then ruffling his hair with her hand. "And mind you don't disturb the guests."

Thomas caught her hand, bowed deeply and kissed it. She waved him off, laughing, and gave him another hug. "Now get going!" she said, picking up her basket. "And be ready to tell all when I get back!"

She headed down the path to the gate. Neal gave Thomas another slap on the back, then followed their mother. Thomas turned to go inside but was stopped by Brian's hand on his shoulder. "Your father suggested that it would be better for you to use the side door in your present condition," said Brian. "I believe he is worried your appearance might cause some disturbance among the guests."

Thomas had a sudden image of a dozen or so merchants thinking they had been set on by bandits. He laughed. "He may be right."

Thomas gave a wave to his mother and brother and another up to his father, then headed to the side of the house. Brian opened the servant's door and led him up the narrow back stairs and into the hallway on the second floor. The changes in the place were remarkable. When he had left, the floor had still been plain, darkly-stained wood and the plaster on the walls was beginning to yellow with age. Now a thick carpet ran the length of the hall, the walls were smooth and gleaming white, and even the spots behind the candle sconces were clean of dirt or soot. The wood of the doors was newly-oiled and shone. The handles were brightly polished brass.

Thomas, used to the dust of libraries and the dirt of the city, found himself suddenly uncomfortable in his own home. He wished he'd had time to bathe and change into the clean clothes he had in his bag, but it was too late. They were already before his father's study.

Brian knocked firmly on the door, and John Flarety's deep voice called for Thomas to enter. Brian pushed the door open and stepped aside. Thomas started to go in, but found his feet had stuck themselves to the floor of their own accord.

Nervous, thought Thomas. *Of all the silly things.*

"Your father is waiting," Brian reminded him, his voice gentle. Thomas guessed his nervousness was showing on his face and felt heartily embarrassed. Brian bowed once more. "Welcome home, Master Thomas. It is good to see you again."

"Thank you, Brian," said Thomas. He straightened himself up, hitched his bag to a more comfortable place on his shoulder, and stepped through the door.

His father was glaring out the window when Thomas came in. At least, Thomas assumed that he was glaring because the expression on his face was too annoyed to be used for much else. John Flarety was a tall, broad man who had passed his shape onto his eldest son rather than his youngest. Thomas waited a long moment, then said, "Hello, Father."

John turned his glare from the window and onto his son, taking in the scuffed and worn boots, the tattered clothes, and the rapier. John's eyes lingered on the sword for a good length of time before returning to his son's face.

"So," said someone from the corner, "this is your youngest son."

Thomas jumped in surprise and spun. He had not even noticed the two men standing beside the door when he'd come in. The first was both taller and heavier than Thomas's father, and wore his size with an air of authority that made him a very imposing figure. He was dressed in the green robes of a high-ranking priest of the High Father. The man behind him was pale and blond and dressed in black from head to foot. A rapier hung at his side, and Thomas's eyes went to it of their own volition. It was much higher in quality than Thomas's blade, and the man wore it as if it were an extension of his body.

Thomas switched his attention back to the clergyman, who was watching Thomas with a slight smile on his lips. "Well, young man," he said. "Who am I?"

Thomas was pretty sure he knew, but looked down to the man's hands anyway. The thick gold ring with the large ruby in the middle, symbol of the man's office, confirmed what he'd thought. "Bishop Malloy," Thomas said. "First of the servants of the High Father. Your Grace honours our household."

"Thank you." The bishop extended his hand and Thomas bowed to kiss his ring.

"I knew that there was company in the house," Thomas said as he straightened, "but I had not expected my father to be in a meeting."

"Indeed." The bishop's voice was light, surprising in a man of his size, but with a smooth tone that insinuated its way through the air. "I had thought as much. Or, at least I had assumed that you would not normally appear before your father's guests in this condition."

Thomas felt a sudden need to straighten his ragged clothes. He suppressed the urge, knowing it wouldn't do any good. "I have been travelling, your Grace—"

"And sleeping in ditches, I should say." The bishop turned his attention to Thomas's father. "If this is where your money is going, I would say it is not well spent."

"I am certain that my money went to the lad's schooling, rather than his wardrobe," said John Flarety, his voice flat. Thomas recognized the tone and guessed that whatever business his father had with the bishop, it was not going well.

The bishop raised an eyebrow. "A young man who dresses in tatters and carries a sword hardly seems the type to do much studying, though I suppose one shouldn't judge a man by his weapons."

He certainly is a pompous creature, Thomas thought. With a deliberate motion of his head he took his gaze from the bishop to the man standing behind him with the rapier at his side. "No, one shouldn't."

The bishop followed Thomas's gaze and his eyes narrowed ever so slightly. "Randolf is my familiar; my personal servant. He has chosen to give himself and his blades to the church."

Randolf bowed to the bishop, and when he straightened, his eyes were on Thomas. They were as grey as Thomas's own, and as cold and dead as the sea under a winter sky. "It is my pleasure to serve," he said, his voice as cold as his eyes, "in *whatever* capacity his Grace requires."

Including running me through on the spot, Thomas thought. A shiver started to work its way up Thomas's spine. He suppressed it and turned to the bishop. "Perhaps your Grace should permit me to withdraw, so I may change into something more presentable."

"No, no," said Bishop Malloy. "After all, if you consider this the proper clothing to see your father in, why should it not be fit enough for me as well?"

Thomas risked a glance to his father, who was looking less and less pleased. "Still, I should hate to interrupt your conversation—"

"Your father and I were merely discussing business." The bishop turned to John Flarety. "He is attempting to convince me that the price he offers for his cloth is the best he can give."

"It is, your Grace," said John Flarety, his tone still flat. "In fact, it is the best price you will find in the county."

"I am afraid your father is finding me harder to convince than most," the bishop said, smiling. "What do you think, Thomas?"

"I'm no merchant," hedged Thomas. "That is why I was sent to study."

"You must have an opinion," said the bishop, his eyes still on Thomas's father. "All the Royal Academy's scholars have opinions, no matter their knowledge of the subject."

Thomas took a moment to swallow the first, very succinct reply that leapt to his mind and measured out a response. "My father is an honest merchant and a good man. If he says that the price he is offering is the best he can give, then that is the truth."

"I think you can do better, John Flarety," said the bishop. *"I think the price can come down a little more, don't you?"*

Thomas started. The motion caught Bishop Malloy's eye. He turned, and for a second Thomas thought he saw fear, then excitement in the bishop's face. Both vanished, and the man's voice sounded perfectly normal when he said, "Is there something the matter, young Thomas?"

"Your voice..." Thomas stopped, not sure how to explain it, or if he really wanted to do so.

The bishop schooled his features and waited. When Thomas didn't say anything more, he repeated. "My voice? What about my voice?"

"It was..." Thomas couldn't find words, and the bishop was staring at him. "I don't know."

Bishop Malloy moved closer to Thomas. "Do you not like my tone?"

"No, your Grace, I just..."

"You just what?" The bishop was too close now. "Did you hear something unusual?"

Thomas felt the sudden urge to back away, and forced himself to stay where he was. "I just... I'm very tired from the road."

The bishop stopped moving for a moment, then took a step back. "Indeed." The bishop's expression was smooth again, his tone unreadable. He held out his ring. "Why don't you wait outside the door until your father and I are done talking?"

Thomas looked to his father. The man nodded, shortly and abruptly. Thomas nodded back, then bent and kissed the ring. "Yes, your Grace."

He backed out, keeping his eyes on the bishop until he had pulled the door shut behind him. The silence of the hallway was a relief. Thomas leaned against the wall, willing the tension out of his body.

What did I hear? Thomas wasn't sure. It sounded as if the bishop's voice had dropped an octave and doubled in volume, though Thomas was sure neither of those things had happened. But *something* had. The bishop knew how to use his voice, certainly, but training couldn't account for the sudden surge of power Thomas had felt coming from the man.

Maybe I'm just tired, Thomas thought, automatically adjusting the bag on his shoulder to a more comfortable position. He thought better of it a moment later and let the bag fall to the floor. He was home, after all. He didn't need to keep carrying it.

The conversation in the study went on for some time. Thomas tried to listen, but the heavy wood of the door muffled the words. His father spoke only occasionally, while the bishop went on at length. Thomas was half-tempted to put his ear to the door and listen, but the thought of getting caught was too mortifying. He stayed where he was, waiting.

At last the bell attached to the pull-cord in his father's study rang twice, sharp and demanding. The study door opened a moment later and John Flarety stepped out. He glanced at his son briefly then turned to look down the hall. Almost immediately, Brian was there, coming up the stairs at a trot.

"The bishop wishes to speak with his men," said John Flarety. "Escort him to them."

The bishop stepped into the hallway, pausing to nod at Thomas. "We shall see you later, Thomas Flarety."

"I look forward to it, your Grace," lied Thomas, bowing low. Privately, he was wondering if there was any way to avoid the man entirely for the rest of his stay. Thomas doubted it. He sighed silently and straightened up.

The bishop was already walking away, and Randolf had taken his place. His eyes bored into Thomas, though he was smiling politely. Thomas returned the stare, feeling uncomfortably like a mouse before a large cat. Randolf inclined his head in a motion that felt far less respectful than it looked, then broke contact and turned away, following his master down the hall.

Thomas watched the two go, then picked up his bag and stepped into the office. His father was already sitting behind his desk, his face a shade of red that Thomas recognized at once. John Flarety was angry.

"I see what you meant about him," said Thomas, putting his bag down. He smiled and started coming around the desk, his arms out. "It's good to see you, Da."

"I assumed that you knew I would have guests today."

John Flarety's chill tone made Thomas freeze in place. His father glared at him, waiting for an answer. Thomas pulled himself together enough to say, "I only learned when I arrived, Father."

"Guests who expect that I maintain my house with decorum, that I clothe my children properly, and that I have raised them not to be hooligans." John Flarety leaned forward in his chair. "Guests like the bishop."

It took a moment for that to sink in. When it did, Thomas was stunned. "He's our guest? I remember you said he would be in town—"

"Yes. *Our* houseguest, not the nunnery's." John slowly rose to his feet, his eyes never leaving Thomas's. "Do you know how important that is to our family?"

Considering that the nunnery owned the land that Elmvale sat on, and that the abbess was in fact the true authority of the county, it was very important indeed. Thomas nodded. "Aye, it's amazing—"

"And *this*," John Flarety's hand cut the air, taking in Thomas's ragged state in a single wave, "*This* is his first impression of my youngest son! A young bravo who comes to my house, carrying a *sword* of all things, and looking as if he has stumbled on foot down the road from the Academy!" He glared at his son. "How *did* you get here, Thomas?"

Thomas braced himself, "I walked."

His father's face turned darker red. "There are a dozen boats going up and down the river every week, could you not have taken one?"

"I could have," said Thomas. He reached into his bag, pulled out a small purse, and put it on the table. "I thought I'd save the money you sent instead."

"Save the money?" John Flarety's hand came down hard on the desk, making Thomas jump. "What about the money that I've been sending you every month? Where did you spend it all, that you come home looking like this? Fifteen silver pieces a month should have been more than sufficient to keep you in a manner fitting the son of one of the wealthiest trading houses in this part of the country!"

Thomas had no idea what his father wanted him to say. "The Academy is expensive, Father—"

"I dare say it is, if you spend your time brawling rather than studying. Tell me, how much of that money went to settle gambling debts? How much for wine? How much for keeping you out of jail?"

Thomas felt as though he'd been hit, hard, in the pit of the stomach. He stared at his father, unable to speak.

"Well?" John Flarety demanded.

"I do not brawl," said Thomas, keeping his words slow and even. "I have drunk wine and I have gambled, but not enough to bring disgrace on myself or this house."

"Then where is the money?" John Flarety's hand hit the desk again. "What have you spent it on?"

"Books!" Thomas nearly shouted the word. With an effort he contained himself and started again. "There are so many books, Father. Most nights I can hardly sleep for reading. I feed off books the way my body feeds off food. Dr. Fauster—he teaches philosophy—talks about books written over a thousand years ago that have just now been rediscovered. And new books are being written all the time: commentaries on the old philosophies, writings about new philosophies." Thomas could hear himself speeding up in his excitement. He picked up his bag and dug into it, coming up with two battered, leather-bound books, each only slightly bigger than his hand. "Look at these, Father. The first is a dictionary, translating the language of ancient Perthia. The second is a book of Perthian philosophy in the original language, with space in it for a student to write a translation."

His father didn't even look at the books. "This is what you waste your time on?"

"Waste?" Thomas was appalled. "It's not a waste!"

"It is a waste," John Flarety repeated. "It is a waste of your time and of my money."

Thomas's legs felt weak, like he'd been standing in the ocean, fighting the tide. Something was wrong. He tried again. "Father, you sent me to learn."

"I sent you to be educated," corrected his father. "I did not send you to waste your time studying philosophy—"

"I don't just study—"

"And I certainly didn't send you to spend your money on swords!"

Thomas looked down to the blade at his side. "Is that what this is about? This?" He grasped the scabbard and raised the sword up. "I wrote about this. I won it at a fencing tournament. It didn't cost a thing."

"And who gave you permission to study fencing?"

"Everyone at the Academy studies fencing."

"We do not. We are merchants. Not soldiers, not ruffians, and not fops." Thomas's father started pacing the width of the room. "I should never have sent you there. The city is a corrupt place, filled with corrupt people. You were sent to develop your mind and to learn a trade, not to study swordplay and become a ruffian."

"I'm not becoming a ruffian—"

"I will deal with your behaviour later," said John, ignoring Thomas's words entirely. "Now, we must solve the problem of what you shall wear in this house."

"I have clothes in—"

"Silence!" The word thundered through the room. "Return to the village. The tailor will be open for several hours yet, and will measure you for clothes appropriate to your station. Tell him you will need them for tomorrow night."

John picked up the purse from where Thomas had placed it on the desk. He opened it and eyed the contents a moment, then tossed it back to Thomas. "This should more than cover the cost of the clothes. Use the rest to buy your supper. I expect that the tailor will keep you long enough that you will not join us for dinner."

Thomas stood where he was, mouth open, staring at his father. John Flarety frowned. "Well, boy?"

Thomas, stunned, could only say, "I'll do as you wish."

"And use the side entrance. I'll not have our guests seeing my son like this."

"No." Thomas shouldered his bag and stumbled to the door. "No, of course not."

Chapter 2

What, in the names of the Four, is going on here?

Thomas had stumbled down the back stairs and out of the house without seeing anyone, which was just as well. He wasn't sure he could manage to be civil if he did. Now, brooding his way down the road back to the village, Thomas tried to make sense of what had just happened.

There had been *nothing* in his father's letters to suggest a greeting like this. The man had practically *begged* him to come home. He had been full of praise for Thomas's success, as well he should be. Thomas had gotten top marks in all his classes. The reviews from his professors had all been glowing, and Thomas had sent them all home. It was exactly what his father had wanted from him.

True, he had walked when he had the money to ride and he was wearing a sword, but those should have been the subject of a little good-natured scolding. Instead, his father had treated him like a servant caught stealing money.

It doesn't make any sense.

Certainly he was not dressed appropriately for guests, but he had better clothes in his bag. A bath and a shave for him and a quick press for the clothes and he would have been more than prepared to greet the guests. As it was, the clothes were still in his bag, the bag was still on his shoulder, and a bath was nowhere to be found.

His mind kept going in circles all the way to the village. It wasn't as though he hadn't written. It wasn't as though he hadn't told them how he was living. His family probably knew more about his life than his friends at the Academy. He had described nearly everything that was fit to share, and would have told his older brother the rest had he not been certain that his mother would read the letters as well. And now, his father was complaining about him doing what he had been sent away to do? It wasn't fair.

The tailor shop was closed.

Of course, Thomas thought, staring at the locked door. *Now what?*

Common sense told him the tailor would be at the fair, and that's where Thomas headed. It was only when he reached the edge of the town common and looked at the crowd that Thomas realized that he had no idea what the tailor looked like. For a moment he felt completely at a loss. He shook it off. Someone would know where the tailor was. All he had to do was ask.

Eileen's voice, yelling words of encouragement, grabbed his attention. He cast about and spotted her standing beside the wrestling pit, shouting at the top of her lungs. Thomas, guessing what the shouting was about, went over to stand beside her.

The pit was fifteen feet square, surrounded by a transplanted pig-fence, and had a thick layer of hay on the ground for the contestants to land on. In the middle of it, George was struggling with Liam. They were in a tight wrestler's clinch, bodies straining against one another. Liam was taller than George, and had once made his living from wrestling. He had even wrestled at the royal court some fifteen years before. He was attempting to use his height to lever

George backwards and while he was succeeding, he was not having an easy time. From the look of it, what George gave the other man in height, he took back in strength.

"Come on, George!" shouted Eileen, trying to rally her brother as the taller man slowly forced him to his knees.

"You can't think he'll win," said Thomas. "No one beats Liam."

"He nearly beat him last year," Eileen said without looking. A moment later she turned, mouth open in surprise. "Thomas! What are you doing here?"

Thomas couldn't even begin a reply to that, and a roar from the crowd saved him from the need. George, moving faster than seemed possible for a man of his bulk, had dropped down to one knee and, with a quick thrust of his hand through the other man's legs, lifted. The small crowd cheered lustily as George raised Liam high into the air. "Get him!" screamed Eileen. "Get him, George!"

George grunted loudly and shifted his grip, obviously meaning to throw Liam to the ground. It wasn't to be, though. Liam, upside down though he was, secured a tight grip around George's waist. With a mighty pull, Liam slipped off George's shoulders, got his feet on the ground and with a quick twist, threw George across the pit. George cried out in surprise then hit the ground with a solid THUD that made those around the pen wince. Liam jumped on him and pinned him. Cheers erupted and Liam was declared the winner.

Eileen and Thomas looked on as Liam pulled the gasping George into a sitting position. "You'll be fine, laddie," he said. "You did well this year. Had me worried there for a bit, you did."

George gasped a little longer then relaxed as the air flowed back into his lungs. "Nearly had you down, I did."

Liam laughed. "Don't fool yourself, laddie. It'll be a few years more before you beat old Liam at his own game. Why I once—"

"Wrestled in front of the king," George finished for him "Aye, I know." Liam grinned and held out his hand. George took it, and Liam pulled him to his feet and gave him a clap on the back. The young smith hopped over the fence as Liam called, "Right, who's next?"

"Good match!" said Eileen. "You nearly had him!"

"Nearly," agreed George. He looked at Thomas. "What are you doing here? You should be at home eating supper."

"My father didn't think so." said Thomas. "I hardly got in the door before he sent me out again."

"Sent you out?" repeated Eileen. "What for?"

"A better wardrobe."

George looked him up and down. "You are a little scruffy," he said. "In fact, I wouldn't wear those clothes digging for clay. Still you'd have thought he'd have fed you first."

"Why wouldn't he let you stay?" asked Eileen.

"I don't know!" Anger bubbled into the words and Thomas took a deep breath to control it. "I didn't even get a 'welcome home.' Just 'aren't you a mess' and 'how could you waste all your time and money on books and school?'"

Eileen looked confused. "I thought he was proud of you."

"Me too," said George. "Why, you can hardly get a word in when your father comes into the tavern for all the chattering he does about his son at the Academy."

"Well, today he thinks his son is a ruffian, who isn't up to the standard for sitting at his table."

George was appalled. "You're joking."

"He took one look and sent me packing to get new clothes and eat at the tavern." Thomas pulled out the pouch and showed it to his friends. "I walked for three weeks so I could save this. He didn't care."

"Thomas—" began George.

"I say we drink in the tavern all night then rouse the tailor at dawn, since that's what he expects." He adjusted the bag on his shoulder with an angry shrug. "Coming?"

George and Eileen exchanged a worried glance, but said nothing as they followed him through the fair. The juggler's stage was between Thomas and the tavern, and the gathered crowd was blocking the path. He started skirting around them when the juggler bellowed, "Scholar! Come to me, Scholar!"

Thomas stopped in surprise. The juggler was a short man, with clothes as worn as Thomas's own, and pale hair poking out in all directions from under his many-coloured cap. The smile he turned on Thomas looked to be infectious, judging from the number of people in the crowd who were wearing it. "Aye, I'm talking to you, Scholar. Come to me."

Thomas spared a glance for his friends then started walking closer. "How did you know I'm a scholar?"

The juggler's grin grew wider. "It's the talk of the town, Scholar! The young man come home, clothes in tatters, sword on hip, and mind full of ideas and learning! Tell us, Scholar, where did you study?"

"The Royal Academy of Learning."

"The Royal Academy!" The juggler's voice dripped mock-admiration, even as his smile took the sting from it. "A true seat of learning, that!" He paused, leaned forward, dropping his voice to a stage whisper. "You did learn something there, didn't you?"

Thomas, still rankling from his father's comments, managed a stiff, "Aye, I did."

"Anything useful?"

Not according to my father. "Some would say so."

"Meaning some would not." The juggler grinned at the crowd. "Well, we shall see what you have learned." His voice grew louder, filling the fair. "I challenge you to the greatest test of learning! I challenge you… to *riddles!*"

Oh, by the Four, thought Thomas as the audience applauded. The juggler had been out to snare someone and Thomas had walked right into it. He really did not want to begin a game of anything. "I don't suppose we could do this tomorrow?" he asked. "I have an errand at the tailor's shop."

"The tailor's is shut!" called a well-dressed man from the crowd—the tailor, at a guess. "But if you beat him, I'll open it for you!"

The crowd cheered, and Thomas knew he was sunk.

"Good luck," said George from the side of his mouth. "He riddled Mayor Tomson into the ground."

"I really don't want to do this," muttered Thomas.

"Surely you can beat him," said Eileen. "After all, you're a scholar."

Thomas fixed a glare on her, and was met with a pair of blue eyes glittering with mischief.

Oh, why not. Raising his voice for the whole crowd to hear, he called back, "Fine. Challenge accepted!"

The crowd clapped loud and the juggler called over them, "And who do I have the honour of challenging?"

"Thomas Flarety."

"Timothy, at your service!" The juggler gave a florid bow. "And because you accepted the challenge, you may begin!"

Thomas thought hard. Riddle games were not common at the Academy — drinking games involving obscure quotations or laws or mathematical formula, certainly, but no one did riddles. It was beneath them. Unable to think of anything else, Thomas pulled out a riddle from his childhood:

> *"I saw a creature, carrying plunder,*
> *From a raiding foray, to his home,*
> *To set up a bower at the top of a tower,*
> *In a fortress tall, he would go.*
>
> *Then came a creature, from over the tower,*
> *Familiar to all in the world,*
> *It snatched away his plunder, and drove the wretch yonder*
> *Far from his path he was hurled."*

The audience turned almost as one back towards the juggler. Timothy stood centre stage, legs wide, arms crossed, with one hand holding his chin. "A good one, that!" he said, scratching at his beard. "Though hardly a difficult one."

"Then answer it!" called someone from the crowd.

Timothy grinned. "I will! It is a bird and the wind!"

Thomas nodded. "It is."

The crowd applauded and cheered. Timothy took another bow. "Well, then," he said, "I am not so scholarly, but I have one that will stump you. Tell me:

> *"A strange thing hangs by the thigh of a man,*
> *Under its master's cloak,*
> *Stiff and hard and pierced through the front,*
> *It waits for the man to raise up his robe,*
> *For then the head of the hanging thing*
> *Will be poked into a hole of matching length,*
> *Where it has often been poked before!"*

Catcalls and chuckles followed the juggler's riddle, and all eyes went to Thomas. "Well, Scholar?" the juggler asked, "What could this strange thing be?"

Thomas looked at his friends. Eileen was blushing and giggling. George was laughing. Thomas shook his head, and smiled at Eileen. "Well, there is only one thing that rises up in my mind—" The crowd roared and Eileen looked at the ground, her blush turning bright red. "—and that would be a key."

"Aye! That it is!" the juggler crowed. He shook a finger at his audience. "And shame on the rest of you!" The crowd laughed louder. "Your turn, Scholar, if you can come up with another one!"

Thomas struggled to think of another riddle; something Timothy wouldn't know. The problem was that the juggler probably knew every riddle ever told by the hearth and some that weren't. The chances of Thomas thinking of something the little man had not heard before were slim indeed.

If he stuck with riddles.

> *"Sword and axe, but not of steel;*
> *Teeth and claw, but not of bone.*
> *Leaf and vine, but not of wood;*
> *Wall and tower, but not of stone.*
> *Ever on guard, ever sleeping;*
> *Beyond all pain, ever weeping."*

The crowd went completely silent and furrowed brows appeared throughout. Beside him, Thomas could see the blank expressions on Eileen and George. Timothy was staring, open-mouthed. Thomas casually folded his arms and waited.

The crowd's eyes were riveted on Timothy. The juggler stood a moment longer, then began pacing back and forth. He pursed his lips. He swung his arms. He opened his mouth only to close it again. He took off his hat and scratched his head. The tension built with every passing moment. Finally, Timothy stopped where he was and raised one hand. "Right!" he said. "I have no idea at all!"

A laugh rippled through the crowd, and all eyes swivelled expectantly back to Thomas. Cries of "What's the answer?" rang out.

"Well, Scholar?" asked Timothy. "What is it?"

"It is the poet Beothin's description of the tomb of King Adolphus of Perthia," said Thomas, "which has a stone carving of the king, standing as if on guard, sword and axe in hand, surrounded by the grape vines of the region, standing over the body of the dragon he slew, weeping tears for the loss of his love. And behind him, inlaid in brass, is the castle of Grenvillis, where he died."

The entire crowd stared, dumbfounded.

"You learned this at the Academy?" ventured Timothy.

"Aye."

"And is this knowledge considered useful or not?"

"Completely useless," said Thomas, with a deep bow. "Until now."

Timothy stared, agape, then burst out laughing. A chuckle ran through the crowd, then applause—led by George, Thomas noticed. Timothy called out, "The scholar wins!"

The crowd roared and clapped, and Timothy waited until the noise died down before continuing. "And since I have been beaten, I must now do something to redeem myself! Something impressive! Something exciting! Something far better than riddles! Ladies and gentlemen, today I will show you something that few in our days have ever seen! I shall show you *true magic!*"

The crowd's attention was on the juggler again. Thomas turned to George and Eileen. "Come on. Let's get the tailor and get going."

"Wait!" called Timothy. "Don't leave, young Scholar! I need your help!" He made shooing motions at the crowd between them. "Make way, make way! Let our young scholar approach the stage."

Thomas stood where he was, uncertain. He really wanted nothing more than to leave, but all eyes were on him and the juggler was gesturing him forward.

"Come, Scholar!" said Timothy. "We must have the opinion of someone with wisdom."

Thomas shook his head. "I have no wisdom. And I need—"

"No wisdom?" said the juggler, grasping his chest and miming shock. "What does one go to school for, if not wisdom?"

The crowd waited expectantly. Thomas sighed. *Trapped again.*

"Knowledge," said Thomas, walking through the crowd towards the stage. "One goes to school for knowledge."

"Well, if we can't have wisdom, then knowledge will certainly do." Timothy grinned broadly at the crowd. "Now, Master Thomas Flarety, student of the Academy, source of all knowledge, have you ever seen magic?"

"Everyone has seen magic," said Thomas, reaching the stage.

"Everyone has seen sleight of hand," corrected Timothy. "Everyone has seen a flower appear out of the air for a pretty girl." He flourished his wrist, and a flower appeared in his hand. He tossed it just behind Thomas. "A blossom for a blossom," Timothy said with a wink. Thomas looked over his shoulder and saw Eileen and George right behind him.

"But not all magic is trickery!" The juggler raised his voice, gathering in more passers-by as his words filled the fair. "The High Father who watches over us all has three who watch with him: The Loyal Consort, who stands by his side and helps those in need and who gathers us in when our time has past. The Rebel Son, who gave man the gifts of knowledge and invention, and suffered great torment before his Father forgave him." He looked at Thomas. "Who is the fourth, Scholar?"

"The Blessed Daughter," Thomas said, wondering where Timothy was going. "Giver of poetry and music."

"And magic!" said Timothy. "True magic!"

The crowd drew closer, forcing Thomas and his friends right against the stage. The juggler took off his hat and placed it on the stage. His jacket and shirt followed a moment later. "Fear not, ladies," he said with a wink, as he took his time folding his shirt. "I'll not offend your eyes by removing more. I just wanted the Scholar here to be certain that I had nothing up my sleeve."

He knelt on the stage before Thomas. "Now look, young Scholar. Look closer than you've ever looked before. Your friends as well." He extended his right hand, low enough for them to watch, but high enough for the audience to see easily as well. "Look at my hand, lads and lassie. I'll show you a trick you'll never see again."

Thomas cast a doubting glance up at the juggler's glee-filled face then turned his attention back to the man's hand. On either side, George and Eileen leaned in close. The little man's eyes narrowed and his breathing became deep and even.

Timothy passed his left hand above his right, and a glowing ball of light appeared in the palm of his right hand.

The light shone turquoise blue, and swirled around itself, giving the ball its shape. It could almost have been a jewel, but the outer edges seemed fuzzy, as though they were fading into the air rather than ending. Timothy rose to his feet and raised his hand higher. The entire crowd leaned forward to look.

"And now," said Timothy, raising his empty hand above the one with the ball, "Allee-oop!"

The ball leapt from his palm into the air. The crowd gasped.

Timothy kept the ball floating between his hands, and raised it slowly until it floated just below his eye level. Slowly, the ball began to spin in place. Timothy let it alone for a time, then with a gesture from his left hand, made the ball start orbiting first around his right hand, then his arm. All the time he kept his left hand close, as though he expected the ball to fly away and needed to be ready to catch it. He raised his hands higher, and the ball whirled around above his head. He tilted his face up to the sky and the ball's orbit shrank smaller and smaller until, finally, it spun in place just above the tip of his nose.

"Witchcraft!" whispered someone, their voice carrying through the silent, staring crowd. "It's witchcraft!"

The little ball slowed its rotation then gently came to a stop. Timothy knelt slowly, keeping his hands on either side of the hovering ball. The crowd leaned forward even further.

Suddenly Timothy's hands clapped above the ball, making it disappear in a flash of light and silvery powder. The crowd gasped collectively then everyone started clamouring at once. Some were cheering the trick, others demanding to know how it was done. The whisper of witchcraft became a shout, and soon it was coming from a half-dozen throats. Timothy stayed where he was, hands high, watching. Arguments began to break out, and an ugly tension began to build.

Timothy's high, ridiculing laugh cut through the noise. He pulled himself to his feet and walked to the front of the stage. He continued laughing as he pulled on his shirt, then his jacket. The entire crowd was staring at him now.

Timothy waited a moment longer before asking, "What's the matter with you lot?"

"Witchcraft!" shouted one man from the back. "You're using witchcraft!"

"Witchcraft?" Timothy laughed again, the sound cutting through the silence like a knife. "What sort of a fool notion is that?" He turned to Thomas. "Scholar! Did you hear what they said? Witchcraft!" He shook his head. "Tell me, in the opinions of the knowledgeable is there even such a thing as witchcraft?"

Thomas was staring wide-eyed at the juggler. He could feel the eyes of the crowd boring into the back of his head, could see Timothy's relaxed, amused expression. Timothy winked and smiled, waiting for his answer.

"No," said Thomas, slowly. He stopped, unsure for a moment, then repeated loud enough for everyone to hear, "No. Though witchcraft is still on the laws of the Church of the High Father as dealing with the Banished for powers beyond what man should have, and though the church holds it to be a grievous sin, in the opinion of the knowledgeable, there's no such thing as witchcraft."

"Well, there you have it," crowed Timothy, pointing to Thomas. "See? No such thing!"

"Then what was that?" demanded the same man from the back. "What did we see if not witchery?"

Timothy pursed his lips and put a hand to his mouth as though thinking, then opened his lips wide. A turquoise-blue ball seemed to come out of his mouth and into his hand. He held it up for all to see. The ball was painted with lighter swirls, and coated with many layers of shellac, so that the ball shone in the light, almost as if glowing from within, and the edges seemed to fade into nothing. With a derisive laugh, he threw it down on the stage, putting force into it. The ball hit with a loud *crack* and bounced back up. He caught it, covered it with his hands then pulled them apart. The ball floated in the air between, and this time Timothy turned his hands to show them the thin threads that held it to his fingers.

"A fine trick, isn't it?" he asked. He caught the ball and put it into his jacket. "It gets them every time, it does. *And I got you all but good!*"

A sheepish groan ran through the audience, followed with applause and cheering.

"And let that be a lesson to you all!" Timothy shouted. "Don't believe everything you see, for you never know when you might be fooled!" He made a showy gesture with his hands, then smoke puffed out from the stage and he vanished. The crowd gasped and surged forward again until those in the front pointed out the trap door. A few moments later the crowd broke up, leaving Thomas and his two friends standing at the edge of the stage.

"Well," said George, grinning, "he certainly had me going for a while there. I thought he really did have magic or something. Didn't you?"

"Or something," agreed Eileen. She turned her attention to Thomas. "Well, I'll bet that made you forget your troubles for a while, didn't it?"

"Yes." Thomas was still staring at the stage. "Yes, it did." He shook his head, forcing himself out of his reverie. "It really did. We've got to grab the tailor." He started scanning the crowd. "The offer for supper at the tavern is still open, if you like."

"Oh, we like," said George.

"Indeed we do," agreed Eileen, "though you'll have to mind George doesn't eat you out of all your pocket money."

Thomas nodded absently and turned his eyes to the crowd, searching for the tailor. His thoughts were still with the little man on the stage. He had seen many magicians in the city. They performed on street-corners for change thrown from the crowd. One night, he'd even managed to get one to teach him several tricks.

Thomas had never taken his eyes off Timothy. Even while the crowd was getting boisterous and angry, Thomas had kept watching the little man, hoping for some clue that would show him how Timothy had done the trick.

Which is why Thomas, paying attention to the man's hands when no one else was, saw Timothy slip the little blue wooden ball out of his jacket pocket *after* the trick was over.

Chapter 3

The tailor, whose name was Alistair and who told Thomas to address him as such, please, insisted on taking them all to the pastry stand in honour of Thomas's victory. Thomas, now quite hungry, hadn't argued, and the three munched on blueberry jam pies as the tailor led them to his shop. A suit for Master Thomas? Oh, yes, of course. His father had already brought the fabric and paid for the work. If Thomas would just accompany him back to the shop…?

"He already paid for it?" asked Thomas, following in step beside the tailor.

"Indeed. He came in not two weeks ago, bringing fabric from his own warehouse, and mighty nice fabric at that. And he ordered boots to match, though the cobbler said he needed your foot size first, since he hasn't measured you since you were fourteen—he's at home by now, so you should drop by him next. Your father said it was to honour your work at the Academy."

Thomas was quite confused and said so.

"Oh, he's very proud of you. Why, he even bragged about that sword you have. Said you won it at a tournament which shows you weren't wasting your time there." The tailor chuckled. "Not that he approved of wearing swords, he was quick to add."

"I thought you said your father was furious at you." Eileen sounded as confused as Thomas felt.

"He was," said Thomas. "He was practically foaming."

"Could he have been pretending?" asked George.

"I don't think so." Thomas thought about it; shook his head. "No. Not a chance. Remember when he had the surprise party for my twelfth birthday? He couldn't think up a lie good enough to keep me distracted for half a day."

"I don't understand, Master Thomas," said the tailor, looking the very picture of mild consternation. "He never stops boasting about you."

Thomas shook his head again. "I don't understand, either."

* * *

The tailor measured Thomas thoroughly, cut the rich blue fabric John Flarety had chosen, and draped it on Thomas. Around a mouth full of pins, he promised that he and his assistants would work through the night. The suit would be ready for fitting the next morning, and done the next night, just as John Flarety had asked. Thomas thanked him and stood, dazed, as the fabric was pinned, marked, and taken away.

Thomas's head was spinning as they went to the cobbler's shop. The cobbler was as accommodating as the tailor. The leather had been selected and dyed, all it needed was to be cut and pieced together. The cobbler measured out Thomas's feet and promised him boots done by the next evening.

By the time Thomas was seated in the pub, his mind felt like a ship rolling in a high sea. Eileen and George let him alone, ordering their drinks and his, and talking to each other as he sat staring into space, his mind foundering in the events of the day.

His father was angry. His father was proud. The bishop said Thomas was a rogue and Thomas's father agreed. Timothy created a ball of light from nothing. His father thought Thomas was wasting money at school but wanted him to spend more money to come home sooner. His father had spent even more money on a fine new suit and boots, but wouldn't let his son sit at table with his guests. Timothy created a ball of light from nothing.

Timothy created a ball of light from nothing.

Too much education distracts a man from what's important, Thomas thought, quoting the favourite excuse at the Academy for dragging students from their studies to the taverns. His father was acting very strangely, and all Thomas could focus on was Timothy's trick. A dozen times he went through it in his head. It was not possible to make a ball of light, and certainly not to make one appear from thin air. Yet, he was certain that the juggler had done just that.

And it was a ball of light, not a ball of wood.

He knew that as sure as he knew he was breathing, and not just because he saw Timothy pull the wooden ball out of his jacket after the trick was over. Timothy could have had two, using the first ball for the trick, and then pulling the second one out for his finale, but that wasn't what happened. Thomas had stared at the ball of light, and knew for certain what it was.

Gavin sniffed right behind him.

The sound, so familiar from years of childhood studies, yanked Thomas from his reverie. He found himself sitting up straight and paying attention out of sheer habit. Gavin was standing beside the table, looking down his nose at the three of them. His hands were clutched tightly at the edge of his cloak, raising it to keep the hem off the floor. He spared a brief nod to George and Eileen then turned to Thomas. His brows were drawn tight together, and his lips pursed. Thomas braced himself for the lecture that usually accompanied the expression. It didn't come.

"I have a message from your father," Gavin said, instead. "You are to use the money he gave you to pay for the cost of your room."

"My room?" Thomas repeated. "Why do I need a room?"

Gavin's brows knitted further. "Your father thinks it best that you take a room for the night."

"What?" Thomas stared at Gavin until comprehension came, smashing into him like a wave. "WHAT?"

Gavin stumbled backwards in surprise. Thomas realized that he was on his feet, his hands planted hard against the table. Everyone in the tavern was staring. He didn't care. "Why?!"

"He didn't say, Master Thomas," said Gavin. "Only that he requests that you come for dinner tomorrow night, and that you present yourself in a more appropriate fashion."

"Present myself? I was coming home!"

"Master—"

"Don't 'Master' me! Do you know how long a walk it was? I've been rained on, chased by dogs, half frozen! I've been sleeping in barns and ditches for three weeks!"

George reached for him, "Thomas…"

Thomas shook him off. "No! All I wanted was to see my family. Yes, I look like a vagrant, but I can clean up quick enough!"

"Which is what your father wishes you to do," said Gavin, using his best school-master tone. "And when you have done so, you may present yourself to your family and their guests. He suggests tomorrow night. At dinner."

Thomas grabbed his bag and started for the door. Gavin took two quick steps and got in front of him. Thomas gritted his teeth to keep from shouting. "Get out of my way."

"Please do not attempt to go home tonight, Master Thomas."

Thomas tried to push past him, and Gavin stepped in his way again. "Thomas, he will have you turned away at the door."

Thomas stared at Gavin in shock. In that moment, he realized that his old tutor's pinched expression was for John Flarety. Gavin was angry, all right, but not at Thomas. Instead, the thin, awkward man put a hand on Thomas's shoulder and lowered his voice. "Your father left instructions with Brian, Master Thomas. You're not to be admitted into the house tonight." He squeezed Thomas's shoulder gently. "I'm sorry."

Thomas searched for words, but none came out. Everything around him seemed to fade.

"Take care of the lad," Thomas heard Gavin say, probably to George and Eileen. The school-master tone was gone, replaced by concern. "Please. The matter will be resolved by tomorrow night, I'm certain."

He gave a short bow, then turned on his heel, lifted his cloak higher, and carefully threaded his way out of the inn.

George's hand replaced Gavin's on Thomas's shoulder; led him back to his chair. Thomas sank into it, stunned.

"This isn't right," said Eileen. "He should be welcoming Thomas home."

"He must have a reason," George kept his hand on Thomas's shoulder. "It's not like him, at all. Even when he and Da fight, he's better behaved than this." He stopped, then amended, "Well, usually."

"I don't understand," Thomas said. A tremor started in his body, and he ruthlessly suppressed it. "What have I done?"

"Come home with us," said George. "Da will surely let you stay for the night."

"Aye, he will," said Eileen. "He and Mum will want to see you anyway, so why not tonight?"

"Come on," said George. "You can have supper at our house."

Thomas shook his head, trying to clear away his confusion. "No. No, we eat here. And we drink here." He looked at the mug of beer before him, then picked it up and drained half of it before setting it down. "I'm here with my friends and tonight we eat and we drink and we celebrate. Tomorrow, I'll get myself cleaned up and dressed up and go home."

"The forge will heat water faster than anything else around here," said George. "We'll get you a hot bath and you can show up at your father's door looking better than any of his guests."

"Good." Thomas drained the mug. "Tomorrow, I go home," he said, gesturing for the bartender to bring more drinks. "And then I find out what's going on here."

* * *

The sun set long before Thomas led his two friends, stumbling and laughing, out of the woods and to the old grain mill with its waterwheel and the stream above, and its deep pond below. "There!" he declared. "Found it!"

"And after only a quarter-hour of looking," laughed Eileen. "You missed the path entirely!"

"True," agreed Thomas. "But I found it!"

They had sat in the tavern for hours, drinking far more than was good for them, and eating far more than they should. Thomas spent his silver liberally, feeding his friends soup and roast beef and fresh bread and berry tarts hot from the oven. His father would be appalled, Thomas was sure.

He had shoved the events of the day firmly to the back of his mind and bought a round for the tavern, declaring his homecoming an occasion for celebration. He demanded to know what had happened in Elmvale over last four years and listened as everyone told stories and jokes. He had to force himself to enjoy it at first, but as the evening wore on, he found himself having fun. George and Eileen told stories on each other that had Thomas gasping for air, he was laughing so hard. The innkeeper had thanked them as they left, and told them to come back the next day for fiddling and dancing. Thomas, still laughing, bowed deeply and promised solemnly to return.

Now Thomas was staring at the mill pond where he and George used to swim years before. In the dim light of the quarter moon, the mill and the woods were shades of grey and silver. The waterwheel was still; a black shadow against the night-darkened stone of the mill. The trees stood silent; no whisper from their leaves or stir from their branches as they reached thin fingers of twig and leaf out over the pond. The wood behind them was a mass of grey shadows, barely distinct and fading to black after only a few feet. On the edge of the pond, a single large stone, the perfect size and shape for jumping from, sat anchored, half in the wood, half in the water. There was no breeze to ripple the pond, and the smooth dark surface reflected the moon and stars back to the sky. Thomas stood at the edge of the water, feeling the pleasant warmth of the evening fading with his friends' laughter. The creatures of the woods began making their night sounds again as the three friends fell silent, filling the gentle air with a sonorous buzz.

"We should head home," said Eileen, after a time.

Thomas snorted. "Wish I could."

"You'll go home tomorrow."

"Why not tonight?" Thomas demanded. The pain that had been simmering since dinner boiled over, "Why shouldn't I be home tonight? I used to live there, didn't I?"

"You still do," said George.

"Then why can't I go home?!"

"Shhh!" Eileen said. "You'll wake the entire village, you will."

"Or worse," said George, "my father."

"We're too far from the village to wake anyone." Thomas lowered his voice as he said it, though. He squatted on his haunches and turned his eyes back to the water. George sat down on the ground to one side of the stone, Eileen on the other.

"I used to sneak out here at night to swim." Eileen said. "The pond looks so black when you're above it, but once you're underneath, the moonlight turns everything silver."

"What?" George leaned back and raised his eyebrows at his sister. "What would Mother say about that?"

"About the same as she would have about you and Thomas, if she'd caught you." Eileen said tartly. She looked back at the pond. "Sometimes I'd just sit out here and watch the moon dance on the pond when the wind blew."

Thomas took a deep breath, willing his anger and frustration down. It sank back, still lurking beneath the surface, but not so overwhelming. "Did you sneak out often?" he asked.

Eileen shook her head, smiling. "I didn't want to get caught. Besides, if you do something special too much, it isn't special anymore."

Thomas nodded. Silence fell again, but not as heavily as before.

Eileen was the first to break it. "What's the city like?"

Thomas thought about it. "Noisy," he said. "The first thing you notice is the noise. There's thousands of people moving around all the time, though not so much at night, and they all make noise. The people there don't know each other well enough to care about each other, so everyone treats everyone else as a stranger."

"And you like it there?" asked George, sounding rather unimpressed.

"Aye, I do." He let his weight sink back and half-sat, half-fell on the ground. "It's noisy and smelly and the sewers back up when it rains and there's people who wouldn't give food to a starving man, but I like it. I like getting up in the morning and buying bread from the baker and fruit from the fruit sellers and sitting by the dirty river looking at the towers of the church and watching the people go by."

He looked out across the water of the pond and in his mind saw the city on the other side. "There's times, when it's been raining all day. The sun breaks through the clouds just before it goes down. Everything has been washed clean by the rain and then the sun hits it and all the grey buildings and all the dirty streets are suddenly paved in light and gold." He remembered, then, standing on the roof of his apartment, looking out. "The palace is roofed in bronze, and so are the High Father's church and the city hall. And when the sun comes out it hits them one at a time, lighting them like fire. And they stay that way until the sun goes down and they fade like embers." He blinked and the city faded, leaving the dark mill pond before him. Thomas shook his head. "I talk too much when I'm drunk."

"Aye, you do," agreed George. "You make it sound good, though."

"It is," said Thomas. *No matter what my father says about it.*

"I'd like to visit," Eileen said, her voice quieter than before.

George snorted. "Aye, I know. Every time Thomas's father starts talking about it, you start going on about how you want to visit." He waved a hand at her. "You just want to sneak into that Academy of his."

Thomas shook his head. "They wouldn't let you in."

"I know," said Eileen. "Girls aren't allowed to learn anything."

Thomas heard the bitterness in her voice. "The Academy really isn't that much to look at, you know," he said, trying to lighten her mood. "Half the rooms haven't been repainted in two hundred years and the other half they don't let students into anyway."

"What about the library?" asked Eileen. "It is really as big as your father says?"

"I don't know how big he says it is," said Thomas. "It's five stories tall, and has thousands of books in it. The main floor is all tables for people to sit and read and columns to hold up the rest of the place and windows so you can see. In the afternoon, you can spend an hour just watching the dust dancing on the air."

Eileen's voice was wistful. "Sounds wonderful."

"To you," snorted George. "Me, I don't think I could stand it there."

"Not much for reading?" Thomas asked.

"Nor for writing," said Eileen. "He wouldn't have learned either if Da hadn't made him."

"Unlike her," snorted George. "Ever since the nuns taught her to read, she's had her nose in whatever books she could borrow."

"The only one I have with me is in Perthian," said Thomas. "Next time I come back, I'll bring some histories. You'd like them."

"What's that?" said George, pointing into the woods.

Thomas turned to look and saw a thin flicker of light moving far off in the trees. "I don't know."

Eileen stood up to see. "Looks like a torch."

"Shouldn't be," said George. "There's nothing over there. Besides, everyone should be inside asleep, saving their energy for the Fire tomorrow night."

"Shush," said Thomas. "Listen."

George cocked his head. "I don't hear..." He stopped. The woods had fallen silent. All the night creatures had stopped their noises and everything was still, as if holding its breath. A moment later, Thomas caught a shout, faint and distant, then another. He pushed himself to his feet. "Come on."

"Not that way," said George, catching his arm. "There's a path on the other side of the pond."

The three slipped into the woods with George soundlessly leading them. Thomas was aware for the first time how much noise he made when he walked. He paid more attention to how he was stepping, and soon found himself moving, if not actually quietly, then softer, at least. Ahead, the torches began to get brighter. Thomas could hear voices, angry and demanding.

"Come out of there, you little rat!" a man yelled.

The reply was muffled, but it seemed to anger the speaker.

"You think we won't burn you out? I'll torch that pretty wagon and listen to you squeal."

"No need to torch it," said a second man. "It's a waste of a good wagon. I say we smoke him out. He'll beg us to let him come out into the air."

"There's no time," a third one said. "Bash in the door."

The three friends reached the edge of a small clearing with a wagon path running through it. On the far side of the clearing a dark horse jerked nervously back and forth on its tether. There were three men standing in the clearing, all with rough faces that showed clearly the fights and privations they had survived. Their clothes were plain and dark, but not travel-worn or ragged as one would expect of bandits. Two held torches and daggers in their hands, the third had an axe. They were surrounding a large box wagon covered in colourful, swirling designs that the flickering yellow light made ugly and garish.

"We're about a mile from the common," George whispered. "That's the juggler's wagon."

"What do they want with him, do you think?" asked Eileen, speaking no louder than George.

"Nothing good." He looked around, "Never a stick around when you need one."

"Last chance!" called the shorter of the two torch-bearers. "Come out. His Grace is waiting for you."

"I'll die before I go near him!" shouted Timothy from inside the wagon.

"No, but you'll wish you had, I'll bet. Billy, start on the door."

"We have to stop them," whispered Thomas.

"Three on two," mused George. "I think we can do it."

"Three on three," hissed Eileen.

"Two," said George, glaring at his sister. "I'll not be risking your life."

The axe sunk into the wagon's door with a dull thud.

Thomas looked closer at the three men. "There's only the one axe," he said. "The other two just have daggers. Come on."

"One moment." George looked around him, then reached up and grabbed a low, thick tree branch some six feet long. The branch bent in his hand, then split from the tree with a loud "CRACK!"

"By the Four," said Thomas. "Remind me not to get on your bad side."

George grinned, and Thomas turned his attention back to the men in the clearing. The three men had all spun around, and were now peering into the woods. Thomas took the moment to step out of the woods and into the light of the torches, his hands on the grips of his rapier and dagger.

"Well," Thomas said, raising his voice to fill the clearing, "here's a bunch up to no good!"

No one moved for a moment, then the biggest of the men stepped forward. "Run off, lad, before—"

The metallic hiss of blade leaving scabbard stopped him. Thomas's rapier and dagger gleamed yellow in the flickering light. "I think not."

The other two men in the clearing shuffled nervously, looking to the big one. George stepped casually out of the woods beside Thomas, using his knife to strip the last twigs from the branch. Eileen stepped out beside him, doing her best to look defiant. George took his time looking over the three rough men before saying, "And what do you think you're doing disturbing a guest of our village, then?"

"Leave," Thomas said, "or my friend and I will keep you busy while the young lady runs back to town and fetches the watch."

The big man sneered. "They'll not reach here in time."

"To save your lives?" Thomas asked. "Probably not. Want to find out?"

The man frowned, his face crushing in on itself. His two companions were not at all happy with the idea of a fight, to judge from the way they were shifting their feet. George finished stripping the twigs from the branch and, after examining it a moment, snapped off the thinnest two feet from it, leaving him a four foot club. He swung it experimentally.

The biggest of the men stepped forward and threw his torch at Thomas. Thomas ducked to one side, and when he straightened the man was already running into the woods. His companions followed, dropping their torches on the ground before vanishing into the trees. Thomas grabbed up the torch that the first man had thrown, stomping out the small blazes it had left on the ground. George ran forward and grabbed up the other two.

"City folk," snorted George as he stomped out the small licks of flame on the ground. "No country man tosses a lit torch to the ground in the woods."

"Well, they can't all be smart," Thomas said. He sheathed his blades, realizing he was grinning like an idiot. Alcohol was said to make men both brave and foolish, and he'd been a prime example of that tonight.

"It worked!" Eileen crowed. "They ran off! I can't believe it!"

"They weren't ready for a fight," Thomas felt breathless. "They just wanted to get at Timothy."

"You were sure of that, were you?" George asked.

Thomas's grin grew wider. "No."

"Fool of a scholar," said George, punching him lightly in the shoulder.

"Aye." Thomas took a deep breath, releasing tension he hadn't known was there as the air came out. "But it worked."

George walked up to the wagon, examined the axe marks on the door. He whistled. "Nearly got through, there." He raised a big hand and knocked at the door. "Juggler? Juggler! It's safe to come out now."

"Go away!" shouted Timothy.

"It's all right," said Eileen, going to stand beside her brother. "They're gone!"

"Just go!"

Thomas went to the wagon and knocked on the door. "Timothy? It's Thomas, the scholar. Are you all right?"

"If you're still scared, we can take you into town," George offered. "We'll hook up your horse to the wagon, and move you into our back yard."

"I don't want to be in your back yard!" Timothy yelled. "I want to be left alone!"

"At least come to the door so we can see you're all right," said Thomas. "After that we'll leave you alone."

There was a long silence, then the sound of slow movement inside the wagon. The door opened a crack. Timothy peered out at them then opened the door wide. Even in the dim light of the torches he looked pale and shaky. He leaned against the door frame, his breath ragged.

"Are you all right?" asked Eileen.

"Aye, I am." He scanned the clearing before stepping out of the wagon. "I can't say as I'm liking your village folk too much, though."

"They weren't from our village," said George. "I'd have recognized them."

"Maybe they were bandits," suggested Eileen. "Though there's not been a bandit around here for twenty years."

"Maybe they're with the bishop," said Thomas. "They said they were going to take you to 'his Grace.' "

"The bishop has no reason to want the likes of me." Timothy's words spilled out in a rush. He waved the idea away with a quick, jerky gesture. "No reason at all. They must have wanted me for something else."

Timothy moved slowly into the clearing, head swivelling back and forth, eyes darting in all directions. He was obviously shaken up and scared and Thomas didn't press him with any questions. Thankfully, neither did Eileen or George. If Timothy didn't want to speak, Thomas wasn't going to try to make him. The little man reached the centre of the clearing and turned in a slow circle. Thomas watched a bit longer, then turned to his friends.

"Well," Thomas said. "We'll go."

George and Eileen muttered assent and started for the woods.

"Don't!" Timothy's voice was loud and frightened. He stopped and looked at his feet. A moment later, he breathed deep and straightened up. He smiled, the expression slightly forced, but with real pleasure behind it. "Such a night of adventures!" he said, the showman's tone back in his voice. "I think it calls for a drink, don't you?" Timothy turned to George. "Build up the fire, lad, and I'll get a bottle and some mugs. We'll toast your victory over the forces of darkness." He stopped, and some of the confidence was gone from his voice when he said, "You will join me, won't you?"

Thomas looked to his friends. George nodded first then Eileen, a little hesitantly, a moment later. "Gladly," said Thomas.

Timothy moved lightly back across the clearing and into the wagon. George tossed the two torches into the fire-pit, then started adding kindling and branches from the pile Timothy had beside the pit. Thomas tossed his torch in beside the other two. Timothy came back moments later with a bottle and mugs in one hand, a lute in the other, and blankets over his arms.

"Take these, would you, Scholar?" he said, waving the bottle. "We may as well be comfortable as not."

Thomas relieved him of the drink, while Eileen took the blankets. The fire began to blaze up. George fed several larger logs into the pit, then sat back to watch the results.

"That's it," said Timothy, looking at the fire. "Well done! Now, one blanket for the lassie, one for each of you, and one for me. And mugs all around. Be careful pouring, Scholar; that's a strong whiskey. Just the thing to end a night of adventures."

In short order everyone was seated on a blanket and all were sipping at the whiskey. Timothy tuned the lute then began strumming gently. Only the faint shaking of his hands betrayed his state of mind, and the tremor quickly stilled as he expertly ran through chord changes and finger exercises.

"Here's to you three," he said after a time, taking one hand from the lute and using it to raise his mug. "Without you, I'd probably be beaten and robbed and my wagon burnt down around me." He drank deeply. Thomas followed his example, as did George. Eileen did the same and nearly choked, making George grin. She stuck her tongue out at her brother once she got her breath back, then sipped at the whiskey.

"Tell me," said Timothy, looking at the three young people, "not that I'm not grateful, but what in the names of the Four are you doing out on a night like this?"

"Taking Thomas to our house for the night," said George. "I saw the lights and Thomas heard the shouting. So we came to have a look."

"And thank the Blessed Daughter, Granter of Wishes, for that," Timothy took another drink of the whiskey. "Why were you taking the scholar to your house?" He looked at Thomas. "Thought you'd just come home, lad. Don't your parents want you?"

"Not tonight, they don't," said Thomas. He took another swallow, shuddered, and changed the subject with, "By the Four above, did you make this yourself?"

"Nay, got it two years ago from a seller of spirits in exchange for a song."

"A song?" Eileen leaned forward. "What sort of song?"

"Oh, it's a depressing one," warned Timothy. "He lost his love while he was serving in the king's fleet and wanted a song about her. Not a great one for late nights by the fire."

"I'd like to hear it," said Eileen. "I've never heard a song played by the person who made it."

Timothy shrugged. "Well, if the lads have no objection."

"None."

"None at all."

"Then I'll sing it." His voice was a light baritone, and his fingers roved skilfully over the lute as he worked his way through the lyrics:

> "Alas, my love has gone away,
> And I must wait here many a day.
> Love, I cannot follow your way
> Until in the ground I lie.
>
> "I was to sail across the sea
> She begged, 'Sir, come back to me.
> For you know I will love only thee
> Until in the ground I lie.'
>
> "As my love watched and cried,
> I sailed off to see the world so wide,
> And my poor love fell sick and died,
> And now in the ground she'll lie.
>
> "So sleep, my love, do not despair,
> For the Mother I know keeps you fair,
> And soon my love I will join you there,
> And in the ground I will lie."

"He must miss her terribly," whispered Eileen as the lute's notes carried them through the last chords of the song.

"I heard that played in one of the taverns in the city," Thomas said. "I never knew where it came from."

Timothy grinned. "How could you, lad? I hadn't told you." He shifted his fingers on the lute and began playing a jig. "Here, let's lighten up our moods before we all get depressed. And refill those glasses!"

He made the strings dance as he played, and soon his small audience was clapping and singing along with him in the choruses as he went from one dance tune to another. He played until he claimed to be tired then took to telling stories for a while. They listened, enraptured, until the lateness of the hour and the strength of the whiskey began to claim them. George, who'd been imbibing rather freely at the tavern before, ended up stretched out on his blanket, snoring. Eileen fell asleep as well, and Thomas rolled up his own blanket to act as a cushion for her head.

"Well, it grows late, lad." Timothy said at last, looking around him. "Or rather it grows early. The moon is down."

"Aye," Thomas agreed, looking at the sky. "Darkest before the dawn."

"It always is," said the juggler.

Thomas took another sip of his whiskey. He had drunk more than enough already to make him careless of words, and there was something that he really wanted to know. "Timothy, can I ask you something?"

"About what?"

Thomas glanced down at Eileen and George. Both were sound asleep. He lowered his voice and took the plunge: "About what you said today, about the Blessed Daughter…"

Timothy laughed. "It was a story my mother used to tell. Said she got it from her mother. One time, long ago, the Four were equals. Not a family, but Gods together, and they each had names." He took another drink, mused on his story a moment. "The names are gone now, of course, but she said that, back when they had names, they all created the world together. The Mother created the earth and the sea and all living things. The Father created the sky and the weather and the forces that make the earth shake and the tides roll. The Son put iron in the ground and gave man fire and the knowledge to use it. And the Blessed daughter, well, she gave the world music and joy and magic.

"And the Banished had names, too. They were the first of the Four's creations; beautiful and immortal and doomed. They tried to overthrow the gods and were driven below ground, to lie in torment until the end of time, able to venture out on the earth only when summoned by those who would use their power."

Timothy reached forward and stirred the coals of the fire, then sat back. "Then, of course, the Church of the High Father got the ear of the king." He reached for the bottle again, found it empty, and set it aside. Grinning at Thomas, he said, "What happened next, Scholar?"

"The Church of the High Father began to rise in strength and declared itself to be the one true religion," said Thomas, remembering the history and theology classes he'd taken. "Took two hundred years and a half-dozen wars.

The other gods were declared to be lesser beings who assisted the High Father in his creation, but who were not worthy of worship themselves. The High Father became creator of all, the Mother was reduced to his consort. The son became the Rebel Son, whose gifts to man were against the will of the High Father. The Daughter became the image of frivolity."

Thomas took another sip of his drink. "It didn't work, completely. The nunneries are all dedicated to the Mother. Smiths and miners and carpenters all have shrines to the Son, who brought man tools and taught them to use them. The theatres all have images of the Daughter carved into their stages. Of course," he added carefully, "I never heard about the daughter giving man magic."

"No one has, laddie," said Timothy, raising his empty glass to Thomas. "It makes a great yarn, though."

"Aye, it does," said Thomas. "Do you believe it?"

Timothy lowered his glass. His eyes, which had been gently unfocused with the alcohol, were now looking sharply into Thomas's. "Now why would I believe it?"

"Because you have magic."

In the dim light of the last flames, Thomas saw Timothy go pale. "I have no magic, boy."

"You made a ball of light appear out of your hand," said Thomas. "You made it float, and you made it disappear afterwards."

Timothy waved the idea away with a harsh slash of his hand at the air. "Nonsense! All I did today was fool the lot of you."

"I was watching you," Thomas said slowly, "after the trick to see where you were hiding the ball."

"Were you now?" Timothy looked away. Abruptly he got to his feet. "And what did you see?"

Thomas suddenly felt nervous. He plunged on anyway. "I saw you take that ball out of your jacket pocket after the trick was over."

Timothy's hand was shaking when he raised his mug to drink again. He realized it was empty, and tossed it onto the grass. "Look, lad, I don't know what you thought you saw—"

"Magic, you said."

"Illusion," corrected Timothy. "Tricks to deceive the eye."

Thomas shook his head, remembering what he saw. "Magic."

"Dammit, boy!" Timothy snapped, bringing Thomas upright with his sudden vehemence, "It was a trick! It was my best one, but it was still just a trick!"

"It was real," Thomas insisted.

"It was a ball on a thread!" Timothy was sweating now, "and you'll get me burned if you keep noising about witchcraft!"

"I'm not talking about witchcraft, I'm talking about magic!"

"And who but a scholar knows the difference?" demanded Timothy. "And who but a scholar cares? Everyone else would be happy to burn a man for witchcraft if they knew about it!"

"They don't burn you for witchcraft," Eileen said in a soft, sleepy voice. "They hang you."

Both men stared at her in surprise and she blinked back at them, her eyes half-open. As they watched, she snuggled her head against the blanket. "Is it time to go home yet, Thomas?"

"Aye, I think it is," Thomas said, still looking at the juggler.

"Well, tell me when to get up." Her eyes closed again.

Timothy's voice was much quieter when he next spoke. "Look, Scholar, you said there's no such thing as witchcraft."

"Aye," Thomas nodded. "I did."

"There you go, then. There's no such thing." He rose up and began kicking dirt into the fire. "It's time you left."

"Timothy," Thomas forced himself to think through the alcohol. "I didn't say you used witchcraft..."

Timothy said nothing, just kept kicking dirt on the fire until the last of the flames died and the only light was the dim red glow of the embers beneath.

"Please," Thomas said. "All I want to know is if it's real."

Timothy stopped kicking at the coals and stared at the ground for a time. The thin red light made his face old, bringing out every line of worry and strain. "Those three you chased off also asked about witchcraft, lad."

Thomas heard the fear in Timothy's voice, saw it in his face. Timothy didn't say anything more, just stood there, looking into the dying fire. With a sudden movement he kicked once more and smothered the last of the coals.

"I'm sorry," said Thomas into the darkness. "I won't talk about it again."

It took Timothy a long time to answer, his voice floating out of the night to Thomas. "Do you promise?"

"I do. And I'll swear by the Four as well if you like."

Timothy chuckled. "No need, lad. If you can't take the word of a scholar, whose is worth taking?"

Thomas managed a smile back, though he was sure Timothy couldn't see it. "Will we see you at the fair tomorrow, then?"

"You will. Now let's wake up that big lump of a friend of yours."

Chapter 4

The smithy and the house beside it stood on the edge of town. George's father had built both with his own hands. Thomas, who had spent nearly half his childhood in and around their house, remembered it very well. It was a pleasant home, well lit and sunny, even in the loft that George used as his room. It was also the single worst place in Elmvale to try to sleep off a hangover.

The morning was achingly bright, even through Thomas's closed eyelids. His mouth was dry and fuzzy all at once, and his head felt like Lionel's hammer was pounding away inside it instead of on the anvil outside. George's father had always said, "A smith's work is never done, from break of day to setting sun," and true to his word, the man was putting hammer to anvil with what Thomas considered far too much vigour for this time of the morning.

Thomas opened his eyes and discovered that the sun had just cleared the woods and was shining directly into his face. He thought about crawling completely under the blankets, but gave it up. He could escape from the sunlight, but the noise from the forge wasn't going to stop and it would take far more than the blanket to block it out.

Thomas cursed Lionel's industriousness and reached for his breeches.

A few moments later, his feet bare and his shirt in his hand, Thomas stumbled through the kitchen, into the backyard, and over to the well. He hauled on the rope to bring up the bucket. It was half-full when it came up. Thomas took the few steps to the trough that George and Eileen's father kept for visiting animals, bent forward, and poured the contents of the bucket over his head.

The water was cold. Thomas gritted his teeth against the sudden shock of it. His entire body erupted in chills and his head felt like it was simultaneously swelling inside and being crushed from without. He pulled himself away and stumbled back, gasping. After a moment, he forced himself upright.

The headache was still there, but the world was no longer a blur. The yard was as it always had been: a patch of earth stamped hard by continuous foot traffic and cleared of all vegetation for fear of sparks from the forge catching on dry grass. The smithy still had stone walls blackened by flame and soot and doors wide enough to admit a horse for shoeing. They were wide open, now, and Lionel had stopped his hammering to wave at Thomas. George, working the bellows and showing no sign of disability, did the same. Given how much his friend drank the night before, Thomas wondered how he was standing at all, let alone working away.

Thomas waved back, then shook the water out of his hair. The movement sent little jolts of pain through his head. He put on his shirt and headed back to the house, hardly stumbling at all until he reached the threshold and tripped into the kitchen.

Thomas had always loved their kitchen. It wasn't a large place; the wooden table that served both as eating and working surface took up most of it. The smooth stone floors were always swept clean, the walls wiped free of any grease or soot from the hearth. The shelves were full with plates and bowls and mugs and the pantry off to the side was fairly bursting with food. A good number of Lionel's customers would pay in barter, and as a result, Thomas had never visited to find a bare pantry. Thomas breathed deeply and smelled what was no doubt a very good breakfast in the making. He turned towards the large stone hearth that took up most of one wall and saw Eileen and her mother both watching him. Her mother shook a spoon at him.

"About time you woke up," said Magda Gobhann.

Eileen's mother had red hair like her daughter, and was almost the same size, though the years had added a pleasant stoutness to her build. With great embarrassment, Thomas realized that they must have been standing there when he'd stumbled through the kitchen moments before. He opened his mouth to apologize, but was swept into Magda's arms for a hug and kissed on both cheeks before he could say anything.

"You are too thin," she declared, stepping back and looking him over with a critical eye. "We'll do something about that right now." She turned to Eileen. "Go fetch your father and brother from the smithy."

"No need." George stepped into the kitchen, looking none the worse for wear save for slightly bloodshot eyes. Thomas was amazed and envious all at once. "We spotted him in the yard." George grinned. "How are you this morning, Thomas?"

"I've been better."

"I'll bet you have," laughed Lionel, clapping Thomas heartily on the back and sending him stumbling. The smith was a match for his son in height and several inches wider. His face had the well-earned wrinkles and scorches of a man who spent his years before the forge.

"George told us something of last night," Magda said, catching Thomas's arm and pulling him upright. "Though how you ended up here instead of at home with your family is beyond us." She held up a hand to forestall Thomas's answer. "You can explain it all to us over breakfast."

"She'll have five pounds on you before you leave the house tonight," said Lionel, smiling. "And good thing, too; your father will never recognize you looking like that."

How very true, thought Thomas.

"Now go and finish getting dressed," said Magda. "Breakfast will be on the table when you come down."

* * *

Thomas did not do much talking after he sat down at the table. He tried, but the food grabbed his attention and held it. The table was stout enough to knead dough on without making it shake, and strong enough for twelve-year old George to stand on before his mother caught him. Today, though, Thomas was certain he could hear it groan under the weight of the food Magda had put on it. There was crisp bacon and hot, honeyed porridge and fried eggs fresh from the hen-house and a loaf of bread that was so fluffy that Magda must have let it rise on the hearth overnight. Thomas worked his way through two helpings of everything.

"That," he said finally, mopping up the last bit of egg with a slice of fresh bread, "was the best breakfast I have eaten in two years."

"Now, surely you exaggerate," beamed Magda.

"Not in the slightest," protested Thomas. He held up the bread. "In the city, a warm piece of bread in the morning is considered a luxury."

"No wonder you're so thin," said Magda. "Your mother must be appalled."

Thomas had managed not to think about his family at all while he was eating. The mention of them brought back all that had happened the day before and turned the taste of the fresh, warm bread to ashes in his mouth. It took him a moment before he could force himself to swallow. "She was."

If his tone revealed his feelings, Magda hadn't noticed. "And speaking of your mother, you'll be heading home right after breakfast," she scolded. "Your first night home and you spend it here! And did you really think you could all sneak in at dawn without waking us up?"

Magda threw a glare around the room, pinning her own children to their chairs. Thomas, hoping for some defence from his friends, quickly realized none was forthcoming. "One had hopes—"

"Aye, I'm sure you did." She smacked him lightly on the back of the head with the flat of her hand. "And that's for not letting us know what the three of you were up to. Bringing my daughter home so late." She shook a finger at Thomas. "If her brother hadn't been with you, I'd have had Lionel take the stropping leather to you!"

Thomas wasn't sure if Magda was actually angry or just teasing him until Lionel caught his eye and winked at him. Thomas breathed a sigh of relief and rose to his feet. "I beg your pardon," he said, giving the best court bow he could manage. "I assure you that nothing of the sort shall happen again while I am a guest under your roof."

Magda rolled her eyes and did her best not to smile. "There's an easy promise to keep, since I'm sending you straight home."

Thomas looked to his friends. Neither looked at all comfortable, and Thomas guessed that neither had told their parents what had happened. Thomas tried to find words, but in the end only said, "I'm to go home tonight."

"Tonight?" Magda shook her head. "No, you'll be going home right after breakfast, if I have to drag you there myself."

Thomas took a deep breath. "I can't."

"Can't?" repeated Lionel. "Why not?"

His conversation with his father came back to Thomas in a rush. He had no desire to explain, he realized. He tried to keep his tone light as he said: "My father prefers me to come home tonight." He smiled around the bitter words. "Properly attired, to meet his guests."

" 'Properly attired?' " Magda's voice rose on the words. "If it was George or Eileen, we'd have the doors open to them if they were dressed in rags and the king himself was here."

"Aye, well…" Thomas avoided Magda's eyes and took his seat again. "Father probably just wants to give me a proper welcome. You know, throw a big party; have his son make a grand entrance." *Assuming he lets me in the door.* "He even had me get a new suit for the occasion."

"Did he now?" asked Lionel.

"A very nice one, from the fabric," said Eileen. "The tailor will have it ready for him this afternoon."

"Well, he must have something planned, then," said Lionel, leaning back and taking a sip from his tea.

Magda shook her head. "Stranger and stranger. Still, if that's what your father wants…" She turned a critical eye over Thomas's travelling clothes. "Do you have something other than that to wear?"

"In my bag," said Thomas.

"Then get it." Magda poked George's shoulder. "Take Thomas out to the smithy and get some water heated up for a bath. And loan him your razor. We'll have you looking presentable, Thomas. That way your father will have no cause to complain."

"Not that he won't anyway," Lionel snorted. "Did George tell you what he said to—"

"Now you stop that," scolded Magda. "The boy has enough trouble as it is." She turned back to Thomas. "Get yourself cleaned up, then spend the day at the fair."

"We'll keep him out of trouble," promised George.

Magda looked at her off-spring and snorted. "You two? You'll put him in it, you mean."

"We never got Thomas into trouble," said George.

"True," agreed Eileen. "It was always his idea."

"It was not!" protested Thomas to the laughter of the siblings.

"Enough!" Magda shooed them all towards the door. "Out!"

Still laughing, George and Eileen led Thomas out of the house. Thomas waited until they were out of parental earshot before speaking. "I take it you didn't tell them about Timothy."

"I told them as little as possible," said George, leading Thomas towards the smithy. "Said we spent the night drinking at the tavern, then sat by the mill pond talking until dawn."

"Good thing, too," said Eileen. "Ma hates it when we get in fights."

"And do you get into fights often?" asked Thomas, remembering her habits of throwing rocks and kicking shins when he and George teased her.

"Not anymore," said Eileen, smiling sweetly at him. She scooped up a bucket and tossed it to him. "Now hurry up. There's a fiddler at the tavern today."

* * *

It was most of an hour later when Thomas emerged, clean, dry, and wearing a clean white shirt and brown pants from his bag. The bath had been steaming hot and exactly what Thomas needed. He had shaved away the scruffy beard and scrubbed at his body and hair until all of the dirt from the road was gone, then sat back in the large tub and soaked until the water turned tepid.

After calling a quick good-bye and thanks to Magda and Lionel, Thomas followed his friends down the wooded lane to the town common and the fair. The sound of happy voices chattering and music playing floated through the air to call them forward.

"Took you long enough," complained George.

"It's been a long time since I had a proper bath," said Thomas.

"Aye, we noticed," said Eileen, smiling to take the sting from the words. "You smell much better now."

Thomas smiled back. "I'm sure I do."

"So what do we want to do at the fair?" asked George. "There's races and archery this morning."

"First, we make sure Timothy is all right," said Thomas. "Then we should find the Reeve and tell him what happened. Is it still old Bluster?"

"Aye," George grinned. "It will probably make his day. He's had nothing to deal with but the occasional tavern brawl for years."

Timothy was on his stage, looking none the worse for the night's adventures and imbibing. He spotted them as they passed by and gave them a jaunty wave with one foot—he was standing on his hands—then flipped to his feet and bowed deeply. When he came up, he had three balls in his hands that he began juggling while reciting a rather bawdy poem.

"He looks all right," said Eileen.

Thomas waved back. "Aye, he does."

"He's fine," George said. "Come on. Let's find Bluster before Timothy there challenges Thomas to another round of riddles."

They left the juggler and quickly found Bluster sitting on a stool underneath a tree at the edge of the town commons. He was a thin man, of average height, in his later years. He had been appointed Town Reeve, in charge of maintaining order in the village, some thirty years ago by the Abbess. He had kept his position by keeping the peace firmly in hand. Nothing more than the occasional brawl disturbed the town, and those ended as soon as Bluster stepped into the room. He sat, smoking a pipe and looking for all the world as if he was ready for a nap. His eyes never strayed from the crowd, though. Thomas was certain that, if asked, Bluster would be able to tell them everything that had happened since he began his watch.

"George, Eileen, and I believe Thomas," said the Reeve, sitting up and smiling as they came close. He looked over Thomas, head to foot. "It has been a while since we've seen you around these parts, has it not, laddie?"

"It has," Thomas agreed.

"I thought your father had packed you off to the city to keep you out of trouble."

"He did."

"And he's allowed you to return, then?"

More or less, Thomas thought, but before he could answer, George stepped forward. "Nay. I wrote Thomas and asked him to come back so we could have another go at rafting the mill stream."

Bluster snorted. "Wonderful. I'll need a mighty big hook to pull you out of the water this time." He turned his attention to Eileen. "You need to steer clear of these two. Why, this one—" he hooked a thumb in Thomas's direction, "—has taken to carrying a sword, I hear. Where is it, by the way?"

"At George's house."

"Good thing, too. A silly city fashion, it is." Bluster leaned back against the tree. "All right, you three, what did you come here for? I know you wouldn't be talking to an old grump like me if you weren't after something."

"We're not after anything," said Thomas, "but something happened last night we thought you should know about."

Bluster raised an eyebrow. "And what would that be?"

"There were three men in the woods last night," George said. "Strangers. They attacked Timothy."

"Timothy?"

"The juggler," explained Thomas.

"They were going to kill him," added Eileen.

"And before you say it, I've grown too old for pranks like this," finished George.

"Oh, I didn't say it was a prank," said Bluster. He crossed his arms. "What happened? From the beginning."

"We were by the mill pond late last night," said Eileen. "We saw torches and heard voices so we went to look."

Bluster nodded. "And seeing three men attacking the juggler, what did you do?"

"Well," Thomas began, "I did have my sword, then."

"And I was bigger than all of them," said George.

"And all they had were daggers," added Eileen.

"Except the one with the axe."

"But he was using it to break down the wagon's door, not fight."

Bluster waited for the comments to stop, then leaned forward. "Was there a fight, then?"

"No!" all three chorused.

"They saw the three of us and decided it wasn't worth the effort," said Thomas.

"Humph." The Reeve leaned back again and tapped the ashes from his pipe. "And Timothy will say the same?"

"He will," said Eileen. "Though he was hiding in his wagon for most of it."

"Humph." Bluster put fresh weed into his pipe and tapped it down. "Bandits. Haven't had bandits here in twenty years." He lit the pipe and took a puff. "Trouble seems to be following that one around."

"What do you mean?" asked Thomas.

"I mean that little display yesterday," said Bluster. "Witchcraft has been the talk of the village this morning. Half of them think he's in league with the Banished and want me to put him under arrest for it. The other half is ready to sneak out into the woods to have him read their fortunes or cast charms on their neighbours."

"Him?" snorted George. "Good luck. He's got no more magic in him than Da has in the back end of his anvil."

"Really?" said Bluster. "Then what were you doing out in the woods last night?"

"Talking," Thomas said. "We were at the tavern until it closed, then we headed back to George's house."

"Which is nowhere near the mill pond."

"We know," said Eileen. "But the scholar here decided he wanted to go there and thought he could find it in the dark." She rolled her eyes. "Took him long enough, too. We'd just gotten there where we saw the bandits' torches and went to look."

"I see." Bluster crossed his arms once more and gave the three a long stare. After a time, he nodded — whether to some decision he'd made or in agreement with Eileen's story, Thomas couldn't tell. "Right, then. I'll send a messenger to the sheriff in Lakewood, let him know we may have bandits." He took another puff on his pipe, then pointed the stem of it and a warning glare directly at them. "As for you three, stay away from things you don't understand. Witchery is not something to be trifled with, real or imaginary."

"There was no witchery at that wagon last night," said Thomas. "Only three strangers picking on a man for no reason other than that he was alone."

Bluster fixed his eyes on Thomas, who met them without hesitation. There *hadn't* been any witchery the previous night, no matter what had happened on stage the day before.

"As you say," said Bluster at last. "I'll keep my eye out for those men tonight, and I'll give an invite to the juggler to stay on the common." He chuckled. "Though, what with this being Fire Night and all, there might be more people around him if he stays in the woods."

George and Eileen snickered, and Thomas, relieved that the man wasn't prying anymore, managed a smile. "Very true."

"Come on, Thomas," said George, taking his arm. "Let's get to the fair."

"Aye, let's," agreed Eileen. "Have a good day, Reeve."

"And you three." Bluster puffed on the pipe again, then called after them, "And stay out of trouble!"

*   *   *

It was amazing, Thomas thought, how time knew to move at a crawl just when you were hoping it would speed past.

As soon as they were done with Bluster, Thomas went to the tailor for final fittings. After that, the day was theirs.

Thomas did his best to be good company. He watched the races and played games of chess and chance with George and Eileen. He listened to the fiddler at lunch and tried the knife-throw and other games in the afternoon. George and Eileen kept up a steady stream of conversation and gossip, and did *their* best to distract him. It all should have made the day pass merrily away. Instead, time dragged its feet. The hours moved past as slowly as children heading home for chores. No matter what else he tried to focus on, Thomas's thoughts kept circling back to his father, and from there leaping to the evening ahead, which he was dreading.

It was just as the afternoon was waning into the evening that the tailor found them. The suit was ready, Alistair told Thomas. He and his assistants had spent most of the night and all of the day working on it but the results were well worth the effort.

After his first look at himself in the tailor's mirror, Thomas could do nothing but agree. The suit was extravagant. The deep blue jacket flowed long to matching breeches. The shirt was glowing white, with lace at the collar and wrists. The crushed velvet hat, also a deep blue, sported a silver badge and a pair of white feathers, too long to have come from any native bird. The boots and belt, which the cobbler and leather-worker respectively had dropped off that day, matched perfectly.

Thomas stepped out of the fitting room and into the main shop. Eileen's jaw dropped. George's eyebrows rose up high on his forehead. Neither said anything until Thomas prompted them with, "Well?"

George shook his head and let out a low whistle. "Amazing," he said. "If you didn't still look like an underfed bird, we'd never have recognized you."

"Aye," said Eileen. "You're too fancy to be walking with the like of us. We'd best stay a step behind, like servants."

"You do and I'll have Gavin lecture you on the intricacies of the wool trade," threatened Thomas. "Now really, how is it?"

"You look wonderful," Eileen said. The moment the words left her mouth she looked away. She seemed to be turning slightly red for no reason Thomas could fathom. "That is... it's very good."

"Your father must be very pleased with you," said Alistair. "No one in this town has ever looked better for their homecoming."

Pleased? Thomas thought of his father's words the day before. Certainly nothing the man had said indicated any pride in his son whatsoever. The opposite, in fact. Thomas shook his head and took one last look in the mirror. *At least I'll show him I can clean up well enough.*

Thomas thanked Alistair, gave him the money, and left the tailor's shop. George and Eileen walked beside him, taking great care not to touch his suit for fear of leaving a stain. George carried Thomas's other clothes, and promised to keep them at their house until Thomas sent for them. Neither of them said anything, and Thomas had no words to fill the space. The dread that had gnawed at him all day was now ferociously chewing on what was left of his nerves. The closer he got to his house, the worse he felt.

The house came into sight and Thomas stopped. He could feel his heart beating hard and fast and he took a couple of deep breaths to calm himself. "Well," he said, when he was done. "This is it, then."

"Maybe we could come in with you?" suggested Eileen. "I don't mean to stay, but just to see you to the door. Your father can't object to two old friends walking you home, could he?"

It was not a good idea, Thomas knew, but he was immensely grateful for the suggestion. Fortunately, George saved him from having to reply. "Bringing uninvited guests to his father's party won't help Thomas's cause. He's better off going in alone."

Thomas nodded, desperately wishing his friends *could* come in. "I probably am." He tried a smile, which he doubted looked at all sincere. "Though, if it goes like yesterday, he'll disown me and I'll be joining George at the smithy."

George grinned. "Not with those chicken wings you won't. But don't worry. The Mayor will probably take you on as a school-teacher for the young ones."

"Don't even joke about it," Eileen said, slapping her brother's arm with considerable force. She turned to Thomas. "Your father was probably in a mood of some kind. Today, it will have passed and all will be well again. You'll see."

"I hope you're right." He took another deep breath. "Well, from here we can all be seen from the house, and…"

"And it wouldn't do to be seen with the lower classes," said George, his smile showing he didn't mean it at all. He reached forward and gripped Thomas's hand. "Come tell us all about it at the Fire."

"If he lets me out of the house, I will."

Eileen stepped forward. "We'll see you tonight, certain," she said, taking his hand when her brother let go. "Even your father wouldn't let a bad mood keep him away from Fire Night." She squeezed Thomas's hand. "Good luck."

The feeling of her fingers wrapped around his sent Thomas's thoughts well away from his father and in a direction that discomfited him in an entirely different way. He did his best not to show it and squeezed back, keeping his eyes on hers. "Thank you."

Eileen smiled, held his hand a moment longer, then let go. She and her brother turned away and headed back down the road to the village. Thomas watched them go. About twenty paces away, Eileen looked back at him. She saw him watching and looked away at once. Blushing, Thomas thought, though he couldn't be sure at the distance. Between that and the warmth in his fingers where her hand had squeezed his, Thomas found himself completely distracted.

Don't be a fool, Thomas thought, as he walked towards his father's house. *She's just being nice. Besides, she's George's sister and you have enough trouble as it is.*

He reached the front gate, and all his thoughts of his father came crashing back to him. It took him several tries before he could bring his legs to march him forward. Once they got moving, though, they seemed in a desperate rush. Before he knew it, he was standing in front of the polished hardwood of the front door, wondering what to do next. The windows of the sitting room were open, and he could hear conversation within. He picked out his brother's voice, then his mother's, then Gavin's. There were others, but Thomas didn't recognize any of them. He reached for the door, stopped, mustered his courage and reached again.

He couldn't bring himself to open it. He felt like an unwanted visitor, rather than a family member coming home.

Fine, he thought. *If he wants to treat me like a stranger, I'll act like one.*

Thomas reached up to the knocker and rapped it firmly against the door. Inside, the voices fell into a hush, broken only by a single set of boots moving across the floor. Brian opened the door. He looked at Thomas in surprise.

"Master Thomas? Why didn't you just—"

"I'm home, Brian," His voice felt ready to break, and he forced it to be steady and calm. "Would you tell my father?"

Brian nodded once and stepped back from the door. "At once."

"Well, don't stand there, Thomas," said his mother, coming to the door. "Come in."

Madeleine was dressed in a fine green gown trimmed with gold thread. Her hair was done high, her hands adorned in rings and her face schooled into the expression she wore when she was not at all happy but couldn't show it. She reached out, took Thomas's arm, and led him inside the house. There were several guests Thomas didn't recognize, talking to his brother and each other in the main parlour.

"Gentlemen," Madeleine announced, "it is my pleasure to present my youngest son, Thomas. He has just returned from the Royal Academy of Learning."

"Of course," said the nearest, a fat man whose wide face burst into a large smile. "Your father told us you would be returning today. I'm surprised he didn't declare the dinner to be in your honour."

"Thomas, this is Frederick Needham, head of the weaver's guild."

"A pleasure," Thomas shook the man's hand.

"I hadn't expected you to look so civilized," said a second man who seemed to have been the source for Needham's extra weight, as he had so little of his own. "Why, when my boy came back from the Academy, he was thread-bare, thin as a rake, and talking philosophical nonsense for hours on end."

"Glen Tripoli," his mother interjected. "Master of Horse. He supplies the animals for our carts."

"Pleased, I'm sure."

The rest of the introductions went by in a blur. Thomas missed most of the names, but did his best to be polite. All of them asked about the Academy, and he did his best to answer their questions, talking about his classes, his friends, and the city itself. The conversation eventually switched back to merchant matters and Thomas's mind began to drift. His father had ideas about Thomas working for one of the merchant houses when he was done his study of the law, but the more Thomas listened to them talk, the less likely it seemed.

One more thing to disappoint him with, thought Thomas. He immediately quashed the thought. Self-pity wasn't going to help him figure out what was going on. He could indulge in it later. *Say, while I'm working at the forge with George.*

That thought brought a smile—a cynical smile, but a smile nonetheless—to his face, and he wore it as he circulated the room.

Thomas's mother went back and forth between the sitting room and kitchen, talking to the guests one moment and directing the cooks and the servants the next. Neal circulated through the room, making certain everyone's drinks stayed full and chatting with the various merchants and suppliers. Thomas watched them in moments between conversations. Both were very tense, though both were covering it up well enough that none of the guests noticed it. Thomas was sure it had to do with his sudden departure the day before, but knew there was no way to take either of them aside to find out. Both were too busy being hosts. Instead, Thomas passed his time pretending to be interested in the other men's conversations and anxiously awaiting his father's arrival.

It was very unlike John Flarety to not already be in attendance. Even in his worst mood, Thomas's father normally wouldn't dream of leaving his guests alone for any length of time. This day, though, he was nowhere to be seen.

It was only when his mother announced dinner that John Flarety stepped into the room. He came through the hall door, and had the slightly rumpled look of a man who had been working at a desk. His clothes were even finer than Thomas's, though the colours were sober, as befitted a wealthy merchant. Thomas expected him to smile at his guests, at least. Instead, his expression was flat, and void of emotion. His eyes went over his guests as though they were market-place cattle. He walked into the room, nodding briefly at his wife. For a moment Thomas thought his mother was going to snap at his father, but she held her tongue. John Flarety moved through the room, shaking hands and muttering words of greeting until he came to a stop in front of Thomas.

Thomas suddenly realized how desperately he was hoping his father would welcome him; that he would show some of the pride he had put in his letters. He found himself standing straighter, holding his head high.

John Flarety surveyed his son from head to foot as if calculating the worth of a measure of cloth. At length, he nodded. His look, when he met Thomas's gaze, was cold and hard. Thomas could feel his stomach sinking and his hopes for a welcome fading as he stared into his father's eyes.

"Well," said John Flarety at last, "it is good to see that you can dress properly when the occasion calls for it."

Thomas had no reply.

"This is how my son should look when he comes home." John turned towards the doorway he had come through. "Do you not agree, your Grace?"

All eyes followed John Flarety's to the bishop. "Indeed I do," said Bishop Malloy. "One can scarcely recognize you without the dirt, young Thomas."

Thomas managed to keep his tone civil. "I am glad your Grace approves."

The bishop turned to the others there. "Before yesterday, I was beginning to think John Flarety only imagined the existence of his second son." A polite chuckle circled the room, dying before it reached Thomas's father. The bishop smiled at Thomas, his tone remaining politely amused. "Shall we talk later, you and I? I understand that those at the Academy have some rather... *interesting* opinions of the Church of the High Father. I would love to hear yours."

And won't that be fun. "I will look forward to it, your Grace."

"So will I." The man stepped forward and held out his ring. Thomas looked at it a moment. No one else in the room was being asked to make formal obeisance and he had no doubt no one else was going to be. Just behind the bishop, Thomas could see his father watching him. His eyes flicked to the bishop's face. There was something burning in the bishop's eyes.

What is with this man? Thomas wondered as he bowed and kissed the ring. *What did I ever do to him?*

"Now," said the bishop, as Thomas straightened, "I believe that you announced dinner, did you not, madam?"

* * *

"There is a weakness," said the bishop, as the final dishes were cleared from the table, "in the moral fabric of our youth."

Dinner had been five courses, and each had been excellent. Hot, fresh bread and butter followed by a clear, fragrant onion and beef soup served in cheese-covered bowls. Brook trout in a lemon sauce came next, then a slow-cooked venison in a rich pepper sauce that melted in one's mouth. Dessert was a tart that was half berries, half alcohol and served with brandy-infused whipped cream. Wine had flowed freely, with a different vintage for each course.

Thomas, while eating the last of his tart, had calculated the cost of the meal to be at least equal to two months' rent on his apartment. Lemon and pepper both had to be imported. Venison was scarce and hunted only by commission. The wines alone represented a huge investment. His father was obviously out to impress his company and was sparing no expense to do so. Thomas wished the evening had not been so tense. He would have loved to eat the same meal without the feeling of impending doom.

Thomas's father had not said much to him during dinner, but had held court with the merchants and the bishop, keeping their conversation easy and free flowing. Those seated next to Thomas had been quite polite, and continued to ask Thomas about his time in the city and what life was like at the Academy. Thomas had the distinct feeling that several of them were looking for a new lawyer and were wondering if he would fit the bill. Thomas's father would stop talking and listen on these occasions, and while a frown never actually crossed his face, Thomas could almost see it building up in his eyes. Bishop Malloy had listened to it all without comment until Thomas, at the request of Glen Tripoli, started listing his favourite pubs. Now, the bishop's words were certainly having an effect, for the entire table fell silent and turned towards him.

Glen Tripoli was the first to respond. "Well, I'm not certain about that—"

"I am," said Bishop Malloy. "The morals of our youth are not the morals of their parents. Where we have focused on the High Father who leads the Four, they have focused on the Rebel Son, who lives for this world, and the Blessed Daughter who gives us frivolity. Where we focus our eyes to the betterment of those around us, they focus on amusing themselves, usually at the expense of others."

Frederick Needham smiled. "It's a common disease. It's called being young."

"Nonsense," John interrupted, surprising Thomas both with his tone and his agreement with the bishop. He had heard some stories of his father's youth, and knew that John Flarety was not one to talk. "The problem," John continued, "is that these young folks have lost their sense of what's right."

"Quite correct," agreed the bishop, warming to the topic. "Not to reflect on you, Merchant Tripoli, for I am sure you tried—" the words slid out of the bishop's mouth in a way that was just this side of insulting, "—but you have to admit that the young of today are much wilder than what they were. And what's worse, rather than keeping them close to hearth and home, where they can be properly disciplined, fathers are sending their sons away and placing their education in the hands of those whom they barely even know. Thomas here," a pair of fingers flicked quickly, dismissively, in Thomas's direction, "for example."

"And a sad example he is," agreed John. "I sent him away for schooling and he comes home penniless and threadbare and as near as I can tell, hasn't learned a thing."

The words were like a knife, driven into Thomas's stomach and twisted. He opened his mouth to protest, then firmly shut it. There was nothing he could say that his father wouldn't refute, and Thomas had no intention of arguing with the man at the dinner table. Whatever was going on, *he* wouldn't be the one to embarrass the family. He could see the very tight expressions of his mother and brother and guessed that they were thinking very similar thoughts. Around the table, all the other guests were looking distinctly uncomfortable.

"I know he dresses up well enough," John Flarety continued, "but you wouldn't have known it yesterday. The boy was a disgrace. Holes in his jacket and a ragged bag on his shoulder. He looked like a vagrant."

"Sadly true," said the bishop. "Isn't it, young Thomas?"

I will not *start a fight at this table.* "Apparently, your Grace."

"And what's worse," said John, "he was carrying a sword! And a duelling sword at that! That wretched school took my money and my son and sent back a vagrant and a brawler!"

The tension in the room was almost visible. Thomas had to struggle to catch his breath, the air felt so thick. The bishop looked unperturbed by it all. He sipped at his wine and surveyed the various faces in the room before turning to Thomas. "And what do you have to say about this?"

"I will admit to being threadbare," Thomas said, keeping his eyes on his father. He forced himself to speak quietly. "And I will admit to carrying a sword. But I am not a vagrant and I am not a brawler."

"Indeed?" The word rolled off the bishop's tongue, and the condescension that came with it put Thomas's teeth on edge. "Then how did you waste all your father's money?"

Waste? Thomas was starting to intensely dislike the man. "I didn't waste it. I'm a student. I spent it on books."

The bishop smiled and leaned closer, like a snake getting ready to strike. "And what sort of books do you read, young Thomas?"

"Philosophy, mostly."

"Pagan philosophy, no doubt."

"*Ancient* philosophy," Thomas corrected.

"The ancients were pagans," the bishop said. "They did not believe in the High Father or his gifts. They had their own, false gods." He turned to the others at the table. "And here you see the root of the problem. The Academy teaches the young the supremacy of pagans over the teachings of the church!"

Thomas felt his teeth clenching. "No. The Academy uses ancient philosophy to teach us the importance of logic and reason, not—"

"And they teach it to be more important than belief in the High Father!"

"No—"

"The ancients gave man nothing. The High Father gave man the world!"

"The ancients gave us philosophy to help us understand the world," snapped Thomas, giving up on being polite. "And words to describe it!"

"Hubris!"

"Like that one, which means the arrogance of comparing oneself to the gods."

Bishop Malloy, mouth opening to say more, stopped, then closed it. Thomas took some brief satisfaction as he watched the man's brows come together and his eyes narrow. When the bishop spoke again, his tone was once more calm and no less contemptuous. "You parrot your teachers admirably."

Thomas inclined his head graciously. "As do you."

"Thomas!" His father's voice cut through the air like a whip. "You will apologize to the bishop at once!"

The bishop did not look offended to Thomas. If anything, he looked ready to attack. Thomas bowed his head to his father anyway. "As you wish—"

"Do not bother," the bishop said. He leaned back in his chair and sipped at his wine again. "After all, my teachers were servants of the High Father. To say that I speak after their manner is high praise indeed. You, on the other hand, speak after the manner of poor, worldly men who do not know to what depths they sink."

Pompous, pretentious, self-serving... "Perhaps we should move to another topic, as this one seems to be distressing my father—"

"Oh, I don't think that the topic is distressing your father. I think it is your sorry state and sad lack of respect that is distressing him." He turned to John Flarety. "*Is that not so, John Flarety?*"

Thomas nearly jumped out of his seat. The bishop's voice had become deep and commanding, filling the room with its power just as it had done in John Flarety's study the day before.

"Indeed it is," said John Flarety. "The lad was brought up well enough by his mother and I, but these four years away from home have been the ruin of him. Still, he'll not be traveling away anymore."

"What?" Madeleine Flarety's head snapped around to her husband. "What do you mean?"

"*Tell them,*" said the bishop, smiling at Thomas. His voice rolled through the room like a wave, buffeting Thomas with its strength.

"What did you just do?" Thomas demanded, staring at the bishop.

The bishop tilted his head and put on a puzzled expression. His voice was perfectly normal when he said, "I beg your pardon?"

"Your voice," said Thomas. "You did something with your voice when you spoke to my father."

The bishop's head straightened and the smile on his face changed from just unfriendly to almost feral. "Indeed."

"Thomas!" John Flarety barked. "Don't talk nonsense!"

Thomas turned to his father. The man was red in the face. "But I heard it," Thomas said. "Didn't you—"

"I heard no such thing, nor did anyone else!"

"The lad apparently thinks that he did," the bishop said, his smile widening. "Or perhaps he is just making an excuse for ignoring his father. *Why don't you finish, John Flarety?*"

The power oozing off the words nearly made Thomas sick. He looked for some sign that the others at the table were feeling the same, but no one else seemed at all disturbed. It was as if they hadn't noticed; as if no one else had heard anything different. They were all just watching Thomas's father, waiting for him to speak.

"You will not be returning to the Academy after this summer," Thomas's father said. "I'll not have you study there anymore."

Thomas felt the world open up beneath him; felt himself plummeting from a great height, though he hadn't moved at all. "What?"

"You heard me."

"But... you can't—"

"Can't?" John Flarety's face turned beet-red. His voice doubled in volume. "Can't! How dare you! How dare you speak to me in that way!"

"I'm three years from finishing my studies!"

"I don't care!" The man's fist thundered down onto the table, making his glass jump and tip and the last of his wine splash in a blood red stain on the tablecloth. John Flarety shoved his chair back and came to his feet. "You will not argue with me in front of my guests! Go to your chambers!"

"My chambers?" Thomas was on his own feet, now. "I don't even know if I live here any more!"

"Thomas, please," his mother was at his side, taking his elbow.

"No!" He pulled away from her and advanced on his father. "I have worked hard at the Academy! I have—"

His father banged the table again. "You have disgraced us!"

"How?" demanded Thomas. "By studying the law like you wanted? By learning other languages?" He looked frantically around the room. The guests were still in their chairs, their faces frozen in expressions of embarrassment and concern. Thomas's brother was coming around the table at high speed. The bishop was sipping his wine again. Thomas rounded on him. "What in the Names of the Four is going on here?"

Neal grabbed his arm, started pulling him backwards. "Thomas, come."

Thomas fought to stay in place, to face his father again. "Every letter you wrote said how pleased you were with my work at the Academy! You were raving about the improvements I could bring to the business and how much you enjoyed hearing about my philosophy classes and would I send you a copy of one of my books! You said you wanted me to come home so you could show me off!"

"That was before I learned that the Academy was making you into a drunk and a reprobate!"

"Says who?!"

"*Enough, John Flarety.*" The bishop's voice stopped John like a leash on a running dog. "Let the boy go from the table. I will speak to him later, to calm his mind."

The last thing Thomas saw before Neal hauled him from the room was the bishop, his eyes on Thomas, his face twisted in a smug smile, and his hand on John Flarety's shoulder.

Chapter 5

"What in the name of the Banished is going on?" demanded Thomas, throwing himself out of his brother's grip.

"Calm yourself," Neal said. He took after their father physically and surely had no fear of being overpowered. Even so, he stayed back as Thomas paced back and forth through the kitchen.

"Calm myself? Calm myself?! 'Your life is ruined, good-night.' How am I supposed to calm myself?"

"You can start by taking control of your tongue," his mother said from the door of the kitchen. She sighed. "You may have my build, but you've certainly got his temper."

"Mother, when was it decided I was leaving the Academy?"

"I don't know." She closed the door, found one of the kitchen stools, and sank down onto it. "I gave him a piece of my mind after he sent you away yesterday. And another when he decided you should stay at the inn. He avoided me all night then spent all morning with the bishop. I didn't see him until lunch. And then he was grumbling about how you looked and the Academy and did I think you should be there and how could you wear a sword in our house—where is that sword by the way?"

"At George's."

"Good place for it. No need to wear it, I say—"

"Mother..."

"Sorry. Well, after that he's back with the bishop for the entire afternoon. I didn't see him until he came down for dinner."

"He didn't say anything?"

"No, he didn't, and a good thing, too. I was angry enough already. I wasn't going to have him spoil your homecoming." She sighed again. "Well, he did it anyway."

Thomas found another stool and collapsed onto it. None of it made any sense to him. "I thought he was proud of me."

"He was," said Neal. "Right up until yesterday. When you wrote that you were going to walk home, first he gets all huffy about how you should ride upriver instead. The next thing you know he's down at the tavern bragging how his youngest would rather walk home than make his father spend an extra penny."

"Well, he certainly didn't think that way yesterday."

"I don't understand it, either," Madeleine said. "It's nothing to do with the money. He has your tuition and expenses saved up for the next three years, and enough money to start you on as an apprentice in any trade you want, from lawyer to doctor to instructor at the Academy."

Thomas put his head in his hands. Half of him wanted to weep about it and the other half wanted to scream. "Did either of you notice anything tonight?" he asked without looking up. "About the bishop's voice changing, I mean."

"How do you mean, changing?" asked his mother. "I heard you at the table, but it made no sense."

"His voice changed," Thomas said. "I'm sure of it. It was deeper and louder and... almost tangible. As if you could almost see it moving through the air."

"I didn't even hear him change his tone," said Neal. He grinned suddenly. "Though I thought he would explode over that parroting comment."

Thomas's head came out of his hands. "He started it."

"And you certainly finished it," said Madeleine. She raised a hand to forestall Thomas's reply. "Understandable, though. He certainly has a dislike for the Academy."

"He hates it!" Thomas snorted. "I wouldn't be surprised if he put all that rubbish about the Academy into Father's head."

There was a knock, then the kitchen door opened and Gavin stepped in. He sounded almost apologetic as he said, "Your husband has asked that you accompany the bishop and himself down to the Fire."

"His Grace is attending?" asked Thomas.

"His Grace is giving the blessing," Neal said. "And a jolly speech it will be, I'm sure."

"His Grace is also introducing the new priest to his congregation tonight," Madeleine reminded her eldest son as she rose to her feet. "And don't you speak down about him, either. He's still the bishop. Now, hurry along and get your cloak. You too, Thomas."

"Master Thomas is to remain," Gavin said. "His father wishes him to be in his room tonight. In prayer."

"On Fire Night?" Shock filled Madeleine's voice.

"In prayer?" Neal sounded no less surprised. "When did father start advocating prayer?"

"It is his order," said Gavin. "Also, his Grace has offered to return here after he has spoken at the ceremony, to help Thomas face his spiritual crisis."

"What spiritual crisis?" Thomas demanded. *And when DID father start advocating prayer?*

"If Thomas isn't going to Fire Night, you can be certain that we won't be either," Madeleine said. She put her hands on her hips and glared past Gavin down the hallway. "And neither will John if I have to hold him here by the ears."

Thomas shook his head, "Mother—"

She turned on him. "If he thinks—"

"Mother, please!" Thomas rose from his stool. "Go to Fire Night. Take Neal. I'll be fine here."

Madeleine looked unconvinced. "You shouldn't be alone on your first night home."

Thomas managed a smile. "Don't worry. His Grace is coming back to keep me company."

"You should be with your family."

"Mum, please. Just go."

"Madeleine! Neal!" His father's voice rang through the hallways. "We have to leave. Now!"

Madeleine looked back at Thomas, then gave him a quick hug and stepped away. "I'll talk to your father," she said. "I promise."

Neal waited until Madeleine and Gavin had left the room before he turned to his younger brother. "So, what are you really going to do?"

Thomas looked him straight in the eye. "I have no idea what you're talking about."

Neal snorted. "Right. Don't get caught."

Thomas forced another smile. "I'll be back before the fire dies down. I promise."

"Don't promise," Neal said. "Just keep yourself safe." He headed for the door, then turned and added, "And don't trip over anyone in the woods on your way back, either."

Thomas watched him go. The guests' voices faded and the sound of the front door closing rang through the house. Thomas waited, listening. No sound came. He turned heel and headed for the back door. It was only a short walk to George's house, and he had to change before he went to the fire.

*   *   *

Everyone from the town was on the commons, readying themselves for Fire Night.

Thomas moved quietly through the crowd, giving polite greetings to those who recognized him, but doing his best to not draw attention. No one had been home at George's house, but the door was unlocked as usual. The clothes Thomas had worn that day had been sitting, folded, on the mat he'd used as a bed. He'd changed into them as fast as he could and headed for the town commons.

The entire village was there, waiting for the fire to be kindled. Even the nuns, down in a flock from their nunnery, were there to share in the ceremony. The young men were crowded together, betting on who could jump the highest and furthest. On the other side of the fire, the girls were gathered and giggling. Everyone over the age of twelve would go over the fire, believing, or pretending to believe, that their energy would go into the ashes which would be scattered on the fields in the morning. After that, many couples would disappear into the woods, to offer their strength in an entirely different way. Thomas wondered how much of a damper Bishop Malloy would manage to put on the second ritual. The answer, he suspected, would be none.

He found George at the back of the crowd, bragging with the other young men. George claimed that he would jump through the flames at their height and not return home until after the ash-spreading ceremony the next morning. There were several demanding to know who he would be spending the night with, but he refused to answer.

"A gentleman must keep his peace," he was saying as Thomas approached.

Someone called out that they only wanted to know which piece he was keeping, and Thomas took advantage of the ensuing laughter to grab George's arm. The other turned, saw, and was delighted.

"Thomas! You made it! Does this mean everything is all right with your..." He stopped, looked his friend over. "Those clothes were at our house."

"Yes."

"Oh."

"Something strange is happening, George." Thomas scanned the crowd. "Where's Eileen?"

"Right behind you and shame on you for not noticing."

Thomas turned. Eileen was indeed right behind him, but was covered head to foot with a long cloak. Thomas shook his head. "Not even your father could recognize you in that get up."

"Well, let's hope he doesn't when he sees what I'm wearing to jump the fire."

Thomas looked at George, who shook his head. "It's my fault," he said. "She bet me that she could jump the flames at their height, and foolish man I am, I took it."

"Your dress will catch fire," said Thomas.

"It would—"firelight and mischief danced in Eileen's eyes, "if I was wearing it."

She opened her cloak, showing off breeches and a shirt that Thomas recognized as soon as he stopped staring at the shape they revealed.

"Those are mine," Thomas said.

"Fresh off the line. And right wet they were, too."

Thomas looked at the clinging fabric. "Aye, I noticed."

Eileen stuck out her tongue and closed the cloak. George shook his head, mournfully. "She'll be the scandal of the evening," he predicted.

Thomas looked across the crowd to the small stage that had been erected on the far side of the fire-pit. His father and the bishop were stepping onto it, the Reeve and several others following behind. "I wouldn't bet on that, if I were you."

"Silence, please!" Bluster called. He had to repeat himself half a dozen times before the crowd stilled themselves. "We are honoured," he said when the clamour had ceased, "to have Bishop Malloy here with us tonight. It has been a sad few months for this village, since Father Martin —" he indicated an old, white-haired priest who had come on the platform behind him, "— announced his desire to retire to the Cloisters for the remainder of his life. He served us well for many years, and shall be missed. Still, we asked that his wishes be granted, and the bishop here has done so. Your Grace?"

The bishop stepped up to the front of the small stage, a younger man in the robes of the Church of the High Father beside him. The bishop's familiar, still wearing his sword, stood just behind them. The bishop gave a gracious nod to Bluster. "My thanks."

"Thomas," Eileen whispered as the bishop began his speech, "What happened at your house?"

"Nothing good," Thomas whispered back, keeping his eyes on the bishop.

"Well, that answers it, doesn't it?"

He turned to her. "Can I tell you after?"

She took a close look at his expression and nodded. "All right."

"Eileen!" someone hissed.

Eileen looked in the direction of the voice. "Oh, no."

Thomas looked. Two nuns were bearing down on them, looking very stern. One was gesturing at Eileen.

"Who are they?" asked Thomas.

"Sister Brigit," Eileen whispered, ducking her head as if to hide herself, "and Sister Clare. I was hoping they wouldn't recognize me. They'll tell my father!"

"Eileen!" Sister Brigit had a loud whisper that carried clearly through the crowd. "What are you doing there, standing among these boys?"

The young men around them quickly backed away. Thomas started to do the same, but Eileen grabbed his arm.

"I was standing with my brother," whispered Eileen back, holding the cloak tight around her. "I thought it would be the safest place."

"I'm sure." Sister Brigit was old, with deep lines in her face and a glare of steel. She applied the latter to Eileen. "Why are you wearing such a long cloak?"

"Have you met Thomas?" Eileen shoved him forward. "John Flarety's youngest son."

"Ah, yes. The Scholar." She surveyed him. "You're too thin, you know."

Thomas bowed politely, hoping that the bishop didn't notice the goings-on in the back of the crowd. "Yes, Sister."

"...and so, I present to you Father Allen Ferguson," Bishop Malloy said, drawing Sister Brigit's attention away, "who will take up the burdens of Father Martin."

The man who stepped forward was in his early twenties, and looked nice enough, though Thomas was ready to view anyone in the bishop's company as suspicious. Father Ferguson bowed briefly to the audience, kissed the bishop's ring, then began speaking. "I know that this night is of great importance to this village," he said, "so I shall be brief."

Sister Brigit snorted. "That will be a first."

"The sisters aren't pleased with the new priest," Eileen whispered as Father Ferguson began his speech.

"It's not that we're not pleased," said Sister Clare, whose hearing was obviously better than Eileen had credited. "It's just that now we'll have to train him. New priests never know how to deal with nuns."

"Besides," Brigit said, "This is not a ritual of the High Father. It's a ritual of the Mother."

"The Mother?" Thomas asked.

"The Mother," repeated Clare, her tone icy, though she kept her voice quiet. "Before she was the Loyal Consort, she was the Mother of All, who brings us in to this world at the beginning and gathers us up at the end, and this ritual was hers."

"It should be we who are giving the blessing," said Brigit. "Not him."

"...And though I know that I can never replace Father Martin," the young priest continued, "I will do my best to follow in his footsteps." He took a deep breath. "And now, it is time for the blessing of the fire. Father Martin asked me to do this tonight, but I have spoken with his Grace, and he has graciously agreed to give the prayer tonight." He turned his attention to the bishop. "As you know, your Grace, tonight we each give an offering of our strength to the High Father that he may bless us and provide us with a bountiful harvest for next year."

"Indeed I do know," Malloy's voice rumbled through the assembled crowd. "Just as I know that it is the custom on this night for the people of this town to go into the fields and woods to couple together, with or without the blessing of the High Father on their union."

The silence was as wide as the sky above the common.

"It is a shame," continued the bishop, "that decent servants of the High Father should take so important a night—a night where all minds should be turned to the High Father, and to those gifts that He bestows—to take license with one another on the unseeded earth like animals."

People shifted where they stood, but no one said a word. As Thomas had guessed, the bishop was not about to give an easy blessing to so pagan an event. He sneaked a quick glance around him as the bishop continued. Both nuns were looking furious, and Sister Brigit looked to be working very hard at not speaking her mind directly to the bishop. George was slightly shamefaced, and many of the young men had become very interested in the ground at their feet. Thomas's eyes went to Eileen, and found her looking right back at him. She bit her lip and turned away at once. Thomas looked away as well, telling himself it was to avoid making her uncomfortable, as his eyes wandered over the crowd.

Timothy wasn't there.

The juggler had said he wouldn't miss Fire Night for the world, but there was no sign of him. Thomas glanced back to the stage where Timothy had performed. It sat empty in the dark. He let his eyes wander over the edge of the forest, watching for anything out of the ordinary. A slight movement beside a tree caught his attention. He stared at it until a shadow resolved itself into the shape of a compact little man.

Timothy was standing just at the edge of the circle of torchlight, half-in, half-out of the woods. A torch flickered, casting a brief light onto Timothy's face. He was staring, eyes narrowed, at the bishop, his head craning forward to catch the man's words. Timothy had said that the bishop couldn't possibly be interested in him. Apparently the reverse was not true. Thomas swung his eyes back to Bishop Malloy.

"Sin!" The bishop was obviously hitting the high point of his speech. "Sin is something from which we must defend ourselves. It is something from which each of us must ask the protection of the High Father, that he may bring us purity of heart. It is something from which each of you must protect yourselves tonight." He stopped, and let the silence drag on for a long time. Everyone froze under his gaze, and all muttering stilled. The crowd seemed to hold its collective breath, as if wondering whether Fire Night would be blessed this year, Thomas eased himself behind George as the bishop's gaze roved over the crowd.

"There is one young man," continued the bishop, "the son of this fine merchant—" Thomas stuck his head out from behind George to see the bishop gesturing at John Flarety "—who has returned home with his soul in such a grievous state that he has chosen to remain home this night, in prayer, rather than imperil himself further with the temptations that may come to him after jumping the fire."

You miserable son of a...

George, Eileen, and the two nuns had all turned to look at him, and for a moment Thomas wondered if he'd actually said the words out loud. Fortunately, the bishop began speaking again before Thomas had to start explaining himself.

"Therefore," the bishop's voice was louder now, his words carrying clearly over the crowd, "let us bow our heads in prayer. Pray to the High Father that He may grant each one of us the resolve of this young man. Pray that, as each of us jumps the fire, the High Father will grant each of us the will to resist sin, and grant all those who dwell here a bountiful harvest!"

He led the crowd in the ritual prayer. Eileen used the moment to sidle up beside Thomas. "So, what are you doing here?"

Thomas kept his eyes on the bishop. "Offering my strength."

"But he said—"

"He lies."

"—And the High Father guide and protect us all!" finished the bishop. A joyous cry went up from the audience, and a man and woman—Liam and Mary Flanders—stepped forward and thrust their torches into the pile of wood. Straw, dried since fall for just this purpose, caught at once, and the flames spread rapidly until the whole pile was burning brightly. Flames leapt into the air. The bishop waited for the roar of the crowd to die down then spoke again, his voice rising over the sound of the crowd. "I will jump with you, and offer my strength to the High Father!"

Those in the crowd roared their approval. The bishop smiled at them and waved down the noise. When they quieted he said, "I am too old to make it over the flames at their height. However, I am given to understand that it is considered a sign of good fortune if a stranger jumps first."

His eyes rose up, past the crowd, to the woods. "Juggler!" the bishop called. "Lend the village your strength!"

Thomas and several hundred others followed the bishop's gaze to edge of the forest. The bonfire's light had not only filled the town common, but had lit the woods with a wavering, yellow glow that left Timothy in plain sight and made his shadow dance on the tree trunk behind him.

Timothy licked his lips, and Thomas could see sweat beading on his forehead despite the relative cool of the evening. He didn't move. "I would be honoured," he said, "but I don't think I could make the leap."

"Oh, come now," said the bishop. "Master Flarety hired you on the strength of your tumbling. *Will you not go first?*"

Thomas's head snapped back to the bishop. The man's voice had changed again. Thomas could feel—could practically see—the words sliding through the air, the seduction and the threat in them flowing across the clearing together like honey on the edge of a razor. Thomas looked back to Timothy. The man was sweating, his brow furrowed. One leg was twitching forward, as if moving of its own accord.

What is going on? Thomas watched in horror as the twitching leg jerked forward a bit, and Timothy's expression became desperate.

"Jump," the bishop said. "*And after the fire, you may join me at John Flarety's house.*"

The bishop's words still slid through the air, but the honey had vanished from them, leaving only the razor and the threat of something terrible. Even in the firelight, Thomas could see Timothy go pale.

The bishop will kill him. The thought rushed into Thomas's head, unwelcome and absolute. Thomas had no doubt it was true. *I have to help.*

Thomas watched Timothy take another slow, twitching step forward. Thomas thought of jumping the flames himself, first, to distract the bishop, but the crowd was too thick around the fire, and wouldn't let him before Timothy got his chance to give the village his strength. That and Thomas was sure his father would descend upon him the moment he stepped into the open.

My father…

Twenty-five years before, John Flarety had jumped the fire with Mary Findley, back when she had been Mary Lissell and the two had been courting, because village lore held that when a young man and woman together were the first to jump the fire, their strength would make the harvest bountiful beyond measure, and the village fortunate beyond all others.

It would certainly be a distraction.

Thomas grabbed Eileen's hand. "Jump with me. Now."

Eileen's jaw dropped. "What?"

"It's the best luck of all, isn't it?" Thomas started pulling her through the crowd. "Better than if Timothy jumps."

"What do you think you're doing?" demanded Sister Brigit, hustling along beside them.

Thomas ignored her. "Well?"

"But—" Eileen looked to the fire. "—the flames are too high."

"You wanted to jump them at their height," countered Thomas. "Tie up your hair, you'll be fine."

"Don't be silly, girl," said Sister Brigit. "You'll cook yourself!"

"Please," Thomas took both Eileen's hands and pulled her towards him. She stopped with her face only a foot away from his. "It's important. Please."

Eileen looked from him to the fire, to the nun glowering at her with a stern, disapproving frown. She pulled her hands out of Thomas's, pushed back her hood, and started tying her hair into a knot.

Thomas could have kissed her. He stopped, looked across the common and the crowd to the bishop standing on the stage and shouted, "Wait!"

The entire village turned to look. On the stage, Thomas could see the bishop's jaw nearly drop, then the man's entire face become rigid as he hid his surprise. Beside him, John Flarety's eyes were wide and his hands were clenched shut in what Thomas could only guess was rage. His ignored it and ploughed on.

"I am Thomas, son of John Flarety, and I have come to offer my strength to the village."

The bishop stepped forward to the edge of the stage. Thomas was impressed at how calm he sounded when he said, "Thomas. Why are you not at home praying?"

"Because the High Father has moved me to come here," said Thomas, stunning himself with his own audacity. "As He moves all men throughout their lives and as He has moved this young lady to come with me."

"Eileen?" Magda's voice rang out above the sudden, excited buzz of the crowd. "What do you think you're doing? You'll be burned!"

"Clear the way!" Thomas shouted in a voice which would have made his fencing instructor, whose commanding barks could be heard the length and breadth of the Academy, very proud. "We will jump together, to ask the Four's blessing on the harvest!"

The buzz grew to a roar and the crowd began to part, leaving a clear path across the common to the raging fire. The blaze was high, and for a moment Thomas wondered if he was going to be able to manage the jump. He forced the thought out of his mind and turned to Eileen. "Ready?"

"I'm not sure."

"Go head first. Do a dive-roll, like we used to when we were little." He took her by the shoulders. "Can you do it?"

Eileen looked at the fire again. She was pale, and Thomas could feel her trembling through the cloak. She bit her lip, and for a moment he was certain she would refuse.

She didn't. "Yes. Yes I can."

Thomas felt a wild grin break over his face. "Right." He turned to the fire, holding her hand. "Run beside me. On three."

"Eileen!" Sister Brigit's face was red. "You will not jump with a boy!"

Eileen looked at the nun, then back at Thomas. From beneath the fear in her face a small, wicked smile rose to her lips. She let go of Thomas's hand, swirled her cloak off her shoulders and threw it into Sister Brigit's arms. Sister Brigit's jaw dropped and the crowd's roar changed to a cry of surprise and several catcalls when they saw what she was wearing. "That will show her," Eileen whispered, taking his hand again. "Start counting."

Thomas felt a heat rising in his face that had nothing to do with the fire. "Right. One."

Eileen added her voice to his for, "Two!"

"Three!"

They ran. Straight forward, hard and fast, hands still tightly clasped. Thomas's boot pounded against the packed earth of the common. The fire grew larger with every step, as if it was racing forward to meet them. Faces flashed past. George was cheering. The nuns looked furious. Eileen's parents looked stunned. Up on the stage, John Flarety and the bishop had identical, thunderous expressions.

The fire rushed towards them and their hands unclasped and they *leapt!*

Fire surrounded Thomas. They had jumped high enough to clear the wood, but not the flames. For a moment all Thomas felt was the heat all around him and saw the world turn yellow with fire. Then they were through and he was hitting the ground hard and rolling to his feet. He turned at once, saw Eileen rolling to her own feet beside him. He grabbed her, spun her, looking for fire in her hair or her clothes. There was none.

"Am I on fire?" she asked, her eyes large.

"No. Am I?"

She looked him up and down then spun him around and back. "No."

"We did it." The wild grin came back, spreading across his face. Eileen answered back with a wild grin of her own. "We did it!"

Eileen let out a scream and they wrapped together in a huge hug. The crowd let out its collective breath in an enormous cheer. Thomas hardly heard it. His arms were tight around Eileen's body, hers around his, and for that moment, nothing else was important.

There was a shout of warning, and Timothy flipped over the fire, clearing the top of the flames with a good foot to spare and landing on his feet beside them. "You did it!" he crowed. "By the Four, boy, you did!"

The cheering crowd surged forward, surrounding them and shaking his and Eileen's hands and slapping them on the back. Eileen linked her arm with his and moved them back from the fire, holding tight as the jostling crowd threatened to knock them apart. George was next over the fire and ran straight for his sister. On the other side of the flames, Thomas could see the other young men of the village lining up to jump.

Thomas turned from the fire and found the bishop still up on the stage, his smile set like stone on his face. He looked straight at Thomas first then shifted his gaze to Timothy. He turned and said something to his familiar. Randolf nodded, and made his way off the platform.

A small, strong hand pulled him around. "I must go, Master Scholar," Timothy said, shaking Thomas's free hand. "Thank you."

"Why is he after you?" Thomas demanded. "And what does my father want with you?"

"Your father?"

"Up on the stage," Thomas pointed.

"Him?" Timothy looked confused. "He just asked me to come out for the festival. Paid my way, in fact."

"And the bishop?"

"Doesn't like jugglers," Timothy said. He looked around quickly to make sure no one was paying attention, then leaned in and added, "Or magic."

Thomas felt his mouth fall open. Before he could put together a question, Timothy released his hand. "I must go. Good luck and protection of the Blessed Daughter to you."

The little man turned and vanished into the crowd.

Thomas, watching him go, was nearly yanked off his feet by a sudden pull in the other direction. When he had recovered his balance, Eileen was no longer on his arm. Sister Brigit and her mother were wrapping her cloak around her, haranguing her in no uncertain terms. Worse, Lionel was bearing down on him. Even in the yellow light of the fire the smith's face looked red as a radish at its ripest. Thomas, who had spent half his childhood in the smith's house and knew

Lionel's temper, turned to run.

George grabbed him. "Don't."

"Are you joking?"

"Don't," George warned. His hands were like iron shackles, holding Thomas in place. "If you run from him, he'll chase you down, tie you to a tree and whip you like a thief. Stand up to him and the worst you'll get is a bit of bruising."

Thomas glanced back, seeing the crowd part for the angry smith. "You sure?"

"It's the way it usually works," George grinned. "Besides, after that, you deserve what you get."

Thomas hardly had time to give him a dirty look before Lionel was upon him.

"By the Four above! What were you thinking?!" the smith bellowed. "She could have been burned!"

"A good thing she wasn't, then," Thomas said, without thinking. "Otherwise you'd have a reason to be angry."

"Angry?!" The man grabbed him by the front of his shirt and hauled him onto the tips of his toes. "Angry?! I'll show you angry!" He shook Thomas like a terrier with a rat. "You could have killed her! She could have been burned to death just so you two could show off!"

"Is that why you did it?" asked the bishop, stepping into the rapidly clearing circle around Thomas and Lionel. "Just so you could show off?"

Thomas grabbed one of Lionel's arms for balance and turned his head towards the bishop. "I said why—"

"I heard," the bishop's face was stern, his voice brooking no argument. "Pity it wasn't the truth."

"It was!"

The bishop ignored Thomas. "He didn't jump the flames to show off," he said to Lionel. "*He did it to steal the virtue of your daughter.*"

"What?!" Thomas heard the bishop's voice change, felt the power in it that would make the accusation seem almost reasonable to Lionel's ears.

"What?!" Lionel echoed, his voice booming over the crowd. "What was that?"

"Ask him." The bishop leaned close to Thomas, "Tell us, what were you planning to do with the maiden after you two had jumped the fire?"

"I wasn't—"

"You want to bed my daughter?" demanded Lionel. "You risked her life just for a chance to lie with her?"

"I swear—"

"He did," the power in the bishop's voice left no room for argument. Thomas could feel the words fly across the clearing and bury themselves in Lionel. "*He has betrayed your family to lie with your daughter.*"

"You little bastard!" Lionel yelled. He shoved Thomas away. "I'll whip your hide off!"

Thomas hit the ground hard as the smith went for the thick leather belt around his waist. Eileen yelled at her father, tried to reach him, but Magda held her back. George stood, rooted in place, obviously helpless. The people around them were now well back and watching nervously. From the back of the crowd, Thomas could hear Bluster, shouting and shoving his way forward.

Thomas scrambled to his feet, ready to run despite George's warning. He caught sight of the bishop backing away with the rest of the crowd, a tight, self-satisfied little smile on his face.

It was the smile that did it.

Well, Thomas thought, *George said stand up to him.*

In the loudest voice he could manage, Thomas shouted, "Apologize!"

The smith looked up from his belt. His mouth was open and his eyes bulging. "What?!"

"I said, apologize!" Thomas closed the distance between them, praying his mind would stay one step ahead of his mouth. "Your words are an insult to me, and worse, an insult to Eileen's virtue and I will *not* tolerate it!"

Lionel was frozen in place, his mouth working for words. The man looked apoplectic. "You will not tolerate it?" he repeated. "YOU?!"

"Aye, me!" Thomas stepped to within inches of the huge man, ignoring the fact that he only came up to the other's chest. He kept his voice loud and steady. "I have no designs on your daughter. She has no designs on me. To say otherwise is to insult the both of us to the greatest degree and I will not tolerate it." He looked deliberately over to the bishop. "From *anyone.*"

Thomas raised his voice even more, making it carry over the entire crowd. "I swear that I did what I did for the glory of the Four, for the strength of this village, and with the intention that harm come to none! If anyone says otherwise, they will be answered with steel!" Thomas turned his eyes back to the smith and watched the man's expression change from anger to surprise. "Well?"

The smith's jaw dropped. "By the Four, you're serious, aren't you, boy?"

"I am." Thomas's heart was pounding in his chest. He raised his voice again. "I will retire to my father's house, to resume my prayer. Those who wish to dispute what I have said may deliver their challenges tonight, and meet me here with their swords at dawn!"

He took a deep breath, surveyed the now-silent crowd. The bishop's smile was gone, Thomas noticed, and the observation did him a world of good. "To the rest of you, good night. May your own leaps over the flames be just as successful, and cause much less stir." He stepped back, bowed his best formal bow, then turned on his heel and walked into the woods.

Chapter 6

What, in the name of the Four, was I thinking?

Thomas stumbled through the woods towards his father's house, his body shaking with shock. After four years away, Thomas wasn't certain he knew the woods well enough to make his way home in the dark. He was certain, however, that he'd rather be wandering in circles forever than meet the bishop or his father on the road.

He was stunned at his own recklessness. What if he hadn't made it through the flames? Worse, what if Eileen hadn't? What if she had been burnt and scarred for life? The thought made him shudder. Small wonder her father had been angry with him. He was lucky the man hadn't beaten him to death on the spot, especially with the bishop egging him on.

At least he'd put stop to that, though the audacity of what he'd done appalled him. What if someone actually answered his challenge? What if they killed him? It would be very annoying to have made it through four years in the city, only to come home and be killed by someone he'd known all his life.

Thomas forced himself to move faster, ignoring his shaking legs. He had to beat the bishop and his father back to the house. He had said that he was returning home to pray, and he had no intention of putting the lie to his own words. His father would be angry enough. There was no point in making it worse. As it was, Thomas was expecting a scene that would make what had happened at the dinner table seem like polite conversation.

Assuming, of course, that I find my way.

The woods might have been familiar, but in the dark Thomas could scarcely tell. Part of him wanted to be lost; to be stuck in the woods until the bishop moved on. His father would still be angry, certainly, but he wouldn't have the bishop putting ideas in his head and making him do whatever he was told.

He couldn't really do that, could he?

The idea was outrageous, or would have been if Thomas hadn't felt what happened when the bishop's voice changed. Thomas shook his head. No one could control a person with their voice. It wasn't possible.

And Timothy's ball of light is?

He remembered the way the bishop's voice had practically pulled Timothy forward, moving him like a marionette. The thought made him shudder. The Church of the High Father had stood solidly against magic for years. For the bishop to use it would go against everything the bishop claimed to believe.

Of course, he might not care.

The woods parted and Thomas found himself at the edge of his yard. The house was dark. All the servants were at the Fire, Thomas realized. They probably wouldn't be back until the next afternoon. He jumped the low stone wall and made his way across the yard. Exhaustion was taking over, threatening to make him collapse before he even got inside. He promised his body that it could rest if it would just make it to the family prayer room.

He looked to the road and found it empty. There was no sign of anyone arriving, no sound of horses. Relief swept through him. He rounded the corner of the house, heading for the back door.

The fist came out of nowhere, crashing into the center of his face and breaking his nose. Thomas went sprawling to the ground. Strong hands grabbed his arms and hair and pulled him to his feet. The fist came again, and another joined it, crashing into his face again and again. He tried to protect himself, but the hands had pinned his arms behind him. The fists switched targets, coming out of the darkness to strike at ribs, at stomach. Blow after blow landed, taking the wind from his lungs.

Everything stopped. Thomas shook his head, tried to see who it was.

The blurred shape holding his left arm spoke, "Think he's had enough?"

"Not yet," said someone in front of him.

A booted foot slammed into Thomas's groin. He nearly collapsed, retching, but the hands held him upright, and another foot, this one from behind, kicked his legs apart. The boot came a second time, harder than the first. He collapsed again, and this time the hands let him fall.

"Now he's had enough."

Hands grabbed his legs and started dragging him, face down. Thomas wished he could pass out, but each bump he hit sent a new shock of pain through him, keeping him awake. He wanted to resist, but he could barely move. The men, whoever they were, dragged him up the back stairs of the house and into the hallway. He got caught on the door-frame and they brutally hauled him loose. That nearly did him in. The rest of the ride was a smooth pull down the hallway and through one more door which he didn't, thankfully, get caught on. They forced him to a sitting position, and shoved his back against a wall.

"Here he is, your Grace," the first voice said. "Just as you wanted him."

"Thank you. I think his father and I will be able to take it from here. Why don't you attend to that other business that needs resolving?"

"Yes, your Grace."

"I will join you once I have finished here," said the bishop. "Afterwards, leave the town. We will meet you on the road."

"As your Grace wishes."

Heavy boots tramped out of the room.

A hand grasped Thomas's chin; forced his face upwards. "Well, young man, it seems we beat you home."

Thomas tried to make his mouth move, but could not.

"In the future, I suggest you remember that horses on roads are generally faster than shortcuts."

Thomas tried once more to answer but no words came, only blood, drooling from where his teeth had cut his lips.

The hand released his chin. "He seems in need of stimulation."

A blast of cold water hit him hard in the face. His eyes snapped open with shock and everything came into hard focus. The bishop was standing over him, victory and amusement playing across his face. John Flarety was behind him, dipping a small pot into a large bucket. Thomas tried once more to make his mouth work, but didn't manage it before a second pot full smashed into his face. The chill of it made Thomas's head ache. He raised his hand as his father went back for a third pot full. He managed a moan, then words. "Enough. Father, please."

"Your father is very disappointed in you," the bishop said. "*Aren't you, John Flarety?*"

"Disappointed?" John Flarety's voice raged through the room, making Thomas wince. "Infuriated! Are you aware of the embarrassment you've caused me?"

"Father," Thomas worked hard to find words, to make his aching mouth wrap around them. "I need help, Father."

"The smith will never talk to me again—"

"Father, they beat me—"

"And only the Four know what sort of lies they'll be spreading about you and his daughter!"

"Father—"

"Do you know what you've done to my reputation?"

"Father!" Every word hurt. Thomas forced them out anyway, making them as clear as he could. "They beat me! Why did you let them beat me?"

"Your father thought you needed a lesson," said the bishop. "I suggested the means of it."

"Aye," John Flarety nodded. "Aye, a lesson."

The bishop was smiling. There was something cruel and vile and self-righteous in the expression and Thomas would have wiped it off the man's face, if he could only have stood up.

"Well, boy?" his father demanded. "Have you nothing to say for yourself?"

"Yes, *boy*," the bishop repeated. "Haven't you anything?"

Clarity was returning, and with it, a cold anger that didn't so much dull the pain as direct it. "Aye." Thomas said, eyes never leaving the bishop. "Get out of this house. Leave my father alone and get out."

"THOMAS!" His father's hand flashed forward, slapping him hard on the face. Light flashed behind Thomas's eyes. The world slipped sideways and faded to grey. John Flarety raged, "How dare you speak to him like that?! How dare you?!"

"Father, please." Thomas shook his head, forcing the grey back. He pushed against the floor with his feet, found the wall with his back and began to stand. "You were proud of me. Proud of what I did at the Academy."

"This has nothing to do with the Academy!"

"It does!" Half-way up, Thomas's legs gave out. The collapse hurt more than he thought possible. He kept talking anyway. "Why are you doing this?" He waved a barely-controlled hand in the bishop's direction. "Why are you listening to him?"

"He is not listening to me," the bishop intoned piously. "John is listening to the High Father's law, *aren't you, John?*"

Even through the haze of his pain Thomas could hear the man's voice deepen, the sound becoming almost tactile.

"Exactly!" said John Flarety. "I'm following the High Father's law!"

Thomas swung his head toward the bishop. "You're making him say that!"

The bishop leaned closer. "What do you mean?"

"I can hear it in your voice! Let him alone!"

The bishop stepped back, considering. John Flarety stood, staring at the bishop like a dog waiting for its master's voice. The bishop smiled. He held out his ring to John Flarety. *"Go speak to your family. Tell them Thomas will be out in a moment, to apologize for his actions."*

John kissed the man's ring and left the room without a look back. The bishop watched him go; watched the door swing closed. With one large hand he reached down, pulled Thomas up to his feet then shoved him hard against the wall. "What do you mean, you can hear it?"

The grey was blotting out Thomas's world again. He forced it back. "Your voice changes. I can hear your voice change."

"No one else can, boy." The bishop let go, and Thomas fell to his hands and knees. He slowly pushed himself upright, kneeling on the hard wood floor. The bishop was at the door, talking to someone just outside. Thomas caught a glimpse of black clothes, heard Randolf say, "Yes, your Grace."

The bishop closed the door. "I wondered if it would be hereditary."

Thomas forced himself to focus on the bishop's face.

"It makes sense, now," said the bishop. "Why your father sent you away. Why he put you in that Academy." He paced back and forth across the room. "We have long known that the Academy was a breeding ground for dissent and blasphemy, but this..."

He stopped pacing, and knelt on one knee beside Thomas. "You have a corruption in you. Just as your father did. Just as that juggler does."

"Timothy?" Thomas's mouth would have gone dry, save for the blood in it. "What do you want with him?"

"Not me." The bishop shoved himself back onto his feet. "The High Father."

There was noise coming from outside the door; voices raised in argument, moving closer.

The bishop was pacing again. His words came out with the same intensity as his sermon on the stage before the Fire. "Just as He delivered your father, just as He will deliver the juggler, the High Father has delivered you to me so that I may take your corruption and turn it to His work." He stood over Thomas once more. "You seek to embrace the workings of the Banished. You must not. You must give it to me."

Thomas stared at him. "What are you talking about?"

The bishop grabbed Thomas and once more hauled him to his feet. Thomas flailed out for balance as he was shoved against the wall once, then again, then slapped hard across the face. Thomas's world spun in place for a while, and when it stopped, the bishop's hand was on the centre of his chest. "Give it to me."

Thomas tried to push him away and the bishop leaned closer, his bulk blocking out the light of the candles. The shadows hollowed out his cheeks, turned his fleshy face gaunt. His eyes, sunk deep under their overhanging brow, were glowing deep, blood red.

"It must be given to the High Father's service." The bishop's voice was a sibilant whisper. "*Give it to me! Now!*"

"Give what?" Thomas demanded. "I don't have anything!"

Madeleine's voice cut through the air. "I don't care if the bishop wishes to be alone with him!" she yelled, the sound ringing through the house. "There's blood on the floor! I want to see my son!"

Randolf made some reply, but Thomas couldn't make it out. His world had narrowed to the size of the bishop's face, his awareness locked into the man's eyes.

A pulling started inside Thomas's chest.

"*Give it to me,*" the bishop repeated. Thomas looked down. The man's hand was still pressed against his chest, but it felt as though it was reaching inside. "*Give it to me!*"

"Give what?!"

"*GIVE IT TO ME!*"

The pulling became ripping. Something inside him was being roughly, slowly, torn out. The pain was incredible.

My soul, Thomas thought, though he had no idea where the idea came from. *He's taking part of my soul.*

His hands rose up to his chest, desperate to hold in whatever it was, but there was nothing to grasp at, only the bishop's hand, pressed flat against his chest. Bishop Malloy was grinning now, his face twisted into a leer. *"You will give it to me!"* he said, *"NOW!"*

Thomas tried pushing against the hand that pinned him to the wall, but couldn't move it. The ripping grew stronger, agonizing. *"NOW!"*

There was shouting outside the door, and the sound of a scuffle.

"NOW!"

Thomas pulled together the last of his strength and attacked.

His fist moved first, arching up in the narrow space between them and catching the bishop on the base of his beaky nose. The man's head snapped up. Thomas raised his boot and smashed it hard against the bishop's knee. Something popped and Bishop Malloy screamed. He stumbling back and fell when he tried to put weight on his leg.

Thomas felt his soul snap back into place, the searing pain instantly subsiding to a dull ache. He slid to the ground. The bishop was curled in a ball around his knee, whispering something over and over to himself. Thomas ignored him and started to crawl away.

The door swung open. His mother was standing there, his father and the bishop's familiar right behind her. Randolf immediately shoved past her and ran to the bishop, kneeling beside his master. Thomas saw his mother's face go white, then bright, angry red. "What in the name of the Four is going on in here?!"

Madeleine was on her knees before she finished the sentence, drawing Thomas up and cradling him in her arms as best she could. "John! Get bandages! Thomas, can you hear me?"

"Mum?" The word came out broken, like a beaten child pleading for mercy. He was starting to cry, he realized, and could do nothing about it.

"Hurry, John!" She started to rise. "Can you get your feet? We'll take you to the kitchen."

"He will be perfectly well here," the bishop said, the melody of his voice tinged with pain.

"He will not!" There was ice in Madeleine's voice, cold and hard as the pond in mid-winter. "What did you think you were doing in here?"

"I was redirecting the boy's education," The bishop tried to stand and collapsed, crying out. Thomas watched him put his hands on either side of his knee and start whispering again. White light glowed from the bishop's hands, sinking into his leg.

"Is that what you call it?" Madeleine demanded. She pulled herself to her feet and dragged Thomas up with her. "You beat him near senseless." She turned on her husband. "How could you let him do this?!"

"You must not allow this, John Flarety."

As soon as the words left the bishop's mouth, Thomas knew what was going to happen. For a brief moment, he wished he had the strength to hit his father, hard.

John Flarety's hands came down on his shoulders and dragged him out of his mother's grip. "I will not!"

"*Your son is tainted,*" said the bishop. "*He must be removed from this house. No matter who wishes it otherwise.*"

"And he will be!" John Flarety hauled Thomas out of the room and half-pulled, half-dragged him down the length of hall.

"You let him go!" Madeleine demanded.

"I'll do no such thing!" John turned on his wife. "I'll have no one talk so to me in this house, do you hear? I will brain the next one who tries to thwart me!"

"John," Madeleine's voice was low and hard, like a volcano's last rumbles before it explodes. "John, he is our son; he is hurt. We have to take care of him."

"No!" The word came out almost as a scream. "I will not be thwarted!" John turned around and began dragging Thomas down the hall again. "I will not!"

"Please!" Madeleine grabbed at his sleeves and was shoved aside. "He is our son!"

"He is nothing!" They reached the back door and John Flarety kicked it open.

"He is our son!"

"He is *nothing*!" He shifted his grip to the front of Thomas's shirt. "You hear me, boy? You are nothing here! Not my blood! Not my son! I cast you out!"

He shoved, hard, and Thomas went sprawling down the steps into the dirt. All the night's hurts flared up into new pain. "Get off my property, boy!" John Flarety yelled, "Or I'll have Bluster lock you in the tower for the magistrate!"

The door slammed, leaving Thomas in the dark. He heard his mother yell something, but couldn't make out the words. Even through the door, though, he could clearly hear the slap that followed and his mother's cry of shock and pain. Fear for her gave Thomas the strength to push himself to his feet and back to the door. He pounded on it and shouted, his voice hoarse with pain and tears.

From somewhere inside, he heard the bishop's voice.

Fear overtook Thomas. He cursed himself for a coward even as he stumbled away to crawl over the fence and be swallowed by the dark woods on the other side.

Chapter 7

It was very, very late when Thomas reached the smith's doorstep.

He had no idea how long the journey through the woods had taken. Every second step had ended in a stub, or a trip, or a stumble that turned the dull aches of his body into sharp, jarring pains. He fell several times, and each time a darkness that could have been momentary or hours long claimed him. He had desperately wanted to give in; to find a hollow in the earth and sleep. Fear kept moving him forward. Fear of what his father had done to his mother. Fear of the bishop and those bravos who beat him. Fear, most of all, that he was hurt inside as well as out, and that falling asleep would mean not waking up again.

Dark windows gazed down on him as he stumbled to the smith's door. No sound came from inside. The family was still at the fire, along with most of the village. Thomas leaned against the wall of the house and wished he had never left; that he was still standing beside the bonfire, watching people jump and getting shouted at by Lionel.

The house hadn't been locked earlier, and he knew it wouldn't be locked now. He could go inside and wait, but after the scene at the fire he wasn't sure if he was welcome anymore and getting tossed out of two houses would be more than he could bear this night. He turned his back to the door, leaned on it, and sank down on the step. He would wait and beg Lionel's forgiveness. If the man still wanted to kill him, fine. At least he'd die among friends.

It was almost funny.

* * *

"Thomas? Thomas!"

The voice was a near-scream. It pierced through Thomas's sleep and left his head aching. He tried to force his eyes open. The lids would only go half-way, and the effort of doing that was almost enough to make him go back to sleep. He fought off the urge and blinked a few times to try to clear his vision.

The sun was soon to rise, he was sure, but it hadn't broken the horizon yet. The sky was the colour of cold steel and the early morning air chill on his skin. Someone was running towards him, but he couldn't quite see far enough to be sure who it was.

He blinked again, and when he opened his eyes Eileen was falling to her knees beside him. George was a few steps behind, and looked horrified. Magda and Lionel were coming quickly behind, shock plain on both their faces.

I must look terrible, Thomas thought. He could feel the blood, dried on his skin and his shirt. He ached from head to foot. His nose throbbed and his ribs stabbed at him every time he breathed.

Eileen reached out for him then pulled her hand back, unsure of what to do. "Thomas." Her voice broke as she spoke. "Who did this?"

"Eileen, move," snapped Magda. Eileen backed away. For a terrible second, Thomas thought that Magda was going to order him away. Instead, she turned to her husband. "Get him inside."

To Thomas's everlasting gratitude, Lionel didn't say a word. He just picked Thomas up like a child and carried him, gently and easily, into the kitchen.

"Get the fire started," Magda ordered, and Eileen hurried to the hearth. Lionel placed Thomas in his own chair, and began opening his shirt. Thomas hissed in pain. Lionel stopped and looked at Thomas's body. He whistled, low and quiet, his eyebrows coming together and worry plain on his face. Thomas looked down and saw the red and purple bruises that covered his ribs.

Magda took his chin in her hand and raised his head. She had a mug in her other hand and held it out. Thomas raised an arm to take it. She gently pushed his hand aside and stroked his hair back out of the way before holding the mug to Thomas's lips. He swallowed greedily, thinking it was water. The whiskey burnt its way down his throat, sending him into a coughing fit. Pain knifed through his ribs, doubling him over. Lionel held him until the spasm passed.

"His nose is broken," said Lionel. "He probably couldn't smell it."

Magda nodded. She put her hand on the back of Thomas's head once more and held the mug to his lips again. This time, ready for it, he managed to get the whiskey down.

"Thank you," Thomas said. His voice was heavy and nasal, and there was a painful pressure in his head.

"George," Magda's voice was harsh, the words clipped. "Go to the nuns. Tell them Thomas has been injured, and we need their help. Now."

Thomas heard George's footsteps, hard and fast, and the door slamming closed behind him. "I'm going to get some water," said Magda. She turned and walked out the back door, grabbing the bucket with an angry snap of her hand as she passed.

Lionel started once more to peel the torn, stained shirt off of Thomas, moving slowly to keep from hurting him too much. By the time he was done, Eileen had the fire going, and Magda was coming back in with the bucket of water.

"Let me," said Eileen, rising from the fire. She grabbed a bowl from a shelf, and a cloth from the counter. Magda took the bowl, dipped it in the bucket to fill it, then handed it back. Eileen wet the cloth then gently began cleaning Thomas's face. The water was cold and the feeling of it sent shivers through him, and he could feel the tremor in her hand. She wiped at his face, loosening the caked-on blood. He tried to smile at her, but just then she touched his nose. A bolt of lightning went off in his brain. He yelped and pulled his head away, the movement sending pain shooting through his skull and turning the yelp to a moan.

Eileen recoiled, yanking her hands back to her chest "I'm sorry, Thomas!" Tears welled up in her wide eyes and her lips began to tremble. "I'm sorry. I'm sorry."

Her mother shushed her gently, and Thomas nodded his acceptance of her apology until he could find his voice. "It's all right," he said at last. "Truly, it's all right."

"I didn't mean to—"

"It's all right," Thomas repeated, leaning back in the chair again.

"Oh, Thomas." Eileen was crying hard now and shaking. "What happened?"

Thomas opened his mouth to tell her and realized that he had no idea how to explain it all. The bruises and the blood were real enough, and his memory of how he got them was as vivid as the pain he felt, but he could not understand *why*.

There was no question in Thomas's mind that the bishop had some kind of magic; no question that he was controlling Thomas's father or that he had tried to control Lionel at the Fire. But why? What could the man possibly be hoping to gain out of it?

And what did he mean by "give it to me?" Thomas wondered, feeling the ache deep in his chest. *Why did he want part of my soul?*

Eileen was still looking at him, still waiting. He couldn't tell her about the magic; couldn't tell anyone. They'd think he was insane.

"I had a disagreement," Thomas said at last. "With my father."

"John?" Magda's voice was filled with disbelief. "He wouldn't. He couldn't."

"He did." Thomas heard his voice shaking, and tried to steady it. "That is, someone did it for him."

There was a long moment's silence. Lionel's face grew dark with anger, his expression becoming very similar to the one he'd had the night before. Thomas was wondering how he'd ever managed to stand up to the man. Lionel turned on his heel and headed for the front door.

"Oh no you don't!" said Magda, stepping in front of him. "Nothing good would come of it."

"Nothing good will come of *that*, either," Lionel snapped, pointing at Thomas's face. He made to step around her, but Magda blocked his way.

"Pity you didn't think of that last night when you were ready to do the same," Magda snapped back. Lionel swelled up, his face growing even darker. Thomas could see Eileen shrinking back, and braced himself for an explosion. Magda was easily as furious as her husband, though, and was obviously in no mood to back down. She stayed where she was, eyes fixed on Lionel, waiting.

Lionel let out a long, slow breath. His body deflated and the red in his face lightened a shade. He took in another breath, let it out. By the third his face had almost returned to his normal colour. "Aye," he said quietly, shame in his voice. "Aye. You're right."

"I am," said Magda, her own tone lightening just a bit. "Now fetch some more wood for the fire, and we'll wait for the nuns."

Lionel nodded and headed out the back door. Magda sighed, then looked at Eileen. "Standing there crying won't help anything," she scolded, though her voice was gentle. "Help Thomas get cleaned up. And mind his nose."

Eileen wiped the tears from her face, then bent herself to the task.

It took a long time before she had wiped the last of the blood from his face, and longer still for the nuns to come. Magda brewed up tea in the meantime and made Thomas drink some. Between it and the whiskey Thomas was more than ready to fall asleep by the time George returned with Sister Brigit and Sister Clare in tow.

Sister Clare, explained Eileen as the nun pushed her aside and started examining Thomas, was the town's healer. Sister Clare grunted an assent while poking and prodding at Thomas and making all his aches come newly alive. Sister Brigit left her to it and turned her attention to Lionel, laying into the man with the sharp edge of her tongue. No matter what Thomas had done, she said several different ways and in no uncertain terms, it was certainly no excuse for Lionel to go and do *this*.

Lionel waited until she stopped for breath then explained. Sister Brigit 'humphed' and promised to have a talk with Thomas's mother at once. Sister Clare finished her examination of Thomas's face and ribs then demanded to know where else it hurt. Thomas remembered the two kicks he'd suffered the night before, but saw Eileen anxiously awaiting his answer and decided that there was no way he was going to mention them. He shook his head.

Sister Clare grunted again, then turned to Lionel and Magda. "No permanent damage," was her verdict. "Two black eyes and bruised ribs, and that nose is going to have to be straightened."

"Straightened?" repeated Thomas. He reached up and touched his nose for the first time. It was lopsided. Badly so, in fact, and the pressure that was building up behind it showed no signs of going down.

"Aye, straightened," said Sister Clare. "Else you'll never breathe out of it again."

"Thought as much," said Lionel. "I'll take care of it."

Thomas's eyes widened in horror and he was about to protest, but Sister Clare beat him to it. "Now it's not something just anyone can do, you know."

"I do know," said Lionel, pointing at his own, oft-broken nose. "I've done it a dozen times, and the stronger the pull, the less it hurts."

Sister Clare looked dubious, but allowed that Lionel was right. After a few more words, and thanks from the entire family, Magda saw the nuns to the door. Once they were gone, Lionel sent George for more water from the well. When George brought it, Lionel soaked the cloth with it and made Thomas hold it against his face.

Thomas pushed the towel as firmly against his nose as he could manage, desperately wishing it was winter so he could rub his face in the snow until no feeling was left.

"Well, lad," said Lionel after the third application of the towel. "Are you ready?"

No, thought Thomas, but he took a deep breath through his mouth and nodded.

Magda took the towel. Lionel put one hand against Thomas's chest to hold him in place, then reached out and placed a bent finger gently on either side of Thomas's nose. Thomas winced. The man began squeezing his fingers together. Thomas closed his eyes, forced himself to breathe as the pain began to get worse and worse.

The smith suddenly squeezed hard and *pulled*. Thomas yelled out and tried to pull away. A moment later he was free and the wet towel was being pressed to his face. Thomas, eyes still shut, grabbed at it and used it to staunch the new flow of blood coming from his nose. The pressure in his head was easing, draining away with the blood. Thomas opened his eyes to see Lionel still standing in front of him, looking rather pleased with himself.

"I think you enjoyed that," said Thomas, his voice muffled behind the bloody cloth.

"Not in the..." Lionel stopped his protest in the middle and for a moment said nothing. When he spoke again his tone was stern. "Aye, I did, actually," he said. "You scared the life out of me, boy. You and her, jumping the fire like a pair of fools. You could have killed her."

Thomas didn't apologize. Their jump had distracted the bishop long enough for Timothy to escape. He couldn't be sorry for that. Still, he remembered the look on Lionel's face the night before; the fear and the anger that were running through him even before the bishop had started talking. For that, he could apologize. "I am sorry we frightened you."

"Well, I'm not," Eileen protested. "I was going to jump the flames at their height anyway. Thomas just made it more exciting."

"Eileen—" Magda warned.

Lionel looked down the length of his nose at his daughter. "Were you now?"

"I said as much last night," said Eileen, her voice rising. "Not that you were listening since you were having such a fine time planning what you were going to do to Thomas."

"Eileen," the warning in Magda's tone was unmistakable. "Enough."

Lionel waved his hand at his wife in a gentle, silencing gesture. "It's all right, love. She's right enough in what she says. I was furious all right, boy, and was certainly ready to give you a piece of my mind, but then..." He shook his head, shame creeping back into his voice. "I don't know what happened. Suddenly I was ready to beat the hide off you, boy. I could have killed you right then, and I nearly did. I have no idea…"

I do, thought Thomas as Lionel trailed off. Out loud he only said, "I know."

Lionel shook his head again, shaking the confusion off his face and replacing it with a stern look. He turned back to his daughter. "As for you, we had hopes you would grow up somewhat less reckless than your brother."

"Hey!"

"Quiet, George." Lionel didn't take his eyes off Eileen. "After last night, however, I can safely say that that you haven't. What you did was dangerous and careless and could have gotten you killed!"

Eileen looked rebellious, but said nothing. Lionel glared at her until she wilted and turned her eyes to the floor. Lionel glared a while longer, then sighed. "At least you've got courage enough to make up for what you lack in sense. Both of you," he added with a nod to Thomas. "And what, pray, gave you the idea of challenging me to a duel? Me, who is close to you as your own kin?"

"Well—"

"Not to mention twice your size."

"Well—"

"And then challenging the rest of the village and the bishop?"

"Well," Thomas said a third time, speaking slowly and clearly to make the words heard through the thick towel he was keeping pressed to his face, "I thought I might have a better chance against your sword than your belt."

Lionel's eyebrows went up, then he snorted with laughter. "True," he said, "though I might just surprise you come dawn tomorrow."

"Now you stop that," Magda scolded. "The boy's had enough grief already without you teasing him."

"Teasing?" The smith looked about ready to protest further, but left off at a glare from his wife. "Fair enough, then. How's the nose, boy?"

"Better. Still bleeding, though."

"We'll wait for it to stop. Then I think we should pay a visit to your house and talk to your father."

"I'm going with you," said George. "I want to know what's going on."

"You'll do no such thing," said Magda, looking from father to son. "I'll not have you making a mess over at Thomas's house."

"I wasn't going to," protested Lionel.

"You're not going to get the chance," said Magda. She took the cloth from Thomas and handed him a fresh one, then shook a finger at Lionel. "And don't bother arguing. We'll none of us be doing anything at all until after we've all had breakfast and a nap. It's been a long night and there's not one of us who's had any sleep. After that, we'll talk about what to do."

Lionel looked at his son. "She does make a good argument."

"Aye, she does."

"Aye, I do. So get this boy off to bed—sitting up, mind you—while we get the kitchen sorted and breakfast made."

* * *

Thomas didn't get up until noon. He had thought he would sleep the entire day away, but his dreams were ugly and violent. Men he couldn't see grabbed at him, hit him, and the bishop's face with its sunken, deep red eyes leered at him until he forced himself awake and out of the bed.

His bruises and sore muscles had stiffened nicely while he lay there, and he could barely manage to get up. He made himself move, preferring the pain to the dreams. He dressed himself in the shirt, breeches, and boots his father had given him. He would rather not have worn them, but they were the only clothes he had that weren't covered in blood or smelling of the fire.

When he came down the ladder, the entire family was at the table, speaking in low voices that hushed the moment they saw him. Thomas managed a smile. "Talking about me?"

"Aye," said George. "And your father."

"Come to any decisions?"

"None," said Lionel. "Though not for lack of arguing." Magda raised a warning finger at him, and Lionel left the topic. "How are you feeling, lad?"

"Sore, stiff and tired," said Thomas. "Thank the Four and you that I can breathe through my nose or I'd be feeling worse than I did this morning."

"The stiffness will pass," said Lionel. "Sit."

Thomas did as he was told, feeling the bruised ribs pull as he eased himself into the chair. There was silence a moment, as Lionel and Magda shared glances that plainly said *you go first* to the other.

"Mother wants to tell the Reeve," said George before either of his parents could say anything. "Da would rather go talk to your father himself."

"Someone has to go talk to the man," began Lionel.

"Aye," Magda said, cutting him off. Her tone made it quite clear that she'd said as much several times already. "But it won't be you!"

Thomas had a vision of how badly that particular conversation would go. "I don't think that's a good idea, Lionel. Father's not in a mood to listen right about now."

"What about your mother?" asked Eileen. "Or your brother? Could they talk to him?"

Thomas shook his head, "Not right now. He's angry enough that he won't listen to anyone."

"He was last night," said Magda. "Do you think he will be still this morning?"

"Aye," said Thomas. *And as long as the bishop still has him.* "I do."

Someone knocked, loud and sharp, at the front door and everyone around the table started. For a moment, Thomas was certain it was his father or the bishop, come to get him. He was half-way to his feet when Bluster called from outside. "Lionel! Magda! Are you in?"

"Aye," called Lionel back. "Come in."

Bluster opened the door and stepped in. He was flushed and sweaty, like a man who had run a fair ways, and looked very tired. He waved at them all and walked across the house to join them in the kitchen.

"So you are here," said Bluster to Thomas. "I thought as much."

"Aye," said Thomas, wondering what he'd done to rate any attention, especially the day after Fire Night. He was surprised Bluster wasn't still in bed.

"Your father said he didn't know where you'd gotten to," said Bluster. "Said you'd left last night in a huff and didn't say where you were going."

Thomas did his best to keep his voice neutral. "Really?"

"Aye." Bluster took a long look at Thomas's face. "He didn't mention any black eyes, though."

"Was it his father who sent you to find him?" asked Lionel, stepping between them.

"Nay," Bluster shook his head. "John was asleep when I got there. Said he's not so young as he can stay up all night without feeling the consequences. No, I actually went there looking for this one here. And since he wasn't at his parents' house, the only other place he could be..."

"Would be our house," finished Lionel.

"Aye."

"Why did you want to see me?" Thomas asked.

"Wanted to talk to you about that juggler," said Bluster. He looked over at George and Eileen, "All three of you, actually, so it's just as well you're here, Thomas."

Fear opened a hole in Thomas's stomach. "What about Timothy?"

"It seems that he was planning to leave last night."

Other business, the bishop had said. Thomas had barely heard it through the haze of blood and pain the night before. His throat was suddenly dry, and it took him a moment before he could manage to say. "Planning?"

"Aye. We found his wagon a ways up the road. A right mess it was, too."

The hole in Thomas's stomach became a yawning pit. "Where is he?" Thomas heard the tremor in his voice, tried to suppress it. "Where's Timothy?"

"Under the wagon," said Bluster, regret in his voice. "We didn't dare move him what with the condition he was in."

The pit pulled his strength into its depths and spat out fear to take its place. "Where?"

"Half a mile north—Hey!"

Thomas pushed past him, running.

"You can't help him, lad!" called Bluster.

Thomas ignored him and ran on, leaving the house behind. It was a rough, limping run that felt like it barely covered any ground at all. Every movement stretched protesting muscles; every jolt shot pains through his body. Thomas told himself the pain was unimportant and tried to force his legs to a faster pace. He stumbled instead and nearly fell.

A strong hand attached itself to his elbow, pulling him upright. George, who hadn't been able to beat Thomas in a race since they were ten, had caught up and was keeping pace. Eileen was right behind him. George kept his grip on Thomas's elbow and helped him keep his feet.

Thomas, immensely grateful, could only manage a nod. His attention all went to the road in front of him and to keeping upright.

They ran through the centre of the town. George was beginning to puff, and Thomas could hear Eileen's strained breathing behind him, but neither slowed. There were people out, now, cleaning up from the fair and going about their business. Thomas managed to avoid running over anyone, though he had to dodge around several. George, still holding Thomas's arm, knocked at least one person off balance. The man's angry words and Eileen's shouted apology followed them out of the village and across the town common. They reached the road and followed it back the way Thomas had come only three days before; up the hill and around the bend into the woods.

Timothy's wagon lay in the dirt at the side of the road. Two of its wheels turned in the air, the other two were dug deep into the earth, miraculously unbroken beneath the weight of the vehicle. Underneath, near the front, Thomas could see Timothy in his brightly-coloured, patched clothes. Sister Clare was kneeling beside him, cradling his head. Sister Brigit, Liam, and four or five of the village men were also there, standing back and looking at a loss. Thomas stopped in front of the wrecked wagon. "Don't just stand there," he demanded, between gasps of breath. "Get it off of him!"

"We can't," said Liam.

"It's killing him!"

"It's already killed him," said Sister Clare, quietly. "He's bleeding underneath the wagon. Moving it will only make it worse."

"How can it be worse?" Thomas demanded. Timothy's face was grey, his eyes closed. Underneath the wagon, his legs were flattened, his pants stained dark red and wet. A pool of blood was overflowing by the little man's waist, sending a thin trickle of red twisting slowly through the dirt of the road. "Timothy! Timothy!"

"Let him sleep," admonished the nun. "It will make his passing easier."

"Passing is already easy," said Timothy. He sounded hollow and distant, as if talking was bringing him back from some place far away. His eyes opened and squinted at the young man beside him. "Can't feel a thing."

"Timothy!" Thomas crouched down beside him, hissing in pain from the motion. "We'll get the wagon off you. We'll stop the bleeding—"

"No, you won't," Timothy said. A coughing fit took him as soon as the words left his mouth. Blood flew from his mouth as his neck and chest twisted. The effort took his strength away, leaving his eyes unfocused and his mouth gaping as he tried to force air into his lungs. Thomas wanted to grab him, to shake him back to life even though he knew it would do no good at all. At last Timothy's eyes came back into focus. His voice was fainter than before. "Sit a while, lad."

Thomas knelt on the wet ground next to him, trying to hide the pain the motion cost him. Timothy saw anyway, and his lips pulled into a shape that could have been a smile. "Rough night all around, then."

"Aye." Thomas could feel tears starting to well up. He forced them back. "Timothy, who...?"

"Same as before..."

Another round of coughing shook the juggler and left him once more gasping for breath. Thomas blinked hard, felt the tears rolling down his face. He was about to dash them away with his sleeve when Timothy's hand shot out, and closed painfully tight on Thomas's hand.

"A word, lad," Timothy's voice was hoarse, his breathing laboured, "in your ear."

Thomas leaned over the heaving chest and put his face beside Timothy's. Timothy licked his lips. The first word was incomprehensible, and the little man tried again. "It's true. The magic...ball of light...true." A shudder passed through the man's body. His grip tightened. Timothy gasped for air again then continued. "No one ever saw... You did."

Thomas strove to make sense of the words. "I don't—"

Timothy interrupted. "Bishop...bastard...took the best part of me." He fought for breath again. "Wants the small magics. Will take..."

"What?" The little man was in great pain now, his eyes rolling back and his face contorting. Thomas held him as best he could. "What will he take?"

"Ailbe," Timothy gasped. His eyes lost their focus then came back, sharp and clear, but not truly seeing. "Want sky." His voice was scared, child-like. "I want to see..."

Thomas sat back. Timothy's face contorted with the effort of getting air into his lungs. His hand, still gripping Thomas's, clenched painfully tight, then relaxed. His twisted features smoothed and his wide-open eyes stared, sightless, into the blue sky above him.

Thomas sat there, crying, until George helped him to his feet and away from Timothy's body.

* * *

Bluster arrived at some point, though Thomas wasn't sure when, with Lionel behind him. Lionel and the other men from the village pushed the wagon upright, freeing Timothy's body. The two nuns wrapped Timothy in the blankets he had shared with Thomas and his friends only two nights before. Bluster and the others lifted the body up into the back of the wagon. Eileen sat beside Thomas, her face wet with tears. George paced back and forth, swinging his big arms helplessly.

Bluster came over to the little group, looking solemn. "A bad business this is," he said, surveying the three young people. "Bad all around."

"It was the ones we scared off." George kept pacing while he spoke, his arms still swinging. "They came back. They did this."

"Aye, as you say." Bluster laid a hand on George's arm, stopping the swinging. "Not your fault if it was, lad."

George stopped pacing; stopped all movement and stared at the little man. His anger was plain, and he looked more than ready to contradict Bluster. The Reeve held his place, keeping his eyes and George's locked together until George's expression softened. "Aye," said George at last. "I suppose not."

They were in my house, Thomas thought, staring through his tears at the back of the wagon, and the small man's corpse that lay in it. *The ones who did this were in my house.*

"I'll want to talk to you three," said Bluster, pulling him away from his thoughts. "As soon as we get the body back into town. We need to talk about Timothy, then I need to send a messenger to the sheriff in Lakewood."

I can tell Bluster, Thomas thought. *I can tell him everything and let him go to my house and...*

And do what?

The men were gone. Thomas remembered the bishop ordering them out of the room. Thomas could see in his mind what would happen. His father would refuse to let Thomas in, or the bishop would deny everything and use the power in his voice to make Bluster believe him. Worse, the bishop would get Bluster to put Thomas in chains where he couldn't get away, and then...

One hand went to his chest of its own accord, and the dull ache there made Thomas shudder.

"Thomas?" said Bluster. Thomas looked up, saw the man staring down at him. There was pity on his face, and worry. "We need to go. Now."

Thomas nodded. At least Bluster would send word to the sheriff, whose demesne extended fifty miles in all directions from Lakewood. Elmvale itself, if it had not been on the nunnery's lands, would be part of his domain. With luck, the man might lay his hands on the bishop's men, at least.

Thomas scrubbed hard at his tears, carefully avoiding his broken nose, then gathered his strength and pushed himself to his feet. It hurt far more than he expected, and he nearly fell over. Eileen stood up at once, letting him lean on her. Thomas tried to bring in a deep breath and found that his nose was bleeding again. He used the edge of his sleeve to staunch it, wincing at the pain.

"Come on, then," said Bluster, "let's get this over with."

Lionel and Liam and two others began pushing and pulling the wagon back towards the town. The Reeve and the nuns fell in behind. Thomas, not having any alternative, followed. He would tell the Reeve as little as possible. Until he had some proof, anything else would make the whole mess worse.

The walk back felt far longer than it possibly could have been. Thomas's body ached. Pain jolted him with every step. His energy was nearly gone. Thoughts flitted through his head like birds unable to decide whether to settle to earth or to fly to distant lands.

George and Eileen walked on either side of Thomas each holding an arm and helping to keep him upright. Eileen's face was still streaked with tears which she didn't bother wiping. George just looked lost. In front of them, the wagon with its still-bleeding cargo moved slowly ahead. Sister Clare and Sister Brigit walked with Bluster beside the wagon, talking in low tones. Every now and then, Bluster would look back at the trio, sweeping his piercing eyes across them before settling on Thomas. He would stare a while, then turn back to the nuns.

"Why does he keep looking back at us?" asked George.

"He's talking to the Sisters," said Eileen. "They're probably telling everything they know about what happened to your face."

"Aye, well, that's precious little," said Thomas.

"He's going to ask you about it," said George, "once this business with Timothy is done."

"Aye."

"What are you going to tell him?"

Precious little, thought Thomas. He didn't answer though, and George let the matter alone.

The procession was spotted as soon as they broke free of the woods, and by the time they had crossed the town common, a half-dozen curious folks were there to meet them and learn what had happened. Liam told them about Timothy and several of them left at once.

"Must they tell everyone?" said Eileen watching a women scurrying away down the street.

"Everyone will find out sooner or later," said George. "It may as well be sooner."

"They shouldn't carry it like gossip," said Eileen. "It's not right."

Bluster led the grim group to the old watchtower where he kept his office, collecting a crowd of the curious in their wake as word spread through the town. By the time they stopped, nearly a quarter of the village had gathered around them, from children too young to understand what was happening to old men and women looking for gossip to share by the fire.

Magda pushed through them all to reach her husband, who took her hand as soon as he put down his side of the wagon's tongue. Thomas searched through the crowd for his own family, hoping to see his mother or brother and talk to them. Neither was there.

It doesn't mean anything, he thought, trying to force himself to believe it. *Most of the village isn't here. There's no reason they should be.*

Bluster stepped up onto the tower stairs and called for silence. The crowd muttered a few moments more, then stilled. Bluster outlined the events of the morning and the muttering began again, this time laced with shock and horror rather than curiosity. Bluster raised a hand for silence once more, and this time got it much faster than before.

"The important thing," said Bluster, "is that we all keep our eyes open for the next while. The men who did this could still be around, and if they are, there could be danger. Now I'll be needing to talk to anyone who was in the woods last night—"

"That narrows it down," someone said in the back of the crowd. No one laughed, but many heads nodded.

"—who thinks they heard anything unusual," Bluster finished, ignoring the interruption. He paused, then added, "And I don't mean Liam's grunting, though we could certainly all hear that."

The chuckle that ran through the crowd sounded more obligatory than amused; an attempt to raise spirits lowered by the sight of the corpse in the wagon. Bluster exhorted them once more to be careful, then waved the crowd away. They broke off in knots, people speaking in low tones as they went. It would be the talk of three counties by the end of the day, Thomas was certain.

"Now," Bluster said, turning to Thomas and his friends. "Come inside and tell me about these men again."

*   *   *

The inside of the watchtower was dark and cool. Sunlight came in long, thin shafts through long slits in the walls once meant for archers to fire through, though the platforms they would have stood on had long since vanished. Now, there was no structure in the tower save for the stairs that ran in circles all the way up to the roof and the thick beams that reached across the empty air from wall to wall, keeping the tower upright. Dust motes danced in the light as the beams fell across the room to land against walls as grey inside as they had been out. There was a single chair and a table that Bluster used as a desk, and two long benches for furniture. On one section of the wall a half-dozen leg- and armchains dangled off iron rings.

Thomas, George, and Eileen were on one of the benches, Magda and Lionel on the other. None of them had moved for the better part of two hours, or spoken save to answer Bluster's questions. Bluster sat behind his desk, a quill in his hand, scratching notes on the paper in front of him as he led the three friends through their memories of the men who attacked Timothy's wagon, making each one of them tell their version of the story twice. Bluster peppered them with questions, searching out the smallest details about what had happened.

Thomas said nothing about the bishop, nothing about the men being at his house, nothing about magic. He kept to what he'd remembered of the night the men attacked Timothy, and felt like a coward for doing it.

There's nothing else I can do, Thomas told himself. *No one will believe me. Not against the bishop.*

"All right," said Bluster at last, putting down the quill, "I'll send a messenger to the sheriff over in Lakewood, let him know what's happened."

"Do you think you'll find them?" asked Eileen.

"I don't know," Bluster said. "If they stay around here, I'll find them, but if they've left..." He shrugged, then stood up and stretched his back. "Long time to be sitting." He walked around the desk. "There is one other matter, though," he said, putting himself directly in front of Thomas. "What happened to you last night?"

Thomas looked at his feet and didn't say anything. Bluster waited a moment, then continued. "Now, my money would have been on that one—" Bluster pointed at Lionel. Lionel rose to protest but stopped when Bluster said "—but the nuns told me he had nothing to do with it."

"I didn't," said Lionel, sinking back in his seat. Shame crept into his face again. "I wouldn't."

Bluster raised his eyebrows at that, but only said, "Do you know who did?"

"I think it's Thomas's story to tell," said Magda.

"True enough," agreed Bluster, turning back to Thomas. "So what happened?"

Thomas wished desperately for a way to explain it all; a way to tell the story that would sound even remotely plausible. There wasn't one. In the end, he could only say what he had said to Lionel and Magda. "I had a disagreement with my father."

Out of the corner of his eye, Thomas could see Bluster pressing his lips together, making them a thin line of white on his face. Thomas waited. At last, Bluster said. "When I talked to your father this morning, he said that when he came home, you two had an argument and then you ran out of the house."

Thomas remembered the feel of his father's hand on his collar, shoving him out of the back door and into the dirt. "I didn't run out. He threw me out."

"Bishop Malloy was there as well," Bluster's tone grew colder with every word. "And he said the same as your father. And that you were in a violent rage and that you threatened them before you left."

Of course he did, thought Thomas. *Of course he would make everything my fault.*

Bluster's strong hand came under Thomas's chin and forced his head up. "Why don't you tell me what happened last night?" said Bluster. "Begin after the Fire."

Thomas wanted to pull his head out of Bluster's hand; to stand up and walk out. Instead, knowing Bluster would stop him if he tried to leave, he met

Bluster's cold stare. "I went to my father's house after the Fire. I got beat up. My father threw me out. I walked through the woods to George's house."

Bluster tilted Thomas's chin higher. "And no one saw you."

"Unless I tripped over someone on the way."

"And you say you were beaten at your father's house."

"Aye."

"And why wouldn't your father mention this?"

Because then he'd have to say why, thought Thomas. *And the bishop won't allow that.*

"The problem, lad, is that all I've got is your word for that," said Bluster, still hanging onto Thomas's chin. "And I've got the word of your father and the bishop saying otherwise. This means that someone is lying. And when someone lies about events on the night a man got murdered, that makes me worried."

Thomas felt his eyes widen of their own accord; felt a dozen protests rise up at once and get stuck together in his throat. Behind him, Thomas heard Magda's intake of breath; heard Lionel rise to his feet and felt George and Eileen stiffen on either side of him.

Bluster's upraised hand stopped any words. "Now I'm not saying you killed the juggler, but I'm thinking you're knowing more than you say, and I'll be wanting the truth out of you." The grip on Thomas's chin grew tighter, pushing hard at the bruises there. "Who did this, lad?"

The same ones that killed Timothy.

The words wouldn't pass Thomas's lips. He had no proof, and the bishop and his father would refute any accusation he made. Instead he said, "It was dark. I couldn't see."

The grip tightened further, bringing tears to Thomas's eyes. "And you're sure you were beaten before you left your father's house?"

"Aye."

"Not after?"

"Aye."

"You don't need to hurt the lad," began Lionel.

Bluster cut him off, his voice rising as he kept the pressure on Thomas's chin. "The bishop and your father say otherwise, lad. And of the three, you are not the one I'm inclined to believe. So unless you have some way to prove it—"

An image of John Flarety, pushing Madeleine away, blazed up in Thomas's mind.

"My mother," said Thomas between gritted teeth. "Ask her."

Bluster's head tilted to one side, his eyes narrowing as he considered it. "She was there?"

"Not for all of it," said Thomas. "But for enough."

"And she'll say the same as you?"

More, thought Thomas, *if my father will let you speak to her.* "Aye. She will."

Bluster stared at Thomas a while longer, then let go of his chin and stepped back. Thomas's head fell forward, the relief from the pain making him gasp. "All right. I'll speak to her." He stepped away and turned to Magda and Lionel. "You said Thomas is staying with you?"

"Aye," said Magda, her tone leaving no doubt as to how much she disapproved what she had just witnessed. "Until he can go home."

"Take him, then," said Bluster. "He looks to be in need of rest."

"He is," agreed Magda, stiffly. "Come on, everyone."

Eileen and George reached to help Thomas to his feet, but he stood before they could. It hurt, but not as much as it had before. Bluster went to the door and held it open for them all. Thomas let everyone else go first, then stopped in the doorway. "What will happen to Timothy?" he asked Bluster. "To his body, I mean."

Bluster shrugged. "The nuns will ready him for the grave," he said. "I'll send notices out when I send word to the sheriff. If no family comes for him in three days, we'll bury him."

"Where?"

"I don't know," said Bluster. "The nuns will take care of it, unless you have an idea?"

"No, I just..." Thomas remembered the night by the fire; the mugs of whiskey in their hands and Timothy's clear, strong voice singing to them as his fingers danced across the lute. Tears threatened to well up again, but Thomas forced them back. "I just want to see him laid down right."

Bluster was watching him again, but there was no accusation in the look, only curiosity. "What was he to you, lad?"

Magic. "A friend," Thomas said. "A new friend, but still a friend."

Bluster nodded, and for the first time that day, Thomas saw something resembling sympathy in his expression. "Aye. Well, we'll see him buried properly, whatever happens."

Chapter 8

Thomas woke at the touch of a gentle hand on his shoulder. He opened his puffy eyes and squinted. It was early evening, judging from the light slanting through the room, and Eileen was standing by the edge of the bed.

He smiled at her. "Hello."

"Hello."

"Have I missed dinner?"

"Mother kept some warm near the fire for you."

"Good." He started to sit up, felt his ribs and stomach muscles protest.

"Thomas..."

The tone of her voice stopped him. "What's wrong?"

"Your brother's here."

"My brother?" Thomas tossed back the blankets and rolled out of the bed, groaning at the pain the movement caused. Eileen jumped back, her mouth opening in what Thomas guessed was a protest. It went unvoiced when she saw he was still wearing his breeches. Thomas took the moment to run his hands over his head, attempting to bring order to his unruly mop of hair, then found his shirt and began pulling it on.

"How long has he been here?"

"He only just arrived," said Eileen. "He's talking to Father in the smithy."

Thomas finished with the shirt and bent over to pick up his boots. He grunted and groaned his way through getting them on, then stood up. Eileen offered a steadying hand but Thomas managed to rise without it. He looked across the room to his sword belt, sitting on top of George's trunk.

"Is he alone?" Thomas asked.

"I don't know," said Eileen. "I think so."

It's my brother, Thomas thought. *I don't need a sword to talk to my brother. If he's alone.*

He picked up the weapons and headed down the stairs.

In the kitchen, Magda looked disapprovingly at the sword belt in Thomas's hand but didn't say anything. She pointed out the back door. Thomas could see George and Lionel talking to Neal by the smithy. Thomas took a deep breath, then stepped out of the house and crossed the yard.

"Thomas!" Neal took a few steps forward then stopped. "By the Four! What happened to your face?"

That made Thomas stop. "You don't know?"

"I was in the woods all night," his brother said, blushing. "And I spent the day at warehouses, organizing an order for the end of the week."

"Have you seen Mother?"

"I haven't seen anyone save Father. He stopped me when I walked in the door." Neal looked confused and held up a letter. "He told me to deliver this to you. Thomas, why aren't you staying at home?"

"I'm not welcome there."

"Because of what you did at the Fire?" Neal waved a hand in dismissal. "Don't be daft. Father did the same thing, and not with Mother, either—"

Thomas cut Neal off before the other could start asking for explanations Thomas couldn't give. "Neal, what does the letter say?"

"I don't know. Father sealed it. Said I was to give it to you, and get your reply. I thought the whole thing was ridiculous myself, but..." He handed over the letter. Thomas broke the seal and started reading.

"What does it say?" asked Neal.

Thomas didn't answer. He read every word in the letter twice. By the second time through, he was starting to feel dizzy. He handed it back to his brother without a word. He should have been furious, he knew, but the anger wouldn't come. Too much had happened too fast.

"Well?" said Neal.

Thomas, feeling numb and unsteady, walked past him to lean his back against the smithy wall. "Read it yourself."

Neal scanned the letter quickly and his jaw dropped. Then he started at the beginning of it again. "Surely he's joking."

"I doubt it." Thomas closed his eyes.

"But he can't be serious!" said Neal. "You haven't finished school!"

The dark behind Thomas's eyelids soothed him, lulled his body into stillness. Still the emotion wouldn't come. He wished for something, anything for him to cling onto in the dark blankness of his mind.

"What does it say?" asked Lionel. "Thomas?"

"My father," said Thomas, his eyes still shut, "wants me to go at once to Berrytown, where the bishop is going to be in one week's time. There, I am to go into the church and spend my time in solitary prayer until the bishop's arrival. When that blessed event occurs, I am to throw myself at his feet, beg his forgiveness, and ask to be taken into his service."

"His service?" It was George asking, disbelief in his voice.

"And me not even a Theology student." Bitterness came, cold and bile-filled. Thomas let it feed him, let the anger that followed it give him strength.

"His service?" Lionel repeated. "What would you do in the bishop's service?"

"Oh, it gets better," said Thomas, opening his eyes. The words felt like venom, burning his mouth as he spoke them. "You see, if I don't, my father will go to the magistrate. He will claim that I have forsaken my education, my family, and my responsibilities. Then he will demand repayment at once, in full."

"You can't afford that," said George. "Can you?"

"No." Thomas pushed himself off the wall and fumbled with the sword belt. "Which is why he'll have me sent to the debtor's prison."

He straightened out the belt and settled it around his hips. The weight of the weapons was a cold, hard comfort.

"Thomas?" George's eyes were on the weapons on Thomas's hips.

"I'm going to see my father." Thomas said in reply to the unasked question. *Even if it means facing down the bishop.* "I'm going to talk some sense into him, and if that doesn't work..." Thomas saw the fear in the eyes of those around him, fear for him and for what he was going to do.

"If that doesn't work," repeated Thomas, "then I'll tell him to go to the Banished and take the bishop with him."

"Thomas?" Neal's voice called after him as he walked. Thomas ignored it. "Thomas!"

Thomas heard Neal's running steps on the road behind him, and a moment later his brother was walking beside him. "I'm going with you," said Neal. Thomas thought briefly about protesting, but kept his mouth shut. If the bishop was there, the man might think twice about attacking him with a witness present. Besides, maybe Neal could talk John Flarety back into his senses.

The Four know I haven't been able to.

Neal badgered Thomas for details all the way home, demanding to know everything that happened after Thomas left the Fire. Thomas said nothing about the magic, but let him know everything else, including what he'd heard once he'd been thrown out of the house. Neal's eyes grew wide as he listened, and by the time the two reached their yard, he was furious. "I can't believe this. Our father isn't like that."

"Our father wasn't like that," corrected Thomas. He stopped in front of the main door and raised his hand to knock.

"What are you doing?" asked Neal, stepping past him and pushing the door open. "We live here, remember?"

A pain that had nothing to do with the bishop blossomed in Thomas's chest. He dropped his hand. "I forgot."

Neal looked ready to say something about that, but didn't. "Come on," he said instead. "Father should be in his study."

The brothers strode quickly through the main chambers of the house and up the wide front stairs. There was no sign of anyone. Thomas was relieved. Servants were traditionally given the day after Fire Night off to recover, but Thomas hadn't been certain of the guests. They probably had all headed home that morning, leaving John Flarety to himself.

They moved in silence, their footsteps muffled by the carpet that ran the length of the hallway. Thomas pushed himself ahead of his brother as they approached his father's door. A lifetime of parental training nearly made him stop and knock. He ignored it, grabbed the handle and pushed the door open. John Flarety, sitting behind his desk, came to his feet. On his first step into the room, Thomas realized that his father was not alone. On his third, he realized who was with him.

Thomas stopped, suddenly unsure of himself, then rocked forward as Neal ran into him. He managed to keep his balance, but lost the last of his composure. Behind him, Neal was also still.

"Thomas," said Bluster, rising to his feet from the chair in front of John's desk. "What are you doing here?"

"I told you that he would not be able to resist coming," said John Flarety. "And armed, too."

Bluster nodded. "Aye, you did."

Neal stepped around Thomas, his eyes on his father. "What is the Reeve doing here?"

"Waiting for Thomas's answer," said John Flarety. "And from the weapons your brother brought, I'd say we know what it is."

"Don't be hasty," Bluster fixed Thomas with his piercing glare. "Why are you armed, lad?"

"Because he's a ruffian," said John. "And now he's dragging his brother into it."

"He's not dragging me anywhere," protested Neal. "What happened here last night?"

"Don't you start—"

"Quiet!" Bluster's word cracked like a whip through the room, silencing them both. "Now, Thomas, what brings you here?"

A dozen thoughts leapt through Thomas's brain at once, but none pulled themselves out of the pack long enough to be articulated.

"It's obvious what the boy is doing here," John said. "He doesn't like the decision I've made for him, and now he's come to protest it with his weapons. Arrest him!"

"I'll not be arresting anyone who hasn't done anything," said Bluster, raising a warning finger. "And I want *Thomas* to tell me why he's here."

"But—"

Bluster fixed his glare on John Flarety. "Thomas, I said."

John fell silent, but the muscles in his jaw twitched and his eyes were still burning with anger.

Bluster stepped forward cutting off Thomas's view of his father. "Come on, now, lad. Why did you come here?"

"I want..." *I want to know what the bishop has done to you, Father.* The words were on the tip of his tongue, but there was no way to let them out. Bluster would demand to know what he was talking about, and if Thomas started spouting about magic he could say goodbye to any chance of sympathy. He had to get his father talking.

"Well, lad?" said Bluster.

"I want to know why you invited Timothy to the May fair."

It was certainly not what John Flarety had been expecting. "What?"

"Timothy," said Thomas. "The juggler. Why did you invite him here?"

John Flarety looked suddenly nonplussed, and when he answered he sounded perplexed, rather than angry. "The bishop suggested him."

The bishop planned his murder, Thomas thought. "The same way he *suggested* I leave the Academy?"

John's face began turning red and the confusion vanished from his tone. "The bishop had nothing to do with that decision. You need direction in your life!"

Thomas forced his voice calm. "I have a direction."

The red darkened to purple. "You dare question me?"

"Yes!" Thomas stepped forward, but the Reeve blocked him with an outstretched arm. "Father, I have done everything you asked of me. I have written home every month. I've passed all my classes. I've gotten honours in Languages and Philosophy and Law. I even took that course on Engineering so I could build improvements for our wagons! Why do you want me to stop now?"

"I don't need to answer to you."

"Yes, you do! You're asking me to give up everything I've worked for! Everything you've *paid* for! Why?"

"I'll not be subject to this!"

"Yes, you will!"

"Calm down!" snapped Bluster. "Both of you!"

John was in full rage and certainly in no mood to listen. "You miserable creature!" He stepped around his desk and closed the distance between them. "How dare you speak to me in this way! I am your father and you will do exactly what I wish!"

"Father—" began Neal, stepping in front of him.

"Be silent!" John pushed Neal aside and came face to face with his younger son. "You dare question me?"

Bluster, behind John Flarety, put his hand on the man's shoulder. "Back away, John."

John shrugged him off. "I will not have my son disobey me!"

"Father," Thomas kept his voice level and slow, "these are not your words."

"Insolence!" The slap was aimed right at the bruises on his face and was hard enough to rock Thomas back on his heels. Thomas stifled a cry, then was jolted forward as his father grabbed his shirt and pulled him forward. "You will do exactly what I say, or I will have you jailed! Do you understand me?"

"I am not going to serve the bishop!"

Bluster grabbed at John's shirt, but the man was already pushing Thomas backwards.

"You're going to do as I say!"

"The bishop's twisted you!"

"That Academy has twisted you!" shouted John, shoving Thomas hard against the study wall. "It has turned you into a creature beyond redemption! The bishop has helped me see the truth!"

"What truth? That you should have me beaten senseless?"

"I did nothing of the kind!" John snapped. "I asked two of the bishop's men to help him with his prayers, and in the midst of it, he attacked them!"

"Thomas?" said Bluster. "Is that true?"

"No!" Thomas pulled at the hands on his shirt. "He lies!"

"Lies?" John pulled him away from the wall then shoved him back into it. "Lies, you little bastard?! Get out of my house! Out!" John dragged him to the study door. "Out!"

"Stop it, Father!" Thomas yelled, struggling against the hands on his shirt. John let go with one hand and slapped Thomas again. Thomas's head rang with it, and blood began running from his nose.

"Father!" Neal attempted to step in. John shoved him aside, then put both hands onto Thomas's shirt and threw him out of the office and against the far wall of the hallway. Thomas bounced off it, saw his father coming towards him, hands raised in fists.

"Enough, Father!" Thomas cried, desperate to stop the man.

"Don't you tell me—"

The steel edge of Thomas's dagger hissed against the metal rim of the scabbard. The blade came up between them, stopping John Flarety cold. Thomas, knees bent in a knife-fighter's crouch, never took his eyes off his father as he raised the blade. "I said, *enough!*"

John Flarety was staring, hatred naked in his eyes. Behind him, Thomas could see Bluster reaching for his truncheon. Neal was standing beside him, his mouth gaping.

John sneered at Thomas. "Why don't you draw your sword as well?"

Thomas stayed in his crouch. "The hallway's too narrow."

"Thomas," warned Bluster, stepping out of the study behind John. "Put the weapon away, lad."

"Nothing has changed," John said, his voice as cold and hard and unforgiving as stone. "You will not go back to the Academy. You will go to the bishop. You will beg his forgiveness, and you will enter his service."

"No."

"Then you are no longer my son."

The words cut far deeper than Thomas's dagger would have. Thomas felt the breath leave his body. *It's not him talking,* he reminded himself. *These are not my father's words.*

John looked down at the dagger, then back to Thomas's eyes. "Now get out of my house."

Thomas didn't move. "I want to see my mother."

"She's not here," said Bluster. "She's up at the nunnery visiting the nuns."

"When is she coming back, Father?" asked Neal, stepping between John and Thomas.

John didn't take his eyes off Thomas. "She didn't say."

Thomas heard the pain in his father's words, buried deep under the rage, but there nonetheless. Thomas dug at it. "You hit her last night, didn't you?"

"Father?" Neal's voice had a scared, angry edge. "Father, did you hit Mother?"

John's eyes went to his eldest son. "What happened is between your mother and me. No one else."

"I heard someone get hit," said Thomas, "and there's no marks on you."

Neal's face started turning red, very much like his father's had. "I'm going to the nunnery," he said between clenched teeth. "I'll go see her and find out."

"It has nothing to do with you!" snapped John. "Leave it alone!" He spun on his heel, shouting at Bluster. "Will you get that vagrant out of my house!"

Bluster stared at John until the man stepped back, then advanced slowly on Thomas, his truncheon swinging at his side. "Lad?"

Thomas realized then that the dagger was still in his hand. He straightened up and let the blade drop to his side. He thought of saying more to his father, but John Flarety's expression had not changed. Nothing short of murder was going to change the man's mind, and Thomas knew it.

"I'll come see you in the morning," said Neal. "I promise."

Thomas sheathed the dagger, then turned and walked away from the study. He forced himself not to look back. Forced himself not to do anything but walk. Out of the house and on to the road. Across the road and into the woods, following the half-remembered path he'd taken the night before.

Anger had control of Thomas and held him tight all through the woods and past the smith's house. He waved curtly at George and Lionel in the forge, but didn't slow his pace at all. He was in no fit condition to talk to anyone. His brain was whirling and any thoughts he tried to hold on to were torn away and lost in the maelstrom that filled his head.

He followed the path he had taken with George and Eileen two nights before until he came to the mill pond. The water looked deceptively shallow in the late-evening sunlight, but Thomas, who had swum in it for years, knew better. He stripped off his sword-belt, boots, and shirt, then dove in. The cold water shocked his body and his mind, tensing all his muscles and driving all thought from his brain. He forced himself further under, swimming as deeply as he could. In the middle of the pond he stopped and held himself still in the water. The light was green and murky. The water around him deadened all sound.

Thomas used to love diving deep like this. George and he would have contests to see who would reach the bottom first. It was nearly fifteen feet deep. Thomas remembered the way his lungs would ache as he struggled to reach the bottom and the time that he had nearly passed out on the way back up.

He floated in the cold silence. Slanting rays of evening sunlight played off the weeds on the bottom of the pond. Silvery movement nearby told him that there were minnows swimming with him. He rolled onto his back and stared up at the surface. The world on the other side was a blur, the sunlight bouncing off the still-rippling surface. Thomas stared at the shimmering light and tried to put his thoughts in order.

His father was being controlled by the bishop.

There was no question in Thomas's mind about that. His father had *changed*. The rage he was showing was way beyond anything Thomas had ever seen. At his worst, John Flarety had been given to brief fits of yelling. Now though?

Despite the rage Thomas had seen that afternoon, despite John's threats and violence, the image that kept coming back to Thomas's mind was from the banquet the night before.

John Flarety had been rude at the dinner table.

It was a strange thing to dwell on, given everything else that had happened, but it was the point that drove home. John Flarety was always courteous and entertaining and if anything were to go wrong, his guests would never know it. Before, he would have been positively charming even if he had been completely furious.

In fact, it was his father's charm that Thomas remembered most. Time and again, Thomas had watched his father talk people out of their moods. He had charmed everyone from grumpy fishwives to other merchants to angry suppliers. He could even persuade Lionel to listen.

Thomas remembered a day when he was thirteen. Two wagons needed new wheel-irons. John Flarety and Lionel had been bickering, and Lionel was in no mood to do extra work. Thomas had been visiting when his father came in, and was certain that Lionel would not change his mind, no matter what.

Thomas remembered his father's voice, flowing like fresh, warm honey. He remembered feeling it fill the forge like something tangible, imagining that he could see it, wrapping around Lionel. By the time John was done, Lionel had forgiven him and set aside other projects to help.

What if I didn't imagine it?

The pieces started falling together in a way Thomas found totally unacceptable.

Timothy could create a ball of light out of air.

John Flarety could persuade anyone of anything.

The bishop could tear apart a man's soul.

And I saw it all.

I'm the only one who could see it.

Thomas rolled in the water and kicked hard upward. He broke from the water like a dolphin breaching the surface of the sea and hauled air into his starving lungs. His muscles, already reacting to the cold, protested mightily as he stroked towards the shore.

Thomas had spent four years studying logic and reason. Four years arguing with theology students about the nature of divinity, and whether the High Father was truly the prime mover for all things in the universe. Four years denying that anything like magic could even exist. Now, though, he couldn't see what else it could be.

Small magics, Timothy had called them.

He reached the water's edge and stepped out into the cool air of the evening, wiping the water from his face and body with his hands.

If the bishop could steal the small magics, could tear them out of a man's chest, what would happen to the person afterwards? Did they fall under the bishop's control? Given the way John Flarety had been behaving, it seemed very likely to Thomas, which made Timothy's fear all the more reasonable. Thomas wondered when the bishop had taken John Flarety's magic and if his father had ever had the slightest idea what he had lost.

Thomas remembered the look on the bishop's face when he had tried to take Thomas's magic. The thought of being under the man's control made him shudder even more than the evening breeze against his wet skin.

Of course, Thomas thought, *now that I know this, what am I going to do?*

Thomas needed proof. More than just words from a dying man that only he had heard. More than half remembered feelings or what he'd thought he'd seen and felt when he was beaten half-unconscious. He needed something tangible.

Thomas picked up his shirt and boots in one hand and gathered his weapons with the other. He started walking back towards the smithy. He would dry off by the forge, he decided, and he would sit there until he had figured out a way to find the proof he needed. Then he could tell someone.

His feet weren't used to being bare, and the stones and roots that he had never noticed as a child now dug in to them with every step. By the time he reached the smithy, Thomas was limping. He was also quite positive that immersion in cold water as the sun goes down was just about the worst thing one could do to a still-injured body. He could barely move, he was so stiff.

He stepped inside the smithy and the heat washed over him like a wave, digging into the aching muscles and soothing the pain. Lionel was there, banking down the fires. The big smith saw the puddle forming under Thomas's feet and raised an eyebrow.

"Don't tell me your father dunked you in the pond."

"No." Thomas found a stool in the corner and pulled it close to the forge. He closed his eyes and let the near-blistering heat suck the moisture from his body and clothes. "No, I dunked myself."

"By the Four, lad, why?"

"I needed to clear my head."

The smith's eyebrows went higher. "Did it work?"

A half-smile quirked Thomas's face. "Aye."

Lionel snorted. "If that's what it takes to be a scholar, I must say I'm glad not to have gone to school."

Thomas said nothing, only revelled in the heat. The smith snorted again, and told him to close the flue when he was dry, and not to forget the dinner that waited for him inside.

Thomas waved at the sound of Lionel's voice and abandoned himself to the heat.

Sit still, breathe, and listen. It was an exercise he'd learned on the first day of his first philosophy class. The first step to wisdom, he had been taught, was to pay attention, and the first step to that was clearing the mind.

He inhaled deeply, the acrid smell of the forge filling his nostrils. The coals, which had spent the day roaring under the wind of the bellows, were quiet now, only occasionally crackling as they split under their own heat. Beyond that, he could hear the voices from inside the house; the evening birds giving their last chirps of the day; and further off, barely audible, the strains of a fiddle coming from the village inn. Thomas listened to it all, breathing deeply.

Images raced through his head: Eileen jumped the flames beside him. Timothy laughed at his expense then gasped for air beneath the wagon. His father screamed hatred at him while Bluster swung his truncheon at his side. The men beat him again, and again the bishop stood over him, trying to pull the magic from Thomas's soul.

One by one the images came, and one by one Thomas set them aside, consciously turning his attention outward, to the sounds around him and his own breathing.

The heat was bringing a sweat to his body, and he embraced it gratefully, feeling the last of the chill and stiffness leave his muscles. He continued breathing and listening to the world beyond while the world within calmed itself. It took a long time, but in the end his mind was clear and all he was focusing on were the sounds of the forge, the noises from beyond the doors of the smithy and, he realized, the breathing of somebody sitting beside him.

He opened his eyes. Eileen was sitting on another stool, looking at him, her expression unreadable. He smiled at her. "Hello."

She blushed. Thomas, not expecting that reaction at all, waited. After a moment, she said, "When Father said you were out here, I came to bring you your supper." She pointed to a bowl of stew, sitting near to the forge to keep it warm. "The way you looked, I didn't want to disturb you."

"Really?" Thomas had never done that exercise in front of anyone before. "How did I look?"

"Beautiful." Eileen blurted. At once she blushed even more and looked away. "I mean, peaceful."

Thomas realized that he was blushing himself, and that it was spreading to his bare chest. He quickly pulled on his shirt. "Aye. It's a relaxation exercise. Helps you clear your mind."

Eileen managed to look at him. "Can you teach me?"

Thomas hesitated. "Can I do it later?"

"All right." Eileen watched him as he put his shirt on. "What happened with your father?"

The bishop is using magic to control him, and now he's disowned me, Thomas thought.

He really needed to speak the words out loud, but who would believe him? Eileen might humour him, but she'd never really believe him. George would call him insane. Their parents would call in the nuns. He wished suddenly for his friends back at the Academy. They wouldn't believe a word, either, but they'd listen and offer answers anyway. All he'd have to say was, 'Just suppose...' and they'd be off on a wild night of speculation and logic games. Here, though, that wasn't going to happen. He needed *proof.*

An idea came into Thomas's mind. It wasn't a particularly good idea, he realized, but it was all he had. "Could you get George and bring him out here?"

"Sure," Eileen stood up and went to the door of the smithy. "Will you tell us what happened?"

"As much as I can, aye."

"All right." She headed for the house. Thomas picked up the hot stew bowl and set it on the anvil. He started to pull up the stool, realized his backside was still wet, and decided to eat standing with his back to the forge. He had enough to worry about without George making fun of him.

The stew was delicious, and Thomas had it polished off before Eileen managed to drag George away from the table and back out to the forge. Thomas had also put the flesh to the bones of his idea. It still wasn't a very good idea, but at least it was something.

George took Thomas's stool and sat on it. "So, what happened?"

Thomas leaned back against the anvil and took a moment to gather his thoughts. "I think I know what's going on with my father."

George's eyebrows went up in a perfect likeness of Lionel. "Well, tell us."

"I can't," said Thomas. "Not yet. I need your help first."

"Our help?" Eileen pulled up a second stool and sat beside her brother. "To do what?"

Thomas took a deep breath before saying, "To search Timothy's wagon."

"What?" Eileen's mouth dropped open and stayed there. "What for?"

"Proof that I'm not insane."

Eileen's mouth dropped open even wider, and stayed there. George's eyes widened, then narrowed as his eyebrows squeezed together in a frown. The siblings exchanged a quick look, then turned back to Thomas. A very long, very uncomfortable silence filled the smithy.

"Please," said Thomas, when it became clear neither of them was going to say anything. "I know how it sounds—"

"No, you don't," said George, shaking his head. "This is a really bad idea."

"I know," Thomas said. "But it's the best I can come up with." He turned to Eileen. "Please. I'll do it by myself if I have to, but I would really rather have help."

There was another long, uncomfortable silence. Thomas looked from one to the other, but could not read anything from their expressions.

"If we do this," Eileen said at last, "you tell us everything. No matter what."

Relief swept through Thomas. "I promise." His turned to her brother. "George?"

George's frown was still there, and stayed on his face while George thought it through. Finally, George sighed. "All right, but you get to explain to Bluster when we get caught."

Thomas was amazed at how relieved he felt. "We won't get caught."

"You hope."

"What do we do?" asked Eileen.

"We'll need a candle to search his wagon," Thomas said. "And we'll need to tell your parents we're going down to hear the fiddler, and that we might be late coming back."

A smile ghosted across Eileen's face. "Not going to leave them wondering?"

"Oh, no," said Thomas. "There's enough people angry with me already."

Chapter 9

The bench outside the tavern was hard and worn smooth from years of use and provided a perfect view of the watchtower. Thomas and his friends had spent the better part of an hour sitting there, waiting. The sun had gone down, and the last of its light had left the sky. The grey cylinder of the watchtower had faded to a vague black shape against the darkness of the night sky. Only the orange and yellow fire-light spilling out the inn door lit the night for them. Inside, the fiddler was playing a fast-paced reel that was nearly drowned out by clomping feet as the villagers whirled and danced. Thomas paid it scant attention. The bench provided a perfect view of the watchtower, and Thomas wasn't taking his eyes off it.

"What if he comes for a pint before he goes home?" asked Eileen.

"Then we say hello, and wait for him to go inside."

Thomas wished he could have brought his rapier. He knew that the bishop and his men were gone, but there was nothing to say they wouldn't come back and Thomas had no desire to face them unarmed. He did have his dagger, hidden under his coat, but had left the rapier behind. Being the only one wearing a sword was the surest way to attract attention, and Thomas had no desire for more of that. Bad enough that everyone who passed stared at his bruises.

"Isn't there any other way?" asked Eileen.

"No."

"Well, maybe if you told us why, we could think of something."

"If I told you why, you'd think I was insane."

"We're thinking that now," said George, stepping from the inn with three mugs of beer in his hands. He handed one to Thomas and smiled. "And more so as the night wears on."

Thomas snorted. "Wonderful."

"Don't worry." George handed the other mug to his sister and took a seat on the bench. "We won't do anything until you start chasing the moon."

"That might be later tonight, if I'm wrong about this," Thomas warned.

"There," Eileen said. "He's coming out."

Thomas could see Bluster, a lantern in his hand, coming out of the watchtower. The man stopped at the door and locked it behind him, then made his way down the stairs and down the rise towards the houses. Thomas watched him go until the light disappeared among the houses of the village, and put his mug on the bench. Eileen did the same. George quaffed his, first.

Thomas took a quick look to be sure no one inside the tavern was paying attention to them, then pushed himself to his feet, groaning with the effort.

"Sure you can walk?" muttered George.

"I'll be fine," said Thomas, stumbling the first few steps until his legs began working properly again.

The noise of the tavern faded quickly behind them, and by the time they got to the watchtower the night hum of the insects and the wind gently rustling through the trees sounded louder to their ears than the fiddler's music. They walked around to the wagon and the stone bulk of the watchtower muffled the last sounds of the fiddler and hid the lights of the village from their sight. The night suddenly felt far darker and far quieter than it should have.

The designs on the wagon's sides were nearly invisible in the darkness. The dark wood door at the end looked almost ominous to Thomas, as if it was about to spring open of its own accord.

Thomas took a deep breath and willed down the butterflies dancing in his belly. He took the time to examine the wood around the hill to make sure no one was lurking around, then reached forward and pushed gently at the door of the wagon. It was unlocked.

"Wait," Eileen whispered, grabbing his arm. "What if his body's in there?"

That thought sent Thomas's stomach plummeting and brought a whole new crop of butterflies flying about. He swallowed, took another deep breath. "Bluster said the nuns were taking him," Thomas whispered back. "They'll have done that by now."

He pushed the door again. It swung open, revealing a small, dark space, empty of corpses. Thomas sighed with relief. "Light the candle."

Eileen had the candle, and it took her a few tries for her flint to spark the tinder. The wait seemed interminable. The tinder blazed, small and yellow, and Eileen used it to light the candle. She raised it and shuddered.

The dim yellow light shone onto the floor of the wagon by the door. A dark stain that had once been red covered it where Timothy's body had lain. The stain looked black in the light of the candle, and didn't shine the way it would have when it was still wet. Thomas reached out a hand, hesitated, then touched the edge of the stain. His fingers came away dry. The wood was old and starved for moisture and had sucked Timothy's blood into itself.

Thomas held out his hand for the candle and Eileen passed it to him, the flame shielded by her hand. It took another moment and another deep breath before Thomas had gathered the nerve to step up and pull himself into the wagon. He took a step in, then turned to shut the door, but Eileen pulled herself in before he could.

"There isn't room for both of us in here," protested Thomas.

"Twice as many makes twice as fast," said Eileen. She turned to her brother. "Keep watch, George. Let us know if anyone is coming."

She pushed the door closed before Thomas could argue further. "Well?"

The inside of the wagon was very narrow, and the two were standing almost body-to-body in the space by the door. Thomas, suddenly very aware of their proximity, stepped back and promptly kicked something with his heel. The noise made them both jump and clutch at each other.

"What is going on in there?" George hissed from outside. "What was that?"

Thomas caught his breath. "It's all right," he whispered back. "It's just a mess in here from being knocked over."

"Well, don't do it again. You scared me half to death."

"Me, too," Eileen whispered. She looked around the small wagon. "What are we looking for?"

"I don't know," Thomas turned and made an inspection on the wagon's interior. It was certainly a mess. Many things—mostly vegetables and dried fruit, which were once hanging from the ceiling—were now on the floor, as were the contents of several shelf baskets. Despite the clutter, Thomas was certain that whoever had killed the little man had not searched the place. The door to the thin cupboard in the corner was still latched shut, and the chest that sat underneath the narrow shelf the little man had used as a bed was unopened.

"You take the cupboard," Thomas said, "I'll look through the chest."

"What are we looking for?"

"Anything unusual."

"That helps," Eileen muttered. Still, she went to the cupboard and, after some quick wrestling with the door, pulled it open and began searching.

Thomas pulled the chest out from underneath the bed and opened it. He saw only clothes. One by one he pulled them all out, searching between them and stacking them on Timothy's bed until the chest was empty. He searched the chest, itself, looking for any sign of hidden compartments. There was nothing. Thomas put all the clothes back, and pushed the chest back under the bed.

"Nothing here," Eileen whispered, closing the closet. "Now what?"

"Keep looking."

They searched every alcove, nook, and cranny of the little wagon twice. They found balls, clubs, the smashed remains of the man's lute, and a half-dozen knives he used for juggling. None of it was what Thomas was after. He rapped on the walls and floorboards of the narrow space, looking for hidden compartments, but found nothing. For a moment Thomas seriously considered banging his head on the floor to see if that would help. At last, concealing the candle in his hand, he opened the wagon door.

"Well?" hissed George, his nervousness clear in his voice. "Did you find what you were looking for?"

"No." Thomas swung down, and turned to offer a hand to Eileen, but she had already jumped down.

"So what were we looking for?" Eileen asked.

Thomas didn't answer. He had been desperately hoping for something to show them—something to show himself—for proof. Instead of answering, he turned away from them and reached inside the wagon to pull the door shut.

Something inside glinted in the light of the candle.

Thomas stopped, but the glint had already vanished. He pushed the door back open and ducked his head, moving the candle back and forth until something inside caught the light and reflected it back. It was under the juggler's bed, whatever it was, near the front of the wagon. Thomas realized that when he put the chest back, he'd shoved it under the end of the bed nearest the door, instead of where it had been. Otherwise, there was no way he'd be able to see whatever was reflecting the candle's dim, wavering light.

"Thomas," Eileen grabbed his sleeve. "What were we looking for?"

Thomas shook her off and pointed. "Look there."

Eileen let him go, followed the line of his arm with her eyes. "What is it?"

"Don't know." he said. "Do you see it?"

Eileen leaned further forward. "Aye, I do." She squinted. "Why didn't we see it before?"

"The chest was in the way."

"And because there's no way to look at it without being this close to the floor," George said, looking over his sister's shoulder. "What do you think it is?"

"I'll tell you in a moment," Thomas said. He handed George the candle, then crawled back into the wagon, keeping himself close to the ground. The movement made all his ribs hurt, but he wasn't about to give up. He kept his eyes on the light reflecting off the metal. George was right. If he moved his chin more than a foot off the floor-boards, the glint would vanish.

"Well?" hissed Eileen.

"There's something here."

"We know that. What is it?"

Thomas reached forward cautiously. His fingers touched a thin metal key-hole. He ran his hand around it, found the edges of a small compartment. The space was as wide as his forearm was long and perhaps six inches high, with the key-hole at the bottom.

He thought a moment, then pulled his dagger and slipped it into the space between the edge of the compartment and the floor. Praying the steel would hold, Thomas pried against the little lock. At first there was only pressure then something moved. Thomas pried harder. There was a tearing of wood and the little door popped open with a noise that made Thomas jump and, to his ears, felt loud enough to wake the entire village and the residents of the cemetery beyond. He waited for George and Eileen to shush him, but they said nothing, and gradually Thomas realized that the sound hadn't gone beyond the confines of the wagon.

Thomas waited until his breathing returned to normal, then flipped the little door up and reached into the opening. He found a small cloth sack which jingled when he pulled it out, then a wooden box, and finally a single book, almost as wide as the space itself and rather thick. He took them all, pushed what was left of the little door back into position, then started crawling backwards out of the wagon. It hurt worse than crawling in. He stopped on his way and pushed Timothy's chest back where he'd found it to hide the evidence of the burglary.

"What did you find?" George asked.

"Not here." said Thomas, groaning as he straightened. He put the three items under his jacket. "Douse the candle and let's get back to your house. And not by the way we came, either."

*   *   *

George took them on a long, round-about path that circled the village before leading them back to the forge. Once inside, they closed the doors tight, leaving them in near-darkness, save for the dull red glow from the banked coals. George lit the candle from the coals then put it on the anvil. Eileen pulled three stools out from under a table. Thomas sank down onto his with relief. He was not nearly healthy enough for what they had done, and his body was telling him so.

"So what is it?" Eileen demanded. "What did you find?"

Thomas placed his prizes on the anvil. They were not much to look at, even in the dim light of the coals and candle. The sack was coarse brown fabric, tied shut with a bit of old ribbon. The box was painted red, and held closed only by a small latch. The book was plain and leather-bound and wrapped shut with twine.

No one said anything or moved. Thomas was acutely aware that the man—the friend—who had valued these things enough to hide them away had been murdered. From the looks on their faces, George and Eileen felt the same way.

George moved first, picking up the little bag and jingling it. He opened the ribbon and poured a half-dozen coins into his hand. George stared at them a moment, shifting them back and forth across his palm, then put them back into the bag. "Bad luck to rob the dead," he said, his voice quiet.

"We'll put them back," said Thomas. "I promise."

George nodded. He put the little sack back on the anvil. "Not much for a lifetime, is it?"

"No," agreed Thomas. "It isn't." He picked up the box and opened the latch. Inside were a dozen pieces of paper, folded and wrapped in a ribbon. He pulled the first out of the bundle, and scanned it.

"Songs," Thomas said. He passed the first to George, then unwrapped the others. "They're all songs."

George read through the one Thomas gave him, his lips moving slowly, then handed it back. "It's that sad one he sang to us."

"What about the book?" asked Thomas, putting the songs back in the box.

Eileen paged through it. "It's his journal, I think. It's all hand written... There's mentions of towns he's visited... some notes on people he's worked for... some recipes..." she took a closer look, "...for cooking rabbit." She flipped the pages until she reached the back of the book. "There's a ledger in the back. Like what your father uses to collect his accounts."

Thomas took the book. It was exactly what Eileen had said; a common journal, listing engagements and accounts and recipes for rabbit. Thomas closed it and set it down. Depression, heavy as the anvil, weighed him down. He had hoped for proof; something that would make his story at least plausible. Instead, he had nothing and his friends were staring at him.

"Thomas," Eileen said at last, "why did we need to see these?"

Just suppose... "You won't believe me."

"Try us," said George.

"You said you'd tell us if we went with you," said Eileen. "You promised."

Thomas sighed. "I did, I know."

"So what is this about?" demanded George. He tapped a finger amidst Timothy's possessions on the anvil. "Why did we steal these, Thomas? What were we looking for out there?"

Thomas sighed, knowing what their reaction was going to be. "Magic."

"What?!" the two chorused, voices loud and eyes wide with surprise.

"You can't be serious!" said George.

"I am." Thomas took a deep breath. "Bishop Malloy has magic. He's using it to control people and he's using it to steal magic from others. He took the magic from my father and twisted him, and he killed Timothy to get his magic."

"Thomas!" Eileen's tone was equal parts exasperation and disbelief. "In the first place, there's no such thing, and in the second, the bishop is a priest of the High Father. He wouldn't kill Timothy, and he certainly wouldn't use witchcraft."

"Magic," corrected Thomas. "And he did. I felt it."

"What do you mean, you felt it?" demanded George. "When did you feel it?"

"Every time he tried to control someone," said Thomas. "I could feel the power in his voice like it was a living thing. He did it to Lionel after Eileen and

I jumped the Fire."

"I was there," argued George, "I didn't feel anything."

"That's because you can't feel magic," said Thomas.

"And you can?"

"Aye," said Thomas, "and that's *my* magic."

"Oh, by the Four!" George stomped to his feet. "You don't have any magic!"

"I do!" protested Thomas. "That's why the bishop is after me! That's why he's twisted my father so badly and why he had me beaten senseless!"

"You said your father had you beaten senseless," Eileen protested.

"I said I had a disagreement with him," said Thomas. "I was beaten up by three men—the bishop's men. They hit me until I couldn't stand, then they dragged me inside my house to the bishop. He put his hand on me and it felt…" Thomas looked for some words that would make it sound reasonable. There were none. All he had was the feeling from that night. "It felt like he was pulling out part of my soul."

There was a long, long silence after that. George and Eileen were both looking at him with expressions reserved for those less than sane.

"How hard did they hit you?" Eileen asked at last.

"I'm serious!"

"You're cracked!" said George. "No one can pull out your soul."

"Not my whole soul. Just part of it."

"Well, no one can do that either!"

"He did!" The memory made Thomas almost sick. "He put his hand against my chest and I could feel my soul ripping apart." He shuddered, practically feeling the bishop's hand on his chest again. "He was trying to take my magic."

"You don't even *believe* in magic," said George. "You said so to Timothy three days ago."

"I said I don't believe in witchcraft—"

"And now you do?"

"No! It's not witchcraft, it's magic."

"It's the same thing!"

"No, it's not!" Thomas could practically hear Timothy again, saying that no one knew the difference. "Listen closely. One hundred and twenty years ago, in the Council of Carlyle, the Church of the High Father decided on a very specific definition of witchcraft. When a man or woman makes a compact with the Banished to gain unnatural powers, that is witchcraft. Do you understand?"

George and Eileen looked wary, but both said, "Aye."

"So, can you imagine my father making a compact with the Banished?" demanded Thomas. "Or Timothy? Or me?"

"I can't see your father doing witchcraft at all," said George. "He's too ordinary." He looked troubled. "I didn't know the juggler that well, though, and you've been gone for four years." He stopped himself. "This is stupid."

"It isn't!" said Thomas. "Remember when we were thirteen, and your father and mine got into a huge row? Two of my father's wagons broke wheels just when he needed them. Lionel said he wouldn't repair them even if the High Father himself came down and asked him. Then my father visits him and apologizes and the next day, Lionel's fixed them both. Remember that?"

"Aye," said George, sounding uncertain.

"And does that sound like your da?"

"Well…" George thought about it. "No. He would have made him wait a week, normally."

"So why didn't he?" asked Thomas. "Why did he help him?"

"I don't know," said George. "Changed his mind, I suppose."

"And how often would your father change his mind on something like that?"

"Not often," said Eileen. "But that doesn't mean anything."

"How often," persisted Thomas. "How many times?"

Eileen thought about it. "Maybe half a dozen that I can remember."

"Aye," said George. "Me, too."

"And every time he changed his mind, it was for my father, wasn't it?"

Eileen and George both had to think about that one, and neither looked too happy when they nodded. "Aye," said George. "It was."

"I knew it," said Thomas. "And how many other people did the same thing? How many changed their minds or did something for him and don't even know why they did it?"

Neither sibling spoke for a while and when Eileen finally did she was looking very troubled. "Your father bought a section of the nunnery's lands for his warehouses. Sister Brigit said that the Mother never sold off anything as long as she could remember."

"But she sold it to him," said Thomas.

"Aye," said Eileen. "He visited her once a week for six weeks. When she gave in, it was the talk of the nunnery for a month. She never changes her mind on things like that."

"He kept me out of the gaol," said George, his voice quiet. "When I was sixteen. I'd gotten in a fight with a couple of the butcher's apprentices."

"I remember that," said Eileen. "You were drunk and you tore up the tavern."

"Bluster was going to keep me chained to the tower wall for a month," said George. "Said it was the only way to teach me a lesson. Da tried to talk him out of it, but he wouldn't listen. The next day your father showed up and talked to him for an hour. At the end of it, Bluster let me go."

"You were so lucky," said Eileen. "Bluster doesn't let anyone…" she didn't finish the sentence, and looked even more troubled.

George shook his head. "All this proves is that your father has a gift for gab," he said, crossing his big arms and looking stubborn. "Nothing else."

"Aye," Thomas seized on the phrase. "A gift for gab. The gift to make others listen to him more often than not."

"And you think it's magic?" asked Eileen.

"I do," said Thomas. "I'm sure of it."

"But you can't prove it," said Eileen. "You can't prove any of it."

"No," said Thomas. "I can't prove any of it."

George raised his chin high and set his face into a stubborn expression. "I won't believe your father's a witch."

"He's not," said Thomas. "Remember what witchcraft is."

"I don't care what witchcraft is," said George. "I can't believe your father would do that."

"I don't think he knew," said Thomas. "He probably had no idea what he was doing."

Eileen shook her head. "How could he not?"

Thomas threw up his hands. "I don't know! How could I not connect the way his voice changed with the way people did things for him? It was the way things were. Maybe because no one else saw it, he couldn't see it himself."

Neither of his friends said anything, though the confusion in their thoughts was so apparent it was practically audible. The light from the coals was almost gone, now, and the wavering flame of the candle cast George and Eileen's faces into deep shadow. Thomas could see them struggling to come to terms with what he had said. Given that they had not experienced any of it, Thomas didn't blame them for their doubts.

Thomas let them alone with their thoughts and picked up Timothy's journal once more. He opened it to the back where the ledger was, and ran his hand down the columns of numbers.

Ailbe.

Thomas bent over the page. Beside her name was only a series of numbers, all but one of which was crossed out. Debts paid and still owed, Thomas guessed. Ailbe's name and six others had been put into a column under the heading *Lakewood*. Thomas knew the place. It was some thirty miles away by the road, or ten by the forest. He and George had hiked there when they were fourteen, just to see what the place looked like. As Thomas recalled, the name said it all: woods on a lake.

Lakewood was on the way to Berrytown.

A chill colder than the water from the pond ran down his spine. He jumped to his feet, wincing at the pain the movement caused and making both his friends start. "I've got to go."

"What?" George jumped to his own feet. "Why?"

Eileen looked at the ledger in Thomas's hand. "What did you find?"

"A name." Thomas said. "Ailbe."

"Who's Ailbe?" asked George.

"Timothy said her name," Thomas picked up the bag and the box. "Under the wagon, when he was dying. He said the bishop would take something, then said her name." He headed for the door. "We've got to get this stuff back in Timothy's wagon. Then I've got to go to Lakewood and warn her."

"Warn her about what?" asked Eileen. "You don't even know if the bishop is after her."

"I don't know that he isn't, either."

"Tomorrow," George said, stepping in front of him. "You can't go tonight."

"I have to," Thomas stepped around George and wrestled with the door. The effort of pulling it open made him stumble. He cursed himself, desperately wishing he was in better condition. "If he is after her, he might kill her like he did Timothy."

"No, Thomas," Eileen shook her head. "You can barely walk. You won't make it to Lakewood tonight."

"I can walk just fine," Thomas snapped, knowing it was a lie even as the words left his lips.

"It's been a day since the bishop left," George said. "On horseback. If he was headed to Lakewood, he's already there."

George was right, and Thomas knew it. The last of his energy left him with the realization, and suddenly he wanted nothing more than to curl up in a corner. He fought the urge. "I still have to try."

"In the morning," said George, putting a big hand on his friend's shoulder. "We'll get these things put back, then get some sleep. That way, we'll have a good start in the morning."

"Aye." Thomas turned to the door then stopped and turned back. "You aren't coming with me."

"Aye, I am," said George. "I'll have Mum pack us some food, and we'll leave word with the Reeve so he doesn't come looking for us."

"You shouldn't—" began Thomas, but Eileen stopped him.

"We're your friends," she said. "We're coming."

Thomas looked from one to the other. "Does this mean you believe me?"

"Not a word," said George, taking Timothy's things from Thomas, then holding the door for his sister.

"But don't worry," said Eileen as she walked past them and into the darkness, "we'll look out for you anyway."

Chapter 10

Despite what George and Eileen had said, Thomas was determined to go to Lakewood by himself. He wasn't sure what he would find there and he had no intention of putting his friends in danger. He didn't say anything more about it, though. He just followed them to the wagon to return Timothy's possessions, then back to the house. He crawled into the bed, and made plans while George fell asleep. He had originally thought to set out that night, but George had been right; he was too tired. Instead he decided to wake up at sunrise and be packed and gone before anyone else was awake. He closed his eyes, telling himself over and over to wake before the dawn.

The sun was streaming in through the window when George shook him awake.

"Get up, you slug," said George. "We're ready to go."

Oh, I'm an idiot. Thomas blinked in the glare of the morning sun and cursed himself thoroughly. "Why didn't you wake me sooner?"

"You needed the sleep," said George. "Besides, we were having a talk with our parents. About the trip."

Thomas rolled himself up to a sitting position and rubbed at his face. Visions of Lionel and Magda's reaction passed before his eyes. The images made him wince. "I'm surprised I slept through it."

"So am I," said George, grinning.

Thomas reached for his breeches. "How are they with the idea?"

"Not happy." George tossed him his breeches. "Father wants to talk to you."

"Wonderful." Thomas stood and pulled the breeches up, then reached for his shirt. "How much did you actually tell them?"

"About magic and that?" George snorted. "Not a thing. And neither should you, if you want to go anywhere. See you outside."

Thomas finished dressing, packed his clothes into his bag, and took it and himself down the stairs. There was a steaming bowl of porridge on the table, with a hot mug of tea beside it. Lionel was sitting on the other side of the table, watching Thomas as he came down the ladder. The man looked older than he had two days before, Thomas was sure. The lines around his eyes and mouth were more pronounced, and his lips and brows were pressed downward in a frown.

Thomas spotted two small bags sitting by the door and put his own bag down with them. He looked at the porridge, then at Lionel.

"Oh, sit down," said Lionel, his tone coloured more with amusement than irritation. "I'm not going to bite you, and your breakfast is getting cold."

Thomas did as he was told. The porridge smelled wonderful and his appetite should have been better, but Lionel's gaze was making his stomach roll. Even so, he picked up the spoon and dug in.

"George says you're taking a little trip."

Thomas, caught with a mouthful of porridge, swallowed it down before saying, "Aye. To Lakewood for a few days."

"To see a woman."

"Ailbe," said Thomas. "Timothy said her name when he was dying. I thought she might be kin."

"I see." Lionel looked at the bags by the door, and his frown deepened. "Are you coming back?"

That startled Thomas. "Why wouldn't I?"

Lionel didn't say anything. Thomas could see him putting his thoughts in order and waited. At last, Lionel said, "Lad, I've known your father for a long time. He always drove a hard bargain, and the High Father knows we disagreed on most things, but I thought he was a good man. What he did to you, though..." Lionel shook his head, leaving the sentence unfinished. Instead, he said, "After you three went out, Magda and I talked about what happened and what your father is doing with this threat of the magistrate and all and, well... we decided that, should you want to leave town for good, well, we won't be telling the Reeve where you're going. All right?"

Thomas nodded, feeling a lump in his throat. "I appreciate it."

"Aye. Well then," the smith reached into his shirt and pulled out a small pouch, "these are for you. They're not gold, but they'll get you a few meals on the way back to the city."

Thomas nearly refused, then changed his mind and took the purse. He wasn't staying away, he knew, but he had no idea how long he was going to be gone. "Thank you." He put the purse in his bag. "I didn't ask George and Eileen to come."

"I know. They said you were ready to head out by yourself, last night."

"Maybe it would be better if I went alone."

"After all the work they did to convince their mother and me?" Lionel chuckled. "No, lad, they'll go with you as far as Lakewood."

"But..." *I don't want them getting hurt.* "What about the bandits?" Thomas asked. "The ones that killed Timothy?"

"Magda brought them up," said Lionel. "George managed to convince her that they were city folks, and that the three of you would be fine, as long as you took the path instead of the road."

"And did he convince you, as well?"

"Aye, he did." Lionel stood up and headed for the door. "Don't worry, lad. George and Eileen will be with you to Lakewood."

Thomas nodded. "I'll take care of them."

"And they'll take care of you," Lionel picked up George and Eileen's bags, "for as long as you're with them. Now hurry up with your breakfast. The lass was about ready to burst, last time I looked."

Eileen did look ready to burst when Thomas stepped out the door. George was managing to look slightly less impatient, but the tapping of his foot against the ground was a giveaway. Both had walking sticks in their hands—George had two—and both hurried forward to get their bags from their father. Magda, who had been standing with them, had another bag in her hand and the same look of foreboding she'd worn the time Thomas and George had announced they were going to make a raft.

"Are you ready?" Eileen asked, taking her bag from Lionel.

"I am," said Thomas, "but you two don't have to come with me."

"We know," said George, taking his own bag. "We're coming anyway."

"I still don't like it," Magda raised a warning finger at all of them. "The last thing I need is to be worrying about the three of you."

"It's only Lakewood, Mother," George protested. "Thomas and I went there by ourselves when we were fourteen, remember?"

"Aye, and I didn't like it then, either." She gave a long glare at the three of them, then handed George the bag. "Here's lunch for you."

"Thanks, Mum," said George, looking inside.

"Leave it until lunch," his mother warned, her tone making George close the bag quickly. She turned to Thomas. "And you. Did Lionel talk to you?"

"Aye, he did." said Thomas. "Thank you. For everything."

A worried frown took over Magda's face. "Are you sure this is the right thing to be doing, Thomas?"

Thomas nodded. "Aye, I am."

She nodded, then pulled him into a tight hug, holding him hard for a time, before stepping away. "Good luck to you, then."

She turned away, rubbing at one of her eyes, then hugged her own children. Lionel shook Thomas's hand and clapped him on the shoulder, then said goodbye to all three. Taking Magda's hand in his own, he led her back into the house.

"What was that about?" said Eileen as she put her bag on her shoulder.

"They don't think I'm coming back," Thomas said. "They think I'm using this trip to run away."

George looked startled. "I hadn't thought of that." He handed Thomas a walking stick. "Are you?"

Thomas took the stick. "You think I'd give my father the satisfaction?"

George snorted. "No, I don't think you would." He shouldered his bag, adjusted it. "Come on, then."

George led them away from the house and up the road. Thomas kept pace, surprised at how easily he was moving. The night's sleep had made a world of difference. Walking still hurt, but it was only a mild, distant ache. His ribs were better, too, as long as he didn't reach too far in any direction. His face was still very tender, as he discovered when he slapped at an insect on his cheek. George and Eileen rightfully laughed at him for that, and Thomas did his best not to touch his face again.

George stepped off the road and led them up a nearly-overgrown path into the woods. He stopped a dozen yards into the woods. "Right, then." He reached into his bag, rummaged a moment, then came up with two long daggers in sheaths.

"Where did you get those?" asked Thomas, stepping closer to have a look.

George grinned. "Da and I make a batch of knives and daggers every year, to sell at the summer markets." He handed one of the blades to Thomas, the other to Eileen. "Made these ones myself. Father thought they were too big, but I like them."

Thomas drew the dagger. It was as long as Thomas's own, with a thick blade that thinned to a gleaming, keen edge and a needle-like point. He held it up and squinted down the length of the blade. There were no signs of dents or imperfections. "This is very good."

George looked pleased. "Aye?"

"As far as I can tell, aye."

"Thank you." George took back the knife, sheathed it, and started tying it to his belt. "You've got your sword and dagger," he said. "I was thinking it wouldn't be a bad idea for both of us to be carrying something, too."

"Are you starting to believe me, then?"

"Nay, I still think you're cracked," George said. "But it can't hurt to be careful. Now come on, we've a long way to go."

They started up the trail, pushing aside branches and stepping over the roots and shrubs that dotted the path. Thomas took the time to tell them everything that had happened to him since he'd come home. George and Eileen still looked doubtful when he'd finished, but neither called him insane to his face, which Thomas supposed was something of an improvement.

The path to Lakewood was little-used and very overgrown. While the road took a long, mainly flat path around the steep hills that separated the two towns, the footpath ran up and down the hills in a nearly straight line to Lakewood. An hour into the trek, all three were making good use of their walking sticks on the slopes. Thomas was surprised that he hadn't remembered how rough the path was from the last trip he and George took to Lakewood. Further proof, he decided, that memory was selective rather than accurate.

It wasn't an unpleasant walk. They kept a steady pace, and Elmvale fell quickly behind. The day was warm but there were streams to drink from and the leaves were in full foliage. Elms and maples and oaks all shaded them from the worst of the heat and dappled the ground with spots of sunlight that peeked between their leaves. Eileen peppered Thomas with questions as morning wore on. What was the city like? How big was the Academy? What classes had he taken? How many sweethearts did he have? Thomas answered as best he could, but his mind was elsewhere. He was fretting about what he'd left behind as much as about what they would find ahead of them. His replies to her questions became shorter and shorter, and after the third or fourth monosyllabic answer, Eileen gave up.

Just as the sun reached the top of its arc, the path opened into a pleasant glade topping a high hill.

"Half-way," said George, opening up the bag his mother had packed. "Lunch."

They snacked on dried sausage and cheese and biscuits, then went on their way again. Clouds rolled in as the afternoon wore on, covering the sun and making the day a little cooler. They hiked on through the woods, breaking free of them as the sun began setting and stepping onto the road just outside of Lakewood. It was a fair sized town, sitting on the edge of a very large lake that reflected the red and gold of the sunset. There were many small houses spread along the shore and several larger buildings further inland—homes for the Mayor and the district sheriff, Thomas guessed. A large inn stood between the lake and the road. Behind it, twenty or so fishing boats were pulled up onto the shore for the night.

"We should find Ailbe," said Thomas, looking at the houses and wondering how.

George shook his head. "We should find some food, first. I don't know about you, but that lunch stopped filling my belly hours ago."

Thomas could feel his own belly rumbling, but wasn't ready to give in. "She might be in danger."

"How are we going to find her?" asked Eileen. "All we have is a name. We don't know where she lives. We don't even know what she looks like."

"We can ask."

"Aye, we can," said George, moving past Thomas. "And the best one to ask is the innkeeper. Now come on."

The inn was two stories high and large, its shutters and door brightly painted and open wide to catch the evening breeze. The smell of freshly cooked fish wafted out from the kitchens and into the evening air, making Thomas's stomach rumble all the more. The inn was crowded with locals, enjoying the end of the day. All heads turned the moment the three stepped inside. Travelers were not so common that the sight of three new faces would fail to draw attention from everyone in the room. Especially if one of the three was a pretty girl and another had a sword and two black eyes. Thomas, used to the city where strangers would draw no more than a cursory glance, stopped in the doorway. George however, pushed right through, giving polite greetings to those he passed as he headed for the bar. Eileen stayed right behind him. Thomas followed a moment later, nodding to those that were staring nervously at his sword.

"Three of your house best, please," George said to the man behind the bar. "We came from Elmvale this morning and it's a long, dry walk."

"This morning?" the bartender raised an eyebrow. "That's thirty miles by the road."

"Aye, but only ten by the trail, and that's how we came."

The bartender poured three drinks from a large cask, then handed them across. George dropped some coins on the bar, took one mug for his own, and gestured for the others to do the same.

"Thank you," Eileen said picking up her own drink. "I don't suppose there's any of that wonderful fish we smell left, is there?"

"Indeed there is." The bartender beamed at them. "One each, would you like?"

"Two for me," George called. "And some bread and cheese if you have it."

"We do," said the bartender. "Anything more?"

"Not for now," George took a drink, then wiped his mouth and sighed. "Very good. Thank you, kindly."

He led Thomas and Eileen to an open table and, putting his bag under one of the chairs, sat down. Eileen did the same. Thomas took off his sword and hung it on the back of his own chair, as much a sign to those watching that he wasn't after trouble as for his own comfort, and took his own seat.

"So," said Thomas. "Now what?"

"Now," said George, "we get our meal, and then ask for directions."

Thomas chafed at the delay, but knew it was inevitable. He took a swig of the beer and found it to be very good. He also found it woke his appetite to full strength, and when the bread and cheese arrived he dug in with a will.

"So you came over the hills did you?" asked a man at the next table. Thomas, whose four years in the city had taught him not to bother others in a tavern, was quite surprised. The other two were completely unperturbed. The man seemed to be twice as old as any of the others in the tavern, and was missing a fair number of his teeth. "Quite the walk for a young lady."

"Quite a walk for anyone," said Eileen. "Why, both my brother and his friend here were nearly ready to drop with exhaustion by the time they got to town."

"Not that you were much better," chided George.

"And what is it that brings you here?" asked a portly woman from the table on the other side. "Surely not just to taste the fish?"

"Now there's nothing wrong with the fish," protested the bartender. "Why, it was fresh caught this morning."

"And every other morning," agreed the woman. "How about tomorrow you catch some deer instead?"

A general chuckle rolled through the room, Thomas took advantage of the moment to say, "Actually, we're looking for someone."

"Are you now?" said the old man, his interest clearly piqued. Folks around the room leaned closer, ears cocked to listen.

"Aye," Thomas looked around the room in case she was there. "A woman named Ailbe."

"The Healer?" said the barman. He looked ready to say more, but was interrupted.

"And what is it you'll be wanting her for?" asked a man who was slouching in the corner. He was a lean, raw-boned fellow, with a battered face and the green and brown clothes of a woodsman.

"It's a private matter," said Thomas.

Eyebrows raised around the room and a few snickers came from various corners. Thomas looked over the room, certain that they had suddenly become the butt of a joke. Several folks were whispering behind their hands to one another, and others were taking long, appraising looks at the three friends. Thomas turned back to Eileen and George, his eyebrows raised. Both shrugged, equally mystified.

"Many folks see her on private matters," said the woodsman. "But she doesn't see anyone at night. You'll have to wait until morning."

"It really can't wait," said Thomas. "It's important."

"To you, I'm sure," the woodsman glanced over Eileen and George, "but not to her."

"To her, actually," said Thomas, starting to be irritated. "I've news for her."

"News?" the old man at the next table perked up. "What news?"

A ripple of words went through the room, and Thomas felt the crowd's attitude change back to what it had been before. *Odd*, Thomas thought. "News I'd feel more comfortable relaying to her first," said Thomas. "If someone can tell me where she is."

"Bad news," declared the old man, nodding his head. "Got to be bad news, with an answer like that."

"Is it?" asked the woodsman.

"Aye," said Thomas, and his tone made the woodsman sit up straighter. "It's important I talk to her tonight. Can you tell me where she lives?"

"I can take you," said the woodsman. "As soon as you're done your food."

Whispers went around the tavern again, but no amusement accompanied them. A woman came with three plates of fish—one with a double portion—and the three friends dug in. The fish was very good, and George, despite the double portion, had his plate cleared before Thomas was half-way through.

George sat back from the table, took a pull of his beer and turned to the other patrons, "Say, has the bishop come through, yet?"

"The bishop?" repeated the bartender. "Why would he be coming here?"

"I don't know the why," said George, "but he left Elmvale two days ago, heading in this direction."

"The bishop," the barman repeated. "Imagine that."

The crowd buzzed over that for a while, wondering at the bishop coming to their town and reminiscing over the last time a bishop visited. Several folks asked questions about the bishop's intentions, but George could only honestly reply that he had no idea. Thomas, feeling very grateful to his friend for bringing the subject up, dug into his fish. If the bishop had not yet come, there was still a chance.

A chance for what? came the unbidden thought. *You don't even know if the bishop's after her.*

As soon as they had finished eating, Thomas was on his feet, putting his sword back on. He left some coins on the table then turned to the woodsman. "Can we go?"

"Aye, we'll go." The woodsman put down his beer, and stood. "Come on, then."

The four trouped out of the inn and into the town. The sun was gone, and a layer of clouds was hiding any light from moon or stars. The woodsman moved unerringly, as if the darkness was a close friend and dancing partner. The three friends didn't fare as well, stumbling down the rough road behind him.

The woodsman kept a brisk pace, quickly passing out of the town and into the wood beyond. Thomas dogged his heels, afraid he'd be completely lost if they dropped the slightest bit behind. The journey was short, fortunately, and the path was mercifully clear of branches or roots, which meant that Thomas only stumbled a few times before they stepped into a small clearing.

It wasn't until they were half-way across that Thomas could make out the cabin—small and stone with a thatch roof and a covered wooden porch across the front. It was completely dark. The woodsman strode up to the porch, leaving Thomas and his friends waiting in the clearing. He knocked at the door, waited for an answer, and when none was forthcoming, knocked again.

"She should be home," he said "It's early yet and she's not usually out at night."

"Unless she's harvesting moonwart," an amused female voice said. The four turned around and saw a tall woman coming towards them from the edge of the trees.

Ailbe walked past them to the porch, sparked a small brand into life, then used it to light a lantern hanging on the wall near the door. The yellow light was almost dazzling after their walk through the dark woods. She held the lantern up high, revealing a narrow, angular face surrounded by black hair, and a nose that very much resembled Timothy's. "Why have you brought these three here?"

"They need to talk to you," said Shamus.

"At this hour?" Ailbe looked the three over. "What's so important it can't wait until morning? The boy's face needs a poultice, but there's nothing wrong with his big friend." She turned to Eileen. "Is it you, girl? Are you pregnant?"

Young girls must come to her often, Thomas realized as Eileen's mouth fell open and a blush spread right up to the roots of her hair. *No wonder the folks in the tavern were looking at us funny.*

Thomas stepped forward before Eileen could find her voice. "It's not that. It's... news." Thomas realized he wasn't sure how to proceed. He'd never told someone that a person they knew had died. "I'm Thomas Flarety," he said, as much to delay what he had to say as to be polite. "These two are George and Eileen Gobhann." A lump started to form in his throat. He swallowed it and pressed on. "Do you know Timothy? The juggler?"

"Timothy Fihelly? He's my brother."

Oh, by the Four. Thomas felt his stomach drop and the blood rush away from his face. The lump came back into his throat, blocking off his breath and any possibility of speech. *Oh, no.*

Ailbe was waiting for him to tell her what was happening, Thomas knew. He swallowed again, trying to clear his throat. It didn't work. Ailbe frowned, and her tone was cautious when she said. "Is he in trouble?"

Thomas forced a breath into his lungs, then let the words rush out with the air. "He's dead."

Ailbe stood motionless, her mouth half-open. "What?"

"I'm sorry," said Thomas, quickly. "It happened yesterday. In Elmvale."

Ailbe swayed, like a branch in a sudden breeze. All the colour had vanished from her face, leaving it pale and sickly in the yellow light of the lantern. Shamus was beside her in an instant, putting an arm around her waist and taking the lantern. Ailbe caught his arm with a hand, squeezing hard. Her voice was distant when she said, "How?"

"He was... uh," Thomas stumbled on the words, then rushed them out, as if the speed would make it hurt less, like tearing a bandage from a wound. "He was murdered."

Ailbe let go of Shamus and stepped forward to the stairs. She stepped down the first stair, then sat. She was shaking, but Thomas couldn't hear any crying. The light of the lantern behind her silhouetted her to Thomas. Her voice, distant and unconnected, floated from the shadows of her face. "Who would want to kill him? He never harmed anyone. He wouldn't..." her head cocked towards Thomas, though he still couldn't see her face. "Why?"

"They..." Thomas stopped, his eyes going to Shamus. The raw-boned man looked shaken, and his face was bleak. Thomas had no idea how much the man knew, or how much to say in front of him. "They were after something."

"After something?" Ailbe's words came out half-strangled, and the short, harsh laugh that followed them had a note of hysteria. "What did he have that was worth anything? He was a travelling performer! He had his wagon and the shirt on his back!"

"He...uh," Thomas wished desperately for a drink to put the moisture back in his mouth. "He said your name."

"My name?" Ailbe sounded confused. "When?"

"At the end."

Thomas could see Ailbe's body crumbling in on itself, though her face was still in shadow. She began sobbing, her shoulders shaking hard. "Oh!" the sound hurled itself out of her body. ""Oh, by the Four! Oh, no..." the words dissolved into sobbing. Shamus put down the lantern and knelt behind her on the porch. He put his hands on her shoulders and she turned, burying her face into his chest. He held her tight.

"You should go," said Shamus. "Come back in the morning. "

"Uh..." Thomas could see how badly Ailbe was shaking, could hear her sobbing into Shamus's shirt and wished he could leave them be. "We can't."

"What do you mean, you can't?" Shamus's voice was hard. "Let the woman alone for tonight. You can tell her the rest in the morning."

"We can't," Thomas repeated. "The men who attacked Timothy might be coming here."

"What?" Shock replaced some of the hardness. "What do you—" Shamus cut himself off, looking down at the woman in his arms. When his eyes met Thomas's again they looked to be made of stone. "You wait," he said, his voice cold and flat. "You wait right here."

He whispered into Ailbe's ear once, then again. Still crying, she nodded. Shamus gently raised Ailbe up and helped her back up onto the porch, then into the house.

"That was awful," whispered Eileen as soon as they disappeared inside.

"It's going to get worse," said Thomas. "I've still got to tell her about the magic."

"Maybe we should go," George suggested. "The bishop isn't here."

Thomas shook his head. "Doesn't mean they're safe. We need to warn her, at least."

George nodded, but didn't look at all happy. Ailbe's sobs, muffled by the walls of the little cottage, still floated out to them. No one spoke, and the night dragged slowly forward. Eileen sat in the grass, and soon George joined her. Thomas kept his feet, watching the front door of the cottage and waiting. The crying kept going for a long time, rising and falling at intervals until it began to taper off. It took the better part of an hour before the crying finally stopped. Thomas stayed where he was, waiting.

The front door of the cabin opened, and a light shone through. Ailbe stood in the doorway, the lantern in her hand. Her face was still streaked with tears, and she looked pale, but she was steady on her feet and her voice was clear. "You said the men who killed my brother were after something?"

"Aye," said Thomas.

"What was it?"

It was the best opportunity he was going to get, Thomas knew. He braced himself for her reaction. "His magic."

Thomas waited, afraid Ailbe would call him insane or have Shamus drive him off the property, but she didn't. She didn't react at all, just stood there.

Thomas pressed on. "Before he died, he said the bishop took his magic; that he was collecting the small magics. Then he said your name. I had to come in case they were going to come after you, next."

The tears were flowing down Ailbe's face again. She made no move to stop them or wipe them away. Instead, she said, "Why you?"

Not 'What magic?' Thomas thought, *not, 'Why would they come after me?'* "Because," said Thomas, keeping his voice steady and trying not to show the relief he was feeling, "Bishop Malloy tried to take my magic, too."

Thomas waited. The tears ran unimpeded down Ailbe's face. Her eyes were focused far away. Behind him, Thomas could hear George and Eileen coming to their feet, heard them shift nervously once they were up. Thomas was about ready to say something more when she stepped back and opened the door wide.

"Come inside," said Ailbe. "Come inside and tell me everything."

Thomas nodded and, with a glance at his friends to make sure they were following, went up the stairs. Ailbe stepped out of the way and ushered them all into the house. The main room was small. There were only two chairs; a large one in a corner which Shamus was occupying, and another, smaller one near the fireplace that was clearly Ailbe's. A worn rug covered part of the wooden floor, and an open doorway led to a kitchen, while a curtain covered another door that Thomas guessed led to Ailbe's bedroom. Thomas came in and stood by the fireplace. Eileen and George stayed near the door, looking quite nervous and out of place.

Ailbe took her chair, sat down, and took a moment to wipe at the tears on her face with cloth on the arm of the chair. When she was done she said, "Shamus knows all about Timothy's magic," which made Shamus sit upright and look very wary. "Anything you would say to me, you can say to him."

Thomas nodded and told the story, from his arrival home to his first meeting with Timothy to Fire Night and all the events that had happened since. It took an hour, from beginning to end, and by the finish of it, Ailbe was wiping at her face again, and Shamus was leaning forward in his seat, anger clear on his face. George and Eileen had sat on the floor near the door, and were looking awkward and uncertain. Thomas, still standing, was aware of the pain in his feet and the ache in his face and ribs.

"I don't understand why," Ailbe said when Thomas was finished. "What does the bishop want with magic?"

"He called it a corruption," said Thomas. "Said he was going to purify me."

"Aye," said Shamus. "The High Father's church has never had a kind place in its heart for witches."

Thomas forbore mentioning the difference between witchcraft and magic. "If that was it, he'd have brought inquisitors," he said instead. "Or his guards. Instead, he was trusting the work to three ruffians. Besides, he's not just getting rid of the magic, he's taking it for himself."

"Which is odd, if he thinks it is a corruption," said Ailbe. She sighed and turned to Shamus. "What do you think?"

Shamus leaned forward in his chair, the firelight flickering over his craggy features. "I think we should talk to the sheriff. Tell him what happened."

Ailbe shook her head. "How?" she asked. "What could we say? If Thomas is telling the truth, then there's no proof. Besides, who would believe us?"

Shamus grunted his acknowledgement. "Not right," he said. "Not right for the bishop to be doing such things."

"No," agreed Ailbe, suddenly sounding very tired. "It isn't." She looked into the fire and stared there for a time. When she spoke again, it was to herself more than to anyone else. "He shouldn't have died like that."

"He should not," echoed Shamus. "He should have stayed home."

Ailbe shook her head. "You didn't," she said. "Can't expect him to if you didn't."

"He could have come back," said Shamus. "He should have just come home."

"I know," said Ailbe. Her shoulders started shaking again, and the tears began to flow hard. "Oh, he should not have died like that!"

Thomas felt suddenly, extremely awkward. The weight of a past about which he knew nothing filled the room. He looked for something to say, but could find no words. George was looking at the ground, his expression mirroring Thomas's feelings. Eileen had tears on her face.

Ailbe rubbed hard at her face. "I'm tired," she said from between her hands. "I'm tired and my heart hurts." She stood. "You should stay," she said to Thomas. "All three of you. In the morning we'll talk more about…"

She lost her voice. Shamus rose and went to her, holding her in his arms. She let him for a moment, then stepped back and turned back to Thomas. "There's blankets in the chest in there," she said, gesturing with her chin at a curtained doorway. "You can sleep on the porch."

"We will," said Thomas. "Thank you."

Eileen rose to her feet and went to fetch the blankets. George gathered up his and Eileen's bags and stepped outside. Thomas picked up his own bag and headed for the door.

Ailbe reached out and caught the edge of Thomas's shirt. "Are you sure?" she asked, her voice trembling. "Are you sure the bishop had him killed?"

Thomas nodded. "I am. I'm sorry."

Ailbe nodded and turned her face away. "In the morning." she said her voice breaking. "We'll talk in the morning."

Thomas nodded then stumbled outside to the porch. George was already there, setting his and his sister's bags down against the stone wall of the house. Thomas tried to think of something to say, but could find nothing.

Eileen stepped out of the house, loaded down with blankets. "I have never felt so awkward in my life," she whispered as she handed blankets to George and Thomas. She put her own down against the wall of the porch. "Ailbe's gone to bed," she said. "Shamus went with her."

George put his blankets down beside his sister's. "Just as well," he said quietly. "She's had a nasty shock."

Thomas let his blanket fall in a pile on the other side of the door and took off his sword belt. He laid it on the porch floor then sank down beside it, feeling his stiff, sore body protest the movement. Dim light from the fire inside came through the shutters, casting a thin orange glow out onto the porch. "I shouldn't have told her like that."

"You didn't really have a choice," said Eileen.

"It's still no good."

"Aye," said George, putting one blanket onto the porch floor. "Well, it sounds like she believes you, anyway."

Thomas nodded. "Aye." He pulled the blanket up around his shoulders. "Now if I could get you two to believe me..."

"We are trying," Eileen said. "It's just..."

"Not easy to believe," finished George. He lay down and wrapped himself in his second blanket. "Where do you think the bishop is?"

"I don't know," said Thomas. He sighed. "He should have gotten here before we did."

"Maybe he had somewhere else to go."

"Maybe." Thomas looked out into the night. The clouds still covered the sky, blocking any of the light from the heavens that might have shone down. All he could see was darkness and the thin, grey shapes of the trees. A long silence fell.

"Aren't you going to sleep?" asked Eileen.

"I don't think I can, right now," Thomas said.

There was quiet for a time, then the rustling of blankets.

"Hey," said George, "Where do you think you're going?"

"I'm sitting with Thomas for a while." She stepped across the porch to him. "If that's all right?"

"Aye," said Thomas, surprised. "But I'm not going to be good company."

"Neither am I," said Eileen, putting a blanket on the floor beside him, then wrapping another around her shoulder. "But I'm not tired yet and I don't want to lie awake alone in the dark."

"Hardly alone," said George.

"Being awake beside someone asleep is as bad as being alone," said Eileen. "Thomas will at least be awake."

"Fair enough," said Thomas. He looked over at George, who was eyeing them with uncertainty. Mindful that Eileen was George's sister, he asked, "Do you mind, George?"

George eyed the two of them, then said, "No. I don't mind." He rolled over, wrapped himself tightly in his blanket. "Just don't tell Mother I let you alone to talk to a boy at this hour of the night."

Eileen sat down beside Thomas, far enough away that they weren't touching, but close enough that they could see each other's faces clearly in the near-darkness. Thomas leaned back against the wall and turned his gaze back out to the clearing, half-expecting to see the bishop and his men coming.

There was no sign of them, of course, and no sound from the cabin. Thomas expected his mind to go wandering off in all directions. Instead, it went to the girl sitting at his side. He felt awkward, all of a sudden aware that she was a very pretty girl, with a very big brother sleeping on the other side of the porch.

"Thomas," Eileen began, "are you all..." She stopped a moment then started again. "How are you?"

Thomas thought about that question. Part of him wanted to just say 'all right' and leave the matter alone. Instead, he said, "Honestly?"

Eileen nodded. "Honestly."

"Tired. Sore. My face hurts, my ribs hurt. Worried about Ailbe. Scared of the bishop. Scared for my father. Scared that everything I wanted is going to be taken away from me." Thomas stopped, the welter of emotions threatening to rise up and overwhelm him.

Eileen hesitated. "Maybe you shouldn't go home. After we're done here, I mean."

"I have to."

"But, if your father's going to disown you—"

"He's going to do that anyway." Thomas looked at Eileen, her face barely outlined in the dim glow coming from the cabin. "The Academy is everything I ever wanted. If I run away, I don't get to go back. I don't get to read philosophy or study law or be anything. I'll end up as a secretary to some merchant if I'm lucky!" His voice was getting loud, he realized, and he stopped talking. The weight of his feelings was crushing him. Rage and fear held onto him like a weight in his chest. He looked back out into the darkness beyond the cabin. His voice was a whisper when he said, "It's all I ever wanted. I'm not letting him take it away."

Eileen said nothing and sat still for a time. Then she took the blanket from her shoulders and spread it across their legs. Before Thomas could ask what she was doing, she grabbed the side of his, put it over her own shoulders and moved in close enough that her shoulder pushed against his. "Better?" she asked.

"Um... yes," Thomas said, not sure what she meant.

"Good." She leaned her shoulder against his. He took comfort from her warmth and her presence, even though he didn't dare move. "It will be all right," she said. "You'll see."

He felt a lump forming in his throat. He tried to swallow it. "Thank you."

Eileen didn't reply, but left her shoulder where it was, and stayed beside him. Thomas stared out into the woods, searching for something to say, but not finding anything. Soon he felt Eileen's head leaning gently on his shoulder, her breathing soft and regular. Part of him knew he should wake her up and send her back to her brother. The rest of him just wanted to feel someone close by. In the end, he left her alone, drawing what comfort he could from her presence beside him.

Chapter 11

Thomas woke hard and fast as a hand blocked his mouth shut and shoved his head against the wall. The pain jolted him and sent spots of light spinning in front of his eyes. A knife appeared, hanging in the air, its wielder near-invisible in the darkness. He looked past the blade, followed the arm to the face of the man holding his mouth shut. "Make a sound and you die," the man hissed. Thomas recognized the voice at once. He had heard it before, at Timothy's wagon and at his father's house. The man shoved his head against the wall again. "And so does the girl."

Thomas risked a glance at Eileen. The second of 'his Grace's' men had a knife at her throat. His other hand had pushed away the blanket, and was fumbling with the edge of her dress. Eileen was rigid; her breath was short and ragged with fear and anger, and her legs clamped hard together. From the other corner of the porch, a near-animal growl followed by a whispered reply told him that the third man had George. He turned his eyes back to the man in front of him, nodded his understanding.

The man took his hand from Thomas's mouth and wrapped it around his throat. "His Grace wants to see you."

"I won't go." The words came of their own accord.

"You will go." The floating knife suddenly pressed against his cheekbone, "And you will go quietly, or my friend will cut the young lady's throat. Understand?"

The man holding Eileen had found the bottom of her skirt and was moving his hand slowly up her leg. Thomas answered quickly. "Aye."

"Good." The knife flicked back from his face, the edge dragging along his cheekbone and cutting the flesh open. Thomas hissed and twisted, but managed not to cry out. His movement brought his legs up against his sword belt, hidden beneath the blanket. Keeping the rest of his body still, Thomas shifted his hand, still under the blanket, towards the hilt of his dagger. "I'll do what you want," said Thomas. "Just leave her alone."

"But I'm enjoying her," whispered the man holding Eileen.

George's growl shook the darkness, "*Don't* you touch her."

"Shut up!" whispered the third man, and George grunted in pain. The man holding Thomas turned to look, and Thomas took the moment to wrap his fingers around the grip of his dagger.

"Enough," hissed Thomas's captor. "Knock the girl out, then go get that wench from the house."

From across the porch came a sudden, meaty *thud!* and the sound of a body going sprawling. The man holding Eileen yanked his hand free from her skirt and jumped to his feet.

Thomas took the moment, pulling his dagger from beneath the blanket and slashing the edge of the blade across the underside of the wrist that held his throat. The man let out a startled, pained shout and jumped away. Thomas rolled clear of the blankets and to his feet, pulling his sword out of the sheath and nearly falling off the edge of the porch. He could just make out George, moving with the speed that had nearly defeated Liam, rolling over and straddling his attacker, grappling for something Thomas couldn't see.

Eileen delivered a vicious kick towards the knee of the man in front of her, buckling it and making him stumble backwards, as she scrambled to her feet.

"You son of a whore!" she screamed, throwing the blanket at him and pulling at her own dagger.

"Get away!" Thomas yelled.

Eileen ignored him, swore viciously and swung her dagger. The man moved to the side, his own blade flashing out. Eileen screamed, short and harsh, then hit the ground. George let out a terrible bellow and drove his fist into the face of the man beneath him with a sound like a cabbage being hit with an iron hammer.

The man Thomas had cut slashed at him with his dagger. Thomas twisted away from it, then thrust with his rapier, sinking it into the other's flesh. Thomas twisted the blade and pulled it free. The man fell off the porch and to the ground with a mewling sound.

Eileen's attacker jumped off the porch and stumbled, limping into the night. Thomas took off after him. The man reached the edge of the woods just steps ahead of Thomas, then dodged to his left. Thomas saw why and just managed to change his own course. Steel ripped the cloth of his shirt, but missed flesh. Randolf, the bishop's black-clothed familiar, stepped out from the cover of the trees and thrust again.

Thomas, unable to stop his momentum, dove to the side, rolling and coming up with his blades towards the man. He thought he could see a sneer on the other's face, but the dark made it impossible to be certain. The man attacked again. Thomas parried and fought desperately back.

The fight was rough and awkward. Neither could see the other well. They thrust and parried, half-seeing, half-guessing where their opponent was. Randolf kept Thomas on the defensive, his blade nearly finding flesh again and again.

From behind Thomas came a sudden light, throwing the black-clad swordsman into sharp relief. Thomas thrust forward and was parried. Randolf launched a sweeping cut at Thomas's neck, making him parry wildly and retreat into the yard.

The familiar, the sneer on his face clear in the yellow light, turned on his heel and ran into the woods. Thomas, breathing hard, nearly gave chase. He wanted the one who had cut Eileen, but knew Randolf would be between them. The man was very good. He had nearly killed Thomas half a dozen times in the few moments they had fought, and not by luck, either.

"She's bleeding, Thomas!" cried George. "Help me!"

Thomas raced to the porch. Shamus was standing in the cottage doorway, a warrior's axe in one hand, a torch held up in the other, his eyes going to George and Eileen, then the bodies on the ground. "What the High Father's name is going on here?"

Thomas ignored him and knelt by Eileen. "Where is she cut?"

He cast his sword and dagger aside and tried to make her uncurl. His hand touched her stomach and came away sticky. Eileen cried out.

"Hold her still," said Thomas. George grabbed his sister's shoulders and tried to hold her down. Thomas took Eileen's hand. "Eileen, you have to stay still, do you understand? Lie back and stay still!"

Eileen made a keening sound between gritted teeth, but uncoiled her body and did as Thomas asked. George looked to the Shamus. "Help her!"

"I'll help her," said Ailbe, stepping out onto the porch. "What happened?"

"They attacked us," Thomas threw a hand in the direction of the bodies, his eyes on Eileen's stomach. The knife had left a long tear across her flesh. "Oh, thank the Four."

"What do you mean, 'Thank the Four'?" demanded George, and for the first time Thomas noticed the blood pouring from his friend's ear. "She's bleeding! Help her!"

Thomas pulled apart the fabric of her shirt and shift, baring her flesh and the wound. "She's been cut, not stabbed. The dagger didn't go in deep." He looked at his big friend, seeing the naked fear in his face. "She'll live, George. She'll be fine." He took Eileen's hand again. "You'll be fine."

Eileen, eyes closed and teeth gritted together, said nothing.

"She needs stitches," Ailbe said. "Put a blanket under her and get her inside." She looked at the other, prostrate forms. "What about them?"

Thomas went to look. The man he had stabbed was lying still in the grass, a pool of blood spreading beneath him, his eyes empty and staring at nothing. Thomas rocked back on his heels, stunned.

"Thomas!" George called. He and Shamus had either end of the blanket. "We're ready," George said. "Watch them."

Thomas nodded, saying nothing. The men lifted Eileen without effort, and followed Ailbe inside. Thomas watched them go, the horror of what he had done momentarily overriding his concern for Eileen. He stood, lost, looking for something to do but unable to think what.

He saw his weapons on the ground and picked them up. The sword blade was soaked with blood. Thomas looked for something to clean it with, but the only spare cloth was lying on the body of the man he'd killed. Feeling nearly ill, Thomas wiped his sword on the dead man's jacket, then sheathed both weapons and put on the belt.

He went over to the man George had punched. There was a large puddle of blood underneath the man's head, and more from his nose, mouth, and ears. The man's face looked pushed in, and beneath his head the boards of the porch were cracked. Thomas shuddered, thinking of the amount of force it took to generate such a blow, then stumbled back and nearly ran inside.

Eileen was on the kitchen table, Ailbe standing over her. Shamus had her legs and George her arms, holding them still as Ailbe held the bunched up cloth over the wound. Thomas stepped up beside Shamus. Eileen's shirt was gone and her shift ripped open, exposing her from just below her breasts to her hips. Her eyes were tight shut, her teeth locked around a small length of leather. The occasional moaning noise let him know that she was still conscious.

"You," Ailbe ordered. "Hold this cloth over the wound until I tell you. I need to thread the needle."

Thomas took the cloth and did what he was told. Blood was already soaking through the material. He gritted his teeth and told himself he'd seen worse, though he really hadn't. He wanted to turn his eyes away from her body, but did what he was told, instead, catching as much of the blood as possible.

"What about those two outside?" asked George. "They'll get away."

"They aren't going anywhere," said Thomas. He took his eyes off Eileen's stomach a moment and looked to her face. Her eyes were open, and she was looking directly at him. He swallowed. "They're dead."

What was left of the colour drained from Eileen's face.

"Dead?" George repeated. "How can he be dead? I only hit him."

"You collapsed his face," Thomas said, meeting his friend's eyes. "I think you broke his skull."

"By the Four." The big man looked unsteady on his feet. The blood was still coming from his ear, and Thomas realized that the lobe had been cut nearly in two. George didn't seem to notice. Instead, he said, "What about yours?"

"I probably stabbed his heart," said Thomas, remembering the feeling of the blade in his hand as it sunk into the other man's flesh. "The angle was right."

George was shaking. "I've never killed anyone before."

"Me neither."

"Enough talk," Ailbe said. She stepped up beside Thomas. "I'm going to wash the cut, then stitch it. You wipe the blood away. You two hold her still, understand?" Both men nodded their answer. Ailbe took Eileen's face in her hands. "Now, this is going to hurt, lass, but it'll make the wound heal faster, so I need you to hold absolutely still, understand?"

Eileen nodded, then closed her eyes and clenched her teeth on the leather in her mouth. Ailbe let her go. "All right," she said, signalling to Thomas to remove the cloth. "Scream if you like, lass. It makes the pain seem less."

Eileen didn't scream; not when Ailbe washed the wound with an herbal rinse, nor when she started sewing. George kept his eyes firmly on the ground, though his grip was steady as a rock. Shamus looked unperturbed, like one who had seen such things many times before and no longer felt anything at the sight. Thomas, watching the needle going in and out of Eileen's flesh, felt distinctly queasy. Being a surgeon, he decided, was not in his future. Still, he cleaned the blood away when told.

Half-way through the operation a pale, white glow surrounded Ailbe's hands. Thomas nearly fell over. A quick look at George told him the big man hadn't seen anything. Thomas watched the glow spreading slowly down Ailbe's hands like pale, liquid light and flowing into Eileen's wound.

Thomas was no longer frightened for Eileen.

Ailbe finished her work quickly and neatly, tying off the last knot and breaking the thread, then having the men sit Eileen up so she could wrap a long length of cloth around her stomach. At last, the wound was covered. "All right, let her go."

George and Shamus lay Eileen gently back and released their hold on her. Eileen pulled her arms to her chest, hugging them close. "Keep an eye on her," said Ailbe to Thomas. "Don't let her move too much."

Thomas stepped back, feeling sick with horror and relief. George ran a hand over his sister's head, then took the strip of leather from her mouth. Tears glimmered in his eyes. He muttered about getting his spare shirt and stepped away to the porch. Shamus and Ailbe stepped over to the hearth, speaking words too quiet for Thomas to hear. Thomas wanted something to do or to say, but there was nothing. He stayed where he was until Ailbe came back, wrapped Eileen in a blanket, and had Shamus carry her over to the fire.

George came in with his and Eileen's bags in his hand and a haunted look on his face. Ailbe poured a cup of liquid, made Eileen drain it, then took George's shirt from him. She started to strip away Eileen's shift and Thomas turned away, waiting until he heard Ailbe rise before looking back. Eileen was lying on the blanket beside the fireplace, George kneeling beside her, his hand engulfing one of hers.

"She'll be asleep, soon," said Ailbe. "The drink will keep her out until morning." She cocked her head at Thomas. "How's your face?"

"My face?"

"Aye, or did you not know your cheek's cut open?"

Thomas raised a hand to the side of his head, felt the blood and the pain. "I stopped feeling it when the fight started. I forgot about it."

"I bet. Come closer." Ailbe ran professional fingers over his face. "I don't think it needs stitching. Just a poultice and some time. It'll leave a lovely scar, though." She turned to George. "And your ear is about in two, as well. I'll fix that next."

"What about the bodies?" asked Shamus. "We'll be wanting them off the porch."

"We'll do it," said George. His face was pale, and he had a sick look in his eyes, which stared at nothing in particular. Still, he repeated, "We'll do it. We killed them." His hand was still in Eileen's. "As soon as she's asleep."

"Right, then," Ailbe said, pulling Thomas back to the kitchen. "Let's get you two put back together."

Thomas went without protest, and managed not to cry out when she washed the blood from his face and pushed the stinging poultice against his cheek, holding it tight. Thomas once more saw the pale white glow of her magic, surrounding her hands. He could *feel* it, warm and comforting, sliding into his face, soothing the hurt there and the aches in the rest of his body. He let himself relax into her hand, let the warmth spread through him.

"She's asleep," said Shamus, from his spot by George and Eileen. "Go get your ear fixed, lad, then we'll take care of the ones on the porch."

George did as he was told, though he kept his eyes on his sister the entire time. Ailbe put a pair of stitches into George's ear and wrapped his head with cloth. George didn't make a sound through the entire thing. When Ailbe pronounced him finished, George stood and looked to Shamus. "Right, let's get this over with."

Thomas and George went out to the porch. Shamus followed them, lighting their way with his torch. The yellow light cast deep shadows all around them and made the puddled blood on the porch black. George went to the body of the man he'd killed and knelt beside him. His eyes locked on the man's caved-in face, and a shudder went through his large frame, turning into continuous shakes that nearly made the big man's teeth rattle. George stood up and walked into the dark woods. A moment later the sound of his retching reached the cabin.

Thomas looked down at the man he had killed. He lay on the grass, hands still clutching at the wound that had ended his life. Thomas stared at the body, but felt nothing. Given what was happening to George, he decided that he should count his blessings. "What should we do with them?"

"You can put them with the firewood out back," Ailbe said from the doorway. "In the morning we'll send for the sheriff."

George emerged from the woods, looking pale and haggard. He stepped over to Thomas. "I heard," he said. "Let's get this done."

"Are you sure you're up to it?" asked Shamus.

"Aye."

His voice was flat, and left no room for questions. He reached down, grabbed the man Thomas had killed under the arms and hauled him away. Thomas watched then went over to the other man. He was too heavy for Thomas to lift alone. Shamus stuck the end of his torch in the ground, grabbed the man's feet, and together the two carried him around to the back of the house.

* * *

It was nearly dawn when Thomas and Ailbe spoke again.

George was inside, asleep at last on the floor beside his sister. Shamus had retired to the bedroom. Ailbe had spent the night moving back and forth from the small kitchen where she brewed medicines for Eileen to the rug where the girl was lying.

Thomas watched her go back and forth, watched George and Eileen sleeping on the floor in front of the fireplace. He felt useless. He couldn't sleep, couldn't do anything else. At last, he excused himself and went out to the porch. He sat on the step, staring into the darkness and trying not to look at the bloodstains. He felt empty inside.

The eastern sky was just beginning to lighten when Ailbe stepped onto the porch.

"I did say we'd talk in the morning," she said, setting herself down beside him.

"Aye, you did," Thomas agreed. "Though I doubt you meant this early."

"I wasn't sleeping, anyway."

He turned away from the woods to look at her. "I'm sorry we brought all this on you. If I'd known—"

"Just be thankful the girl's alive," said Ailbe, waving away his words. "If that knife had gone deeper..."

"Aye." The thought made Thomas shudder. He changed the subject. "Ailbe, how old were you when..."

"How old was I when what?"

"When you first found out about the magic," said Thomas. "About the healing."

Ailbe went quiet. Thomas waited. At last she said, "Did Timothy tell you about that?"

Thomas shook his head. "I saw it."

"Saw it?" Ailbe's eyes went wide. "What did you see?"

"White light. Going from your hands into the cut."

Ailbe's mouth fell open and she looked at her hands. "I've never seen it," she said. "I can feel it, but I can't see it."

"Timothy said people had gifts. Small magics. I guess this is mine." He sighed. "Or I'm insane."

"That's how I felt," said Ailbe. "I'd just become a woman. I was walking in the forest and I found a bird." Her gaze went far away. "A fox had been at it. I picked it up, wished it was better, and felt... I felt myself making it better." A smile ran over her face, erasing some of the weariness there. "I healed it but its wing was too twisted to fly. I kept it as a pet for years." Her eyes came back into focus. "What about Timothy? What did you see with him?"

"A ball of light," said Thomas. "That trick he does. I saw it was a ball of light, not wood."

"He still does that?" Ailbe shook her head. "I warned him about that trick."

"Everyone in the crowd saw it," said Thomas, "but he showed them his wooden ball and they all believed him. But it wasn't a wooden ball. It was light." Thomas could see Timothy in his mind, laughing at the crowd. "I saw him bring the wooden ball out of his pocket after he'd put his shirt back on," said Thomas.

"You saw that?" Ailbe's eyebrows went up.

"Aye," said Thomas. "He didn't try to hide it that well. I'm surprised no one saw it before."

"They couldn't," said Ailbe. "His gift was making things invisible."

That caught Thomas off-guard. "What?"

"He could make small things invisible. Like a piece of bread or one of my dolls," she snorted at the memory. "I used to go mad looking for my doll and he'd be sitting there, hands in his lap."

"But, I thought the ball of light..."

"No. He learned that."

"*Learned* it?" The idea rocked Thomas. "Where?"

"No idea," said Ailbe. "He just showed up one day with a big grin on his face and a ball of light in his hand. Sent me for a loop, I can tell you."

Thomas leaned back on his arms, thinking. "If he could learn a trick like that..." *Maybe I can learn how to help my father.*

Ailbe wrapped her arms around herself, stared out into the sunrise. "It seems a stupid thing to kill him for."

Thomas couldn't think of any reply to that. He sat still beside Ailbe, watched the sky grow lighter with the coming dawn.

"Why would the bishop kill Timothy?" she asked at last. "Why would he take his magic?"

"He called it a corruption," Thomas said. "When he was trying to take mine, he said something about the Rebel Son and the Blessed Daughter, and that he would turn it to the High Father's work."

Tears were coming down Ailbe's face again. Her whole body shook with them. Grief filled her voice. "How is killing my brother the High Father's work?"

"I don't know." Thomas reached a hand out, wanting to offer comfort but unsure how. He let the hand fall.

Ailbe wiped at the tears. "Is this his gift? To tear out a person's magic?"

"I don't know," said Thomas. "He can do it, I'm sure, but he also controls people with his voice. And he healed his knee by touching it, just like you did." Thomas tried to sort it out. "Maybe he learned it, like Timothy learned to make the ball of light."

"I suppose." Ailbe looked thoughtful for a moment. "Why did he need to heal his knee?"

"I broke it."

"Good."

There was hatred in the word, and in her expression when she said it. Thomas turned away and looked to the east. The sun cleared the horizon, casting yellow light on the trees and yard and bringing the blood, now dried and brown, into stark relief. Thomas closed his eyes, felt the warm light on his face.

"Do you think the bishop will come today?" asked Ailbe.

"I don't know," said Thomas. He opened his eyes and squinted at the sun. "He's not going to be happy, though."

Ailbe nodded and rose to her feet. "I'll get Shamus up. He can head for the sheriff and tell him what happened." She went to the door. "As soon as the sheriff sees the cut on Eileen's belly, he'll know you three were just defending yourselves."

"The cut," said Thomas, getting up himself. "How long will that take to heal?"

"About half as long as average, though it will still leave a scar."

Her parents will never forgive me. Thomas sighed and followed Ailbe inside.

Eileen was still asleep on the rug, wrapped in blankets. George, dozing beside her, blinked awake and looked up at Thomas and Ailbe. Thomas wondered if he himself looked anywhere near as rough as George did. He sat down on the floor beside the fire, while Ailbe went into the bedroom to wake Shamus.

"How are you doing?" Thomas asked his friend.

George took some time to reply. "All right," he said, at last. "Better than Eileen is, that's for certain."

"She will recover," Thomas said. "Ailbe told me."

"Aye, she told me, too." George looked down at his sister. "My father's still going to kill..." He left the thought unfinished, and turned his eyes back to the fire. Thomas waited. At last, George said, "We should never have come."

Thomas nodded. "I suppose not."

"She never would have gotten hurt." Thomas could feel the anger in George, could see the tremors in his hands. "It was stupid to come here." said George. "I don't even believe in magic."

"I know."

"I can't see it. I've never seen it. And now..." he trailed off, started again. "It's not worth killing someone for something you can't even see."

Thomas watched his friend's large body start to shake. He put a hand on George's shoulder. "She will be all right."

George shrugged it off. "We should never have come."

"You saved my life," said Thomas. "If you two hadn't been here, I would be dead. And so would Ailbe."

"You don't know that," George said, still looking at the floor.

"I do," said Thomas. "And so do you."

Thomas waited. George kept his eyes on his sister. It was a long time before he finally mumbled, "I never wanted to kill anyone. Never."

"No one ever does," said Shamus, startling them both. He was standing in the bedroom door, pulling on his shirt. "At least not those with a conscience."

"Have you?" asked George. "Killed anyone, I mean?"

"Aye."

Thomas and George waited for something more, but the man only walked past them to the front door.

"Has he what?" asked Eileen, her voice soft and fuzzy, and instantly grabbing both their attentions.

"Eileen!" George bent down over his sister. "Are you all right?"

She shook her head. "It hurts."

"I'll get Ailbe." George stood and headed for the kitchen. Thomas knelt down in his place.

"Eileen," Thomas began, "I am so sorry—"

"Last night..." Eileen sounded like she was having trouble getting the words to come out. "Was either..."

She trailed off, but Thomas guessed the rest. "No. I went after him, but he got away."

Eileen turned her head away, biting her lips and closing her eyes, squeezing the tears that slid out between the lids. For the third time that morning Thomas felt useless and helpless and numb.

"Let's see you, then," Ailbe said, coming from the kitchen with a steaming mug in her hand. She tapped Thomas on the shoulder with her empty hand. "You should wait in the kitchen, I think."

Thomas did as he was told. George was sitting at the table, staring at his hands. He looked up when Thomas came in. "How is she?"

"I don't know," said Thomas. "Ailbe's examining her."

George nodded and went back to looking at his hands. Thomas sat across the table from him, feeling he should say something but once more having no idea what. He closed his eyes and rubbed his hands across his face, trying to drive away some of the exhaustion, and push some sense back into his head. When he opened them again, George was looking at him.

"Thomas?" George asked. "Could they hang us for last night?"

The thought gave Thomas a nasty jolt. If the bishop wanted to, he could certainly send the law after them. Of course, the bishop would have to admit that he sent the three men, and that would lead to questions Thomas was certain the bishop wouldn't want to answer. "No," Thomas said. "They can't do that."

"Do what?" asked Ailbe, crossing the kitchen and taking the kettle from the fire.

"Hang us," repeated George.

Ailbe shook her head. "The sheriff will take one look at that girl's cut and be on your side all the way. I know him and he doesn't take kindly to the type that would put a dagger into a young girl."

"How is she?" asked George.

"Healing," said Ailbe. George nodded, and Ailbe put a hand on his shoulder. "It will take time, but she will be fine."

George nodded. "How soon can she go home?"

"Tomorrow at the earliest, if you're walking. Two days would be better."

"All right." George rose to his feet, casting his eyes about the room. "So, what can we do now?"

"Wait," said Ailbe. "Go sit with your sister and keep her company. Thomas here can help me make breakfast."

George nodded and headed for the next room. Thomas watched him go, saw the way his large body was hunched in on itself, wrapped around the pain the big man was feeling. He turned back and found Ailbe watching him with concern on her face.

"I'm all right," Thomas said. "It's George who's taking it hard."

"Aye," Ailbe agreed. "That's because George is letting himself feel it. You've hidden it away."

Thomas had no real answer to that. He shrugged. "I guess."

"Are you hungry?"

"No."

"Didn't think so." Ailbe picked up a bowl of potatoes and a knife and handed them to Thomas. "Sure sign a man's upset when he won't put food into his body."

Thomas shrugged and took the bowl. Ailbe pulled some salted bacon down from the rafter and began cutting it into slices. Thomas started to work on the potatoes. At length Ailbe said, "Shamus went for a soldier when he was a boy. Served in the king's wars for ten years."

"Really?"

"He never talks about it, never lets on he feels anything. The saying in town is that if you hit him in the face with an axe he'd not get excited."

In his mind, Thomas saw himself kill the man again; saw Eileen scream and hit the ground. "Lucky him."

"I've seen the nightmares he has. I wouldn't wish them on anyone." She turned her eye back to Thomas. "Don't let it happen to you."

Thomas, still numb inside, could only say, "Yes, ma'am."

"Now hurry up with those potatoes. I'll want to fry them up before the sheriff arrives."

Chapter 12

Thomas heard Shamus returning just as breakfast was being set on the table, and went to the porch to see. The sheriff was right behind Shamus. He was a stout man with an oft-broken nose, wearing the green and black of the king's livery, and leading a large black horse. He tied the animal to the porch, stopped outside to survey the drying blood, then grunted and mounted the steps.

"I'm William Pherson," he said. "Sheriff of the County. I take it you are Thomas?"

"Aye."

The man grunted again and stepped inside. He spotted George first, and looked the big man up and down. "You must be George." He turned to Eileen, who was wrapped in blankets, a large mug of tea in her hand. "Which leaves you to be Eileen, unless Shamus got all his descriptions completely wrong."

"He got them right," said Ailbe from the kitchen, putting a large plate of bacon on the table. "I take it you'll be wanting some breakfast?"

"That would be wonderful," the sheriff said. "But first I'd better see the two outside by the woodpile." He turned back to George and Thomas. "If you two will come with me?"

It was phrased as a request, but was certainly an order. Thomas felt suddenly nervous, and reminded himself that they had done nothing wrong. He glanced at George, and from his friend's expression, guessed he was feeling the same way. They followed the sheriff outside and around to the back of the building.

In the daylight, the skin of the corpses was a sickly white, the blood a dark reddish-brown stain on their skin and clothes. George turned away, taking deep breaths and working hard at not being sick. Thomas still felt nothing, and hated it. He wanted to feel something, anything, looking at the body of the man he killed. All he could find was a void and somewhere far behind it, a white, slow-burning anger.

The sheriff watched both their reactions with interest, then knelt beside the bodies. He took his time examining them. At length he asked, "How did the one's head get smashed in?"

"I hit him," said George, still not looking at the dead men.

"What did you use?"

George held out his hands. "I just hit him."

The sheriff whistled, then pointed to the second man. "This one's wrist is cut."

"Aye," Thomas stepped forward. "I did that to get away from him. I stabbed him when he came at me again."

"With what?"

"My rapier."

The sheriff nodded. "Upwards under his ribs and straight through the heart, I see. Where did you learn that?"

"The Royal Academy of Learning."

"Good teachers you must have had," said the sheriff. "And were these two killed before or after the girl was cut?"

"After."

"Hmm," the sheriff rose up brushing the dust from his knees. "Well, let me look at the girl next, and then we'll sit down to breakfast. Come on."

They went back inside. Eileen showed the sheriff the stitches that ran from just below her ribs to the side of her hip. He whistled again.

"Well, that is impressive." He turned back to George and Thomas. "And this happened before you killed the other two?"

"Yes, sir," they chorused.

"I see. And the one who did this?"

"Got away," said George. "Thomas wanted to go after him, but someone stopped him at the edge of the woods."

"A swordsman," Thomas said, keeping the man's name to himself. "He nearly skewered me."

"Did you see his face?" asked the sheriff.

The sneer on Randolf's face flashed through Thomas's mind. "Aye."

"Would you recognize him again?"

"Aye," said Thomas, "though I doubt it will help."

The sheriff looked askance at Thomas. "And why's that?"

"I'm the only one who saw him."

"So it will be your word against his." the sheriff nodded to himself and grunted one more time, then turned to Shamus. "Well, everything they've told me matches your story, Shamus. And judging from that one's reactions—" he cocked a thumb at George—"I'm pretty sure he's no killer by trade. The other, though..." the sheriff took a long time watching Thomas for some reaction. When none came, he said, "You're fortunate. We don't normally have killings here, so I tend to take everyone involved into the gaol when one happens and sort it out after that. But with these two vouching for you," he gave a nod to Shamus and Ailbe, "and from the mess on the porch I'm tending to believe you myself." He shook his head. "Not right, bandits attacking folks in the middle of the night." He turned his attention back to Thomas. "Though from what Shamus said, you think these ones were more than just bandits."

Thomas risked a look at Shamus, wondering exactly what he had said. The woodsman's expression showed nothing. Thomas turned back to the sheriff. "Aye."

"Well, then, you'd better get me your version of the story while we're eating." the sheriff turned to Ailbe. "I take it breakfast is ready?"

Ailbe led them into the kitchen and served up a large meal of bacon and potatoes fried in the bacon grease, with strong mugs of tea and fresh-baked biscuits. The sheriff and Shamus dug into their breakfast with a will. No one else did. Eileen was restricted to a beef broth and some bread and George only nibbled at the bacon and fried potato slices set before him. Ailbe, claiming not to be a breakfast person, drank only tea. Thomas didn't eat anything. He had no appetite, and the sheriff's questions kept him busy for most of the meal anyway.

Thomas had spent most of the time before breakfast figuring out how much to tell the man. When Bluster had questioned them about Timothy's death, Thomas had kept silent about the bishop's involvement because he had no proof. Now, though, proof was lying dead behind the house, and Thomas had no intention of letting the bishop get away unscathed. Thomas knew he couldn't mention magic, of course, or what the bishop had done to his father or tried to do to himself. But that was no reason not to tell him about Timothy's fear of 'his Grace' and allow him to draw his own conclusions.

The sheriff grunted when Thomas finished, then turned to Ailbe and began questioning her about how Thomas and his friends came to be staying with her. She told him, also leaving out any mention of magic.

"A shame about your brother," said the sheriff, after Ailbe finished. "He was a good man."

"Thank you."

"And you say he was murdered," he said to Thomas.

"Aye."

"Humph." the sheriff frowned, took another spoonful of potatoes, chewed and swallowed. "And you think these three that attacked you are the same ones who killed Timothy?"

"Aye."

"And were they the ones that gave you the black eyes?" asked the sheriff, gesturing with his spoon.

"Aye."

"Can you prove it?"

Thomas shook his head. "They attacked Timothy's wagon. George and Eileen will vouch for that, but as for the rest…" he sighed. "I didn't see who beat me up. It was dark and they caught me off guard. No one was around when Timothy died, but I'm certain it's the same ones who did it all."

"And Timothy said they were working for the bishop," said the sheriff, using a biscuit to soak up some of the grease from his plate, "which, of course, no one else heard him say but you."

"Aye," said Thomas, "but all three of us heard one of them say 'his Grace' was waiting for Timothy when they attacked his wagon."

The sheriff turned to George and Eileen, who nodded their confirmation. "Humph." He cleared the last of the food from his plate and stood up. "Well, then, we'll just have to ask the bishop about it."

"If we can find him," said Thomas. "He was heading to Berrytown when he left Elmvale. He should have passed through here two days ago."

"I don't know about that," the sheriff said, "but one of his men rode into town last night to secure rooms at the inn. Apparently he'll be arriving today."

* * *

Thomas was certain they'd attract a crowd from the moment the sheriff led them back into town. If the sight of three strangers had turned heads the night before, the return of those three with fresh injuries, two dead bodies, and the sheriff as an escort would probably cause whiplash. To his surprise, no one came out on the street to see them. In fact, there was no sign of anyone. The houses were quiet; the streets empty save for a stray dog that shied away, smelling death.

"Where is everyone?" asked George. "The place is empty."

"I was with you," said Thomas. "I have no idea."

"Well, they can't have all vanished," said Ailbe. "Maybe they—"

She was cut off by the rumble of voices lifted together in not-quite unison. It took Thomas a moment to sort out the sounds enough to realize it was prayer.

"From the inn, sounds like," said the sheriff. "Guess the bishop made it in."

He led them towards the inn. The rumbling became recognizable words as they grew closer; responses chanted to the bishop's prayers. When they reached the street with the inn, they found it filled with people. The bishop himself was in front of the inn, standing on something that raised him high enough to be seen above the crowd. He was resplendent in his green and white formal robes, his gold jewellery glittering in the sunlight. He was also not alone. Several other priests and what looked to be several courtiers stood behind him, watching and listening. Randolf, dressed in his customary black, stood to one side, glaring at the crowd. Thomas, remembering the man's speed from the night before, felt a shiver run up his back.

"Now go in peace," the bishop said, ending the service with the ritual words, "And may the love of the High Father, greatest of the Four, be with you!"

He waved a blessing over the crowd, then stepped off the platform and temporarily out of sight. The crowd started to break up, but stopped at the sight of the sheriff, leading his corpse-laden horse. The voices that had been in prayer moments before started muttering speculatively to each other. Several people called out questions. The sheriff ignored them. A few of the mutterers had been at the inn the night before, and they started passing out what little they knew about Thomas and his friends.

"Your Grace!" the sheriff called, just before the man could vanish into the inn. The bishop turned and saw the group walking towards him. A flicker of some emotion—annoyance, perhaps—passed over the bishop's face, then vanished. The sheriff walked forward, the crowd parting before him.

Before the inn was a small stage of the sort that was set up for travelling players. Between it and the inn were a half-dozen guards, dressed in the grey livery of the Church of the High Father. The sheriff motioned Thomas and the others to stop a fair ways back from the inn, then led his horse forward. Two guards stepped in his way as he closed in.

"Let him pass," said the bishop, stepping forward to meet him. Randolf stayed right behind his master, his hand resting almost negligently on the hilt of his sword. The sheriff came forward and the bishop held out his ring. As protocol dictated, the sheriff bowed and kissed it. "The young man I see with you has a reputation for causing trouble," the bishop said before the sheriff could speak. "What has he done this time?"

A retort leapt to Thomas's lips and he locked it away, letting the sheriff take the lead.

"Defended himself, it seems," the sheriff said. "Last night, he and his friends were set upon by four men who intended to do murder."

"Indeed?" The bishop said. "I find it rather surprising how murder follows this one around." He locked eyes with Thomas. "Only two days ago there was a murder in Elmvale. A travelling juggler, wasn't it?"

"It was," said the sheriff. "He told me about it."

"Indeed?" the bishop kept his eyes on Thomas. "How brave of him."

The mockery in the bishop's tone was subtle, but Thomas caught it, and he had no doubt that the sheriff had as well. He kept his eyes level, meeting the bishop's and doing his best to look calm. The bishop stared at him a moment longer, then turned back to the sheriff. "I fail to see, however, Sheriff, why this young man's brawling should be *my* concern?"

"I've been told that these two might have worked for you," the sheriff gestured at the bodies on the horse. "I'd appreciate if you'd have a look at them."

"This hardly seems the place," said the bishop.

"I appreciate the timing is difficult." The sheriff gestured Shamus forward. "However, the sooner we get the matter resolved, the better."

Together, the sheriff and Shamus pulled the bodies off the horse and laid them out on the ground. The crowd buzzed and drew closer. Heads craned to see the men on the ground, and from the protests, several children were being led away.

The bishop stepped forward and surveyed the bodies. "And these were supposed to have worked for me?"

The sheriff nodded. "And the two others who got away."

The bishop shook his head. "I would never hire such men," he said. "Though I believe I have a third of this company in my care."

The sheriff, who had been maintaining a bland countenance until that moment, looked suddenly interested. "Do you, now?"

"My familiar found him on the side of the road, this morning. He had been stabbed repeatedly." The bishop looked once more at Thomas, then down at Thomas's rapier.

The sheriff followed the bishop's gaze. "I see."

"We have engaged a room for him to die in peace."

Thomas ignored them both and fixed his eyes on Randolf. The man's hand was still on his rapier, and his eyes were on Thomas. There was a hint of a smile on the familiar's face that made Thomas's blood run cold.

"You expect him to die, then?" The sheriff's voice brought Thomas's eyes back to the bishop.

The bishop nodded. "His wounds are severe. We were surprised he lived the night. I'm sure his attacker thought he would die, or he would have finished him off."

"This morning?" the sheriff said. "That would be on the road from Elmvale, then."

"From Fog Glen," corrected the bishop. "We left Elmvale two days ago. We were supposed to be here yesterday, but were delayed." The bishop turned to Thomas again and smiled, cold and smug. "There was a young woman there whose soul was in peril. I... assisted her."

Thomas felt his gorge rise. The poor woman would have had no chance at all. He wondered what her gift had been, and if she was still alive.

"And all your servants were with you in Fog Glen?"

"All of them," the bishop said. "Why? Do these folks claim to recognize one of my men as their other attacker?"

The sheriff looked back at the three, and for a moment Thomas expected to be asked who he recognized. The idea of having to accuse Randolf without proof made Thomas very nervous. He had no doubt the man would immediately challenge him to a duel, and Thomas doubted he'd come out as victor.

The sheriff only shook his head. "No. They will need to have a look at this one you found, though."

"Of course," said the bishop. "If you will follow my familiar?"

The bishop raised a hand. Randolf bowed slightly, then turned his back and walked toward the inn.

"Stay here," the sheriff said to Shamus, then gestured the others forward and followed. Randolf moved just quick enough to make Thomas have to hurry to catch up. Eileen, leaning on her brother, couldn't maintain the pace, and fell behind.

The familiar led the small group inside, then up the stairs to the rooms above. He didn't look back, just led them to a small room at the end of the hallway, opened the door and stood to one side. The sheriff glanced into the room, then turned and waited for the rest to catch up. Thomas, hard on his heels, stopped as well. Ailbe was the next up.

The sheriff gestured into the room. "See if there's any hope."

Ailbe squeezed past the others and went into the room. Eileen came up the stairs a moment later, supported by George. The walk had been tiring enough for her, Thomas knew. He imagined the stairs had been no fun at all. Thomas met them at the stairs and offered her his arm. She grabbed it, and used it to help pull herself up the last stair, wincing at the effort. Her walk had a definite wobble to it.

"Are you all right?" asked Thomas, realizing it was a stupid question the moment it left his mouth.

"I can stand," Eileen let Thomas go and reached out to the wall to steady herself.

"You can lean on me, if you like."

"No."

She kept moving down the hall, using the wall to stay upright. George followed behind, a concerned frown on his face. Thomas watched and found himself feeling very alone, and very guilty.

It's not my fault, he told himself. *If she had stayed home she wouldn't have gotten hurt.*

He didn't believe it. He should have made her stay home. George too. The problem was, having them around was so much better than being by himself. They had listened to him and went along with his ideas, even if they thought he was crazy.

Ailbe stepped back into the hall, wiping her hands on a length of cloth. "He's dying," she said. "I'm surprised he lasted this long."

"Can he talk?" asked the sheriff.

"Not even if he was awake." Ailbe finished wiping her hands, leaving streaks of red on the fabric. "One of the wounds is in his throat."

"Handy," grunted the sheriff. He turned to Eileen. "I need you to have a look at him and tell me if he's the one." He held out an arm. "Come on, lass."

Eileen took his arm and a deep breath. He led her into the little room. There was a long silence. Thomas, leaning around George to see, watched as she looked down at the man. She stared a long time.

"It's him," she said at last. She turned away from the bed and stumbled back to her brother, who wrapped her in his big arms. She shook in his grip, tears coming down her face. "Bastard," she whispered. She heaved in a breath, clutched at her stomach from the pain the motion caused. "Bastard!"

Thomas watched, feeling stupid and useless, as her brother gently led her away.

"Thomas," the sheriff gestured him in with two fingers. "I need you to look, too."

Thomas followed the sheriff into the little room. The man on the bed was on his side, bandages wrapped around his throat and torso. A pile of cloths and a bowl of water lay near his head, though there was no sign of anyone there to care for him. The man was drawing ragged, gasping breaths, as if getting air past his injury was a near-impossible task. His eyes were closed, though his face was too contorted in pain for Thomas to believe he was asleep. His bandages, clothes, and the bedspread beneath him were stained deep red with his blood. Thomas looked at it all, and still only felt numb.

"So, lad," said the sheriff. "Is this your handiwork?"

Thomas, staring at the man on the bed, took a moment to realize he was being accused. The anger that burned behind the numbness flared up. "No. I told you, I didn't get the chance."

"The bishop said he had all his people with him," the sheriff's voice was low, meant only for Thomas's ear. "Are you calling him a liar?"

Thomas glanced to the door, knowing that Randolf was just on the other side of it. He shook his head. "I couldn't prove it if I did."

"What I wonder," said the sheriff, "is why he would do this? What does he need to hide so badly that he would kill one of his own?"

The answer to *that*, Thomas knew, would get him into more trouble than anything else.

The man on the bed opened his eyes. His wheezing gasps changed pace, becoming harsher and more desperate. His lips and tongue moved, forming words that had no sound to give them life.

"Ailbe!" the sheriff pulled Thomas out of the room. Ailbe went in, the bishop's familiar on her heels. Thomas stood in the door and saw Ailbe putting her gentle hands on the dying man's face, calming him. Randolf stood right behind her, watching.

"You didn't answer me," the sheriff said, watching from the doorway of the room. "Why would the bishop do such a thing?"

"Thomas," Ailbe interrupted. "Take George and Eileen back to the house. She needs to rest."

"I need an answer," said the sheriff, his tone adding the '*now.*'

"Get it later," snapped Ailbe. "I need your help here. Thomas, *go!*"

The sheriff looked ready to argue the point, but went in to help Ailbe. Randolf was pushed out, leaving him and Thomas alone in the hallway. He stared at Thomas, a sneer on his face and one hand resting on his sword. Thomas bowed to the man and backed away until he was out of sword range. Then, using the opportunity Ailbe had given, he escaped the inn.

He was nearly running by the time he reached the yard. Eileen and George were already there. Eileen was wiping at her tears. Her brother stood with one protective arm around her, looking angry. Thomas told them what Ailbe had said. George nodded and offered Eileen his arm. She took it and the two started walking slowly back to Ailbe's house. Thomas fell in beside them. No one spoke. Thomas wanted to say something—anything—to bridge the gap that was starting to grow between them. Nothing he could think of seemed any good, though, so they walked in slow silence back through the woods.

Once they got to Ailbe's house, George wrapped Eileen in her blanket again, and helped her lay down on the floor beside the fireplace. He sat beside her, holding her hand. Thomas sat in the doorway, shifting his gaze back and forth from his friends to the woods. No one had found anything to say, and the time dragged interminably by. After what felt like hours, Thomas caught sight of movement outside. A moment later Ailbe and Shamus stepped into the clearing, with the sheriff two steps behind them. Thomas got to his feet and out of their way.

"He's dead," Ailbe said as she came in the door. She looked at Eileen, lying on the floor. "How's your stomach?"

"It hurts," said Eileen. "But not as bad as last night."

"Good." Ailbe collapsed into her chair. "Thomas, there's a small keg in the pantry. Draw some beer, will you? For everyone."

Thomas got up, found the beer and a pitcher to hold it, and mugs for all of them. In a couple of trips, he'd brought everything in and filled everyone's mugs. The sheriff had taken Shamus's seat, leaving the woodsman standing against one wall. Thomas took up his spot in the doorway again. Ailbe took her mug and drained half of it in a single swallow. She was looking pale and very tired.

"Well," the sheriff said, looking at Thomas. "It's a right mess you're in, isn't it?"

"Aye," said Thomas.

"Did you know your father's placed a price on your head?"

Thomas felt the air pressing in on him, growing thick and hard to breathe. "No. I didn't."

"Seems your father wrote up the papers and is having them delivered to the nearest three towns in all directions. The bishop had a copy with him."

Anger flared again in Thomas. He forced his voice to be calm. "And what does it say?"

"That you've been stealing money from your father for the last four years. And that you have to either swear yourself to the bishop's service or appear before a magistrate in Elmvale to answer the charges."

"When?"

"Three days from now. After that, you're for the gaol, and anyone bringing you in gets fifteen silver and your father's grateful thanks."

Thomas swore—short, specific and with great feeling, bringing raised eyebrows from nearly everyone in the room save the sheriff, who looked entirely unmoved. "And that means you are going to do what?"

"I'm going to face the magistrate," said Thomas, still seething. "I'm not serving the bishop."

"Because you believe he had Timothy killed?"

It was a good enough reason, Thomas thought, and a much easier one to explain. "Aye."

"And you think he was trying to have Ailbe killed as well."

"Aye."

The sheriff sighed, took a pull on his beer. "Unfortunately, the three that could prove it are all dead."

"*We* only killed two of them," said Thomas.

"So you said," agreed the sheriff. "The bishop seemed to think you stabbed the last one in the back."

"I was too busy fighting for my life, at the time."

"Against someone no one else saw," the sheriff pointed out. "How do I know you didn't just stab the man then come back?"

"Because the bishop said he found him on the road," said Ailbe. "If Thomas had stabbed him he wouldn't have gotten out of the woods. Not with those wounds."

The sheriff gave Ailbe a speculative look. "Is that so?" He took another drink. "And why didn't you mention this before?"

"Because calling the bishop a liar to his face would be a bad idea."

"True." The sheriff leaned back in his chair, took a long look at Thomas. "I don't suppose you can prove the bishop was involved?"

Thomas shook his head. "No. It's only my word against his."

"Which doesn't put you in a good place," said the sheriff.

When the sheriff didn't say anything more, Thomas asked, "So now what?"

The sheriff drained his beer and stood up. "Well, I believe you three were only defending yourselves against the ones you killed, so there won't be any charges on that account."

The relief would have knocked Thomas off his feet, had he not been sitting already. He looked over at George and Eileen and saw the same emotion on their faces.

"I could," the sheriff continued, "arrest you and have you hauled back to Elmvale. But the magistrate hasn't been there yet, which means that you haven't broken any of the conditions of the warrant. You have until tomorrow to get yourselves home."

Thomas pulled himself to his feet. "Thank you."

"Don't thank me, lad," the sheriff warned. "I'll have you in irons if you're still here tomorrow afternoon. And if you go anywhere other than home, I'll have you charged for fleeing the law as well. Understand?"

"Aye. And thank you anyway."

The sheriff grunted and left without another word.

Eileen spoke up for the first time since they'd left the inn. "Does this mean we can go home tomorrow?"

"If you're well enough," said Thomas. "Otherwise, I'll go alone."

Eileen turned to Ailbe, who nodded. "Aye, you can leave tomorrow. I'd like to have you stay here and heal for a couple of more days, but you could manage it. You'll have to rest often, mind you."

"I'll manage," said Eileen. "I just want to get home."

"We can make it a two-day trip," said Thomas. "We'll need to buy some food, though."

"I can get it," Shamus offered, pushing himself off the wall. "Better you lot stay here out of sight."

"Aye, it is," Ailbe finished her beer and pushed herself to her feet. "Take the blankets, too. They'll keep Eileen warm over the night."

"We won't be able to get them back to you," said George. "Not for a while."

"I'll come get them in a few days. I need to go to Elmvale anyway. To collect Timothy."

George opened his mouth, closed it. He looked to be searching for words, but in the end only said, "All right. Thank you."

* * *

By evening, Thomas was feeling thoroughly sorry for himself.

The day had dragged by after the sheriff left. Thomas had given Shamus money to buy supplies for the three of them for their trip, as well as food for all of them for lunch and dinner. Eileen spent most of the day sleeping. George spent it sitting at her side, or talking with Shamus about weather and the woods and other country matters. Ailbe busied herself in the kitchen for the most part.

Thomas had spent the day sitting on the edge of the porch, back against one of the wooden posts that held up the roof, feeling miserable. Thoughts of his father and the bishop and the previous night's violence were all wasps drilling holes into his brain. Worse than all that, though, was that his friends would not *talk* to him. He thought about going in, but couldn't bring himself to face them. Instead, he stayed on the porch, looking at the clouds and willing the day to pass.

Dinner time came, and Ailbe fed them lake trout and biscuits and beer, then shooed them out to the porch so she could clean up. Thomas took the same spot he'd been at all day. Eileen sat on the stair, wrapped in her blanket. She slouched, her loose red hair covering her face. George sat beside her, big arms crossed in front of him, eyes on the woods. Thomas watched the way Eileen leaned against her brother, drawing comfort and strength from him. The distance he felt between them and himself was far larger than the width of the porch. Even at dinner they hadn't spoken to each other, and now, with the sun starting to set, Thomas was desperate to bridge the space between them.

"At least you two will be on your way home tomorrow," he said, wishing he could come up with something better.

George glanced at Thomas, then shrugged and turned back to the woods. "Aye."

Silence fell again. Thomas tried to find something else to say, but couldn't.

Eileen's head came up. "Hang on," she said, her eyes finding Thomas's. "What do you mean, 'You two?' Aren't you coming?"

"What?" Thomas was completely confused. "Of course I am."

"Then why didn't you say so?"

Thomas thought about what he *had* said. "I meant 'home,' not just Elmvale." He leaned back against the wall. "Though maybe I shouldn't."

Now George was looking at him as well. "The sheriff said he'd lock you up."

"I know. I just… Ever since I came home, everything's gone wrong." The flow of words, now started, turned into a torrent. "My father's insane, Timothy's dead, the bishop is stealing people's souls, and Eileen got stabbed. Everything went to pieces the moment I arrived. And every time I try to make it better, someone else gets hurt." He stopped. Both his friends were staring at him. He took a deep breath, and added, "And you two aren't talking to me anymore."

There was a very long, very pregnant silence after that.

"No," said George at last. "I don't suppose we were."

"Why not?" demanded Thomas.

There was another long silence. At last, George shrugged. "Don't know what to say."

"It's all changed," Eileen said, pushing her hair away from her face. "Everything changed."

Thomas sat silent, looking at his friends, waiting for more.

"We killed people," George said, at last. "*I* killed someone." He rubbed at his face, and when his hand came away, Thomas could see the glimmer of unshed tears in his eyes. "I never wanted to kill anyone, Thomas. I never even wanted to hurt anyone that bad. And Eileen got stabbed fighting these men and could have died and..." He shrugged again, the gesture helpless and angry. "We can't even see what we're fighting for."

Thomas looked out to the setting sun. The sky was beginning to change colour now; clouds glowed red and yellow, and the blue began to fade from the sky. His voice was quiet, when he said. "If you two hadn't come I'd be dead."

"You don't know—"

"I know," Thomas turned back to his friends, meeting each one's eyes in turn. "Those four may have been after Ailbe, but they would have taken me as well. And either I would have fought them and died, or they would have dragged me before the bishop and he would have destroyed me. By being here, you two saved my life." George and Eileen looked away from him, something akin to embarrassment in their faces. There was silence again, but not so deep, or so long as before.

"Aye, well," George met Thomas's eyes again, a smile starting to form on his lips. "Someone had to."

"I shouldn't have let you come," said Thomas, feeling as if a weight had been lifted from his chest. "But I'm glad I did."

"Like you could have stopped us," said Eileen, a smile coming to the corners of her mouth as well. She slapped her brother on the arm. "Especially this lummox."

"Me?" George turned on her. "You swore to me you'd run after us pelting us with rocks if I made you stay home."

"Aye, well, the more fool me." She turned back to Thomas. "And I don't see what you're smiling at. You still have to tell my parents."

Thomas closed his eyes and let himself fall back against the floor of the porch with a groan. "Your father will kill me."

"Don't forget Mother," said Eileen. "She'll want your ears, once she learns what's happened."

Thomas sighed. "Is there a bright side to going home?"

"Well, everyone will be able to see how nicely that cut on your face goes with your black eyes."

Thomas sighed again. "I should have stayed at the Academy."

"Probably," agreed George. He pulled himself to his feet and turned to his sister. "And we should probably get you inside to sleep," he held out his hand. "Come on."

Eileen shook her head. "I'll be fine out here with you."

"You will not." said George. "You should be inside by the fire."

Thomas got to his own feet. "He's probably right."

"He's probably wrong," said Eileen, "and he can just go inside and find out."

George opened his hands and raised them to the sky, as if beseeching the High Father for patience. "I can. And I'll be back in a moment to bring you in."

"Do that, then."

George snorted and shook his head, but went inside. Thomas smiled at

Eileen, who smiled back. A moment later, she blushed and looked away. Thomas felt immediately awkward. He thought about going inside himself, but didn't want to leave her alone. He sat down on the stair beside her instead.

Very quietly, he said, "I'm sorry."

She shook her head. "It wasn't your fault."

"It was." Eileen opened her mouth to speak but he stopped her. "You came here for me. It's my fault. And I'm sorry."

"I came here for myself." She half-smiled. Her voice turning mocking. "I wanted to have an adventure."

"Well, you got that," Thomas said, smiling back. "And a story to tell."

"Aye." Her smile faded, and she turned away from him, her eyes going to the sunset. After a time, she said. "I wish I knew how it was going to end."

Thomas nodded. "Me too."

Eileen leaned against him and rested her head against his shoulder. He stayed very still, afraid to disturb her. They sat in silence, watching the sunset together. After a little while, Eileen sighed. "I should go in. Before George comes out to get me."

Thomas, who didn't want to move for the world, forced himself to stand up. He held out his arms. Eileen wrapped the blanket over one arm, then raised her own hands. Thomas took them, steadying her while she rose to her feet. She winced as she stood, and Thomas put one arm around her waist to help her onto the porch from the step. She leaned into him to get up, then stayed there. Thomas stood a moment, awkwardly unsure of what to do next. Eileen started to shake a bit, and Thomas began to back off.

She caught his arm. "Don't," her voice was trembling. "Not yet."

She began to cry, leaning her head against his chest and twisting her hands into the fabric of his shirt. Thomas was frozen a moment, then folded his arms around her. She pulled herself closer, sobbing into his chest. It didn't last very long. He held her until the crying slowed, then loosened his hold and leaned back. She did the same, bringing one hand up to wipe her eyes.

"Are you all right?" Thomas asked.

"I'm fine," Eileen said. "It just... It felt good to be held and I just wanted to cry all of a sudden." She ducked her head, embarrassed. "I'm probably just tired."

"Probably."

"I don't usually cry."

"I believe you."

"Good." She wiped her eyes again then leaned against his chest once more. He wrapped his arms back around her, held her for a moment longer, then kissed her gently on the cheek. She didn't move for a moment, then turned her face upwards, close to his. Thomas could feel her breath against his lips, her body against his. There was a question in her eyes, but Thomas couldn't guess what it was, let alone begin to answer it. He nearly leaned closer, nearly kissed her. Instead, he stepped away. "We should get you in before George comes out."

"George is out," said George from the door, making them both turn to look. His face was neutral, and the taunt Thomas expected didn't come. Instead, George held out a hand to his sister. "Ailbe is waiting for you inside."

"All right," Eileen stayed where she was a moment, then took one of Thomas's hands and squeezed it. "Thank you."

She let go, and Thomas watched her walk inside the house. Something inside him felt much lighter than it had all day. He realized he was smiling just as George tossed a blanket at his head. Thomas caught it with his face. He unwrapped it from his head and started laying it out on the porch. George did the same. Both avoided the broken boards and the patch of blood from the night before. Neither said anything until Thomas pulled his sword free of the scabbard and lay it down beside him.

"You think you'll need that tonight?" asked George.

"I don't know," said Thomas. "Better safe than sorry."

"Aye," George smiled and raised his walking stick where Thomas could see it, then put it down beside his blankets. The two made themselves comfortable on the porch and watched the sun setting. It wasn't until the last of the sun's orb had disappeared behind the horizon that George said, "Thomas... about Eileen..."

"Yes?"

George fell silent, and Thomas waited, watching the last light of the day fading from the sky. At last, George said, "I mean, I know she's going to be kissing someone, but..."

George trailed off again, and Thomas filled in the obvious conclusion. "But you'd rather it wasn't me."

"Aye." George sounded embarrassed. "I mean, you're a good man, but look at the mess you're in. And there's no way she can be thinking straight right now. Not after all she's been through."

"I know." Thomas hugged the blanket closer, trying to use its warmth to fill the empty place that had just opened inside him. "That's why I didn't kiss her."

"Good," said George. "I mean, thanks."

George pulled the blanket over his body, and settled himself into the porch. A moment later he snorted quietly. When he spoke again, Thomas could hear the wry amusement in his voice. "Besides, there's no sense you two starting something now. Once we get back to Elmvale, it'll be years before my parents let you see her again."

"True." The empty place inside Thomas grew at that thought. He sighed and made himself as comfortable as possible with his sword hand free of the covers. "Good night, George."

"Good night, Thomas."

Thomas waited for sleep. It should have come quickly, to make up for the time lost the night before. Instead, memories of all that had happened warred in his head with imagined scenes of what was waiting for him at home. He laid awake deep into the night, staring at the woods and the sky and listening to the night sounds as his brain whirled. At last, with the setting of the moon, he drifted to sleep.

On the other side of consciousness, a man with a knife and a hole in his stomach was waiting. Thomas spent the whole of his dreams killing him over and over again.

Chapter 13

The next morning dawned clear and bright. George looked less haggard, as if his spirit had started healing as he slept. Eileen also looked better and moved a bit easier, though she winced on every second step. Thomas, blurry from lack of sleep and wearied further by the night's dreams, did his best not to be grumpy as they ate breakfast with Ailbe and Shamus. Afterward, he and George divided up their supplies and Ailbe's blankets and the contents of Eileen's bag into their own.

"The sheriff's coming," said Shamus, just as they were finishing. He pointed out the window, to where the sheriff, riding his horse, was emerging into the clearing. Shamus went to the door. "Morning."

"Morning, Shamus," said the sheriff. "Thought I'd tell you the bishop's gone."

"Gone?" Shamus repeated. "What about those with him?"

"Them, too" the sheriff said. "Save the dead man. Apparently, the bishop left enough coin to pay for the burial and his rooms and that was it."

"Did they say where they were going?" asked Thomas, leaning out the window.

"Nay, they did not," the sheriff frowned at Thomas. "Though back to the city would be my guess. And what about you?"

"We're just packing," said Thomas. "Then we'll be on our way."

"Good. Good day to you, Shamus. I'll stop by around lunch."

"Until then," Shamus stayed in the door until the sheriff rode off into the woods, then stepped back inside. "Well, the bishop's gone, anyway." He shook his head slowly. "Doesn't solve much, though."

"No," agreed Thomas. "I don't suppose it does."

"At least the ones who got Timothy are dead," Shamus looked at Ailbe. "That's something."

"Not much," said Ailbe, grief and pain lacing the words. "Are you three packed?"

"Aye." Thomas saw the sorrow in her face and wished he could help ease it. "I'm sorry about the trouble we brought you. And about Timothy."

"I'll see you in a few days," said Ailbe, not answering his words. "Just mind you tell the Reeve I'll be coming for him."

"We will." Thomas picked up his bag and watched as George picked up his own and Eileen's. George and Eileen said good-bye and George led the way out the door, Eileen following right behind him. Thomas wished he could find something better to say, but only managed, "Goodbye," before he turned and followed his friends.

Their progress down the path to Elmvale was slow. Obstacles that had been easily surmounted on the way to Lakewood were now serious challenges. On one particularly rough and steep section of the path, George picked Eileen up in his arms and carried her. Once near the top, though, she insisted on being put down.

"I'm not a complete invalid, you know," she said. "Ailbe said I should be completely healed in a week or so."

"Good," George put her lightly down on the grass. "Injury hasn't made you any lighter, you know."

"Listen to you complain," Eileen turned to Thomas. "He once carried Maggie Stewart on his back for an entire day, just to prove he could."

"Is that true?" Thomas asked.

"It was a bet," said George. "And I won it."

"What were the stakes?"

George glanced over at his sister, and coloured slightly. Thomas, guessing at what George had won, didn't pursue the question any further.

Eileen just rolled her eyes. "Boys."

"You brought it up," George protested. "I was just filling in the tale."

"And did anyone say it needed filling?"

"Well, if you hadn't started it, I wouldn't have finished it."

"Oh, aye, I'm sure."

"Can we argue while we walk?" Thomas asked.

"Aye, surely," George started going again, but Eileen waved a hand to stop them, and set herself down on a nearby rock.

"I think maybe a rest is in order."

"A rest?" George looked pained. "After only an hour? Are you all right?"

"I'm fine."

"Let me check the stitches."

"It's all right, George!" she snapped. "I'm just tired. Ailbe said I would be. I'll be fine in a bit."

"How far do you think we've come?" Thomas asked, looking around in the woods. With only the trail as a guide, and trees obscuring the view, it was difficult to tell where in the country they were, let alone their relation to home.

"About half as far as we would if Eileen wasn't hurt," said George. "We should make that clearing by late this afternoon."

"Why don't we stop there for the night?" said Eileen. "Easy to set up a campfire, and there's a good view. It would be a grand place to wake up."

"It would be," George agreed, "if we can *reach* it by night."

"We will," Eileen pushed herself to her feet with a groan. "Come on."

The rest of the day went much the same way. Eileen stopped often enough to leave Thomas and George chafing with impatience, but didn't seem any the worse for wear. With Lakewood behind them and the bishop no longer an immediate threat, Thomas could and did spend the day worrying about what John Flarety had planned for him. George kept plodding steadily on, his eyes on his sister. Occasional bits of banter broke out between them, but for the most part they walked in silence. Their lunch—yesterday's fish and water—went down quickly, though they rested a while for Eileen before heading down the trail again. The sun was starting to set as they reached the clearing on the top of the hill. George led them to a spot with trees on three sides to shelter them from the wind.

"I'll dig us a pit for the fire," he said to Thomas, "if you can find some wood."

"I'll try," said Thomas.

"And what am I supposed to do?" Eileen asked. "Sit here like a lump?"

"Aye, that's what I was thinking," replied George.

"Good." Eileen put her back to one of the trees and slid down to sitting. Resting her head back against the tree and putting her hands in her lap, she said, "Call me when we're ready."

They made their camp and sat with their backs to the trees and their fronts to the fire, dining on a late supper of cheese, bread, and a flask of wine that Shamus had put into their packs. When the last of the food was gone they sat in silence. Thomas looked out at the hills, watching the light from the setting sun turn the sky into a blaze of red and orange. The few clouds caught the light, changing colours as the sun sank lower.

"That," said Thomas, "has to be the best part of the last week."

"Aye," Eileen's voice was quiet. "It's beautiful."

"Bet you don't see any like that in the city," said George.

"Not many," agreed Thomas. "The closest you get to a view like this is sitting on a rooftop, which is actively discouraged."

"How come?" asked Eileen with a yawn.

"People fall off."

"Oh."

"We still do it, though. Our apartment's nearly high enough to give a view of the entire city. Some nights, when the sun is setting, you can almost believe that it's a beautiful place."

"Isn't it?" asked George. "You said it was, before."

"It has its moments," said Thomas, "but not like this." Thomas waved a hand out, taking in the valley below, the fields and trees coated in gold from the last of the sunlight and the sky above slowly deepening into the dark blue that comes just before night falls. "Not at all like this."

The three fell silent, watching the sky change colours until the sun was below the horizon and the stars had come out from hiding. George fed a couple of more logs onto the fire then turned to his sister. "You should get some—" he began, then stopped. Gently, he reached down and tucked Eileen's blankets around her.

Thomas watched as George made himself comfortable next, wrapping himself in his blankets and promptly falling asleep. Thomas wished he could do the same. All it would take, he was sure, was for his mind to stop running long enough for him to drop off. He had hoped the wine would help.

Thomas sat, watching the stars chart their slow course through the heavens until the last of the flames burnt down to embers, then lay there in darkness until exhaustion finally claimed its toll. The thoughts that had kept sleep at bay for most of the night stayed with him and ran him ragged in his dreams.

* * *

Eileen fared much better the second day, stopping to rest less often and making better time. She was still in pain, though, and any sudden movement would make her hiss through her teeth. Every time she did, Thomas and George were right beside her, asking what was wrong. After the fourth time, she glared at them and snapped, "What do you think?" Still, she managed to keep moving, and by afternoon the three had pushed away the last of the branches that overgrew the path and stepped onto the road that led to the smithy.

Thomas had no desire to face Lionel and Magda. He had even suggested staying at the inn, rather than coming home with them. The other two had refused to hear of it.

"Better to face them now," Eileen said. "Get it over with."

"Besides," George added, "if Father's mad enough, he'll track you down wherever you go."

"Wonderful," Thomas remembered the man's reaction at Fire Night. They rounded the last bend and saw the smithy and house. "You're home."

Eileen's face lit up, and as soon as the three were close enough to be heard, Eileen started calling for her mother. A moment later, Thomas could hear Magda from inside, calling back and shouting to Lionel. By the time the three friends reached the door both parents were coming around the corner of the house, one black with soot from the forge, the other wiping dough off her fingers. The expected cheerful welcome was not forthcoming, however.

"Thomas!" Magda stopped dead in her tracks, shared one horrified look with her husband then snapped. "Into the house! Quick!"

Thomas started to protest, but Lionel grabbed him and shoved him inside. Magda did the same with George and Eileen, making the one protest and the other cry out in pain.

"Are you daft, lad?" Lionel demanded, once he had Thomas inside. "You should have kept going, not come back here!"

"What's wrong with you?" Magda demanded as she pushed Eileen in through the door. "What happened?"

"Your father has a price on your head," said Lionel. "He's demanding you appear in front of the magistrate."

"I know," Thomas's eyes were on Eileen. George had her by the arm and was leading her to the chairs around the kitchen table.

"You know?" Lionel was stunned. "Then what the devil did you come back for?"

"I'm not running from him."

"I'm fine," Eileen told George. "It just hurts."

"He'll have you heaved into the gaol, you young idiot!" Lionel was nearly yelling now. "Of course you're going to run from him!"

"I won't!" Thomas dropped his bag and went to Eileen. "I can't."

"By the Four, why not?!" Lionel looked closer. "And what happened to your face?"

"He promised Sheriff Pherson he wouldn't," said George as he helped Eileen to sit at the kitchen table.

"The sheriff?" confusion was in Lionel's voice now. "When did you see the sheriff? And what's wrong with Eileen?"

"That's what I want to know," Magda's words were hard and clipped and brought silence to the room. "Eileen, what happened?"

Eileen hesitated a moment. "I got hurt."

"Hurt? How?"

Eileen's eyes went to Thomas. Magda and Lionel followed her gaze.

"Thomas," Lionel's voice was quiet in a way that felt far more dangerous than his shouting at Fire Night. "What happened?"

Thomas took a deep breath. "We were attacked—"

"In the woods?" demanded Magda. She turned on her husband. "I told you we shouldn't have let them—"

"In Lakewood," said George, softly. "We were in Lakewood."

Magda looked at her son again, then at her daughter. Neither met her eyes. She turned back to Thomas. "What happened?"

Thomas found he had trouble speaking. He did his best to keep the words clear. "The men who killed Timothy tried to get his sister while we were there. There was a fight."

"And?" Magda demanded.

"We killed them."

Magda's hand went to her mouth, her skin pale. A moment later, Lionel stepped over to his wife and put an arm around her. He was as pale as she.

"Tell it all, lad," said Lionel, leading Magda to one of the benches and making her sit. "From the start."

Thomas did as he was told, trying to tell the entire story as it happened. The tale came to a dead halt as soon as he told them about Eileen's cut. Magda insisted on seeing it at once. Eileen showed her the bandage then opened it to show the stitches. Lionel growled under his breath when he saw it, and started glaring at Thomas and George. "You two were supposed to take care of her."

"They tried," Eileen protested. "It would have been worse if they hadn't."

"Would it?" demanded Magda. "How?"

Eileen said nothing, just looked at her mother until Magda's eyes went wide, and she put a hand on Lionel's arm, steadying herself though she was sitting down. Lionel's face turned dark red. Eileen looked back and forth between her parents. "It didn't happen."

"It could have," said Magda, voice tight. Thomas could see tears in her eyes, though none fell.

"What happened next?" asked Lionel.

Thomas told them the rest, from the man's escape to his subsequent death in the inn. Lionel and Magda listened in grim, angry silence. When he was finished, Magda stood up, and told Eileen to get to bed.

"We haven't had supper yet," Eileen protested.

"I'll bring it in," Magda's tone brooked no argument. "You need to rest."

Eileen went without protest. Magda walked with her. Lionel watched them go then turned back to George and Thomas. "Someone should tell Bluster you're back," Lionel said to George. "Go. Dinner will be ready when you get back."

"But I—"

"If Thomas goes, Bluster might keep him." Lionel said, stopping George's argument. "You go and tell him Thomas is here and staying put."

George's expression suggested that more walking was the last thing he wanted, but he went anyway. Thomas stayed where he was at the table, watching Lionel. The big man looked down at his hands for a time, then back at Thomas. "You sure all three are dead?"

"Aye."

Lionel's expression didn't change. "Good."

"She's in bed," Magda said, coming back into the kitchen. "Where's George?"

"Gone to talk to Bluster."

Magda nodded. Her lips were pressed tight together, the flesh white from the pressure. She turned to Thomas, stared at him. Her eyes were blazing.

"Love—" Lionel began, reaching a hand out to her. She shoved it off without taking her eyes off Thomas.

"What did you think you were doing out there?" Magda's voice was hoarse with anger. "She could have died!"

"I know," said Thomas.

"You should have helped her!"

"I told her to run," Thomas felt sick at the memory of the moment. "She wouldn't listen."

"She shouldn't have gone at all!"

"No," said Lionel, his voice quiet. "She shouldn't."

"She'll have a scar for life!"

Lionel reached out and caught her wrist. "Love—"

"What?!"

"It's not the lad's fault."

Thomas was stunned. He had fully expected both of them to blow up, throw him from the house, and possibly skin him alive. Magda, her eyes still blazing with anger, looked ready to do just that. Lionel, for a change, didn't.

Magda pulled at his grip. "What do you mean, it's not—"

"It's mine."

Magda tried again to pull her hand free. Lionel held it anyway. "I let her go," he said gently. "It's my fault she was hurt. Not Thomas's."

"He didn't have to take her!"

"She wanted to go," Lionel's voice was quiet, soothing. "So did her brother."

"He could have said no!"

"He did," Lionel said. "And it worked about as well as you would expect."

Magda was silent, eyes locked on her husband. He stared back. After a long silence the tears that had been sitting in her eyes began to roll down her face. "That stupid girl!"

Lionel nodded, still holding his wife's hand. "Aye."

Magda didn't cry long. She scrubbed at her face with her sleeve, driving the tears away. Thomas could still see the anger, smouldering behind her eyes. It wasn't all for him, though.

"I need to get dinner going," Magda went to the cupboard and started pulling out potatoes. She stopped a moment later and turned back to Thomas. "Lionel's right. It's our fault she went, not yours." He took a deep breath, and the smouldering anger in her eyes blazed bright. "But I'm still furious at the lot of you! How could you be so stupid! You could have been killed! All of you!"

Thomas, glad he was no longer the sole target of her anger, forbore saying that it hadn't been their idea to fight. Magda turned back to the cupboard and started attacking the potatoes with a knife.

"The Healer said she'll be all right?" asked Lionel.

"Aye," said Thomas. "She said the stitches could come out in a week or so."

"Good." The big man sighed and leaned back in his chair. "You're a packet of trouble, you are."

"I'm sorry, Lionel—"

"All three of you," Lionel added. He sighed again. "But at least you're alive."

"Aye."

"The ones you fought, are you sure they're the same ones that killed the juggler?"

"Aye."

"Well, then, that's laid to rest, at least."

Not even close, Thomas thought. He changed the subject. "Is the magistrate really coming tomorrow?"

"Aye."

"Your father wanted him here as quickly as possible," Magda said.

"He's practically saying you took the family silver," Lionel shook his head. "I swear I don't know what's gotten into the man."

Thomas, who knew exactly what had gotten into his father, said nothing. He took off his sword and put it in the loft, along with his and George's bags. When he came back down, Lionel was setting the table. Thomas helped, and the two of them kept busy and out of Magda's way until she demanded they help with the preparations.

By the time George came back Magda had a stew on, which she ladled out generously to all of them. Thomas half-expected Bluster to come with him, ready to clap Thomas in irons. George came in alone, though, and fell to his dinner like a starving bear. Eileen got hers in bed, despite protests that she was more than well enough to sit at table with the rest of them.

"I don't care if you've walked five miles," was her mother's reply. "You shouldn't have done that, and you'll not be up any longer today."

"But, Mother—"

"No arguments," Magda said. "You should be thankful you're here at all, after a cut like that."

Thomas picked at his dinner. He'd spent the last hour helping prepare it, all the while thinking on what he could say to the magistrate. Neither task had given him an appetite. Thomas waited until George's plate was empty, then traded it for his own.

"Not eating?" George asked.

"Not really hungry," Thomas sighed. "Too much thinking."

Lionel watched George dig into Thomas's dinner and shook his head. "About tomorrow, I take it?"

"Aye."

"Any ideas?"

"Well," Thomas put his thoughts in order. "I need to make the magistrate believe that my father's been proud of me until this week. If I can do that, it will be up to my father to prove I've been a drunk and a thief for the last four years. Otherwise, it will be up to me to prove that I haven't."

"Makes sense, I guess," Lionel sounded dubious.

"I've got his last letter with me," Thomas said. "In my bag. There's enough in it to show he wasn't thinking this way when he asked me to come home."

"You could tell the magistrate how your father talks at the inn," George suggested. "There's two dozen that hear him do it every time a letter comes in from you."

"I've never heard him," said Thomas. "I'd need to get those who have to say so."

"Humph," Lionel sat back in his chair, chewing on his lower lip. "Well, we might manage something. Come on, George."

"Where?"

"The inn. I want to see who remembers John bragging about his son the scholar." Lionel smiled at George, "Unless you're too tired."

"Not for that trip," George said, getting to his feet.

"See you in a bit," Lionel gave Magda a kiss on the cheek.

"Don't stay too late," warned Magda. "And don't forget what you went for, either."

Lionel just smiled and stepped out the door.

Chapter 14

Thomas startled Lionel and Magda by rising with the sun the next morning. Worry had made sleep elusive and the dark dreams that came with it made the night less than restful. Bleary-eyed and foggy, he stumbled to the well and doused himself with a bucketful. The shock of the cold water drove off the fog, leaving his mind clear and his body shivering.

"You know, we can heat water before you put your face under it," said Lionel, stepping out of the forge. "Or is it a scholarly tradition?"

"Usually only after a night of drinking," Thomas shook his head then combed his fingers through his hair to get the water out. "Hot water for shaving would be appreciated, though."

"Shaving?" Lionel's eyebrow went up. "You? You have your father's skin, and he can't grow a beard to save his life."

"Aye, but after a few days, we both begin to look a bit fuzzy."

"Well, we can't have that," Lionel turned to the forge, picked up a bucket and tossed it to Thomas. "Here, fill this up, then put on your best. There's a fair number of people waiting to testify for you."

Thomas, about to drop the well bucket back in the water, stopped in surprise. "There are?"

Lionel smiled. "It was a full night at the inn, lad. Now hurry up and scrape your fuzz. You've got a big day ahead."

That, Thomas thought, *is an understatement.*

He shaved, washed himself, and put on the suit his father had bought. Magda had brushed it and hung it up, and washed the shirt while he'd been gone. He wished he had some other finery to wear, but knew that nothing he owned was as nice. Besides, it underscored his father's pride in his son, if the tailor's tale was to be believed. The sword, Thomas left behind. If John Flarety saw it, he'd claim it as proof Thomas had fallen into bad company.

John Flarety had been in courts a half-dozen times over matters of trade. As Thomas recalled, his father had won all of the cases, and not because he had magic. Thomas had attended one case just before he left for the Academy, and had been amazed at how well his father came prepared. Every scrap of information, every bit of evidence had been properly marshalled and served John Flarety well. In fact, it had been that day in court that had made Thomas think of being a lawyer in the first place.

Thomas sighed and pulled on his boots. He had no doubts that his father was going to show up just as well prepared this time, and no good would come of giving him any extra points to quibble at. Thomas finished dressing, smoothed down the suit, and headed outside.

"About time," said Eileen as he stepped out the door. "We'd thought you'd gone back to bed."

Eileen was wearing a green skirt and bodice, with a white shirt that shone in the morning sun. Magda was beside her, her own dress two shades deeper than the one her daughter was wearing. Lionel and George were wearing grey breeches and jackets with white shirts. They looked like twin mountains. It was the finest Thomas had ever seen them dressed, and the fact that it was for him brought a lump to his throat.

"If appearances were all that mattered," Thomas said, "I'd be declared the most respectable man alive."

The entire family managed to look both pleased and slightly embarrassed at once. "Flatterer," said Eileen, smiling.

"He certainly is," agreed Magda.

"Aye, I am." Thomas felt a lump in his throat. "Thank you. For everything."

Magda patted his un-cut cheek. "You're family," she said. "Family help each other."

Thomas nodded. "Let's hope mine think so." A sudden thought came to him. "How are the black eyes today?"

Eileen grasped his chin in her hand and turned his head side to side. "Not black any more," she said thoughtfully. "More of a purple, with yellow highlights. And the cut sets them off nicely."

"Wonderful."

"How's the rest of you?"

"Not bad." He looked down at her stomach, well hidden beneath shirt and bodice. "You?"

"Getting dressed was no fun," said Eileen, "and neither is taking a deep breath, so don't go making me laugh."

"You won't have to worry about that too much today," Thomas straightened his coat once again, and squared up his shoulders. "Come on. The sooner we're there, the sooner this will be over with."

They walked through the village and up the road to the old watchtower. Folks were already milling about outside, and more were already inside, waiting for the trial to begin. Heads turned to watch Thomas as he approached and voices immediately hushed themselves until he went past, then rose once more.

Thomas sincerely wished that the matter could be dealt with in private, but all trials were public and for a village the size of Elmvale this was going to be the event of the month. Thomas did his best to ignore the crowd and led his friends inside.

The inside of the tower was still dark, the arrow slits letting in hardly enough light to see by. There were lamps hanging on the walls, though they had not yet been lit. Bluster had erected a short stage to put his desk on—the magistrate's podium, Thomas guessed—against the far wall, and put two tables beside each other on the floor five feet in front of it. He'd also brought in enough benches to fill the rest of the room

John Flarety wasn't there. Thomas wasn't surprised. His father had always said that the key to winning in court was not who got there first, but who arrived the best prepared. Thomas, feeling utterly inadequate, made his way to the front. Bluster was standing in front of the platform.

"You've come back, then," was the little man's greeting.

Thomas managed something similar to a smile. "Well, I didn't want to miss my day in court."

"Humph," was Bluster's reply. "After you left for Lakewood I wasn't certain."

"Did George tell you all of it?"

"I think so. Said this Ailbe would come to pick up the juggler's body."

"Aye. A couple of days, she said."

"Good. I told the nuns. Good work on the bandits, too. Their type are better off dead."

Thomas didn't answer that. Instead, he asked, "Where do you want me to sit?"

"The table on the right." Bluster led him over and pulled the bench out for him. He looked at the smith and his family. "They're supporting you, I take it."

"Aye."

"Good."

Thomas looked to Bluster in surprise. The little man smiled slightly. "It's good that you have friends, lad. And good that you decided to come back. When you left town your father was certain that you'd never return."

"Why stop disappointing him now?" The words slipped out of Thomas's mouth almost of their own accord. He clamped his mouth shut. The bitterness that came with the words wasn't a surprise, but it wouldn't do to have it come out in court. He could practically hear the Master of Laws saying that emotional control was as powerful a tool as proper evidence when one stood before a magistrate.

Bluster shook his head but didn't say anything. He showed Lionel and the family where to sit, then turned back to the door. His expression grew harder, and Thomas guessed who had come in. He started to turn, then stopped himself, unsure if he'd be able to keep his composure. Instead, he sat down on his bench and kept his eyes glued to the front while his father came in and sat down.

Thomas heard the rest of the crowd coming in behind his father, and guessed the Magistrate was on his way. Bluster moved away to light the lamps. Voices and the sound of boots against the worn stone floor of the tower filled the air. Thomas took the time to regain some composure, and to plan out his strategy.

A soft hand touched his shoulder. Thomas turned, expecting Magda or Eileen.

Madeleine Flarety was taking a place on the bench behind him. She was wearing a deep blue dress—the colour she always wore when she needed to appear her most impressive—and carrying a small blue bag. Her hair was done high with a silver chain woven in and out of the coils. She smiled at her son, her hand squeezing his shoulder gently. There was a tightness around her mouth, though, and dark circles around her eyes. She was flanked by Sister Clare and Sister Brigit.

"You didn't think we'd make you face him alone, did you?" asked Neal, coming in to sit beside Sister Brigit. He was also dressed in his best, and the look he gave his father was not at all happy.

"I didn't think you had a choice," Thomas said. He risked a glance at his father, hoping to see some sign of expression. John Flarety was looking down at his notes, though, and ignoring his family. Thomas turned back to Neal. "I thought he'd order you to stay at home."

"He ordered your brother to stay at home." Madeleine's voice was cold and hard. "I haven't been there since you left."

"That's why Father wouldn't let us see her," said Neal. "She packed a bag and moved to the nunnery before Fire Night was over."

"He hit me," said Madeleine. Thomas, who had heard the sounds of the blows when he was lying in the yard, still felt his stomach knot at the words. His mother's eyes were on her husband. Though he was only eight feet away and could no doubt hear them clearly, John Flarety did not turn around or acknowledge his family. Madeleine shook her head. "I told him years before we were married I'd never tolerate a man who did that."

"He'll never do it again," Neal said, his voice tight and angry. "I'll see to that."

"No, *I* will see to that," Madeleine's tone left no room for contradiction. She turned back to Thomas. "Did you know that he still hasn't apologized to me?"

"No," said Thomas. "I've been—"

"Well, until he does, he can sleep there alone." She took a deep breath, shook out her skirt and straightened her back. "Now, what are the charges he has against you?"

"I don't know, exactly," said Thomas. "Theft, I think. Wasting his money."

"Well, we'll see," Madeleine took another deep breath then turned to Magda and Lionel. "I'm sorry that I haven't had the chance to thank you for taking care of my son."

"Let there be silence!" called Bluster from the door, instantly stilling the room. "All present rise and pay respect to Magistrate Cauwood."

The magistrate stepped into the tower. He was a man well advanced in his years, though his posture was perfectly erect and he looked very impressive in his black robe and gold chain of office. His hair was white and thin, set over a deeply lined face. He walked to the stage slowly, taking the time to look over the faces of all those in the courtroom, then mounted the platform at the same speed. He sat in his chair, straightened his robes, then nodded to Bluster.

"Be seated," said Bluster, and there was a brief stir of activity as the crowd sank back onto the benches and then silence as the crowd settled down with a hush of anticipation. The magistrate leaned forward and surveyed the room once more.

"I am Jonathan Cauwood," he announced, beginning the ritual words that marked the beginning of the trial, "appointed by his Majesty the King to act in his stead in matters of law. In his name, and by the grace of the High Father, who has called me here?"

John Flarety rose from his seat. "I did, your Honour."

The judge took a long, slow measure of John Flarety, then nodded. "Why have you called me here?"

"To lay complaint against my son."

"For what charge?"

"I charge him with the misuse of funds given to him for his education."

The judge turned his head, and took the same long measure of Thomas. "You are his son, I take it?"

"Yes, your Honour."

"And you are prepared to answer this charge?"

"Yes, your Honour."

Magistrate Cauwood nodded and sat back in his chair. "Then let us begin. The plaintiff may make his case first."

John Flarety did, and in fine style. He spoke at length of his expectations for his youngest son, how the family's money had been invested in his education, how that money had been turned aside and how the boy had turned to drinking and carousing and taking part in fencing matches, rather than paying attention to his studies. Thomas listened carefully, keeping his face blank as he listened for holes in his father's argument. The more John Flarety spoke, the more Thomas's stomach twisted. He longed to shout *liar*; to grab his father's shoulders and shake them until the man came to his senses.

If he thought it would have made the slightest difference, Thomas would have tried it. Instead, he stayed silent.

John Flarety brought his speech to a close, declaring his deep love for his younger son, and how that love had motivated him to tell the boy to enter the priesthood and mend his ways.

"And I take it that this idea does not appeal to you, young sir?" the magistrate interrupted.

"No, your Honour."

"Hmph." He waved a hand at John Flarety. "Continue."

"There is not much more to say, your Honour," said John Flarety. "Thomas has refused every reasonable request made of him. He has disobeyed my orders and flaunted—"

"Murderer!"

The word was a scream that echoed off the bare walls of the tower, and made everyone jump in their seats before whirling around. Thomas recognized the voice even as it was raised again.

"Murderer!"

Ailbe was standing beneath the heavy stone archway that held the tower's door. Her face was ashen; her clothes looked as if they had caught on every bramble on the path between Lakewood and Elmvale. There were scratches on her face and legs and her feet were bare and bloody. Even the arm she held out, extended finger pointing at Thomas, was covered in scratches. Thomas watched in horror as she stumbled forward, leaving bloody footprints behind her. "Murderer!" she screamed again. "Murderer, murderer, murderer!"

Sister Brigit and Sister Claire were on their feet in an instant, and began pushing their way past Neal and Madeleine Flarety. Bluster got to Ailbe first, blocking her way as she stumbled towards Thomas. "Who's a murderer?"

"Thomas!" Ailbe tried to push past Bluster. He held her in place and she jabbed with her extended arm, the finger like a dagger aimed at Thomas. "He murdered the bishop's men and he murdered Shamus!"

A gasp rippled through the room and heads swivelled towards Thomas. George leapt to his feet. "The bishop's men attacked us!" he shouted, fear and confusion rising in his voice. "You were there! You told the sheriff yourself!"

The heads swivelled to George, then back to Ailbe, who was still trying to push past Bluster. Voices raised louder, and a half-dozen people leapt to their feet to try and help Ailbe. Magistrate Cauwood called repeatedly for order. The nuns closed in on her on either side, trying to take her arms. She shook them off, screaming, "Murderer!" over and over.

Thomas had also come to his feet, but was rooted in his place. The full impact of what was happening hadn't hit George or Eileen yet, but it struck Thomas with the weight of a charging horse and left him stunned and immobile.

Shamus was dead.

Shamus had been murdered.

And now Ailbe was here, in torn and tattered clothing, to accuse him of the crime.

Not her, too. Despair nearly overwhelmed Thomas. *Please, not her.*

As if his thought was a spur, Ailbe threw herself past Bluster and the nuns in her way and grabbed both of Thomas's shoulders, shaking him. This close, Thomas could see her eyes were unfocused, almost glazed over.

"Murderer!" she screamed, her voice shrill and ragged. "You killed the bishop's men! You killed Shamus! You killed them all!"

Thomas grabbed her hands to stop the shaking. "Who says?" he demanded. "Who told you to say that?"

She stopped, wavering where she stood, her mouth open.

"Who told you, Ailbe?" Thomas asked again, forcing his voice to be gentle. "Who told you to say I was a murderer?"

"The... I don't..." Clarity flared for a moment in her eyes, then died. Her voice rose to a scream again. "You killed the bishop's men! You killed Shamus!"

Bluster grabbed her from behind and pulled her back, tearing her from Thomas's grip and pulling her away. Thomas followed them, trying to keep eye contact with Ailbe. "Did he take it?" Thomas asked, pushing past Sister Brigit. "Ailbe, did he come back and take it?"

Ailbe, struggling with Bluster, didn't hear him. The crowd was starting to get up, blocking Thomas's way. Bluster, pulling Ailbe towards the door, found his way blocked by a dozen well-meaning but unhelpful people. Thomas shoved several of the crowd aside, earning harsh words of protest. Raising his voice as loud as he could, Thomas shouted, "Ailbe!"

His bellow brought her and everyone else to a sudden stop. Thomas managed to reach out and grab Ailbe, pulling her out of Bluster's grip and towards him. Thomas wrapped his arms around her, put his mouth to her ear. "The magic, Ailbe. The gift. Do you still have it?"

He leaned back, searching her face for an answer. The clarity he'd seen in Ailbe's eyes before came through again, much stronger. She looked down at her bloodied, bruised body, then back to him. When her voice came, it seemed to be from some deep, desperately frightened place inside her. "No."

Bluster shoved him away and started pulling Ailbe outside again. Thomas watched them go, then sank to one of the now-empty benches, put his head between his hands, and cried.

* * *

It was some time before things calmed down enough for the magistrate to order Thomas back to his place. Bluster, once he and the nuns had taken Ailbe outside, had come back and cleared the room of spectators at the magistrate's request. The crowd went willingly, sensing that the more interesting affair was happening outside. George and Eileen had stayed, and both looked pale and unhappy. Thomas could see Eileen shaking, and George clenching and unclenching his hands, as if he could crush the accusations against them. Beside then, Lionel and Magda sat mute, hands clasped and looking at their children. Madeleine and Neal were still there as well, their eyes on Thomas and a question that Thomas could read only too clearly in their faces.

"It wasn't me," Thomas said to his mother and brother as he rose from the bench and made his way back to the front of the court. He sat down at the table, thinking how weak the words sounded, and looked to his father.

John Flarety had not left his place the entire time, and the disdainful look he had been wearing whenever he looked at his son was replaced with horror and disgust. Thomas had no doubt his father believed Ailbe, and no doubt that John Flarety would use what happened against him. Feeling weary beyond measure, Thomas took his seat and waited for the trial to start again.

"Well," Magistrate Cauwood straightened his robe and looked down at Thomas and his father. He took a long moment to contemplate the pair of them, then shifted his gaze over to John Flarety. "Given the nature of the accusations just made, I think it best to leave this matter alone until the other is resolved."

"With respect, your Honour," John Flarety said, rising. "I would rather say that these accusations are only more symptoms of the same problem, and that it is best to resolve this matter at once, rather than give Thomas the time to engage in activities that will bring him into greater trouble."

Anger surged inside Thomas. He clamped down on it, reminding himself that John Flarety's actions were as much the bishop's fault as Ailbe's were, and that losing his temper would do nothing for him in the eyes of the magistrate. *Even so, a little sympathy would be nice.*

Magistrate Cauwood frowned at John Flarety. "I think that this other matter, being a hanging offence, might be rather more urgent to the young man."

Just a little. The shock of the last few moments and the lack of real sleep for the past three days suddenly threatened to overwhelm Thomas. His legs felt weak, and his hands were starting to shake. Too much was hanging over his head, he realized. He wanted *something* to be resolved. Thomas rose to his feet. "Let's finish this, if we can, your Honour."

The magistrate's eyebrows went up, then down, and he frowned at Thomas for a time. At length, though, he shrugged his shoulders, straightened his robe, and said, "Very well, your father has given his argument. Do you have a reply?"

Thomas nodded, and began to speak, keeping his voice cool and measured. "Your Honour, my father's disapproval of my education and my behaviour while at the Academy only began a week ago at most. Previous to that, he was fully supportive. I have his last letter in my possession, which will show this, and the testimony of many members of the town who can confirm what I have said." He glanced back at the nearly-empty courtroom. "If they can be recalled."

"I don't need to be recalled," Madeleine said. Thomas and his father both turned towards her as she rose, her head high. "Nor does my son, Neal. Both of us will testify that what he says is true."

"As will I," said Lionel, also coming to his feet. "The man's been giving nothing but praise of the lad until three or four days ago. Since then, he's done nothing but complain."

John Flarety dismissed Lionel with a quick, angry wave of his hand. "This man is no friend to me. Why only last week he tried to cheat me on the price of iron rods for my carts!"

"I did not try to cheat you!" snapped Lionel. "You offered less than they were worth!"

"I offered far more than they were—"

"Gentlemen!" Magistrate Cauwood's voice cut the argument short. "I'm afraid the plaintiff's point is made. And I am equally afraid that it is impossible for the court to allow a family to testify against each other without collaboration."

"I am not testifying for, or against, my husband," Madeleine said. "I am testifying on behalf of my son."

"It cannot be allowed, since your husband is the accuser."

"Then hear this." She reached into her bag, and pulled out a pouch that, by the way she hefted it, was rather heavy for its small size. "I hold here gold of my own, given to me by my father at my wedding. John Flarety has no claim on it, and I swear now that I will use this money to pay whatever amount will be owing to my husband, should the decision be against my son."

"Mother," Thomas protested. "You can't—"

"What better use do I have for my dowry?" Madeleine demanded. She turned to her husband. "And I say this to you, John Flarety. If you continue with this stupidity, then this money shall be the last thing that you receive from me and this trial the last time that you shall see me. I will go to the convent and I will take vows, rather than return into your house."

John's mouth was open, shock clear on his features. He stuttered once, then again before finding his voice. "The lad needs to go to the bishop," he snapped. "He is a danger to himself and others and needs to be controlled."

"He does *not!*" Madeleine's voice, though no louder, carried a weight that made John Flarety fall silent. "You will drop this matter and you will apologize to your son, or I will *never* forgive you and I will never speak to you again!"

Thomas realized he was holding his breath, but couldn't find the will to release it.

Magistrate Cauwood cleared his throat. "I think," he said, looking down his nose at John, "that you would be wise to consider your options, Master Flarety. I will reserve this case over until tomorrow morning. At that time, you may tell me if you intend to drop this matter or pursue it." The expression on the magistrate's face said plainly that he thought that the former was the reasonable course of action. He turned to Thomas. "If your father wishes to pursue the matter, you may present your witnesses at that time. Is this acceptable to both parties?"

Thomas nodded. "It is," he said.

John Flarety nodded once, hard and sharp. "It is, your Honour."

"Good." Magistrate Cauwood rose from his place. The smith's family were the only ones still sitting, and they came at once to their feet as the man made his slow way down from the platform. When he reached the ground, he turned to Thomas. "As for the other matter—"

"I am innocent, your—"

The magistrate raised a hand and Thomas fell immediately silent. "Be that as it may, you must still answer the charges made. Do not leave this room until the Reeve has arrived, or I will have you declared a fugitive. Do you understand?"

"Yes, your Honour."

"Good. This court is adjourned for now."

They all watched Magistrate Cauwood make his slow way across the tower and out the door. As soon as he was gone, Madeleine turned to her husband, but John Flarety was already on his way out, saying nothing. Anger and horror still twisted his features, but now there was fear there as well. John Flarety was clearly a man torn. He met no one's eyes as he walked across the room, and stepped out the door without a word.

Thomas sat down behind his table and put his head back into his hands. The tears wouldn't come again, but the darkness behind his eyes was a safe haven; a place to hide, if only for a moment.

A gentle hand landed on his shoulder, making him look up. Eileen stood beside him, trying to look brave and not succeeding. Behind her, Neal and his mother were talking in low tones to Lionel and Magda.

"This is ridiculous," said George, leaning forward from his place behind Thomas. "What could Ailbe be doing?"

"It's not Ailbe," said Thomas.

George was taken aback. He stared out the door as if he expected her to reappear. When she didn't, he turned back to Thomas. "It looks like her."

"That's not what I meant," Thomas turned around on the bench and faced his friends, dropping his voice as he did. "Remember how I said the bishop was controlling my father?"

"Aye."

"Well, that's what it's like."

"It's awful," Eileen breathed, coming closer. Her expression lightened suddenly. "Do you think that means that Shamus is still alive?"

Thomas shook his head. "Not likely. If he was, he'd be with her."

Eileen's face fell, and she looked at the floor, biting her lip.

"I'm surprised the sheriff isn't with her," said George, "if she's going around saying you killed Shamus."

"Do you think he's dead, too?" asked Eileen.

"If he were, then Ailbe would have shouted it to everyone." Thomas said. "No, he's still alive, and probably on his way here to hang me."

The tower door opened, and Bluster stepped through. He pulled the door closed behind him and headed straight for Thomas. Lionel attempted to step in front of him but was stopped by a single word and a sharp gesture. Thomas pushed himself to his feet as the Reeve closed in.

Bluster's brows were drawn tight together and storms were running in his eyes. His skin was red and the knuckles of his right hand were white around the grip of his truncheon. He stopped three feet away from Thomas. "All right, lad, let's have it."

"It isn't true."

"Prove it."

"We were with him the entire time," said George, coming to his own feet. "He walked back with us and never harmed anyone."

Bluster didn't take his eyes off Thomas. "Unfortunately, the woman says that you two helped to murder this Shamus, so your word doesn't count for much."

"We'd never kill anyone," Eileen protested.

"These two already have," Bluster moved his truncheon in a slow arc from George to Thomas. "You've been accused of murder, Thomas. You and your two friends. Explain to me how you could be innocent and I'll listen."

Thomas shook his head. "We didn't murder anyone. We killed the bishop's men in a fight. They attacked us and they cut Eileen. George told you all about it."

"Aye. He did. I have yet to see it, though."

Eileen loosened her bodice. "George, help with the wrappings."

George did, and Bluster soon got a first-hand look at the ugly, stitched up gash on Eileen's stomach. It was also Lionel's first look at it, and the sight of it made the big smith go pale. Eileen saw the look on her father's face and dropped her shirt down again. "Is that proof enough for you?"

"Aye." The little man didn't look at all fazed. "It's proof you were in a fight. What about Shamus?"

"We left Lakewood three mornings ago," said Thomas. "It took two days to get here because of Eileen's wound. Shamus was alive when we left. You can ask the sheriff."

"There's nothing to say that a strong pair of lads like yourselves couldn't have doubled back to the house and killed Shamus," said Bluster. "I need proof of your innocence, Thomas."

Thomas's mind raced, looking for a counter-argument. "How long ago did she say Shamus had died?"

"Yesterday morning," said Bluster. "Why?"

"And it made her so distressed that she left without her shoes to come here and accuse us?"

"Aye."

"Did she say she left immediately?"

"Aye, lad. Where are you going with all these questions?"

"Why wasn't she here last night?"

Now it was Bluster's turn to look for a hole in Thomas's argument. It took him a moment before he replied with, "You said it took you two days."

"One of us was hurt," said Thomas. "She was perfectly healthy."

"She wouldn't go off her head like this," Eileen said. "When Thomas told her about Timothy, she didn't react like this, and Timothy was her brother."

"Her brother?" Bluster repeated, his eyebrows going up. "Didn't know that.

She told me Shamus was her lover, though. Maybe his death right after Timothy's pushed her over the edge."

"If Shamus was her lover," Thomas argued, "why is it she yelled about the bishop's men, whom she didn't know, as if they were as important to her as he was?"

"And how did she know those three were the bishop's men?" asked George. "The bishop said they weren't."

Bluster looked from one to the other. "Did he, now?"

"Aye," said Thomas. "Ask the sheriff. He'll tell you."

"I will," Bluster stepped back, and the white in his knuckles around the truncheon faded a little. "I'll send for him now." His eyes narrowed at Thomas. "If she had more proof, you'd be locked up. As it is, I've only got her word, so I'll leave you with these two. But you're not to leave—"

"—town until the matter is settled," Thomas finished. "Strange how used to those words I'm getting."

"Strange how often I've had to say them to you," Bluster said. "Stay in town."

The little man turned on his heel and headed out the door, leaving Thomas and his friends looking helplessly at one another. George summed it up best with, "Well, now what?"

"Now, lunch," Magda said, stepping in with Madeleine Flarety at her heels. "Your mother and brother are joining us, Thomas, so we'll need to pick up some more food before we head back."

"Good," Thomas stepped to his mother and embraced her, feeling relief flood through him. "I didn't know what had happened to you," Thomas said. "I was worried. I wanted to talk to you about what happened—"

"And I to you," said Madeleine. "Come on. You can tell us your version of what happened while we walk to the smithy."

*   *   *

Lunch passed as pleasantly as it could, given the circumstances. After, Magda served tea for them all, and they stayed around the table in the kitchen. Thomas filled in his mother and brother on all that had happened, though he once again left the subject of magic aside. The explanation settled them a bit, though he could still see their apprehension. Thomas changed the subject. "Is the business suffering?" he asked. "I mean, is father's behaviour noticeable?"

"It's the strangest thing," Neal said. "Father is completely normal about everything else. He runs the warehouses the same, he runs the carting the same. The only thing that's changed is his attitude towards you and the city and the Academy."

"That's change enough," said Thomas, ruefully.

"Aye," agreed his brother. "But you remember all the morality talk he was spouting at that dinner? None of it seems to matter in any context but you. And if anyone tries to take your side on any of it, that person instantly becomes his enemy, no matter who." Neal did his best to hide his expression, but Thomas saw the hurt buried there. "It's like he's under a spell or something."

"Now don't you start with that superstitious nonsense," Madeleine scolded. "There's those in this town who might believe you and then where would we be?"

Right on the truth, Thomas thought.

"So, now what?" asked Lionel.

"We wait for the sheriff," said Thomas. "He knows Ailbe. He'll see at once that she's not in her right mind."

"And how long will that take?" asked Madeleine.

"A day for the message to reach him," said Thomas. "Another for him to come back, I would guess. It's thirty miles by road."

"Well, then," Madeleine took another sip of her tea, then put down the mug and patted her son's hand. "We'll see the end of the trial tomorrow, and wait for the sheriff."

"Aye. And Mum?"

"Yes?"

Thomas turned his hand over and squeezed the hand that was patting it. He held it tight for a while. "Thank you for everything."

"There's nothing to be thanking me for," Madeleine said. "We're family." She took another sip of her tea, then smiled and added, "Even if you do insist on wearing a sword."

Thomas, caught completely off guard, managed, "I wasn't wearing it today—"

"And just as well," declared Madeleine, "or the judge would have gone directly over to your father's side."

"Mother!" Thomas's volume rose slightly. Madeleine fell silent, and the worry that the joking hid came back to her face. Thomas squeezed her hand again and repeated. "Thank you. For everything."

She smiled at Thomas and squeezed his hand. The worry was still plain on her face. "Get this sorted out and come home soon, will you?"

"If I can, Mother, I will."

Neal drained the last of his mug and rose. "We should get going."

There was a moment's general confusion as they all rose and said their good-byes. Thomas, not wanting them to go, protested. "Surely you can stay a while longer."

Neal shook his head and clapped his brother on the shoulder. "I've got to get back to the business, and mother needs to get back to the convent."

"Forgive me for hoping that you don't stay there," said Magda, embracing Madeleine. "We'd miss you."

Madeleine smiled, squeezed her friend, then stepped away. "Thank you."

They took their leave, and Thomas stood long in the doorway watching them go. Even after they were out of sight, he remained, watching the empty road. Eventually, Magda came up behind him. "Are you all right?"

"As right as I can be," said Thomas. "Did you know I haven't slept a night in my own bed since I got here?"

"Well, hopefully that will be remedied soon," she said. She turned back to the now-empty kitchen and began to pick up the mugs from the table. "What will you do for today?"

Thomas shrugged and picked up his mug before Magda could get at it. "Wait, I guess. There's really nothing else for me to do."

"Then go help the boys in the forge," said Magda. "That will keep you busy until nightfall, and by then you'll be too tired to worry about anything."

"That," said Thomas, "is a very good idea, though more likely than not I'll be in the way."

"You just get changed, then go out," Magda said. "There's always something to be done."

And there was. Lionel and George were delighted to have the help— especially George, who was nearly a week behind in his work, thanks to their trip to Lakewood. They set Thomas to hauling water from the well and coal from the pile, then to working the bellows to keep the forge hot. The roar from the flames kept talking to a minimum, and the heaviness of the labour kept Thomas's mind as far from his problems as he could manage. The day passed in sweat and coal dust in the blistering heat of the forge. Thomas, who had considered himself strong and fit, was exhausted by the time dinner arrived, and could barely lift his arms to wash them.

"Not bad for your first day," George said as they cleaned themselves at the pump. "Why, another few months, and we could put some meat on those chicken wings of yours."

"Another few months and you'd kill me," Thomas protested. "I'd forgotten how hard all of that is."

"How many years has it been since you helped out?" Lionel asked. "Five, six?"

"Five, I think."

"Still, a good day's work from you."

Thomas smiled. "Consider it my room and board." A thought struck him. "Your money! You'll be wanting that back, I think."

"Now, we gave that to you," said Lionel. "We'll not be taking it back."

"You gave it to me to use if I ran off," Thomas countered. "And since I'm not running anymore, I can give you what's left back easily enough."

"Hang onto it for now," Lionel advised. "When the trial's over, then you can give it to me."

Thomas opened his mouth to argue further, but Lionel stopped him with an upraised finger. "No arguments," he said. "Now hurry up and get washed or you'll be late for dinner."

Thomas, who hadn't felt so hungry in several days, took that advice to heart.

Chapter 15

The world was pitch black when a rough hand shook Thomas awake. "Get up, boy! Quick!"

Thomas, who had only managed to achieve sleep moments before, tried to push the hand away, and was shaken even harder for his efforts. He blinked, focused his eyes, and made out Lionel's profile in the darkness of the loft. "Lionel?"

"Get up!" The hand hauled him out from bed and upright. His clothes were thrown at him while he struggled to gain his balance. "Get dressed, get your gear, and get downstairs, fast!"

Thomas, who still wasn't truly awake, did what he was told, scrambling around the loft and pulling on the road-worn and tattered clothes he'd been wearing while working at the forge while Lionel shook George awake. Lionel kept hissing at them to hurry, and practically pushed them out of the loft the moment they were dressed.

They stumbled down the ladder, bleary-eyed, with Lionel coming down behind them with their travel bags. He herded them into the kitchen. Thomas, holding onto his sword-belt with one hand and his cloak and boots with the other, was about to ask what was happening, when Magda led Eileen out of her room. Eileen's skirt was crooked and her blouse untucked, and her hair tied up for sleep. She blinked bearily at the boys and stumbled forward, one hand on her stomach. Magda threw her daughter's bag on the floor, then started tucking in her blouse.

"What's going on?" demanded George, his voice surly. "I was asleep."

"And a hard time I had waking you up, too," Lionel snapped. "Get your boots on, all of you!"

George grumbled, but did as he was told. Thomas stumbled over to a bench and shook his head, trying to clear the cobwebs, and sat down to pull on his boots. There was a quick, quiet tapping on the door, and a whispered, "Magda?"

Magda, now helping Eileen with her bodice, shoved her chin at Lionel, who went to the door and pulled it half-way open. "Inside, quick!"

Thomas stopped, his boot half-way on, to stare as his brother slipped in through the door and hurriedly close it behind him. "Neal? What are you—"

"No time," his older brother hissed. "Get your boots on. Fast!"

Eileen, now dressed, stumbled to the bench beside Thomas and began pulling her own boots on. George attempted to ask a question and was promptly told to be quiet. Lionel doused the candles and stood, silent, in the middle of the room. They all followed his example and waited.

"There," said Lionel. "Hear it?"

"Hear what?" Thomas demanded. Then he heard it: voices, talking together, and the sound of many footsteps, coming closer. "What is that?"

"It's the bishop's guard," Neal said. "They rode in just after sundown and headed straight to our house. They've got a warrant for arrest for the three of you."

"They can't!" Thomas's head was clearing fast. "They need the Reeve to arrest us."

"Not for witchcraft."

Thomas swore hard. "Does Mother know?"

"She's still at the convent."

Thomas stood and wrapped the sword belt around his waist. Lionel tossed George his stick and Magda gave her children the knives they'd taken to Lakewood. "Take your bags," said Lionel, grabbing up their walking sticks. "This way!"

All three grabbed their bags and followed Lionel to a window facing the woods. He threw the shutters open. "Out. Get to the woods and keep moving. They'll never find you if they don't know the area."

"But what about you?" Eileen protested.

Her mother shushed her and pushed her towards the window. Eileen winced and clutched her stomach, but Magda kept her moving. "We'll be fine," Magda said. "We'll say you left at sunset. Now go!"

George went first, then turned to help his sister through the window. Thomas went next, and Neal took up the rear. Moving as fast as they could in the dark, they crossed the yard and slipped into the woods. Thomas glanced back and saw torchlight, yellow and ugly, lighting up the night behind them. George grabbed Eileen's hand and hissed, "Form a chain so we don't lose each other."

George led them away from the house and deep into the forest. Branches whipped at their faces and bodies, and the roots and undergrowth tripped them as they ran. At one point they found themselves stumbling across a stream that soaked them all to their knees. By the time George pulled them to a stop a half-hour later, Thomas had scratches stinging his face and arms, and his ankle throbbed from one particularly nasty stumble. Eileen was biting her lip to keep from crying. The moment her hands were free she wrapped them around her stomach. George put a hand on her shoulder, offering what comfort he could as his eyes scanned the forest.

"All right," George said. "If I didn't lose my bearings, we should be north and east of the town, somewhere north of the old mill."

"Which way is the road?" Neal asked. "I have to get back before anyone finds out that I'm gone."

"Won't they know?"

Neal shook his head. "The servants won't say anything, and Father went with the bishop's guards to make certain that they caught you."

"Of course he did," Thomas let his anger rise, using the heat of it to give himself strength. "He probably asked them to come."

"No," said Neal. "The guards had a writ dated three days ago, signed by the bishop himself." Neal pressed a bag into his brother's hand. "Here. Mother gave me this before she went back to the convent. She said to give it to you if anything went wrong. It should see you safe to another county. Or another country if you need."

"I'm not going to be run out of the country!"

"Keep your voice down!" hissed Neal. In the silence that followed they all strained to hear sounds of pursuit. None came. "Just keep safe," said Neal, keeping his voice low. "And stay off the road until you're well out of town. They'll be looking for you." Neal grabbed Thomas in a quick embrace. "Good-bye, brother. Be careful."

"Tell Mother I'll be back as soon as I can."

"I will."

George gave a quick set of directions, and Neal took a moment to shake George's hand, then Eileen's, before turning and vanishing into the forest. Thomas listened to his brother stumbling in the dark, and hoped Neal would make it back undetected. When Thomas could no longer hear his brother, he turned to George. "Now where do we go?"

"I don't know," George sounded exhausted, and there was a note of panic creeping into his voice. "I can keep us moving all night but I don't know where to take us."

"Just keep us away from the bishop's men," Eileen's voice shook with pain and fear. "They'll hang us!"

"They have to catch us first," Thomas said. The words sounded nowhere near as comforting as he'd hoped.

"And they will if we don't keep moving," said George. "What do we do?"

"I don't know," Thomas could feel panic rising up inside him. He shoved it down hard, letting his anger rise and drive his thoughts forward. "Let me think."

The dark woods felt like they were closing around him as he stood, sifting through and discarding ideas. He listened the entire time, expecting to hear the cries of the bishop's men, but the only sounds were the night birds and crickets, and the laboured, frightened breathing of his friends. None of the plans he could come up with seemed any better than the others.

"All right," Thomas said at last. "We'll go towards the city until we're far enough that they won't find us. Then we'll find someplace to hide until we can figure out where to go next. Good enough?"

"Aye," George agreed. "Pity it isn't fall, there'd be haystacks to hide in."

"Tonight, I'll settle for a pig barn." Thomas said. "Let's just go."

* * *

In the end, it wasn't even a pig barn. After two more hours of stumbling through the dark woods, George found a small copse of trees close enough together to act as a wind-break and with enough ground-growth to conceal them from prying eyes. From the looks of the well-trampled grass inside, the little space had been used by deer in the recent past. Fortunately, none were there to dispute the friends' claim on the place.

They didn't dare light a fire. They could only wrap themselves in the blankets that Ailbe had given them and huddle close to each other for warmth: Thomas and George on either side of Eileen, who stifled a moan when she lay down and clutched at her belly.

Thomas lay awake, listening for the sounds of searchers, even though he knew the bishop's men would be far away. George, as always, was the first to drop off. Thomas envied him. The man could sleep no matter what happened. Eileen was not so lucky. As soon as her brother started snoring, she started to shake, her breath becoming ragged and hitched.

Thomas reached a tentative hand to her shoulder. She started when she first felt it, then rolled her face into his chest. The move caused her to gasp, and her hands tightened on Thomas's chest as she clung close. She shook against him, silent crying wracking her body. Thomas held her tight until the sobbing subsided, and kept holding her until, much later, she passed into sleep.

The moon was just about down when Thomas slipped out of his blanket. He used it to cover George and Eileen then moved away to the edge of the bower. Sleep was not going to come, he knew. Rather than letting his thoughts drag him through the night, he found himself a place to sit with his back against a tree trunk, and stared out into the dark woods. *Right. Now what?*

Run, hide, fight. Pick one.

At this point, with exhaustion making his head hurt even as the frantic pace of his brain denied him rest, Thomas seriously considered the first two options. The temptation to run to the coast and take ship, knowing he had enough money to leave, was almost overwhelming. He could convince George and Eileen to come with him and the three of them could sail away to see what they could of the world.

The problem is, it isn't just about me. Thomas sighed and rocked his head back, gently tapping his skull on the tree behind him. *Eileen's hurt, Timothy and Shamus are dead, and my Father and Ailbe...* he looked for a word to describe what had been done to them. *Robbed and twisted* came close, but didn't seem to be enough. And they weren't the only ones.

Thomas thought about the bishop's words in Laketown; about a girl in Fog Glen who had needed 'guidance.' Thomas wondered if she had survived, and if so, what had happened to her mind.

How many more? Thomas wondered. *How many more has he torn open? How many has he killed?*

The wind stirred the trees, making the leaves rustle and shiver as they danced in the darkness. The night animals were making their noises; the insects and the owls and the bats and the many animals that crawled across the ground, seeking food. They would have been silent, Thomas knew, if anyone had been coming.

I can't let him keep going.

So how do I stop him?

There is a certain point in exhaustion when all extraneous thoughts vanish, all feeling and ideas are stripped away, and a strange lucidity comes. For Thomas, it came just as the sky was changing from dark to deep blue. Everything made perfect sense.

Or I could be so tired that I'm not making any sense at all.

Either way, Thomas had a plan.

The sun had just broken the horizon when Eileen rolled over and opened her eyes. She had to brace herself with her hands to sit up, and the effort made her groan. She peered around herself, bleary and dazed. Thomas waved at her.

Eileen blinked, shook her head, and slowly pushed herself to her feet. Still wrapped in her blanket, she came over. She was pale in the bright light of the sun, and lines of worry and unhappiness were creasing her forehead. She leaned against Thomas's tree and scanned the wood. "Any sign of them?"

Thomas shook his head. "Not so far."

"Have you been up long?"

"All night."

"Oh." She pulled the blanket closer around her, hugging herself with her arms, and yawned. "I'm surprised I wasn't."

"Must run in the family," Thomas said, looking over to George who was still snoring into his blanket.

Eileen followed his look and smiled slightly. "Probably." She turned her gaze back out to the woods, and Thomas watched her smile fade and the worry lines on her forehead return. "Thomas," her voice was much smaller, "I'm scared."

Thomas reached up and found one of her hands. He squeezed it in his. "Me, too."

She squeezed his back, and Thomas welcomed it, drawing comfort from her touch. The feeling must have been mutual, for she held on to him a long time.

The sun was nearly entirely above the horizon when she asked, "What do we do now?"

"Well, first, you take off your clothes."

Eileen's turned her head slowly towards him, her eyebrows high. "And then?"

Thomas smiled, "And once you've done that, you can put mine on. They're looking for two men and a girl, not three men. It isn't much of a disguise, but it will have to do for now."

She glared at him some more. "I suppose you thought that was funny."

"A bit, aye," said Thomas, pushing himself off the tree and getting to his feet. "Of course, after being awake all night, pretty much anything can be funny." He went over to where George was lying and picked up his travel bag. Rummaging through, he came up with the brown breeches and spare white shirt he'd worn at the fire. "You'll need to find some way to hide…" He found himself unable to finish the sentence.

She watched him, waiting, and Thomas felt himself turning red. "Hide what?" she asked sweetly.

Thomas wondered briefly why, of all times, he chose now to get embarrassed. "You know what."

"Indeed I do, and I'm thankful I'm not built like Marie McNichols, I can tell you that. That girl could fall on her face and miss."

Thomas felt the colour rising higher. "I'm sure."

"I need to tie them down with something," Eileen said, looking around. "Just a moment."

She went over to her own bag of clothes and came up with her spare cloak; plain brown wool, but lined with a lighter, undyed flax material. A quick cut with her knife opened a seam, and she followed it up, ripping until she had a length of the beige cloth in her hands. She cut twice more then tied the pieces together into a single, long length of fabric. "That should do, and not so dark as will show through." She picked up her clothes. "I'll go behind the trees," she said, picking up his clothes, "and don't you dare come looking until I call." She stepped out of the little shelter. "And make sure that lout doesn't come looking either."

"The lout," George said, voice slightly muffled from his blankets, "has no desire to see his sister's skinny backside. Now hurry up so we can get going."

Eileen stuck out her tongue at him, then went to the other side of the trees, while George hauled himself up. He rubbed his face and stretched where he sat. "Any sign of them?"

"Not so far," said Thomas.

"Good."

"I don't suppose you know where we are, do you?"

George pushed himself to his feet, dropping the blanket on the ground and stepping out of the little copse of trees. He took his time looking around before he answered. "More or less. We stayed going east last night, heading towards the city, for all the good it will do. It's two weeks to walk there."

"Three, if the weather is bad," said Thomas, remembering just how much bad weather he'd encountered.

"If we head straight east, we should come to a road," said George. "From there, it's straight south to the nearest town. Greenwater, if I'm right."

"Which is on the river." Thomas remembered coming through it on the way home. "Good."

"And what are we going to do with ourselves?" asked George. "Aside from walking to Hawksmouth?"

"I have an idea," Thomas picked up his bag and settled it onto his shoulder. "Mind telling me?"

Thomas hesitated, "I'll talk while we walk."

"Well," said George, raising his voice high enough for his sister to hear, "if Eileen will ever finish dressing, that might just happen."

For a reply, Eileen stepped half-out from behind the bushes, giving Thomas a quick glimpse of one bare leg as she threw her skirt at her brother's head. Some time later, she stepped out again, dressed in his shirt and breeches, her own boots back on her feet. It looked, Thomas realized, very good on her. The breeches fit snugly across her hips, and Thomas found the sight of her wearing them was raising a flush in his neck.

You are being chased by the bishop's men, he told himself. *Pay attention to what's important.*

"How do I look?" she asked, stepping out and turning. "Can I pass for a boy?"

"Not with that hair," said George.

"I didn't mean the hair." Eileen turned to Thomas. "Well?"

Eileen was a petite girl, fortunately, and had bound herself down enough that the shirt flowed loosely across her chest. Thomas, well aware of her brother standing beside him, tried to look for a polite way to say so. He settled on, "It looks fine."

"Flat as a board," said George. "Not that you had far to go."

Eileen replied by throwing her bodice at him, which he caught, and her balled up shirt, which he didn't. While George was pulling the shirt off his head, Eileen stepped over to Thomas. She reached up and grabbed her thick red hair. Turning away from him, she said. "Cut it off."

"Oh no," Thomas was horrified. "I can't."

"It's a giveaway," Eileen said. "I've cut it before."

"But—" Thomas was surprised at how much the idea disturbed him. "But you have beautiful hair."

She looked back over her shoulder, a small, shy smile playing on her lips. "Do you really think so?"

"Aye," said Thomas. "I do."

He smile widened a bit, then she turned away again and gathered all her hair together at the top of her head, holding it between her hands. "It will grow back," she said, though there was something of a hitch in her voice. "Please?"

Thomas drew a deep breath and his dagger. Eileen was right; it was a giveaway, and they really didn't need to be more noticeable. He put his blade against the hair underneath Eileen's hands. With a swift motion, he sliced through.

Her hands dropped, and she stared at the mass of red in them. For a long time she just stood there. At last, she said "It's only hair," but the assurance was gone from her voice.

"It *will* grow back," Thomas said, quietly.

"Aye, I know." She looked at the hair in her hand a while longer, then tossed it to the ground. A few wisps clung to her hand, and she blew on them to send them off. "Come on. Let's get going." She pointed a finger at George. "And no more words from you."

George, for once silent, handed Eileen her blankets and began packing up his own. When they were all organized, George led them east, away from Elmvale, towards Hawksmouth.

Thomas had intended to tell them his plan at once but the woods, though they seemed much less threatening in the daylight, were no easier to traverse. The underbrush was thick enough to block their view of anything more than twenty feet away, and more than thick enough to trip up Thomas a half-dozen times. George and Eileen moved along easily enough, and Thomas began to wish sincerely that he'd spent more time walking in the woods and less in the library.

Half-way through the morning they found a stream. They stopped to drink and to rinse their faces in the cool water, then moved on again. They had no food, and the water bottles they had taken to Lakewood were back at the house, left behind in the rush. Bellies began to rumble and mouths dried out as the morning wore on. George picked some of the grasses from the forest floor and passed them out for everyone to chew. It helped their dry mouths, but did nothing to ease hunger.

It was nearly noon when, true to George's guess, the group struck a road. It was little more than a cart-path, heading north-south. George, remembering what he could of the area, was certain it wouldn't change direction.

"Now what?" asked Eileen.

"This road is bound to meet up with the main road sooner or later," said Thomas. "When it does, we can head toward the city."

"Well, if it's the road I think it is, we should be a day's walk from Greenwater," was George's opinion. "Of course, if it isn't, then I'll just keep us moving south. We'll end up at the river eventually."

The road ran relatively straight, as George had predicted, and was flat and clear enough to be a relief after the woods. There were still weeds and ruts enough to trip up the unwary, but the walking was much easier.

They walked on without conversation, hunger taking all their focus and keeping them moving. It was well into the afternoon and Thomas was getting to the point where he was wondering which of the grasses would make a full meal before they came upon the first farm. It was just a small house, set back from the road, on a cleared patch of land. No one answered their knock, so George led them around the back, into the fields. They found the farmer and his family, hard at work getting the crop into the ground. Thomas waved and called out to get their attention.

The farmer came over to them, a hoe in his hand and a wary look in his eyes. "Hello to you," he said. "What can I do you for?"

"We're looking for lunch," said Thomas. "We've a long way to walk today, and were hoping you'd have some food to part with."

"And a skin to carry water," added George.

The farmer nodded. "I might." He scratched at his beard and smiled at the three of them. "How much would you lads have to spend?"

Thomas smiled, realizing that Eileen had just passed for a boy. He caught sight of her out of the corner of his eye. From the pleased expression on her face, she had realized it, too. "Well," Thomas said. "Why don't you tell us what you've got and what you think a fair price would be, and we'll tell you if we can afford it?"

The haggling which followed was quick and to the point, and while Thomas was certain that the farmer had gotten the better of him, he was too hungry to complain when the man handed him skin of water and a sack with dried sausages, withered apples, and fresh-baked biscuits. "Made by the wife this morning," the farmer assured them. "Worth the money all by themselves."

Thomas nodded his agreement and opened the pouch his brother had given him. He took one look inside, and promptly closed it again and put it away. The farmer's face darkened, and his grip shifted on the hoe he was still carrying. Before he could say anything, Thomas pulled out the pouch of coins from Lionel. "Picked the wrong one," he explained. He found the proper coins and handed them to the farmer with thanks. Farewells were exchanged, then Thomas led his friends back to the road.

"Aren't we going to stop and eat?" Eileen asked as they left the farmhouse behind.

"Not here," Thomas glanced over his shoulder, then turned back to the road ahead. "A little further down the road."

"Why?" George asked. "And why didn't you pay him from your brother's money?"

"I couldn't," Thomas said, handing the pouch to George. George opened it, then whistled and handed it back. "That's impressive, that is."

"What is?" Eileen intercepted the pouch and looked inside. "By the Father, how much is that?"

"I don't know," Thomas looked behind them again. There was no sign of the farmer or anyone else following. He stopped and opened the pouch, counting the coins into his hand. "Fifty gold coins," he said when he was finished. "Enough to pay for my schooling for the next two years and to set you two up in whatever trades you like."

"Your mother's dowry," Eileen sounded at once impressed and horrified. "She gave you all of it?"

"Aye." Thomas poured the coins back into the bag, feeling sick inside. "She'll have nothing, now."

"Your brother will take care of her," said George. "And your father, when he comes to his senses."

"If he comes to his senses," said Thomas. He looked at the pouch, wondering how to keep it safe. "George, could you put this inside your shirt?"

"Me?" George look appalled. "I've never held that much money in my life."

"Neither have I," Thomas said. "But a pick-pocket's a lot less likely to get inside your shirt than he is to get inside mine."

"I suppose," George didn't sound convinced. "Just give me a moment."

He reached into his bag and came up with extra laces for his shirt. With deft fingers he turned the lace into a make-shift necklace, tied it to the pouch and tucked the whole thing into his shirt. It was nearly invisible between the muscles on his chest. "Will that do?"

"It will."

They found a small rise, shaded by a half-dozen elms, only a little way further down the track. George declared it to be the ideal place for lunch, and sat down. It was a sure sign of how hungry they all were that no one said anything until they were on their second round of the food. Only then did George speak up, "You know, you never did tell us what you're planning."

Thomas had to work around a mouth full of biscuit to say, "That was because you led us through every bramble in the forest."

"And after we reached the road?" asked Eileen.

"I was too hungry to think of it."

"And now?" asked George.

"And now you two are asking too many questions for me to get a word in."

"Thomas…"

Thomas heeded the warning in George's voice. "All right, all right." He swallowed the last of his lunch. "This whole thing's been about the bishop. Everything that happened to Timothy, to Shamus; my father, Ailbe, you," he nodded at Eileen. "It's all been about the bishop collecting the magic."

"So you said." Eileen rubbed at her stomach gently, as if trying to reach an itch without actually touching it. "What do we do?"

"We stop him," said Thomas. "That is, I stop him."

George nearly choked on his food. "You?"

"If you go after him," Eileen said, "he'll have you killed."

Thomas shook his head. "He'll have me killed if I go after him or not. He's already got charges of witchcraft on us. All he needs to do is catch me and I'll either end up dead or like my father."

George managed to swallow his food enough to say, "Surely there's something else you can do."

"Sure," said Thomas. "We can run away. Of course, that leaves my father hating me, my mother in a convent, and none of us able to go home ever again."

George and Eileen both fell silent. For the first time since he'd come home, Thomas could see the family resemblance. Near-identical frowns were on their faces and each one's brow was pulled down in wrinkles. He knew how they felt. He really didn't want to try to stop the bishop, but he literally could see no other way to end things.

George spoke first. "How do you stop him, then?"

"I don't know, yet," said Thomas. "For now, we get to Hawksmouth. Once we're there, I can check the library for books on magic. Maybe I can learn how to stop him."

"And what if you don't?" asked Eileen. "What then?"

"I don't know," Thomas sighed. "It's not much of a plan, I know."

George and Eileen looked at one another. Eileen shrugged, and George nodded, then turned to Thomas. "I want to go home again."

"So do I," the words came out harsher than Thomas intended them. "But as long as the bishop's out to get us, we can't."

"Aye," said George. "We know. So we'll go with you, and we'll help as best we can." He shook his head, "Though the Four know what I'm going to do while you're in the library."

"Same thing you always do," said Eileen. "Haul the water and chop the wood."

George aimed a swat at her, which she ducked without dropping the remains of her lunch. She froze immediately, hissing in a breath and putting one hand against her stomach. George grumbled at her for not taking care of herself, then rose and began gathering the last of the food together. "We may as well get started." He put the food into his bag. "The sooner we start walking, the sooner we get there."

"We'll not be walking all the way," said Thomas. "It took me three weeks to get here, and the three of us won't be going any faster. Especially not with Eileen's injury." He turned to her. "How is it, anyway?"

"Hurts," Eileen rubbed her stomach some more, then got to her feet, "But it isn't bleeding and it isn't slowing me down."

"You'll need to get those stitches out before long," George said.

"A week, Ailbe said."

"And that was three days ago," Thomas thought about it. "We'll find someone to do it on the way." He pushed himself to his feet and slung his bag back over his shoulder. "We'll walk to the river and find the closest town. Once there, we can see about trading one of these gold pieces for silver, then catching the next barge down-stream."

"What about the bishop's guard?" asked George. "What if they're still after us?"

"With luck we'll be on the boat before they search this far."

"Then let's hope for luck," Eileen said. "And let's get moving."

Chapter 16

The rough path that led to Greenwater had turned into a well-trodden dirt road by the time they reached the outskirts of the town. It led to a narrow cobblestone street that meandered towards the centre of town. The streets were almost empty, the residents having retreated home for the night. Smoke rose from chimneys, and the three could hear the residents' voices, slipping out from behind closed shutters.

The sunlight was slipping off the walls and leaving grey shadows in its wake when they reached the main street of the town. A half dozen inns lined the street, their doors open and casting cheery yellow rectangles of light into the oncoming twilight. Beyond the inns, the street turned to wharves and the large, grey swath of water that was the river Hawk, flowing east towards Hawksmouth and the sea.

Thomas, worried about being noticed, picked the largest and most crowded of the inns and secured a small, single room for the three of them. A day of walking on near-empty stomachs made the unremarkable dinner a feast. None of them had the energy or desire to stay in the common room for any time once dinner was done, and they retreated to their room.

There was only one bed in the small, dark, draughty room Thomas had secured. Thomas and George both insisted Eileen take it, and wrapped themselves in their blankets on the floor. Thomas had half-expected to lie awake through the entire night again. Instead, exhaustion won out, though not until well after the midnight bell.

Far earlier than Thomas wanted, the innkeeper was banging on their door and calling them down to breakfast. Thomas rose with the others, feeling grumpy and out of sorts. And after a breakfast of lumpy porridge and weak tea, the three were back on the street, bags on their shoulders, heading towards the river.

The wharves were solid, thick timber that jutted out into the river, their big pilings holding them fast against the current. Fishing gear was scattered on the docks, and several small boats were pulled up to the bank beside them. Three larger vessels were actually tied to the wharf, and it was there Thomas went and made inquiries. The discovery that all three were going up-river did nothing to improve his mood.

"So, now what?" asked George, leaning back against one of the pilings. "Go back to the inn and wait for another boat?"

The idea was very tempting, but Thomas shook his head at it. "We have no idea if another one is coming today, or if the bishop's men are still looking for us. We should push on."

"I don't suppose we could just hide in the tavern?" asked George, though there was no real hope in his voice.

"We can take the river road south," said Thomas. "It's a two-day walk to the next town."

"If I was the bishop's men," said George. "I'd be following the road, too."

"We can see them coming on the road," Thomas said. "We should start walking."

"You would think so," George grumped as he straightened up and adjusted his bag on his shoulder. "It's your favourite way to travel."

They picked up some dried sausages and fruit, and another pair of skins for water, and headed east down the road. The town quickly gave way to farms on one side and the occasional fisherman's shack on the other. The road was sparsely populated with the occasional farmer's wagon and the odd set of labourers heading to their day's work. Other than that, they had it to themselves.

There was little traffic on the river, save for the occasional fishing boat, and those dropped away behind them with the last of the fishing huts and farms, leaving nothing but the green water flowing slowly beside them as the trees closed in.

Oaks and elms vied with ash and pine for space, and their branches shaded the dirt of the road, making the walk cool and green. The river road stretched out far in front of them, following the lazy curves of the river, sometimes in sight of it, other times moving away around a hill or patch of swamp. Occasional flowers dotted the side of the path amidst the thick undergrowth that ended sharply at the cobblestones that marked the road's edge. There was no sign of any other travellers, and no sound save the birds in the woods and the tap of their feet and walking sticks on the road.

"Is anyone going to say anything?" Eileen asked after two hours of walking.

"Why waste the energy?" said George, who was walking easily along and looked to have energy to spare.

"Because I don't want to spend the whole trip counting the flowers," said

Eileen with some asperity.

Thomas, who'd been doing just that, and naming them as he counted, found himself in agreement. "It would pass the time."

"Good," said Eileen. "You start."

"Me? Why me?"

"Because," grumbled George. "I've heard all her stories before."

"I haven't," said Thomas.

Eileen shook her head. "My stories aren't interesting. Tell me about the Academy."

George rolled his eyes. "Here we go again."

"I'll tell mine if you tell yours," said Thomas.

Eileen smiled for the first time, Thomas realized, in a pair of days. "Fine. You go first."

"Right." Thomas thought about the mood that had haunted them all since they'd been in Laketown, and decided to lighten it. "Well, there's the time that Gerrett Plimptin decided that he could eat more breakfast than anyone else in the Academy. The problem was that they were serving spiced eggs that morning..."

By the time they'd stopped for lunch, Thomas had actually made Eileen laugh, which led to her clutching her stitches, and George taking a swat at him. She retaliated in turn by telling of the day when the nuns, to drill the tenets of the faith into her, had spent four hours repeating with her the values of the Loyal Consort. Her story, along with her imitation of Sister Clare, had even George chuckling.

As they sat down and shared the dried sausages among them, Thomas began to think on what she'd said.

"Did they say anything about the Blessed Daughter?" he asked in between chews of the dried sausage.

"Not much," said Eileen. "They focused on the Loyal Consort, and her role as Mother. They hold the belief that at one time she was equal to the High Father."

Thomas chewed a bit more, thought on it. "I'm just thinking of what Timothy said. About the Blessed Daughter being the one who gave men magic."

"Never heard of it before he said it," said Eileen. "George?"

George snorted. "Where would I hear about it? I spend all day at the anvil."

Thomas smiled at his big friend. "And do you have a shrine to the Rebel Son hidden in the forge, by any chance?"

George snorted again and shook his head. "Da's not big on that. He always said that the Four belong in the churches, and the metal in the forge, not the other way around."

"Probably a good way of looking at it." Thomas bit off another piece of meat, reflecting that his jaws were going to get as much work as his legs by the end of the day.

"Besides," added George, "if the Daughter gives magic, why don't we see any of it around?"

"And why is it all called witchcraft?" Eileen asked. "I mean, if it's a gift from the Blessed Daughter, shouldn't it be celebrated?" Thomas tried answering around the mouthful of meat, but found it impossible. He chewed hastily, giving Eileen time to add, "In fact, why is it we never see any services to the Blessed Daughter?"

"Well," managed Thomas, swallowing down the mouthful, "about two hundred years ago, the Church of the High Father began to gain ascendancy, claiming that it was the true faith, and that the other three were lesser gods. Over the course of the next hundred years, they drove the other sects out of power, claiming their teachings were perversions of the High Father's truth. If the Daughter's followers practiced magic, claiming it came from the Banished would be as good a way to discredit them as any." Thomas contemplated another sausage, then set it aside. His mouth was tired enough. "Makes sense, really. If you want to make someone less than you, the best way is to talk about everything they do as bad."

"Pattie Seymour tried the same thing on Maggie Jonston," said George, taking a bite of apple. "It seemed mighty petty, too."

"It is mighty petty," agreed Thomas. "What did Maggie Jonston do to Pattie Seymour?"

"That," said George, "is a long story."

"We've got all afternoon," Thomas pointed out. "Speaking of which, we should get going."

"True," George picked up his bag and started stowing away the food. "Well, it began with Pattie seeing Maggie kissing Billy Tomlin..."

By the time supper came around, Thomas had learned that life in Elmvale was far more interesting than he'd remembered. George turned out to be far more of a gossip than his sister, and had a rather extensive knowledge about who was involved with whom, especially when it came to the village girls.

For his part, Thomas relayed the foibles of a dozen of his classmates and several of his professors by the time they stopped again that evening.

Supper was exactly the same as lunch, and by the time he was finished, Thomas was certain his jaw was going to fall off. The food had not been nearly this bad on his way in, he was sure. Still, they forced it down and the three hit the road again, moving onward until the sun started sinking into the horizon.

They went a fair distance from the road to find a camp spot, more to keep out of sight than for lack of choices. They finally found a comfortable spot well enough away from the road that Thomas felt safe.

"Can we build a fire?" asked George.

There had been neither sight nor sound of anyone else on the road, Thomas knew, and he doubted very much whether the bishop or his men would be travelling by night. "A small one," said Thomas. "Can you hide it?"

"Aye. I'll dig a pit." George pulled out his dagger and started digging into the thick earth. Soon the group was curled up in their blankets, backs to the trees, watching the light of the flames as they danced. The night was alive with noise, but it was all natural; the hum of insects, the gurgle of the brook. No other sounds disturbed them.

"How much further?" asked George.

"Twelve miles, according to the last marker we saw," said Thomas. "That will get us to Highbank. After that, maybe a week on a boat if we can find one."

"I hope so. I'm not sure my boots could manage three weeks of walking."

George cast a mock-baleful glance at his sister. "Or my ears."

"You did most of the talking," she protested. "Why, we could hardly get a word in edgewise for all you were gossiping."

"And when you did, it was to ask poor Thomas about the Academy," George replied with what little dignity he could muster. "Do you not think about anything else?"

"And when *you* spoke it was about girls," Eileen shot back. "Do *you* not think about anything else?"

"Were you two always like this?" Thomas asked before George could reply. Relieved as he was to hear good humour from each of them, he was tired enough not to want to hear it right then.

George thought about it for a moment. "Aye. Pretty much."

Thomas sighed. "How come I never noticed before?"

"Because you two never let me be around before," said Eileen. "You were always sending me away."

"Thomas was always sending you away," corrected George. "I wanted you around."

It was Thomas's turn to protest. "You said she was someone handy to blame."

"She was," said George. "You said she was an infernal nuisance."

"Infernal nuisance?" Eileen repeated, almost managing to sound outraged. "I'm insulted!"

"That was five years ago," said Thomas. "I don't think you're a nuisance now."

"Aye, I know what you think of me now," said Eileen archly. "I saw it in your stare the first time you saw me."

"I was looking at your eyes."

Eileen snorted. "You weren't looking that high."

"I was, too!"

"Really?" Eileen turned her back to him. "And what do they look like, then?"

The words came nearly by themselves. "Like a stream whose water sparkles in the sunlight as it flows over a bed of pure blue cornflowers."

In the silence that followed, Thomas could practically hear George's mouth fall open. Eileen turned back and stared at him. Even in the dim light of the fire, Thomas could see the flush creeping up her face. After a few moments she managed, "Flatterer."

"Whole courses dedicated to it," said Thomas grinning. "Remember?"

"Aye, I remember." Eileen smiled back. "And how long did it take you to make that one up?"

Thomas smiled back. "I found the words the first day I looked upon you," he lied. "And they've been dancing in my heart ever since."

Eileen started giggling. George snorted. "Enough of this." He shook his finger at his sister. "Don't encourage him," George warned. "He'll be writing poems to your eyes next." He rolled himself up in his blankets. "Now goodnight, the pair of you."

Thomas followed George's example and wrapped himself up. He could hear Eileen do the same a few feet away. The fire burned lower and the light grew fainter until Thomas could barely see the branch of the tree above him.

"Thomas?" Eileen's whisper floated out of the darkness.

"Aye?"

"Do you really like my eyes?"

"Aye. I do."

There was a moment's silence, then Eileen said, "I like yours too."

George rolled over, groaned, and pretended to stuff the blankets in his ears. Eileen reached over to hit her brother, then settled herself again. Soon, both were asleep.

The fire turned to embers and the night slowly went silent, save for the occasional grunt from George as he rolled about finding himself a comfortable position. Thomas listened to his friends snoring, then turned his face to the fire, and watched until the embers burnt out and sleep claimed him.

* * *

They rose with the sun, stiff and wet with the dew, finished off the last of their food, and started walking again. The road ran on along the river. The sun shone off of it, turning the green water white with its reflection. The oaks and elms gave way to willows for a distance, and the long branches draped down to brush their shoulders and hair. Wildflowers grew along the road, opening as the morning progressed and giving spots of colour in the deep green and brown of the woods. Thomas led them in word games for the first part of the morning, then Eileen and Thomas took turns naming the plants and their properties as they went.

Conversation lapsed as hunger began to get a hold on them. Noon came and went with no food. The three kept walking, falling into their own thought as they did. George whistled an occasional tune, and Eileen walked with only half an eye on the road and the other half on the plants and the trees.

Thomas's thoughts flitted about in several directions, from the events at home, to his plans in the city, to his father, to the pretty girl who was walking a few paces ahead of him. And despite having shorn her hair and dressed in boys' clothes she was still a very pretty girl.

Thomas shook his head. *We're on the run. This is no time to think about girls.*

Once there, though, his mind decided to stay. Thomas tried to get his thoughts back on his problems or on the road, but he was tired of his problems and the road was boring and Eileen was far more interesting than either. Part of Thomas found it absurd. He was in the most dangerous situation that he could be, and all he could think of was the way her raggedly cropped hair framed her face, or the way her legs swung in the breeches that she filled out far better than—

He put his mind firmly back on the road, and kept it there until they reached The Bend, a small fishing village just off the road, early in the afternoon. Thomas, who had stopped there on his walk to Elmvale, led them at once to the inn. It was mostly empty, and the three got a table and the remains of the inn's lunch, which they fell on like wolves on prey. It wasn't until after the last scrap was gone and the three were nursing second pints that Thomas thought to ask about boats heading downstream. There was one, they were told, but the innkeeper had no idea as to whether or not it was leaving that night.

Thomas and his friends grabbed their bags and headed for the door as fast as their overly-full stomachs would let them. A family of five blocked their way out, and Thomas waited impatiently for them to come in before leading George and Eileen on a fast march out the door and to the river. By the time they reached it Thomas was promising himself he wouldn't eat so much so fast again. They stumbled onto the village dock, gasping and clutching their full bellies. The boat in question was a large river barge, some forty or so feet long. It was half-empty, with a large square of the deck in the centre bare. There were no rails around the deck; only piles of crates and barrels set out at balanced intervals and securely lashed down. A small square cabin with a metal chimney out one side took up part of the back portion of the barge. A young man about their age was leaning against it, looking bored. Thomas called out, and the man came over.

"Is the captain on board?" Thomas asked when the man was close enough.

"Nope," said the young sailor. "He's on his way to the tavern with Ma and the others."

"Ma?" repeated George. "Your mother's on the ship?"

"And my three brothers. We're a family affair, we are." The young man grinned. "And a right noisy one, too."

Thomas groaned, realizing that they'd passed them on the way out the inn door. George and Eileen rolled their eyes and exchanged annoyed looks, which they at once directed to Thomas. Thomas ignored them and turned back to the sailor. "When are you leaving?"

"Tomorrow after breakfast. Father wanted to see if he can get some more cargo in town, make up for the space on the deck. We had a half-dozen horses we dropped off two towns back, and he's been grumpy about the extra space ever since."

"Would three passengers do instead?" asked Eileen.

"It might," said the sailor. "Where are you headed?"

"Hawksmouth."

"That would make him happy, all right. Talk to Father, but make sure Mother's with him. He drives a harder bargain when she's not."

The three said their thanks then headed back to the inn at a much more comfortable pace. Thomas found himself sighing with relief. He had feared there would be no barge at all, and that the three would have had to walk all the way to Hawksmouth. All they had to do was spend one more night on shore and then they would be safe from the bishop—for a little while, at least.

Eileen must have been thinking the same thought, for she asked, "So, what about tonight? Do we stay at the inn, or hide in the woods again?"

"The inn," said George. "You saw how small that cabin was. We'll be sleeping on deck for..." he turned to Thomas. "For how long, anyway?"

Thomas thought about it. "Five days, I think."

"Five days," repeated George. "If this is our last chance to sleep on a bed for five days, I'm going to take it."

"Five days?" Eileen wrinkled up her face. "I don't suppose there's a bath at the inn?"

"I don't think so," said Thomas, "though if you ask them to, they'll probably send a wash-tub and some water up to the room." He grinned. "They'll probably even supply a lad to pour the water over you for a rinse, if you like."

"And won't that be an education for him," said Eileen, tartly. "If I'm going to be spending a week in close quarters, I want to start clean, at least." She gave a critical eye to her companions. "And it's an idea that wouldn't do you two any harm, either."

"No, it wouldn't," agreed Thomas. "We'll talk to the captain first, then arrange the room and washtub."

They reached the inn and headed inside. The captain was sitting near the fire, his feet out and a large mug in his hand. He was a spare man, with no more flesh on his bones than was necessary to hold them together. His wife was cut from the same cloth, save that her hair was long and black, while her husband's was gone. Unsurprisingly, the three young men sitting at the table were also lean, but with tight curls that clung to their heads. All looked up as Thomas and his friends approached.

"I understand you're going downstream," said Thomas.

"I am," said the man. "Captain Richard Gloust. And you are?"

"Thomas. This is George…" Thomas pointed at him, and was just changing his finger's target to Eileen when he realized that he had no idea what to call her. He spoke quickly to cover any hesitation, "and his brother."

"My wife, Vicki," said the captain. "My sons."

The boys waved, the lack of introduction not fazing them in the slightest.

"We're looking for a ride downstream," said Thomas. "Your son on the boat said you had room."

"Well," the captain, leaned back in his chair. "I've got the space, all right, but I'd hate to waste it on passengers. Cargo pays more."

His sons and wife nodded in agreement. Thomas nodded back, recognizing that the opening gambit in the discussion that would decide the price. "If you had cargo it would," Thomas agreed. "As it is, you're only five days from Hawksmouth and have a half-empty boat."

"It could fill up," said the captain. He took a drink, wiped his mouth, then continued. "Three people can take up a fair amount of space." He nodded at George. "Especially one as big as him."

"Think of him as extra ballast," Thomas suggested. A chuckle ran around the table.

"He will be that," said the captain's wife. "Why, we could use him as an anchor, if we needed."

"Aye," agreed George, "though if I'm working for my passage, you'll be needing to pay me, rather than the other way around."

"How far are you going?" asked the captain.

"Hawksmouth," said Thomas.

"All the way?" The captain exchanged a glance with at his family and got several nods. "Well, we might arrange something, if you're going all the way. Of course, it will have to be worth the trip."

"And what would make it worth the trip?" asked Thomas.

The captain pursed his lips, took another drink. "Well, I'm thinking a silver each."

"Each?" Thomas echoed. "That's a bit steep."

"Aye, but think how much you'll save, not having to stay at inns for three weeks."

"Are you going to feed us?"

"Nay. You bring your own." The man's wife gave him a sharp look, but said nothing. Thomas guessed this point was negotiable.

George stepped forward. "I take it we'll be sleeping on the deck, too."

"Aye, unless it storms. Then we all sleep in the cabin, once we get the barge to shore."

"So since you're not giving us food or a roof over our heads," said George, "How can you expect us to pay so much?"

"You see another barge out there?"

"No."

"There you go, then."

"One silver for all three."

"One each."

"Two for all three," offered George. "And meals included at the price."

"You'll eat a silver worth of food yourself," protested the captain. "One each if you want food."

"Two for all three."

"It's a long walk," said the captain, taking another drink.

"There'll be another barge along in a day or two," George sounded supremely confident. "You give us a ride, you come out two silvers ahead and we get there quicker. You don't, the next one will. Up to you."

"Enough," the captain's wife interrupted before her husband could open his mouth again. "Two for all three of you, you buy your own food, and I'll do the cooking. Fair enough?"

"Sounds good to me," said Thomas. "George?"

"Aye."

"I could have gotten another half-silver," grumbled the Captain, and all three sons erupted in laughter. The captain joined in a moment later. "All right. Two silvers it is. But you pay before you get on board, and if you're not on the deck at sunrise, you're walking to Hawksmouth. And my wife is on board, so I'll expect you to behave as decent folk at all times."

"Meaning use the garderrobe and not the edge of the deck," put in one of his sons, earning a glare from his mother.

"And no wandering around without your breeches," said another.

Eileen grinned. "We'll remember."

"You wear that thing all the time?" asked the captain, nodding at Thomas's sword.

"Only on the road," said Thomas

"Well you'll be on my boat as of tomorrow, and I'd appreciate it if it stayed put away."

"Fair enough."

"Right, then. It's a deal."

They shook on it, then Thomas bought the entire family a round, which immediately endeared him to the sons, and earned a frown from their mother. Thomas promised to be at the dock first thing in the morning, then went in search of the innkeeper. In short order the three had a room for the night, and the promise of a bath on its way.

"I was beginning to worry you'd bargain us out of a ride," Thomas said as they headed up the stairs. To celebrate their luck, Thomas splurged and got a room with beds enough for all of them. The inn-keeper, quite pleased at the expenditure, threw in the costs of the baths for free and led them to their room personally, the wash-tub hanging off one arm.

George grinned. "You can't bargain if you're not willing to turn your back on the deal. Besides, I knew he'd come down."

The innkeeper opened a large room with four beds in it and ushered them in. He put the tub on the floor, promised the water would be up as soon as it was heated, and left them. George dropped his bag and began checking the beds. After a few moments, he declared them vermin free and quite comfortable.

"Good," Thomas tossed his bag onto one of the beds. "I could use a night on a mattress."

"We should go get the food," George said. "Before the farmers head home for the day."

"We should," agreed Thomas. He turned to Eileen. "But first, we need to figure out what to call you."

"I thought of that when you tried to introduce me," Eileen said. "Any suggestions?"

"Reginald?" said George.

"Too noble," countered Eileen. "Charles?"

"You don't look like a Charles," said Thomas. "Algernon?"

"No."

"Edward?"

"Mmm... no."

"Eustace?"

"No, George, not Eustace."

"Well, we need something," said Thomas. "You're the one that's going to have to remember it, you pick."

"All right, let me think." She did, then smiled. "Alexander. Alex for short."

"Alex works," said Thomas. "All right. Alex it is." He turned to George. "George, meet Alex."

"Alex," George shook his head. "I'm not sure I can get used to it."

"You'd better," Thomas warned him. "*He's* got to travel with us for at least a week."

A knock at the door ended any further discussion. Thomas opened it and found a rather buxom young woman with a steaming bucket of water in each hand.

"Here it is," She stepped inside and set them down. "We had some heating for the dishes, so we brought it up for you." She looked them over. "Will you all be needing baths, then?"

"Aye," said Thomas.

"I'll need to fetch more water," said the girl. "Will you be bathing together or one at a time?"

"Separately, I think," Thomas turned to Eileen. "George and I will get the supplies while you wash up."

"All right," said Eileen. "Take your time."

The young lady smiled at Eileen. "Would you like some help washing your back, then?"

Eileen's mouth dropped open. "What?"

"It's no difficulty," the girl smiled wider and moving closer, "and only a small fee."

Thomas worked very hard at not laughing as Eileen turned bright red. George didn't bother, and chortled while Eileen stammered out, "No, thank you."

"All right." The girl turned to Thomas and George. "And you?"

"Not me, thanks," said Thomas. "George?"

George took his time replying, and all the while his sister glared daggers at him. "No, I suppose not," he said at last. "Thanks, anyway."

She smiled. "Well, let me know when you want more water." She turned an eye to George. "You'll certainly need an extra bucket or two."

She left, closing the door behind her. Eileen waited until she was gone, then turned on George. "I don't see what you're laughing at!"

"The colour of your face, for one." George's chortling grew louder. "And the look on it when she made the offer."

"And I suppose *you'd* have taken her up on it?"

"Well, she is pretty…"

"That's it," Eileen pushed her brother, then Thomas towards the door. "Out! Both of you!"

Thomas, now laughing as hard as George, let himself be driven from the room. The two stood in the hallway a while, letting their laughter die down.

"Right," said George. "We'd best get supplies."

"And some more clothes for Alex, there," Thomas said. "He won't be happy if he has to put dirty clothes on a clean body."

"He?" George looked confused for a moment, then comprehension came. "Of course. We'll see what we can find for *him*." He grinned again. "It might even be enough to get us forgiven. Come on."

Chapter 17

Two days slipped past like the banks of the river. Thomas and George had presented Eileen with the clothes they'd found for her at the market, and she almost forgave them. The next morning the three shared breakfast with the Gloust family, then brought their food and bags aboard and settled themselves into the corner of the raft they had been given as their own.

The four sons had undone the ropes that held the barge to the dock and pushed it away from the banks with long poles. The river had a strong current, and once away from the dock, the barge moved at a good clip downstream. Thomas sat at the side of the barge, watching the shore drift past for most of the first morning. Sometimes the road was in sight, sometimes it vanished behind the trees. Occasional farms broke the edge of the forest; houses and cleared land coming up to the water's edge. On the second afternoon, a stone circle, smaller than the one Thomas had slept in two weeks before, drifted into view. Time and weather had done their worst, leaving the stones looking like broken teeth, upthrust from the earth.

The water itself flowed clear, the mud of the spring run-off having settled a month before. From his spot Thomas spotted schools of fish and the thick river weeds deep below them. On one occasion, they passed over the remains of another boat, sunk long before. He pointed it out to George and Eileen before going back to his place and resuming his watch of the shore.

There was little else to do on board. The barge moved south at the pace of the current, and while one of the four sons was always on watch for snags or sandbanks, they spent the rest of their time playing at cards or dice, or wrestling on the open space of the deck. Their mother did not approve of this last pastime, and often threatened to toss her children into the river. George watched the wrestling with amusement, but didn't join in.

The boys invited their guests to join them in their card games, and George dove in. After the first day, though, he handed the purse of gold to Thomas and made him solemnly swear not to give it back until they were on land again. Eileen and Thomas joined the games occasionally, but Thomas was far too conscious that he was now holding all the money for the three and Eileen disliked gambling with the boys. She had, she said, a hunch they were cheating, but couldn't prove it.

The boys' father liked to play chess, and Thomas played against him several times. The man was good, though Thomas was better. Eileen also had a few games with Captain Gloust, and the two turned out to be an even match.

Thomas still didn't sleep well.

He had hoped that being on the barge would help. There was no way for the bishop or his men to know where he was, and certainly no way for them to catch him. Once Thomas got to Hawksmouth, he could find his friends and books on witchcraft and a way to stop the bishop. There was nothing for him to do but wait.

Unfortunately, his mind would not accept that idea. It kept prodding at him to do something. Anything. He lay wide awake until nearly dawn on the first night, his mind running him ragged. The second day, after lunch and a pair of chess games, Thomas spent most of his afternoon wandering back and forth in the cleared space on the deck, mind racing and body restless. At last, George told him to either sit down or be sat on.

After dinner, Thomas found a stack of crates near the bow and sat down with his back to them, looking out at the banks of the river and the water they flowed on. He played a game of trying to identify every tree they floated past, but it wasn't enough to calm him or stop his mind from worrying at his problems like a dog with a bone. He stayed there anyway, running through the relaxation exercises he had learned, going over stories and poems in his mind, remembering articles of law and their applications; anything to take his mind away from the constant barrage of worries and fear. He brought out his little book of poetry and attempted to translate the next poem, but couldn't stay focused enough to do it. Nothing worked, and he ended up watching the sunset from his vantage point.

It was long after dark when Eileen touched him on the arm. He turned, surprised to see her still awake.

"Can I sit with you?" she asked.

"Aye, sure," Thomas moved over on the crate. She sank down beside him, crossing her legs tailor-fashion. She was wearing green beeches and vest, though both looked grey in the light of the stars and partial moon. Her white shirt shone in the pale light.

"George is snoring up a storm," she said, leaning back against the wall of crates. "It woke me up."

Thomas cocked his head and caught the clear buzz of George's snoring. He smiled. "I'm not surprised."

"I'm worried about the card games he's playing with those boys," Eileen shook her head, the shaggy hair waving into her eyes. She pushed it aside. "They're going to take all his money, at this rate."

"He seems to be doing pretty well," said Thomas. "At least, he says he is."

"He's breaking even. I wouldn't be surprised if they tried to take it all."

"I wouldn't be either. That's why I'm not playing."

"And why are you not sleeping?"

Thomas turned to her, saw the concern etched in the moonlight on her face.

"You always look awful in the morning," Eileen said. "And you spent half of today wandering about as if you're looking at something different than everybody else. How long has it been since you've really slept?"

Thomas thought about saying it wasn't so bad, or that he always slept this little. Unfortunately, it wasn't the truth, and he had no desire to lie to her. He sighed. "Since I got home." He stopped and a small, bitter smile crept over his face. "Since I didn't get home, I should say."

"That long?" Eileen sounded appalled. "You must be exhausted."

"Not really," said Thomas. "I always have trouble sleeping when I'm worried. That's why I did so well on my exams. I couldn't sleep so I'd get up and study. Cost a fortune in candles and lamp oil, though." He turned back to the dark waters of the river, wondered what was swimming underneath them. "It got worse after Lakewood."

Eileen didn't say anything to that, but one hand crept to her stomach, and something in her expression hardened. She looked away from him, staring into the river the way Thomas had done the moment before.

"It will get better," Thomas said, more to bring Eileen away from her memories than from any real belief it was true. "We'll get to the city and I'll find out how to stop the bishop. I'll sleep better after that."

"That could take a long time."

"It could take forever," Thomas said. "In which case I'll see a lot more sunrises than I used to."

Eileen put her hand on his arm. "You need sleep."

"I know," Thomas sighed. "I'm just not going to get it right now."

They sat in silence for a while. The banks of the river ghosted past, the trees vague shapes in the night. Moon and starlight glanced off the surface of the river. Thomas watched it roll with the ripples of the water.

"Tell me about the Academy," Eileen said.

Thomas shook his head. "I've told you about it."

"You told a couple of stories," she corrected. "Not what it was like. Besides, you need to stop worrying and I need something to distract me from that noise," she gestured back in the direction of her slumbering brother. "What's your favourite class?"

"Philosophy."

"Why?"

"Exactly."

Eileen glared at him. "Very funny. What's your favourite place?"

"The Broken Quill. Best pub in the student quarter. Good food, good music, cheap ale."

"Favourite book?"

"*The Arguments of the Ancients.*"

"How many girls have you courted?"

"Hundreds."

"Any you didn't imagine?"

Thomas chuckled. "Some."

"Any waiting for you?"

"No, not that it's your business."

"Any you spent Fire Night with?"

"They don't celebrate Fire Night in the city," Thomas said, glad the dark was hiding his blush. "And *that* is definitely not your business."

Eileen laughed. "I thought so. Who were they?"

Thomas, feeling the blush rising up even further, tried to counter, "I'll tell when you will."

"I have nothing to tell."

"I'm sure."

"No one dares. Have you seen the size of my brother?"

"Aye, and that wouldn't stop a boy for an instant. Who were they?"

"Aren't we supposed to be talking about you?"

He peered at her through the darkness. "Are you blushing, now?"

"No. Now tell me."

"I said I'd tell if you would."

Eileen looked out at the river. Thomas was sure she was blushing, and wished he could see well enough to know. When she spoke again, her voice was much quieter. "You promise not to tell anyone?"

Thomas felt his heart pick up its pace. "I do."

"Really?"

"Really," said Thomas. "I promise."

"All right." Eileen looked over her shoulder, as if her brother would suddenly appear, awake and listening, then leaned in close. She swallowed, then blurted, "I haven't spent Fire Night with anyone, yet. Michael Pembleton and I got to kissing once, but he was only doing it to make Lisa Grant jealous. And at New Year I let Billy Grant get his hand down my blouse."

"Lucky him."

"Shut up," Eileen hit him. She was definitely blushing, Thomas was sure. "Now you tell."

"You sure you want to know?"

"Aye."

"Well..."

"Thomas, if you don't tell me I'll never speak to you again!"

"All right," Thomas leaned back against the crates. "There were two. One was Christine. She was a shop-girl. It lasted for maybe a month. She tossed me aside for a young noble with more money."

"Nice. And the other?"

Thomas smiled. "The other was Alison Dunlow."

"I take it that went better?"

Thomas, remembering many stolen afternoons with her, smiled wider. "Aye, it did."

"Is it over?"

Thomas caught the change in her tone. "Are you jealous?"

"I am not!" Eileen snapped. She turned away, and when she spoke again, she sounded much more composed. "I'm just asking."

"Aye, it's over. Her father serves the king, and he was moved to another city. We talked about keeping on, but her father didn't really approve of me and...." The smile vanished and Thomas didn't finish the sentence, just waved it all away with a motion of his hand. "It ended."

"I'm sorry."

"So was I."

Eileen didn't say anything to that and Thomas, caught up in his own bittersweet memories, didn't feel like talking. The moon slipped behind a cloud, casting them into darkness. They stayed there, silent, until it slipped out again and its light once more lit the river. Thomas took a deep breath and let the memories flow out of him with the air.

"On Ailbe's porch," Eileen's voice was low, tentative. "Why didn't you kiss me?"

Thomas thought back to that night, to the feel of her in his arms, and the terrible pain in her eyes. "Because you'd just been hurt. Because I'd just killed someone and I didn't know if I was going to hang or have to run away or what." His eyes sought hers in the darkness. "I didn't want to make things worse."

"Oh," Eileen kept her eyes on him a moment, then turned away to stare out at the river again. "Thank you."

Thomas, feeling incredibly awkward, searched around for another topic of conversation. "Did I ever tell you about the worst lecture I ever attended?"

Eileen shook her head, clearing whatever thoughts were there away. "No. What was it?"

"Well, once upon a time, there was a nasty history professor named Dr. Magnus Dodson..."

The story led into another, then into a third. Thomas kept going, telling her tales of the Academy and his friends there, until her eyes began to slide shut and she nodded off against his shoulder. He let her sit there a while, enjoying the warmth of her body beside his. At last, he woke her and led her back to her blankets. He tucked them around her, then lay down on his own and tried to sleep. He didn't manage it for a long time, but at least his mind was filled with the girl asleep next to him, rather than the problems that lay ahead and behind.

When he woke up, it was to the feeling of cold rain falling on his face.

The three quickly scrambled to get their few possessions out of the rain, and took themselves to the cabin. Vicki made them breakfast and kept them dry until the captain and his sons stretched out some fabric for them, tying it to the crates and spreading it wide to keep the rain off a fair sized section of deck.

Thomas and his friends huddled there for the entirety of the morning, talking quietly about inconsequential things, arguing lightly over events from the past that they all remembered differently, and wishing the time would pass faster.

The barge made a landing shortly after lunch, pulling into the dock at a small town. Richard announced that they would all spend the night ashore, and told them where the inn was. Thomas was glad for the chance to stretch his legs, even if it meant getting soaked, and George and Eileen were feeling exactly the same. Thomas reclaimed his sword from the captain, and all three went ashore as soon as the barge reached the dock.

Thomas led them first to the inn to get a room, then the three took themselves throughout the town, finding fresh supplies for the rest of the trip. A few enquires also led them to a Healer and, with a few quiet explanations, they managed to have Eileen and George's stitches removed. After that, they sat in the inn, watching the rain come down and the grey afternoon slip away to dark night, while the fire kept them warm. The four boys, Thomas noticed, were not gambling on shore.

"Not surprising," was George's comment. "They can't cheat here and get away with it."

"So they do cheat?" Eileen asked.

"Aye. Badly. I'm expecting them to try and take me for all they can our last day."

"I told you," said Eileen to Thomas. "I knew they were doing something."

"And if they do?" asked Thomas.

George smiled. "I've got a plan for them."

"Which is?"

George's smile spread to a grin. "You watch and see." He picked up his glass, but found it empty. "We should have another, I think."

"You should have another," Eileen rose from her chair, a little unsteady. "I'm going to see if they can send up a washtub to the room."

"And shall we have a girl to wash your back?" asked George.

Eileen hit her brother in the arm before stalking off to the bartender.

* * *

The next morning dawned as grey and rainy as the one before. Breakfast was warm and very welcome, and eaten as the rain poured down outside the inn. Thomas wished they could stay there for the day, rather than heading back on the river. The captain was not willing to linger, though, and as soon as breakfast was gone, he herded his sons and wife out the door and towards the dock. Thomas and George pulled their coats close, and Eileen wrapped her cloak around herself, and all three followed quickly behind.

The group reached the barge at a quick trot, and George and Eileen hastened on board to where the captain's two youngest sons were making tight the canvas over their passengers' makeshift shelter. Thomas, of a mind to do the same, had to stop while the two elder sons undid the ropes from the moorings and tossed them on board. Thomas hopped on board as soon as they were done, then turned to watch as they pushed the barge away from the docks, skilfully using their feet and poles and jumping aboard at the last second. Their father called from the stern, and the young men bent themselves to pushing the poles against the bottom of the river, forcing the heavy barge away from the shore and out into the current.

There were boats coming down the river towards them.

Two of them, Thomas saw as he squinted into the rain. They were large river vessels, masts empty of sails and oars stroking the water. They had pennants which hung limp against the mast, the rain plastering them down even as the wind tried to make them flap.

Some noble, Thomas thought, *heading for shelter to wait out the rain.*
Lucky them.

The barge moved out into the river and the rain began to come down harder. Thomas was about to join his friends under their makeshift shelter when he spotted a figure standing alone at the bow of the first boat. The man was thin as a whipcord or the blade of a rapier. His black cloak covered him, obscuring any features that the thick rain might have left unhidden.

Thomas felt his heart in his throat.

He stepped back into the shelter of the crates, wishing for just a moment that the pennants of the boats would flap just enough for him to see their insignia. They didn't, and as the barge slipped into the middle of the river, the rain began to pour harder, becoming a thick grey curtain that obscured all sight of the shore and enveloped the boats and the man on the bow.

No reason for it to be Randolf, Thomas thought as he stood, getting drenched and staring out into the thick haze of the rain.

But no reason for it not to be, either.

He went to where his friends stood under the stretched-out canvas, and after a moment's thought, told them nothing. All he had seen was a man standing in the bow of a boat, waiting to come to shore. There was no reason to think it was any more than that. Of course, that didn't stop the idea from staying with Thomas like a persistent itch that would not go away whether scratched or left alone.

The rain kept falling for the rest of the morning and the afternoon and the whole of the next day. The captain offered them crates to keep between themselves and the wet deck, but didn't allow them to sleep inside the galley, saying the weather wasn't bad enough for that, and so they sat, venturing into the small cabin for food, or to pass a moment in warmth. George continued to gamble with the captain's sons and came out slightly ahead every time. Thomas played chess with Eileen or the captain and watched the river go by and worried. Eileen wandered between the various groups. By the end of their fourth day on the river all three agreed that the only thing worse than being stuck in the rain was being stuck on a barge they couldn't leave. Fortunately, that night, the captain pulled them in at another town. Thomas, George, and Eileen practically ran to the inn, revelling at the chance to get dry and warm and stay that way for more than a few hours.

The next day dawned clear and bright, and all three breathed a sigh of relief. They settled onto the barge again, and the youngest of the captain's sons joined them. "We'll be in Hawksmouth by early this evening," he told them. He rattled a pair of dice in his hands and grinned at George. "This afternoon will be our last chance."

"Not in a dicing mood," said George. "Thanks anyway."

"Oh," the young man looked disappointed, then tried again. "We could play some cards?"

"No," said George. "Thanks."

Thomas watched the young man's face fall as he went back to the stern, probably to tell his brothers. Thomas looked at George. "This was your plan? Say no?"

"That's part of it," said George. "The next bit comes when they start getting insistent."

By noon several of the brothers had stopped by, asking him to join them for one more game. George refused them all. In the end, all four came at once, practically demanding he join them at dicing. George took a moment to wink at his friends before pushing himself to his feet and stretching.

"No cards or dice for me, today," he announced. "I've spent too many days here sitting around to want to do more of it." Arms raised above his head, he looked like a giant compared to the four young men in front of him. From the looks on their faces, they were realizing it themselves. "I'm in the mood to be moving," George continued. He pointed at the empty space in the middle of the deck. "Tell you what, though, I'm always willing to wager on some wrestling. Who wants to try?"

The four young men took a fair bit of time looking back and forth among themselves before declining and retreating. As soon as they were out of earshot Thomas turned to George, "That was the rest of the plan, I take it?"

George grinned. "It was."

"How much did you win off them?" asked Eileen.

"Enough to make them sorry for themselves," said George. "And no less than they deserved."

Eileen shook her head and sighed, then went off to find a place to watch the river go by. For the rest of the day the four sons cast grumpy looks whenever they passed George, but none said anything. George just smiled and waved happily.

The day crept by no faster than any of the others, and Thomas amused himself talking to Eileen or watching the river, or playing chess with the captain. He was deep into a late-afternoon chess game with the captain when Eileen cried, "There it is!"

She was standing on the crates at the bow, waving. Thomas gave the captain his next move, then headed for the bow. George met him there and the two joined Eileen in staring at Hawksmouth.

The forest had been giving away to farmland all day, and now there were only a few strands of trees along the banks, and, in the distance, the city. The walls of Hawksmouth were thirty feet high, made of a red-streaked brown granite that had once seen invading armies dash themselves to pieces on its surface. The city had long since overgrown them, however. Now the walls jutted up like a rather ineffective dam unable to hold back the tide of shops and houses and inns that had spilled out from inside and now engulfed its walls.

Thomas found himself filled with relief. For the last four years Hawksmouth had been his home. His friends were here. He had a place to stay that was his own. The bishop did not know he was here, and once inside the city he could vanish without a trace if the need arose.

George and Eileen were staring at the city, a mixture of amazement, fear, and curiosity on their faces. Thomas was sure he had worn a very similar expression four years before. He pointed to the buildings and began naming the ones he recognized. He told them the story of the construction of the High Father's Cathedral, whose steeples rose high above the city walls. He found the royal castle, a thick cluster of towers and walls in one section of the inner city. Thomas quickly put a name to each tower as they glided ever-closer down the river.

"There," Thomas, pointed to a tall group of buildings, rising above the apartments and houses and businesses near the edge of the outer city. "That's the Academy."

"That's the Academy?" Eileen shielded her eyes with her hand. "Can we see where you live from here?"

"No. I'm in an apartment." said Thomas. "You can't see it from here. But that– " he pointed to a domed building, " –is the observatory, and there's the church, and the big one in the center is the assembly hall."

"It looks marvellous."

Thomas felt himself grinning, and for the first time since they'd started running, something like hope was starting to form in his chest. "Aye, it is."

Thomas and his friends stayed at the bow, watching the city grow closer. The farmhouses gave way to clusters of buildings, and the barge was soon floating through the city. Warehouses and docks lined the river, taverns and merchant houses filling the spaces between. Boats and ferries plied the the river around the city, and a pair of large bridges, big enough for even the largest of barges to pass under, spanned the water for foot traffic.

The captain called an order, shifted the rudder, and his sons brought their poles out once more. The barge pulled into the docks on the edge of the great walls, picking a spot as far from shore as possible.

"We aren't going right to the sea?" Eileen asked.

"Nay," said Captain Gloust. "The currents are too strong for the likes of us. We'd be pulled out and it would take a fair number of strong men to row us back. Better to stay upriver a bit."

The barge docked, the four sons jumped to the wharf and tied the large craft to the mooring posts. Thomas and his friends gathered their gear and said a quick good-bye to the captain and his wife. The four boys said good-bye as well, and managed to sound almost civil when they did, which made George grin.

As soon as they were ashore, Thomas restored the purse of gold to George's possession, then led his friends north and east, away from the city walls and towards the stone towers of the Academy.

The streets were filled with people, most moving quickly and not looking at one another. Some stood in the street and talked, ignoring the rush of bodies that dodged around them. A few wretched, scabrous individuals, some missing limbs, sat on corners or at the edge of the street, calling for alms. Men on horseback or driving carts cursed and shouted their way down the road, forcing those on foot to scatter to the sides or risk being run over. The streets narrowed and became more crowded as they went further. Buildings rose on all sides, blocking the view.

"Is it always like this?" Eileen asked.

"It's worse on market days," said Thomas, raising his voice to be heard above the crowd. "Today, it's just those who live here. On market days, the population doubles."

"Awful noisy," George observed.

"Aye."

"And dirty," Eileen added.

"Aye."

"And you love it, do you?"

Thomas grinned at George's reproachful tone. "Aye, I do. Come on."

He led George and Eileen forward and deep into the crush of people, slipping in and out of the moving bodies and down twisting side streets until he found the thoroughfare he wanted. George and Eileen's heads were turning constantly back and forth, their eyes wide as they tried to catch all the sights and sounds. By the time they'd gone half a mile both wore stunned expressions, as if the noise and movement had hypnotized them. Thomas, remembering the day he had arrived, knew exactly how they were feeling.

They moved up the street, and Thomas began seeing familiar places. He pointed out the buildings he knew and was a bit embarrassed when he realized that the majority of them were taverns. The closer he got to the Academy though, the more he could expand on the list. Soon he was pointing out booksellers, clothiers, and bakeries. There was a theatre that was the favourite of the students, and a nearby hall where prize-fights were held and where he'd won his rapier. He told them which streets were safe to walk down at night and which weren't. One side street, wider than the others, held the grand houses and spacious apartments of wealthy merchants that lacked the connections to buy similar dwellings within the city walls.

The street ended at the Academy's gates. The wall that stretched off to both sides wasn't greatly impressive in comparison to the walls of the city. The Academy wall was only twelve feet high and certainly no more than two feet thick. It was nothing that would keep out anyone determined to get in, but it was high enough to separate the Academy from the city that surrounded it. The wide, wooden gates stood open. Through them Thomas could see the clean lawns, neat paths, and well-manicured trees that surrounded the school's buildings. A pair of young men dressed in the black livery of the scholars with steel helmets and long staves stood a casual and bored watch just outside the gates. Several students, robed in black, passed in and out while the three friends watched.

Thomas waved an arm, taking in the gates and the buildings beyond, "This is it. This is the Academy."

"It's huge," said George, alternating peering through the gates and staring up to the buildings that rose above the wall. "It's bigger than Elmvale."

"Why are there guards?" Eileen asked.

"The Academy is owned directly by the crown, not by the city's government. The wall reminds us that we are separate, and the guards are supposed to keep the king's peace among the students."

"Do they succeed?"

"Not often. But they do try." Thomas smiled. "Actually, these days guard duty is punishment for students who break the Academy rules."

"Are we going in?" George asked.

"Not yet," said Thomas. "We'll go to my apartment, first."

"You have your own apartment?" Eileen's eyebrows went up. "Isn't that expensive?"

"It's not just mine. There's two others who stay there as well."

"All in the same room?" George sounded appalled. "The poor folk in the village have it better."

"That they do," Thomas agreed. "But we're not all in the same room. Come on, I'll show you."

He led them a little way down a street that ran parallel to the Academy wall, then turned up a short, narrow alley, ignoring the debris on the ground. A tall, thick gate stretched the width of the alley, attached to the edges of the buildings on either side. Thomas lifted the latch, opened it, and ushered his friends through.

On the other side of the gate, the alley opened wide into a shaded, cobblestone courtyard. The tall brick and wood walls of the two buildings that enclosed it not only blocked the sunlight, but also most of the city noise. They were four stories high, with balconies running the length of each building on every floor. A few were bare, but most were adorned with plants and wind chimes and furniture. Several lines of laundry were strung between the buildings, filled with black robes and white linen. There were young men out on many of the balconies, talking animatedly about classes or books or girls, or playing heated games of cards or chess. A small fountain with two short stone maidens in flowing robes pouring never-ending streams of water from jugs into the pool below stood in the centre of the courtyard. On one side of the fountain a dice game was keeping a half-dozen young men busy. On the other, two students were deep in discussion with a pair of young ladies who were giggling and obviously refusing to go to the young men's rooms.

"This is it," said Thomas, smiling at the chaos. The sense of relief it gave him was amazing. For the first time in weeks Thomas felt that he was somewhere that he belonged. "I'm home."

From above, a voice called, "Thomas?!"

Chapter 18

Thomas looked up. A familiar and startled face was leaning out over the edge of one of the balconies. Even as Thomas wished that his name had not been called across the courtyard, the face and the body it attached to vanished into the building. "He's back!" Thomas heard faintly. A moment later, the same young man and another rushed onto the balcony. Thomas grinned, waved at them, and led George and Eileen across the courtyard and up the outside stairs of the building.

"What in the name of the High Father are you doing here?" demanded the first of the young men as Thomas reached the balcony. He was a big man, almost as large as George, though somewhat heavier around the middle, with a shock of black hair that looked as if he'd just gotten out of bed. He was in breeches and a white shirt and barefoot. "You're not supposed to be back for three months at least."

"Change of plans," said Thomas.

The big man narrowed his eyes. "Good or bad?"

"I'll explain after we get the bags inside."

"Which you won't be doing until you introduce us," said the second student. He was several years older than Thomas, and his clothes were both of better material and more finely cut than anyone else's in the room. His pale blond hair was immaculately coiffed, his face and nose thin and long and marred with a scar that cut diagonally across them. He stepped in front of George and Eileen, the move simultaneously casual and elegant. "Well?"

Thomas sighed. "Can't I put the luggage down, first?"

The blond man waved a finger at Thomas. "Manners before everything. Introductions, please."

"Right," Thomas dropped his bag directly on the toes of the elegant young man's shiny boots. "George, Alex, these are my room-mates. Benjamin—" he pointed at the big student—"and Henry—" his finger moved to the elegant one. "Benjamin is studying Theology, Henry studies Law. Ben, Henry, these are George and Alex, friends of mine from home."

"Welcome," said Benjamin, extending an arm. Visiting, or joining the Academy?"

"Uh, a visit," said Eileen, stepping forward to take the large man's hand.

"And are you merchant's sons like your friend here?" asked Henry.

"No," said George, also shaking Benjamin's hand. "Blacksmith."

"Ah," said Henry, nodding as if he'd had a guess confirmed. "Tradesman, then."

"Lower your nose," growled Benjamin. "Half of us are tradesmen."

"And I hardly hold it against you at all," assured Henry, grandly.

Benjamin sighed. "You'll have to forgive Henry. He was raised to think of himself as our better and occasionally it goes to his head."

"He's the son of the Duke of Frostmire," explained Thomas. "It gives him delusions of grandeur."

"The youngest son," corrected Henry, cheerfully, "and therefore worthy to receive an education, instead of land or money. Nice cut on your face, there, by the way," he added. "Story behind it?"

"Aye."

Henry scooped up Thomas's bag with an easy motion and bowed a deep court bow. "Come in, come in. The prodigal student has returned, and this calls for a drink!"

A cheer rose from several nearby balconies, to which Henry called, "Not for you, peasants!" before turning and leading the others inside.

The apartment had a single, central living space, with four doors in the walls.

Three rooms and the back exit, Henry explained. The big room served as kitchen, dining room, meeting room, and occasional bedroom for those who were too drunk or tired to go home.

"And this," said Thomas, leading them to one of the closed doors, "is mine."

He stepped in and threw the shutters open, then turned back to his friends. Their expressions were carefully neutral. Thomas couldn't blame them. The room truly wasn't much to look at. The walls and ceiling, once white, were now yellow from smoke and blackened in places from candles burning. The sole window, just above the desk, was small and looked out over the roof. There were no curtains. The desk itself was old and splintery and had a piece of wood under one leg to keep it level. The stool before it was no better. The bed beside the desk was rumpled, the sheets unaired since Thomas had left. A shelf above it was overflowing with books, and more lay in stacks on the floor beside it. Everything was coated with a layer of dust.

"You like it here?" asked George as he took in the room.

"It's a place to sleep," Thomas said. "And to study."

George looked dubious. "I suppose, it is."

"I like it," said Eileen, stepping in and taking a closer look at the books. "Are they all yours?"

"Aye."

"Hey," called Henry from the main room. "Put those bags down and get back here! We have drinking to do!"

Thomas took George and Eileen's bags and tossed them on the bed before leading them back to the main room. Benjamin smiled and told them to grab a cushion and a place on the floor.

"It's far more comfortable than the table," he explained, "and much less distance to fall, once you pass out."

Benjamin pulled a bottle of wine from one cupboard and Henry brought a loaf of bread and block of cheese from another. Cups were hastily rinsed from a pitcher of water, the excess liquid dumped off the balcony to the protests of those below. Soon all of them were seated on the floor, cushions against their backs, nibbling on the food.

"So, what we want to know," said Henry, after polishing off half of his first drink, "is what you are doing here, what your friends are doing here, how you got your face cut, and did you bring back anything for us?"

"Hear, hear!" said Benjamin.

"All right," Thomas agreed. "Do you want the short story or the long?"

"Short," declared Henry. "If you tell the long story, we'll be here until midnight."

"Right," said Thomas. "My father had me beaten, kicked out of the house, and charged with stealing his money, the bishop has put all three of us up on charges of witchcraft, my face was cut fighting his men, and I didn't bring anything back for you. So, dinner on me?"

After a long silence that was thick enough to cut and serve, Henry spoke. "You're buying dinner?"

Benjamin glared at him. "You're wanted by the bishop?"

"And the magistrate," said Thomas, enjoying the appalled look on Benjamin's face.

"Why?"

Thomas shrugged. "You asked for the short version."

Benjamin's brow furrowed and his eyebrows came down. "Fine. You want to make a story out of it, we'll listen. But you *are* buying dinner. And the longer the story, the better the dinner."

"Make it as long as possible, then," said Henry, starting to rise, "after we get to the *Broken Quill*."

"Wait!" Eileen blurted. They all turned to look at her, and she blushed. "I mean, I don't think we should talk about this in public."

"Sh—" George stopped and corrected himself. "He's right. Loud talk in a tavern gets around."

"True," said Henry, sitting down again. "Thomas, go out and fetch us supper."

"Me?" Thomas protested. "I just got here."

"You have the money," said Henry. "Still, one of us can go with you, to help you carry." He turned and looked meaningfully at Benjamin, who shook his head and started to rise.

"Subtle, Henry." Benjamin extended a hand to George. "Come on. If we both go, we can probably manage a keg of ale between us."

"We're not getting a keg," warned Thomas, getting to his feet.

"I'll go, too," Eileen said, also getting up. "I want to see more of the city."

"And leave me here all alone?" asked Henry, mock-hurt in his voice.

"It's not our fault you're lazy," said Thomas.

"You are a rude little burgher," declared Henry, "and so to punish you, I will stay here and drink."

"Fine," Benjamin opened the back door of the apartment, revealing a dark hallway on the other side. "We'll buy better and keep it for ourselves."

He led them out the back door and down a dim hallway to an equally dim flight of narrow, worn stairs. What light there was came from above, shining in from an opening in the ceiling. It was a common design, Thomas explained, since landlords in the city refused to pay for more roof than absolutely necessary. The hole was too small to provide any real illumination and the stairs were steep and treacherous. Thomas and Benjamin took them with practiced ease. George and Eileen each slipped, barely catching themselves on the rail before falling headlong down the stairs.

The stairs ended in a short hall that emptied out onto a narrow street. Benjamin led them down it and out into the heavy traffic of the main thoroughfares. They dodged their way across, then down several other side-streets and across another major road. There were people everywhere, milling about, standing in the street talking, and occasionally pushing back against the walls around them to avoid being trampled by a passing cart or rider. At last, the street they were on opened into a large, busy market.

The square was the size of the Elmvale town common, but with easily five times the number of people, and surrounded on all sides by shops and houses. Vendors had tables set up to display their wares, or sat on blankets on the ground. A juggler was tossing flaming torches while a musician played on a flute, and a small crowd clapped in time. Thomas watched a moment, his heart going back to Timothy, then turned away and plunged into the market.

There were fruit and vegetables—most either small from being picked too early or shrivelled from having been stored over the winter—chickens, both alive and cooked, cheese-sellers, bakers with bread and tarts of meat and berries, and people selling crockery and kitchen gear, gloves and cloaks, and a dozen other things besides. It was lively, loud, vibrant chaos from end to end.

"Hang tight to your purses," Benjamin said to George and Eileen. "There's a good number of pick-pockets that work the market, and no doubt they'll grab anything you're not holding tight."

Thomas had already taken a good grip on his purse, and saw his friends do the same. Benjamin plunged into the crowd, and Thomas let Eileen and George follow before bringing up the rear. It was like stepping into a whirlwind. George and Eileen's eyes were darting everywhere, trying to catch everything that was happening. Benjamin looked over his shoulder to George. "First time in the city, is it?"

"Aye," said George, pulling his eyes away from a display of leather goods. "It's busy."

"That it is," agreed Benjamin. "The first year I was here I couldn't keep up with anything. Spent most of my time in the Academy library just to keep my mind straight. You said your father's a smith?"

"Aye."

"Mine's a stone mason." Benjamin stopped abruptly, pointing down one of the aisles. "Found him!"

"Found who?" Eileen asked.

"Him," said Thomas, stepping up beside them and pointing down the aisle. A short, fat man stood in front of a small cart, with several roasted chickens on it. "He is the finest cook in the quarter. And where his stand is, you'll find the stand of the best baker, freshest fruit, and best wines."

"It's a game he plays," Benjamin explained. "Most of the merchants have their own place that they stay in, but he likes to move around the market, just to keep us on our toes."

"Bernard!" Thomas called. The man behind the cart looked around, spotted Thomas, and waved.

"Thomas!" he called back. "I thought you were gone to visit your family!"

"I was," agreed Thomas, "I just got back."

"And the first thing you do is visit me? I'm grateful!"

"Where else would I go? I'm hungry."

"I'll give you a good meal, I promise that!"

"Can you give me a good meal for five?"

"Five?" The man looked impressed. "You must have come home with money."

"Not a lot," Thomas made his voice as casual as possible, "but enough to feed all my friends for a day if you don't drive too hard a bargain."

"I never drive too hard a bargain," Bernard said, widening his eyes in pretended offence. "We will give your friends a good feed." He turned to the stalls on either side. "Come on, you lot. Wine! Bread! And for the centerpiece..." He turned behind him, where a metal trough held several roasts of beef and pork on spits. "Here we are!" He reached back and pulled one of the beef roasts. "Rare and fine. And no doubt you'll want some chicken as well."

"Of course."

"Well then, here you go." A chicken came off another spit. "Your timing is just perfect. I've been getting ready for the supper crowd, and you've beat them to it."

"Good. Benjamin, take the wine cart; George, the bread."

George watched as Benjamin turned and immediately began haggling. Without a second thought, he turned to the baker's cart and demanded the price on two loaves of bread so fresh the steam was still rising from them. Soon, lively discussions were happening on either side. Bernard watched the two squeezing every possible penny, and looked disapprovingly at the young man before him. "Thomas, Thomas, you wouldn't starve an old friend now, would you?"

"Not I," Thomas said. "Alex?"

Eileen stepped forward and smiled at the cook. Thomas grinned. The city may have been overwhelming for George and Eileen, but markets were the same everywhere. He listened a moment as Eileen, feigning complete indifference to the food, began haggling far better than Thomas would have managed. "I'm going for dessert," Thomas said. "Have George pay for it all, then the lot of you meet me at the edge of the market."

* * *

The four returned to the apartment as the last of the evening light was fading. George and Eileen both stopped in the door and glanced back at Thomas in surprise. Thomas, guessing what had happened, pushed them in. The common room had been tidied, the table cleared and set with clean plates and mugs and fresh candles. The bottle of wine, mostly untouched, sat in the centre of the table. Henry, seeing George and Eileen's expressions, smiled at them and bowed deeply. "I may be a pompous ass," he declared, "but I will not have it said I keep a poor table for company."

He quickly relieved the four of their burdens and set them on the table. In a short space of time, he had the meat carved, glasses filled, and was gesturing them all to sit and eat. All five dug in with gusto. Roast beef, chicken, bread, and potatoes all vanished at high speed. Henry kept everyone's glasses filled and all five became quite merry. Thomas attempted to talk about what had happened in Elmvale, but Henry waved him off.

"Business is not suitable talk for the table," he declared. "Now we eat, drink, and be merry. Later, we fix your problems." He turned to George. "So, are you a smith like your father, then?"

Thomas gave up. Henry played gracious host very well, and for an hour or so, Thomas let him. Henry and Benjamin caught him up on the doings of the city, and the conversation ranged from the latest plays to the antics of the professors to a new treatise questioning the position of the nobility in society.

The five finished three bottles of wine by the time the last plate was cleared. Thomas let the others drink the lion's share of it, though he was by no means sober. Henry refilled each mug again and led them away from the table to the cushions on the floor. He took one for himself and sat, swaying all the way down.

"Not a bad dinner at all," said Henry, sipping at the wine. "How many bottles do we have left?"

"Four," Benjamin said, swaying himself as he lowered his bulk onto a cushion. "I bought a lot."

"Good." Henry sipped again and turned to Thomas. "Now. The long version."

"What?" said Thomas.

"Witchcraft and theft," reminded Henry.

"Oh. That." Thomas slid down the wall until he, too, was on the floor, and gestured George and Eileen to do the same. They did, though warily.

"What about witchcraft?" Benjamin demanded, swinging slightly unfocused eyes to Henry.

"Thomas is wanted for witchcraft," said Henry. "He said so before dinner."

Benjamin thought about it. "Right. I'd forgotten."

"So now he'll tell us the long version of the story," Henry took another drink, "and then we will hang him."

"Not funny," Benjamin said, firmly. "Not even if you're drunk. Which you are."

"No, I'm not."

"Yes, you are."

"No, I'm not."

"Yes, you are."

"Fine then," Henry waved Benjamin off. "I'm drunk. Now what's the story? From the beginning."

Thomas managed to tell the story fairly succinctly, up to the point where he'd been beaten by the bishop's men. He stopped there, thinking hard about how much to tell Benjamin and Henry. He'd known them for four years now, and trusted them both. They weren't the sort who would turn their backs on him, though they certainly wouldn't believe what had happened. Thomas took a deep breath and told what happened in the family prayer room, stopping at, "And that's when the bishop tried to tear out part of my soul."

There was a long silence. Benjamin and Henry both looked befuddled. At last, Henry ventured, "You're speaking metaphorically, right?"

"No."

Henry turned to George. "Is he joking?"

George shook his head. "No. And there's more."

"More?" Henry swung his head between the two. "You have something to top that?"

Thomas sighed. "Unfortunately, yes."

He told the rest of the story, watching his friends closely as he did. They stayed silent until he finished, then Henry asked the obvious question.

"You've gone insane, right?"

Thomas shook his head. "No, I haven't."

Henry turned to George and Eileen. "He has gone insane, right?"

The siblings looked at each other and hesitated. It was George who finally spoke. "We don't know."

"What?" Thomas was shocked.

"We're sorry," Eileen said. She turned to Henry. "I mean, everything he said about the bishop being after us is true, and something *was* wrong with Ailbe, but as for the magic..."

Thomas suddenly felt very alone. "I thought you believed me."

"We want to," said George. "It's just that we haven't *seen* any magic."

"What about Timothy?" demanded Thomas. "What about the ball of light?"

George stared at the floor. "All I saw was a ball, Thomas," he mumbled. "I couldn't tell you if it was light or wood. I'm sorry."

Thomas's heart felt like it was being squeezed. "But you were *there*..."

"But we didn't *see* anything," Eileen looked almost as upset as Thomas felt. She turned back to Henry and Benjamin. "And it doesn't change anything, really. The bishop is still after us, Thomas's father still kicked him out, and the bishop's men killed Shamus and Timothy. All that's true, and Thomas thought you would help."

"How?" asked Benjamin. "Other than buying you passage on the next ship out?"

"Help me *prove* it," Thomas tried not to sound as desperate as he felt. He had hoped George and Eileen had believed him, at least a bit, and the news that they didn't rattled him far more than he expected. "I need to find out how the bishop is doing it, and I need to stop him."

Benjamin thought about it. "Are you sure he's using witchcraft?"

"Magic," Thomas corrected. "Not witchcraft."

"All magic is witchcraft," said Benjamin.

"Ah!" said Henry, raising an unsteady finger. "Not according to the Council of Carlyle."

"Exactly," Thomas spoke slowly. "At Carlyle they declared that witchcraft came from the power of the Banished. Magic doesn't."

"Then where does it come from?"

"I don't know," admitted Thomas. "Timothy thought that it was a gift from the Blessed Daughter."

"Can't be," Benjamin shook his head, the movement nearly making him tip over. "The Blessed Daughter gives us music and art, not witchcraft. She doesn't have that power."

"She doesn't now," said Thomas. "Maybe she did, once."

"The gods don't change."

"Yes, they do!" declared Eileen. Everyone turned to look at her, and she blushed. "I mean, the nuns always talked of a time when the Loyal Consort was the Great Mother, giver of all life and death, who ruled beside the High Father."

"That is true," said Henry. "And why were you hanging out with nuns?"

Thomas spoke before Eileen had to answer. "Timothy's mother told him a story of when the gods were equal and had names. She couldn't remember what they were, but she remembered they had names."

"It's not in any of the books I've seen," said Benjamin, stubbornly. "And I've read far more theology than either of you."

"If I was going to make my church supreme," Henry pointed out, "I'd get rid of all the books that say otherwise."

"Exactly!" said Thomas. "I mean, have any of us seen any books written about the Blessed Daughter? Or the Loyal Consort, or the Rebel Son, other than those written by the priests of the High Father? The Church of the High Father has been in ascendancy for the last two hundred years. What if they did it by getting rid of the things that made the other gods important?"

"Like magic?" asked George.

"Aye! How can the Church of the High Father be supreme if the priests of other gods can do magic and theirs can't?"

"It's a good argument," said Henry. "Pity there's no such thing as magic." He nodded at Benjamin. "Or witchcraft."

"It's not witchcraft," said Thomas, quietly.

"How do you know?" demanded Benjamin.

"Because there's no such thing!" Henry repeated.

"It can't be witchcraft," said Thomas slowly, "because if it is, I'm guilty of it, too."

Benjamin was the first to work his way through what Thomas meant. When he had, he looked even more confused. "But you said you only saw him do it."

"That's right. I *saw* him do it. No one else can."

Benjamin stared at Thomas for a good length of time. At last, he leaned back against the wall, holding his head. "I'm too drunk for this."

"We all are," agreed Henry. "We should go to bed and start over in the morning."

"We can't," said Benjamin, sounding very worried. "Because I'm duty bound to report witchcraft to the Master of Theology."

George and Eileen's jaws both dropped at once. Henry's head snapped around to Benjamin. "You can't turn him in!" he protested. "There's no such thing as witchcraft! He's just gone crazy."

"You're not really helping," said Thomas.

Benjamin was at once looking extremely sorry and very stubborn. "The Master of Theology has to know if someone is using witchcraft."

"It's not witchcraft!"

"No one is telling the Master of Theology anything," declared Henry.

"I'm duty bound," began Benjamin, but Henry cut him off.

"Are you going to tell him the *bishop* is using witchcraft?" demanded Henry. "Because all you've got is Thomas's word for it, and he's insane."

"I am *not*—"

"Yes, you are!" Henry snapped, turning on Thomas. "You said that you were the only one that can see or hear this 'magic.'"

"Yes, but—"

"When the bishop commanded your father, did anyone else there notice?"

"No, but—"

"And when Ailbe healed Eileen, did anyone else see the white light?"

"No, but—"

"You see and hear things that no one else does, Thomas. So either you're insane, in which case it's all right, or you're a witch, in which case Benjamin would have to report you."

Thomas was about to protest the difference between magic and witchcraft again, when he realized what Henry was doing. A smile he couldn't help spread itself across his face. "Of course. I'm insane."

Comprehension lit Benjamin's face a moment later. "Of course you are. Completely."

"That's right," Henry said, slapping Thomas's arm affectionately. "Mad beyond all singing of it. Of course, that doesn't help him with his real problem."

Benjamin opened his mouth to speak, then stopped. After a moment, he said, "You know, I've forgotten what that was."

"I'm wanted for murder and witchcraft," said Thomas.

"And he says the bishop is guilty instead," said Henry.

Benjamin's eyes started to glaze over. "Didn't we just have this argument?"

"No, this is a different argument," Thomas assured him. "That argument was theoretical. This one is practical."

"All right, then. Practically, what do you need?"

"He needs to prove the bishop is guilty," said Henry.

"No, first he needs to prove that he's innocent," argued George, "then he gets to prove the bishop's guilty."

"They go together," said Thomas. "And before I can do either, I need to find out what he's up to. I don't even know if he's back in the city, yet."

"I can find out," Benjamin said. "I know the initiates who serve in his house once a week. I'll ask them."

"Good. But he can't find out that I'm here."

"I won't mention you," Benjamin waved a dismissive hand. "Besides, he doesn't talk to initiates anyway."

"Thank you."

Eileen, who had been quiet through the whole discussion, was wearing a very confused look on her face. As her head turned slowly from one student to the other, she said, "So, you two are going to help him?"

"Yes," said Benjamin. "After all, he's insane."

Eileen turned to Thomas. "You are?"

"He is," said Henry, smiling and raising the wine bottle and filling mugs. "At least until he proves otherwise." He filled the last mug then raised his own. "So tonight, we drink until it all feels better."

"Knowing tomorrow the hangover will make it all feel worse," intoned Benjamin.

"Speaking of tomorrow," said Thomas, "I want to get into the library."

"The library?" repeated Benjamin. "What's in there?"

"Some answers, maybe. About the bishop."

"Where?" demanded Henry. "In the witchcraft section?"

"Well, there's got to be something."

"No there doesn't," Benjamin was lilting a bit to one side, now, but sounded fairly clear. "I went through the witchcraft section in the library for one report I wrote on the workings of the Banished in the world and the social impact of those workings on the three estates—"

"Which estates are those?" asked Eileen.

"The three estates," said Henry. "The king, the nobility, and you lot."

"Ah."

"The primary focus of the essay was to determine which acts, ascribed to the Banished, were actually done by them through their witches, and which were actually the results of human stupidity and sheer incompetence." Benjamin stopped for a moment, tried to start again, then stopped once more. "Why am I talking about this?"

"Witchcraft," prompted Thomas.

"That's right," Benjamin nodded several times, then looked lost. Just before Thomas could prompt him he started again. "I wrote a report. And I went through the library and there was very little information there. There's nothing in it except books on how many witches have been caught over the last hundred years, how many converted, how many flogged, how many hung, and so on. Not even any books on how to detect witches or how not to detect witches or how to tell a real witch from a fake one."

"And nothing to tell the difference between witchcraft and magic," guessed Thomas.

"Not a thing."

"Well, that's useless."

"That it is." Benjamin realized he was on an angle, and righted himself, only to starting to listing to the other side. "Though there is one book that talks about body markings and extra hairs and strange behaviours." He looked at Eileen. "Did you know hiccups can be considered a sign of witchery?"

"I did not," said Eileen.

"Neither did I." He righted himself again and this time managed to stay erect. "Nothing in there would be any good to us."

Thomas suddenly felt very depressed. He looked down at his mug, still full, and put it down. Hopelessness grabbed him hard, taking away any desire he had for more wine.

Benjamin shook his head. "No, all the good stuff is in the Theology building."

Thomas sat up straight. "What good stuff?"

"On witchcraft," explained Benjamin, over-enunciating. "I told my professor about the report and he got me into the witchcraft section. Students aren't normally allowed in there." He cast a baleful eye at Thomas. "Especially not philosophy students or lawyers, of which you are both."

Eileen stared at Thomas, her mouth falling open. "You're doing philosophy and law?"

"Aye."

"Is it hard?"

"Not if you're insane," said Henry, raising his mug in Thomas's direction, "which he is."

"We need to get into that room," said Thomas.

"And how are we going to do that?" asked Henry. "We're hardly even allowed in the building, except to take classes."

"I don't know," Thomas picked his mug back up and took a long drink. "But I'll think of something."

Chapter 19

Thomas woke up on the floor of the common room, a cushion lying near his head, and his mug still clutched in his hand. The hangover that he had taken for granted would come was there in full force, and, judging from the sonorous bodies he stumbled over on his way to the balcony, he wasn't going to be alone. He stumbled outside, the fresh air assaulting his lungs and threatening to start a coughing fit as it drove the stifled and squalid air of the apartment from his lungs. Thomas managed to navigate the stairs and cross the rough cobblestones to the fountain without so much as a stumble, much to his relief. Stripping to the waist, he dunked his head underneath the water. It was nowhere near as cold as that from the well at the smithy, but it woke him up enough to realize how miserable he was feeling. He plunked himself on the edge of the fountain, truly thankful that the sun wasn't high enough to light the courtyard.

Despite his declaration that he'd think of something, and the several hours of alcohol-soaked inspiration that had followed it, Thomas had not come up with any ideas at all. He sighed, shook his head and instantly regretted it. At least he knew there were books he could look at. All he had to do was get at them.

Movement from above caught his attention. Squinting up to the balcony, he could see a thin figure in a loose shirt making its way out of the apartment and down the stairs. Eileen, he realized, wearing her trousers and one of George's shirts. It was large enough to look ridiculous on her, but judging by the expression on her face, she didn't much care. She made it down the stairs on not-too-steady feet and walked directly towards him.

"I saw what you did," she said, eyeing the water in the fountain. "Did it help?"

"Some."

"Good." She pulled the collar of the shirt apart wide enough that it slipped past her shoulders. With one hand holding it in place, she leaned forward and dunked her head under. She stayed down for a fair while then surfaced with a splash, gasping for air. She wiped her face with the hem of the shirt, and then sat down on the edge of the fountain beside him. "I feel awful."

"Second hangover of your life, is it?"

"Aye." She rubbed at her face, wincing as she did. "I thought that stuff Timothy fed us was bad, but this..." She looked up to the sky. "Where's the sun?"

"It doesn't reach the courtyard until about eleven o'clock, this time of year."

"Thank the Four." She looked around the silent, empty courtyard. "You have strange friends, Thomas."

"Aye."

"Do they always drink so much?"

"Only when they can."

"Benjamin seems nice enough, but Henry's..."

"Strange," finished Thomas. "Aye, he is."

"Where did he get the scar on his face? Duelling?"

"No," said Thomas. "Frostmire is on the Northern border. He spent three years fighting against raiders before he came to the Academy."

"Oh."

Thomas looked for another subject and took the obvious. "Why are you wearing George's shirt?"

"I got tired of being tied down," Eileen crossed her arms in front of her chest. "It can't be good for them."

Thomas didn't know how to reply to that, and so kept quiet.

"I thought if I put this on I could save tying myself up until we're ready to go out." She squinted at Thomas. "When are we going out?"

"Fairly soon, I should think," Thomas said. "In fact, I'm surprised the bell hasn't rung yet."

"What bell?"

As if in answer to her question, a loud, deep-toned bell began ringing from somewhere not too far off. A moment later there was scurrying movement on the top floor of the building opposite Thomas's apartment. A student, not looking too steady himself, stepped up to what looked like a ship's bell. He grabbed the cord, winced in preparation, and rang it for all he was worth. Much smaller than its counterpart at the university, it nonetheless managed to fill the courtyard with its sharp pealing.

"By the Four," Eileen moaned, holding her head. "What is that for?"

"First bell," said Thomas, covering his ears and wincing. "Classes start in half an hour."

"Half an hour?" Eileen looked around. "No one is moving—"

The buildings around them erupted into sudden, busy life. Doors were flung open, robes hastily tossed on, and dozens of people began making their way down the staircase in waves. Thomas took Eileen by the elbow and moved her away from the fountain. "Come on. We'll try not to get run over."

She did as she was told, keeping well back from the crowd and keeping her arms crossed in front of her chest. Several students stopped to dunk their heads in the fountain; others just splashed their faces or ran straight out the gates. A few were leading girls down the stairs, talking to them quietly in the midst of the tumult. No one looked twice in their direction. Benjamin stumbled down the stairs, his black hair even more messy than the day before, his skin grey and his eyes bright red. He managed a brief wave at them and grunted something that Thomas couldn't understand before joining the crowd streaming for the gate. Thomas waved back, and watched as Benjamin stumbled away.

Eileen turned to him. "Where's all the young ones?"

"They have to stay in the dormitories," Thomas explained. "You can't live outside of the Academy until you've reached sixteen."

"Then everyone does, no doubt."

"Everyone who can afford to," Thomas agreed. "It's expensive."

"Then why do it?"

"No curfew, for one," said Thomas. "And for another…" He pointed to the students kissing their girls good-bye.

Eileen shook her head. "My father would kill me if I stayed out all night."

The bell from above stopped pealing, leaving echoes that rang through the courtyard for what felt like an inordinately long time. The bell-ringer ran down the stairs and was out the gate as the last echo faded.

"Why does he have to ring the bell?" asked Eileen. "Do you take turns?"

"Sort of," Thomas said. "Every two months all the students in the two apartments pick teams and have a football tournament. The team that loses the most games rings the bell until the next tournament." He watched the student making his way across the courtyard. "I think he was the goal-keeper."

"Ah."

The last of the students cleared the courtyard and Thomas led Eileen back up the stairs to the apartment. Inside, Henry was sitting hunched over at the table, his face sour and his eyes red. There was a cup of wine in his hand and another on the table. He carefully poured wine from one of the half-empty bottles into the cup before him.

"No classes this morning?" asked Thomas, coming over to the table. He looked at the cup on the table and shuddered when he recognized the contents.

Henry grunted, took out a small bag and added something powdery to the cup. He stirred, then brought out a small, black bottle and poured a dose of a viscous liquid into the cup. He stared at the cup in front of him a moment, then took a drink from the one in his hand.

Thomas sat down beside him. "You drink too much."

"This from you," growled Henry, adding something black and leafy to the concoction.

"I don't try to keep up with George."

"That's because you have no manners." Henry stirred the contents of the cup, looked closely at it, then stirred again. "You should match your guests drink for drink, not leave them to drink alone."

"George doesn't mind. And even he isn't drinking this early."

"Hair of the dog," said Henry. He drank off the rest from the cup in his hand, then stared balefully at the one on the table. Thomas waited. A moment later, Henry picked it up and swallowed the entire contents in one go. A shudder ran through his entire body, and his breath gasped out, then back in. He shook his head, and straightened up. "Much better. Want one?"

Thomas sighed. "I probably should. Though I'm not sure the hangover isn't the lesser of two evils."

"What is it?" asked Eileen, watching Henry divide a half-dozen ingredients into three more mugs.

"The secret hangover cure of the Dukes of Frostmire," said Henry. He poured wine into the cups, stirring them with a spoon. He added the powder, the viscous liquid and the leaves, and stirred them again. When they'd reached the right consistency, he handed one to Eileen. "To be used only by nobility and those in desperate need."

Eileen sniffed it, made a face, and promptly put it down. "I don't think I need that."

"Benjamin already had his," said Henry. "Trust me; it will make it all better."

Thomas nodded and picked up the second mug. "Unfortunately, he's right."

Thomas took a deep breath and tossed back the slimy contents of the cup. He knew what was going to happen and still wasn't ready for it when something exploded inside his belly, then shook its way out to his extremities in a massive shudder. His stomach turned inside-out, flipped over, then settled itself back. Stars danced behind his eyes a moment, then cleared.

"Are you all right?" Eileen asked.

"I am," said Thomas immediately, though he wasn't sure. He did a quick check on his stomach and head, found he was right. "Your turn."

"Drink it all at once," advised Henry. "Bottoms up."

Eileen took up her cup, smelled it again, and shuddered. Wrinkling her nose up, she took a deep breath of her own and tossed it back. The shudder ran through her, and her face twisted in several unseemly ways before she could speak again. "That," she said at last, "was disgusting."

"True," agreed Henry. "How's your head?"

Eileen, obviously taking stock, took a moment before saying, "Better."

"And your stomach?"

"Also better." She shook her head in surprise. "Thank you, Henry."

"You are welcome," Henry turned from the table and shrugged himself into his robe. "Did you figure it out yet?" he asked Thomas.

"Figure out what?"

"The plan for getting into the witchcraft room in Theology. You said you'd think of something."

"Oh," said Thomas. "That."

"Have you?"

"Not yet, no."

"Wonderful." Henry headed for the door. "I've got a class to attend. Come tell us when you've got it worked out."

"We'll meet you after the third bell," called Thomas after him. "Tell Ben!"

The only reply was the clatter of Henry's feet on the stairs. Thomas shrugged and headed for his room. George was there, sitting up and holding his head. He saw Thomas and managed a wincing, "Good morning."

"Morning, George," said Eileen from behind Thomas, her voice cheerful and just loud enough to be annoying. "How's the head?"

George glared at his sister. "It's been better." He switched the glare to Thomas. "Yours?"

"Much better, now."

George shook his head, wincing again, then looked closely at his sister. "Why is Ei—" he stopped at Eileen's raised finger. "Alex. Why is Alex wearing my shirt, and why is it soaked?"

"We dunked in the fountain," said Thomas.

"Is it as cold as the pump back home?"

"No."

"Good." George heaved himself off the bed like a bear from its winter den and stumbled out of the room.

"Drink the mug that's on the table first," called Thomas. "It will help."

He watched as George sniffed the cup, threw him a glare, and tossed back the contents. After a long, shuddering gasp, the big smith shook his head, glared at Thomas again, and stomped outside. Thomas watched him go, then turned back to see Eileen was looking at him expectantly. Thomas took a moment before he caught on.

"Right," he said, realization dawning. He let her go in, then stepped out and closed the door so she could change in peace.

* * *

The second bell, announcing the start of classes, rang before Thomas, George, and Eileen made it out of the apartment. Eileen wanted to go sooner, but

Thomas kept them inside, worried the Masters would recognize him. In the meantime, they made a breakfast of leftovers from the night before, and Thomas raided his room-mates' cupboards. Henry's robes would be large on Eileen, but many students wore over-sized robes. Benjamin's, on the other hand, fit George quite well. Thomas waited for a few moments after the second bell, and then led his friends down the stairs and across the courtyard. Instead of heading for the main gates, though, Thomas led them in the other direction.

"Aren't we going to go in?" asked George, peering over his shoulder to the gates.

"We are," assured Thomas. "But not that way. There's a smaller gate that goes directly into the dormitory quadrangle. No one watches it. We can sneak you two in through there."

They turned a corner and the sunlight hit them full on, making them all squint and groan.

"Sneak us in?" asked Eileen, holding a hand over her eyes to block the sun. "Why sneak?"

"No one's supposed to be in there except students, Masters, and workmen."

"Why not?"

"I don't know. I think it's supposed to keep out distractions."

"What happens if you get caught?" asked George. "And what happens to us?"

Thomas shrugged. "They shout a bit, I get a reprimand, and you two are escorted out the gate with a stern warning."

"And if they find out I'm a girl?" asked Eileen.

"Longer reprimand," Thomas said. "Flogging if you're sneaking the girl in for indecent purposes."

"Ouch."

"Aye. Here it is."

The place he pointed to seemed more ivy than wall. The green vines covered it top to bottom and left only the occasional glimpse through to stone.

"Where is it?" asked Eileen.

Thomas pointed. Behind one small opening were the bars of a small iron gate. He pushed aside some of the ivy and revealed a passage just wide enough to admit one person at a time.

George looked at it dubiously. "I'm going to have to walk sideways through that."

"Probably," agreed Thomas. He stuck one arm through the bars of the gate, and fiddled until he found the latch. There was a metallic click, followed by a long groan of un-oiled and ill-used metal, and the gate swung slowly open into the passage. Thomas made sure no one was watching, then ducked under the vines and into the passage beyond. Eileen came in hard on his heels, leaving George to turn sideways as he had expected and close up the gate before following.

On either side of the little path, steep, windowless walls rose up—the backs of the dormitories, Thomas explained. The little path led them straight for a short distance, then under an archway and out into a quadrangle. The buildings here were built much like Thomas's apartment, with balconies and stairs on the inside. These, however, were stone, beautifully constructed and spotlessly clean. Even the paving stones underfoot were shiny.

George gazed up at the architecture, his eyes wide. "You moved out of this?"

"No girls," Thomas reminded him.

"Ah, right."

Thomas took them across the compound and down a set of stairs. "This leads us through the baths and out the other side."

"The baths?" George repeated, shooting a look at his sister.

"That's the other reason we waited until after the second bell," said Thomas. "The place is empty this time of day."

"Oh, please." Eileen rolled her eyes. "I do have a brother."

"But not a hundred of them," said Thomas. "Follow me."

The stairs ended in a large open room. The walls were adorned with hooks for towels and clothes, all empty. Four long, thin tables had enough washstands for fifty to have a quick rinse. Beyond that were the pools proper. Each was about four feet deep, ten feet wide and twenty long, tiled with stone and full to the edge.

"How are they heated?" asked Eileen, staring at them. She stepped closer and nearly lost her balance. Thomas caught her.

"From underneath," he explained. "There's a room where they heat the water, which they pump in through the vents on the sides," he pointed to an open vent, just above the surface of the pool. "See?"

"Aye."

"Good. Now be careful. It's slippery."

Thomas led them through the baths and pushed open the rear door of the building. A thin cobblestone path led from the door to a wide thoroughfare that ran through the Academy. There were a dozen large buildings, all of light grey stone cut in large blocks and mortared together. Most were square and squat, like the dormitories, with windows every few feet to let in the light. Thomas identified the different schools for his friends as they passed them. The junior college taught the basic subjects: grammar, rhetoric, and logic; geometry and arithmetic; astronomy and earth science. Another held classes in music and art, as well as the gymnasium, where the physical disciplines, including fencing, were taught. The other buildings held the advanced schools; Theology, Philosophy, Science, Medicine, Languages, and Law. The observatory on top of the Science building was home to the largest telescope in the country, Thomas explained proudly.

There was also a meeting hall, which was a dark, forbidding building, but with a slightly more elegant appearance than the schools themselves. There was a lofty-spired church where services to the High Father were held, a small house beside it where the priests lived, and a sizable graveyard behind. Two dozen smaller buildings stood in a cluster at the far end of the compound. They were the houses of the Masters, Thomas explained. One single grand manor house, by far larger than the others, held the Principal's residence. The rest of the area was covered in grass and scattered with trees and benches.

"I can see why you like it here so much," said Eileen, turning slowly to look at all the buildings. "It's so peaceful."

"It is now," said Thomas. "Wait until class gets out."

"Even so," she sighed, "I wish…"

Thomas, guessing the rest of the sentence, said nothing. He took a quick look to make certain that no Masters were around, and led them swiftly across the grounds to the most impressive building of them all: the library.

It looked almost like a small castle, save that where a castle's walls would be solid stone near the ground, this building had windows every five feet, rising twenty feet high and made of dozens of small panes of glass set in lead frames. George examined the work and shuddered. "That must have cost a fortune."

"That's what they tell us at the beginning of every year," agreed Thomas. "And the Four show you mercy if they find you playing with a ball anywhere near it."

There was a tower on each corner of the building, each with a spiral staircase, Thomas explained. The windows, so plentiful on the lower half, were fewer on the upper reaches of the building to keep the books from fading. In fact, Thomas said, some places among the stacks of books, you had to go searching at a certain time of day, when the sunlight was coming directly through the upper windows, to tell one book from the other.

"And you're allowed to go looking up there?" Eileen asked. "I thought books were too valuable."

"They were once," said Thomas. "Not so much anymore, though."

"What happened since?" asked George.

"The printing press," explained Thomas. "When it started getting popular a hundred years ago, the Academy built their own and used it to make copies of every book in their library. Took fifty years."

"Wow," said Eileen.

Thomas nodded his agreement. "All the manuscripts are under lock and key in the colleges or the Masters' houses. All the books in the library are now pressed, rather than hand-written. It's much cheaper and allows the students a chance to actually use the library."

"Can you take books out?" asked George.

Thomas shook his head. "They're not as cheap as that. You can read them on the main floor, and make notes from them."

"Are you going to go looking?" asked Eileen. "For books about..." She trailed off, obviously not wanting to say it out loud.

"No point," Thomas said. "Ben is a better researcher than I could ever hope to be. If he says there's nothing useful there, then there isn't."

"Then why are we here?" asked George.

"I wanted to show you," said Thomas, his eyes on Eileen. Eileen blushed slightly and smiled back at him. "Besides, we're waiting."

"For what?"

The Academy's bells began pealing again. Thomas smiled. "For that. End of the period; the others should be coming out now."

The peace of the grounds was immediately shattered. Students started pouring from buildings, and the grounds were soon filled with movement. The younger students were shouting and pushing and playing with balls, while the older ones moved more slowly, talking among themselves and occasionally fending off the accidental charges of the younger boys. Thomas moved easily through the crowd, leading the others towards the Theology building. A dozen or so students came out of the gymnasium, robes on their arms and sweat on their faces. A stout, bald man stood in their midst, obviously making a point while the students listened attentively. Thomas immediately angled away from him.

"What are you doing?" asked George.

"That's the fencing master," Thomas kept his voice quiet, fearing the man would hear him.

"And he dislikes you so much you need to hide?" asked Eileen.

"He knows me so well, he'll spot me at once," said Thomas. "I've spent far too much time there."

"Is that why you're not wearing your sword?" asked Eileen. She looked at the other students passing by. "And why isn't anyone else wearing one?"

"You said everyone wore them in the city," accused George.

"In the city, we do," said Thomas. "Not on the Academy grounds. They were banned. Too many duels."

"What do they fight over?" Eileen asked. "They're students."

"Aye, and if you've ever seen a Theologian debating with a Philosopher, you'll know why they took the swords away."

"There you are!" Benjamin's voice boomed across the courtyard.

"So much for being unnoticed," Thomas muttered, hurrying towards him.

Benjamin was just emerging from beneath the thick lintel of the Theology building. He was moving somewhat slowly, but his eyes were focused and he wasn't wincing at the noise. Further proof of the efficacy of Henry's cure, thought Thomas. The four met on the grass, and Benjamin gestured them to follow him.

"I take it that fits comfortably?" asked Benjamin, pointing to the robe George was wearing.

"Very," agreed George, rubbing the fabric. "Thank you."

"You're quite welcome, though I can't quite recall Thomas asking permission."

"I knew you wouldn't mind," said Thomas.

"Fortunately, he's right." Benjamin gestured them forward. "Shall we walk?"

They moved away from the crowd and followed Benjamin towards the church. The large building was surrounded by an even larger garden. It was quiet and pleasant, and obviously meant as a refuge for the students. A few were taking advantage, talking quietly or reading on one of the stone benches, or walking slowly through the garden, voices low as they debated amongst themselves. Benjamin led them through the garden to the hedge that bordered the southern end. There was a low iron gate in the middle of the hedge. Benjamin opened it and guided them into the cemetery beyond.

The cemetery, like the church garden, was immaculately maintained, though unlike the garden there seemed to be little order to the arranging of the stones. Some stood alone, others were clumped together in groups. Some were simple rectangles of stone, others had statues or images or strange designs carved into them. The narrow path weaved among the graves, moving in loops and curves through the length of the cemetery.

"Who's buried here?" asked Eileen.

"The keepers of the Academy," said Benjamin. "Priests, professors, philosophers, and principals. They've been buried here since the place was built three hundred years ago." Benjamin picked a row of stones and led them down it. "No one comes in here," he added as he sat on the ground.

"Too afraid one of them will rise up and lecture them to death," said Thomas.

"That's a blasphemous thought, Thomas," warned Benjamin.

"It wasn't blasphemous," countered Thomas. "It was the truth."

"It was unnecessary, and we need to talk before I have to get back." Benjamin settled himself against a rather ornate gravestone with the constellations carved into it. "I talked to those who are serving in the bishop's house."

"And?" asked Thomas.

"They know nothing. He isn't back yet."

"For this you brought us out here?" asked Henry, startling them all. He grinned as they glared at him, and leaned against a tall, thin gravestone carved as a tree-trunk. "I think you could have imparted that in the middle of a theology lecture and no one would have noticed."

"True enough," said Benjamin. "What did you come up with?"

"An idea." Henry tilted his head towards George and Eileen. "Are you aware that those two aren't allowed to be here?"

"Can you say it any louder?" asked Thomas. "I'm sure someone in the observatory didn't hear you."

"I'll try harder next time," Henry sat himself on the grass next to Benjamin.

For a long moment no one said anything, then Benjamin sighed. "All right, Henry. What's your idea?"

Henry smiled. "We sneak in and steal the books."

Benjamin's eyes bulged. "What?"

"We steal them." Henry repeated. "There really is no other way."

"Are you mad?" asked Benjamin. "It's my college! And the books are forbidden to begin with."

"I know."

"I can't do that!"

"Would you be willing to borrow them for a while?" asked Thomas.

"It's not borrowing if you don't ask!"

"It's not stealing if you don't get caught," said Henry. "Besides, no one will miss them."

"It's against the laws of the High Father!"

"So is murder," said Thomas, allowing some of the anger that had been burning inside him for days escape with the words. Benjamin opened his mouth but Thomas's glare made him close it again without speaking. Thomas measured his words carefully as he kept his eyes locked with Benjamin's. "The bishop's already killed at least two people, Ben. Probably more. I can't tell anyone, and I can't prove it. All I can do is try to stop him." Benjamin bit his lip, almost looking ready to protest. Thomas drove on. "His men tried to kill me and they cut open Alex there. The bishop has control of my father and managed to get us accused of murder and witchcraft. I need to stop him and the answers on how to do it might be in those books. Now, will you help me?"

"I don't know," Benjamin sounded very unhappy. "It goes against everything

I'm supposed to stand for."

"Can you at least not talk about it to anyone?" asked Henry.

Benjamin bit his lip again and stared at the ground. Thomas waited as the man thought it through. "Aye," said Benjamin at last. "I can do that."

"Good." Thomas clapped his friend on the shoulder. "So, we sneak into the grounds, we sneak into the Theology building, and open up the room."

"Three problems," said Henry. "How do you sneak in, how do you open Theology, and how do you open the room itself?" He turned to Benjamin. "I assume it's locked."

Benjamin, still looking at the ground, nodded. "Aye, it is."

"Who has the key?" asked Eileen.

"The Master of Theology. On his belt."

"Oh."

"How does the door open?" asked George.

"Doors," corrected Benjamin. "Double doors. You unlock them and pull the handles. Why?"

"You pull the handles?" repeated George, a speculative look coming into his eye.

"Aye."

"Then I can get us in," George said with certainty. "I'll need some tools, but I can get us in."

"And you're an established housebreaker are you?" asked Henry, curiously.

"I'm a smith," George said. "If the door opens out, then the hinges are on the outside, and if the hinges are on the outside, I can take the doors off."

Henry nodded his approval. "I begin to like this one, Thomas."

Thomas nodded. "So we can get into the room. Now, how do we get into the building itself? We can't rob the Master of Keys, too."

"Well, we could—" Henry started, but Benjamin cut him off.

"No we can't! I'm not robbing anyone else. And I'm not letting you do it either," he added before Henry could argue the point. "Besides, he locks his keys in the gatehouse with him every night."

"But he doesn't lock the gatehouse when he makes his rounds," said Henry.

"He doesn't need to," Thomas said. "He has the keys with him."

Henry grinned, the expression somewhat unnerving and feral. "Not the spare keys."

"What spare keys?" asked Thomas.

"He keeps a spare set of keys in his desk in the gatehouse, in the top drawer."

"And how do you know that?" demanded Benjamin.

Henry's grin widened. "Because I've stolen them."

"*What?*" cried Thomas and Benjamin simultaneously. Henry leaned back against one of the tombstones, smiling as he made himself comfortable. Thomas waited for him to elaborate, but Henry said nothing. At last, Benjamin leaned his bulk, as imposing as George's, forward. "Henry..."

"You won't do anything," Henry raised a warning finger at his friend. "You're on your way to being a priest."

Benjamin leaned closer. "I'll sit on you and watch to see if the High Father lets you keep breathing."

"Oh, all right," Henry said. "When I was a junior and still living in the dormitory, I met a certain young lady who lived in the town—"

Benjamin rolled his eyes. "Do all your stories start like this?"

"Of course."

"Let him talk," said Thomas. "Just keep the bragging to a minimum."

Henry looked somewhat disappointed at that, but went on anyway. "She wanted to see the grounds, and I couldn't very well toss her over the wall. So, I waited for the Master of Keys to be making his rounds, and I searched the gatehouse. He had extras and I borrowed them."

"How did you get them back?" asked George.

"Waited until the next morning when he made his opening rounds, and put them back in his desk."

"That's clever enough to work," said Thomas. Hope started to stir inside him, and he took firm hold of it. If the plan worked he might just have a chance of stopping Bishop Malloy. "I'm impressed."

"As well you should be," Henry said. He crossed his arms and looked down his nose at the four of them. "Now, who's going to get them tonight?"

The others exchanged a look, then all turned back to Henry. He sighed. "I should have known."

"Well, it was your idea," said Thomas. "You should have the honour."

"I'm sure."

A bell began tolling, loud and insistent. It was not the class bell they had heard before, but a different one, sharper and louder. Thomas recognized it at once, and turned instinctively to the sound. Henry and Benjamin did the same. From beyond the wall of the cemetery they could hear shouts and movement.

"What is it?" asked Eileen.

"Call for a general assembly," said Benjamin, standing up. "There wasn't one scheduled."

Thomas felt his stomach sinking even as he got to his own feet. An image of ships pulling into a town in the rain filled his mind. *If it was the bishop, there's no reason he couldn't make it here a day behind us.* "We should get out of here."

"You think it's about us?" asked George, also rising.

"Don't be ridiculous," Henry scoffed. "The world doesn't revolve around you, you know."

"You care to lay any money on it?" Thomas felt his fear rising. He ran for the cemetery gate, Eileen and George on his heels. Benjamin and Henry followed a few steps behind. Thomas stopped just inside the gate and peered out around the bulk of the church. "You two go to the assembly and find out what it's about. We'll wait here until everyone goes in, then head back to the apartment."

"You're being paranoid," said Henry. He stepped out the gate and stepped right back in. "There's a coach coming."

"They don't allow coaches in here," Benjamin stepped forward and looked out, "unless it's a visit from the king or the—"

Thomas knew the alternative. He grabbed George and Eileen and pulled them down behind the hedge. They stayed there while the other two watched the coach go by.

"You wanted to know when the bishop was coming back," Henry said, not looking down. "That would be him."

Thomas cursed silently and forced down the urge to curl into a ball against the earth. "How many men does he have with him?"

"Ten on horse. His personal guard."

"Any ideas?" asked George. His eyes were wide, and sweat was beginning to bead on his forehead.

"Hide here?" suggested Eileen, her voice higher than normal and her breath coming fast.

"Won't work," Henry said. "Not if they come searching. Better to move now. You can hide in the crowd."

Thomas knew Henry was right, even as the thought of stepping out into the open sent shivers through him. "Let me know when he's gone past."

"Wait... Now."

The three fugitives got to their feet and followed Henry and Benjamin across the garden and out into the open. Students were coming from every direction, pouring out of buildings and rising from spots on the grass. Others came running in through the main gates. All headed for the meeting hall. Thomas took over the lead, angling for the dormitory. Professors were emerging from buildings looking peeved at the interruption of their lectures even as they shooed the students toward the meeting hall.

"You lot!" boomed a large voice, ringing through the grounds.

Thomas looked and cursed. "Of all people..."

It was the fencing master, standing at the door of the gymnasium. He was looking directly at them, face stern and arm pointing back towards the assembly hall.

"Maybe he won't recognize you," said Benjamin, his voice low.

"Maybe the sun won't rise," muttered Thomas. "I'm his best student. If he gets close enough, he'll recognize me."

"You there! Go to the meeting hall! At once!"

"Any chance he's not speaking to us?" Eileen asked.

"Not one," said Henry. "And I was his best student."

"Any clever ideas?" asked Benjamin.

"Yes," Thomas hissed, his nerves starting to jangle. "Do as we're told until we can think of something."

The group turned and headed for the assembly hall, moving slowly.

"We can't go in there," Eileen said, panic rising in her voice. "If the bishop sees us..."

"I know," Thomas kept his voice even, kept his breathing slow and willed himself to stay calm. Beside him, George's face was a tight mask of worry. Thomas could see the big man's hands clenched into fists, and could almost feel him shaking, though they weren't touching. "We have to leave."

"Wait for a moment," Henry said. "There's a crowd coming."

Thomas saw another wave of students coming from the buildings around them. It was a long nervous moment before they were overtaken, but soon the group was engulfed in black robed young men talking querulously about the sudden summons. They quickened their pace, keeping with the group.

"Wait until we're opposite the dormitories," said Henry, his voice low. "Then run."

The walk took forever. The bishop's guards, instead of staying at the assembly hall, had turned and were casually riding back along the road. Thomas risked a glance behind them, saw the fencing master starting to head their way.

"We're here," Henry said. "Run."

They didn't wait to be told twice. Thomas led the three in the dash, expecting to hear the fencing master's bellow, summoning them back. It didn't come. Several students looked their way, but no one called after. George cast a glance over his shoulder. "No one's following."

"Good." They reached the door to the baths and ran down the steps. Thomas barely managed to get the latch open before George bashed into the door with his shoulder. The three dashed into the bath hall. Thomas shut the door behind them, and hissed out, "Wait!"

"What for?" demanded George, though he dropped his voice to match Thomas.

"It's slippery, the tiles are loud, and if anyone spots us, we're dead. Keep to the wall, and keep an eye out for Masters."

"All right," Eileen hissed. "Just get us out of here!"

Thomas led them as quickly and quietly as he could. Every footstep on tile echoed through the room, seeming certain to bring discovery. Thomas led them across and to the stairs, then moved up to the top and peeked around the courtyard. It was empty. He gestured sharply, and he and his friends made the quick dash to the short passage. It was empty, the gate unguarded. Thomas breathed a sigh of relief.

"Now what?" asked George as they headed down the narrow lane.

"We go back to the apartment and wait."

"What if they come looking?" demanded Eileen.

"Then we run away."

"Where?"

"I don't know yet," Thomas opened the gate, peered out. "All clear. Come on."

Chapter 20

They waited in the apartment all morning and most of the afternoon, sipping at left-over wine and water, and eating left-over food. Thomas spent the time pacing and glancing nervously over the balcony rail to the empty yard below. He had cast his robe aside and put on his sword. There was something comfortable about it, even though he knew it wouldn't do him a bit of good if twenty of the bishop's guards came after them. Still, he kept his hand on the hilt as he paced back and forth through the room.

George spent the day sitting on the balcony, looking moodily at the courtyard and the fountain below. Thomas didn't bother to ask the big man's thoughts. He was sure they were bleak, and probably focused on who got him into this mess. George, of course, said nothing of the sort. Thomas still felt guilty and morose.

He paced some more, stared off the balcony beside George a while, then went back into the apartment. He went to his room and found Eileen sitting at the desk, reading.

"How are you doing?" Thomas asked.

"Oh, badly," Eileen said, attempting to muster some cheer and not succeeding. "I think I've been reading the same page for the last hour."

Thomas stepped in beside her, once more aware how dingy the room was. "I really should have cleaned more often."

"Probably," she agreed. "I still like it, though."

Thomas snorted at that. "You should be here in the winter. We all sleep in the middle room to keep from freezing."

"Even so." She waved a hand around the room. "Look at these books. Could anything be better?"

"Warmth in winter and fewer insects in the room."

She looked at him, eyes sharp and head tilted to the side. "Would you trade it?" she asked. "For anything?"

Thomas sighed and shook his head. "No. I wouldn't. It's all I wanted to be."

"Me, too." Eileen turned back to the book and shut the cover with more force than it needed. "Of course, I'm not allowed."

"I suppose not."

"Why not?" she demanded. "The nuns tell tales of women who taught at schools or led armies. Why aren't I allowed to go to school?"

"I don't know," said Thomas. "Things have changed."

"Not for the better."

"They're back!"

George's shout echoed through the apartment. Thomas and Eileen rushed to the balcony. Henry and Benjamin were walking rapidly across the courtyard, neither looking at all happy. Thomas tracked their movements all the way.

"Well?" Thomas demanded when they reached the top stair.

"You were right," said Henry, his expression dead serious. "You're in trouble."

"How much?"

Henry ignored him. "Alex, come here."

Eileen stepped forward, warily. "Yes?"

"Turn around, will you?"

Bewildered, she did what she was told. He stopped her when she was facing the back wall.

"See that?" Henry said, indicating her backside to Benjamin. "How could I have mistaken that for a boy's?"

"Hey!" Eileen spun around, indignant.

"I don't see how we missed it," Benjamin looked stern and shook a finger at her. "You are a girl."

"She is rather skinny," said Henry.

"I'm standing in front of you, you know."

"And very flat up top, too."

"I'm tied down, you lout!"

Thomas felt his jaw tightening. He stepped forward, blocking Henry's view of Eileen. "Very funny. Hilarious, in fact. What happened at the meeting?"

"You've been accused of witchcraft and conspiracy to commit murder," said Henry, off-handedly. "Nothing we didn't know." He looked over Thomas's shoulder to Eileen. "You aren't being courted by anyone right now, are you?"

"George!" Eileen turned to her brother. "Do something!"

"Was there any other news?" demanded Thomas. "And stop staring at her."

"I'm sorry," said Henry, "but she has lovely legs."

Eileen headed for the bedroom. "I'm putting on a skirt!"

"Oh, please, don't," Henry stepped around Thomas and in her way, "there's so much more to say."

"That's enough," the rumble of George's voice, low though it was, filled the apartment. Henry saw his expression, and stepped aside, leaving Eileen to huff off into Thomas's room and slam the door behind her.

"So," Henry smiled at Thomas, "is she courting with anyone?"

"No," George replied, his voice sounding like a bear's growl. "And she won't be starting with you. Now leave her alone and tell us what happened."

"The bishop read off a list of charges," said Benjamin. "He says you three were seen in several towns down the river, heading this way."

"He also took the time to inform us of how we at the Academy are a bad influence," interrupted Henry. "Apparently, we are as responsible for your troubles as you yourself."

"He threatened to have the king remove the Theology school," Benjamin said. "To keep the future servants of the High Father from falling into bad company." Worry filled his eyes. "I don't want to leave the Academy."

"He hates this place." said Thomas, remembering the bishop's speech at John Flarety's table.

"Probably wants to keep the clergy from learning anything but the teaching of the High Father," Henry patted Benjamin on the arm. "It could ruin an impressionable young man like you, you know."

"I think it already has," said Benjamin, the worry spreading from his eyes to the rest of his face. "Because when the bishop was talking about removing Theology, I kept thinking about the books in the vault, and what he would do with them."

The idea of the bishop possessing books on witchcraft sent a shiver through Thomas. "He'll use them if there's anything to use, and destroy anything that could expose him." He began pacing again. "We have to get them tonight."

"He's posting guards outside all the Academy's gates," said Henry. "All students entering or leaving will be required to show their faces. Any suspects will be held until the bishop or his familiar sees them."

Thomas swore and paced harder.

"At least he didn't put guards inside as well," said George.

"It's the king's Academy. He needs a writ before he can put soldiers on the grounds," said Henry. "If he tried it without, the students would rise up in protest." He smiled, and the expression was not at all pleasant. "In fact, they're already complaining about the guards outside." Henry turned back to Thomas. "And it gets better."

"How could it?"

"Well," said Benjamin, "the bishop summoned all those Theology students working in his house to attend him at once. We waited for them to get back before we came here. That's what took so long."

Thomas had a very bad feeling. "What did they say?"

"Two things," replied Benjamin. "First, the bishop had all students working in the house come in for confession."

"Is that unusual?" asked George.

Benjamin nodded. "The bishop never does confession for the house. He's too high for that, and certainly too high to lay hands on foreheads during benediction."

It clicked in place in Thomas's mind at once. "He's searching for magic."

"We thought you'd say something like that." said Henry.

"The bishop also told them all to pack the house for another trip," Benjamin continued. "He's moving to the summer house at Seaview early this year."

"What's at his summer house?" asked George.

"Less stench," suggested Henry. "The city gets rather rank in July."

"What *else*?" demanded Thomas.

"The remains of an old battlefield," ventured Henry. "A stone circle, some lovely country, lots of sheep."

"Thank you," snapped Thomas.

"—And the bishop, in three days," said Benjamin. "Those working in his household are excused from classes for the next two to help him pack." He sat down at the table and looked at Thomas. "What are you going to do now?"

Thomas had no answer, but Eileen's appearance saved him the need. She was wearing her green skirt and bodice and a white blouse. Henry whistled appreciatively and received a glare. "That's enough of that," she said. "You'd swear you'd never seen a girl before."

"Not one so pretty as you," assured Henry.

"You're a liar," Eileen went over to stand by her brother. "And a scoundrel, I'm certain. Now, what's happened?"

Several voices joined in the telling, and Eileen was brought up to date. When they were done she, too, looked to Thomas. "So, now what?"

Thomas's mind was whirling. He tried to think of some alternatives, but in the end realized he couldn't do anything except keep going or run away. "I say we keep with the plan; we just need to get past the guards."

"We'll need to change your appearances," said Henry, "or go over the wall."

"The wall," said Thomas. "It's easier."

"We also need to find some tools," said George. "If I'm to open the door, that is."

"Right." Thomas resumed pacing, going back and forth across the apartment a dozen times. "Right. Benjamin, can you take George to the Street of Smiths and get what we need?"

"Are you sure we should go?" asked Benjamin. "I mean, we're not exactly easy to hide."

"Nay, you're not, but they're not looking for two big men, and on the Street of Smiths you'll blend right in."

"He's right," said George.

"He is," agreed Benjamin. "Come on."

"Take the stairs away from the Academy," Thomas added. "There's no sense in letting one of the bishop's guards get lucky."

George nodded. "We'll stay out of sight."

"Just get what you need and get back fast."

"What about me?" asked Henry.

"Go around the Academy. Find out where the guards are posted and then come back and tell me. We'll work out how to get in after that."

"And what are you going to do?" asked Henry, archly, looking at Eileen.

"Nothing that you need worry about," Eileen answered sharply.

Thomas raised a hand to forestall any other comments. "Eileen will stay here. I'll get us food for tonight."

"No you won't," said Henry. "If you're caught, we're all in trouble."

"He won't have guards at the market."

"I didn't think he'd put guards on the Academy," said Benjamin. "But they're there."

"They won't—"

"They might," said George. "And I'd rather you didn't leave Eileen alone, in case they come here."

Thomas tried to think of an argument, but came up with nothing. All his friends' eyes were on him, and all of them were looking very determined. "All right, I'll stay here." He pointed at Henry. "You get the food for tonight."

"And who are you to order me?" asked Henry, pulling his long length upright and raising his nose.

Thomas tossed him a pair of silver coins. "The one who's paying."

Henry caught them, and without changing tone or posture said, "Good enough."

"And no wine."

"No wine?" Henry repeated, appalled.

"No wine," Thomas repeated back. "We all need to be clear tonight."

Henry sighed. "All right. I'll get the food on my way back. And no wine. You two stay out of sight." He smiled. "And don't do anything I wouldn't."

Benjamin and George left out the back while Henry sauntered out the front. Thomas watched the lot of them go, then turned and went into his room. Eileen followed him.

"So," she asked, "What is it that we *are* going to do?"

"Find my map, first," Thomas replied, opening the drawers on his desk and digging through the papers there. "Every new student gets a map of the grounds. If I can find mine, I can figure out the best place to go over the wall. Here!" He came up with a ragged sheet of paper and spread it out on the desktop. "As soon as Henry gets back, we can start planning."

"And until then?"

Thomas found himself at a complete loss. He sank onto his chair. "You know, I have no idea."

Eileen sat on the bed, facing him, their knees almost touching. Worry was etching lines into her forehead, and Thomas had to force himself not to reach out and smooth them. Instead, he smiled at her, trying to lighten the mood.

"You know, you do look much better as a girl."

She managed to force a smile back. "Thank you."

"Though I'll miss the sight of you in breeches."

She leaned forward and gave his leg a swat. "You're as bad as Henry."

"He has been a terrible influence on me."

"I think he has." For a moment Eileen's smile looked a little less forced, then it faded. Worry tried to make its way back into her face, but Eileen pushed it aside, and put the smile back on. "You could hurt a girl's feelings," she said, nearly succeeding in making her tone light, "saying things you don't mean."

"Who says I didn't mean it?" protested Thomas. "You look very pretty."

"I look terrible," Eileen countered, she raised a hand to her head, her fingers catching in the tangled mop. "My hair is a mess."

"You look fine," Thomas felt something deep within coming to the surface. "Even the hair."

She tilted her head at him. "You're beginning to sound like you've come to court me."

Thomas laughed without humour, "Not just now." He pushed the feelings back inside; pushed himself up from the chair and paced the short length of the room. "I don't think this is a good time for it."

"Too bad," said Eileen quietly.

That brought Thomas up short. His heart sped up of its own accord, and he felt suddenly light-headed. "Do you mean that?"

She nodded, not looking at him. "Aye."

Thomas sank down on the bed, as much to keep from falling over as any other reason. His shoulder was touching hers, and the warmth of the contact felt to be spreading through his entire body. "You couldn't have told me on Fire Night?"

"Oh!" Eileen laughed and pushed him. "With you just back and only having spoken three words to me?" She laughed again. "You're lucky I held your hand, let alone jumped with you."

"Why did you?" Thomas asked. "Jump with me, I mean?"

Her eyes twinkled. "For the village," she said, piously. "The village and the luck."

He snorted. "Right."

She giggled some more. "I think I did it mainly to annoy Sister Brigit. And because..." she began to blush, "because it was you."

"Me?" Thomas felt his eyebrows going up of their own accord. "What about me?"

Her blush deepened. "You'll think it's stupid."

"No I won't."

"Aye, you will." She took a deep breath. "It's just that you'd been gone for four years. And suddenly you're back and you're... you were..." she hesitated, then let the words out in a rush. "You were new and exciting and you wore a sword and the first thing you did after four years away was to look at me like I'm pretty."

Thomas felt his own blush rising. "You are."

"So you said," Eileen didn't look at him. "But we all know how pure your motives are."

Thomas sat there for a moment, then reached over and took her hand. Softly, he said, "You are beautiful, and if we were back home I'd court you properly. I'd even bring a gift for your parents and announce my intentions to them."

Her jaw quivered slightly, and she still didn't look at him. It took a long moment before she said, "Like as not, they'd throw you out on your ear."

"Like as not," agreed Thomas. "Would you come pick me up?"

She turned to him at last and met his eyes with her own. "Aye, I would."

Thomas smiled, leaned gently forward, and kissed her lightly on the lips.

He meant to stop there, but when he leaned back, she grabbed his hand, pulled him closer. He leaned in again, kissed her once more. She kissed him back, gently at first, then with more fervour. Thomas responded with fervour of his own and soon their arms were wrapped tightly around each other's bodies, their lips pushing hard against one another. Emotions that had been pent up in Thomas for the last two weeks broke free, releasing themselves in a burst of desperate passion. Eileen's response was as powerful as Thomas's own. Their breath grew short and heated. He kissed her harder, his fingers running through the short rings of her red hair while her hands traced a pattern on his back. One of them, Thomas wasn't sure which, started leaning back. Together, they fell backwards across the narrow bed. Passion added speed to the movement and power to the impact as they hit their heads against the wooden ledge of the shelf with a resounding pair of *cracks!*

Both cried out and swore with pain as they grabbed for their respective skulls. Thomas rolled up and came to his feet, realized it was a bad idea, and promptly sat down again. Eileen fell over onto the bed and lay with her face against the pillow, making some sort of muffled noise and shaking. Thomas, once he had sufficiently recovered, put a hand on her shoulder and asked, "Are you all right?"

She waved him away and kept on making the noises that Thomas slowly realized was laughter. He began to laugh himself, though not quite as hard. At length, she sat up, looked at him and gave him a push. "You idiot."

"Me?" he protested.

"Aye, you. And me." She rubbed her head again. "Just as well it happened though. I'd hate for George to have come in and found us like that."

Thomas snorted. "Or Henry. We'd never hear the end of it."

Eileen took a deep breath, let it sigh out and then took another. "What happened?"

"We hit our heads."

"Before that, you goose."

Thomas shook his head. "I don't know. I'd say we were..." he lost any words he might have had. "I don't know."

"Too much strain?"

"Aye. Probably."

Eileen got to her feet. "I need something to drink."

"Wine?"

"Water," she said firmly, heading out of the room. "Cold water. And you should have some, too."

"I should take a swim in it," Thomas muttered as he rose to follow her out of the room. She poured a mug of water, handed it to him and then poured another for herself. They each drank it down before speaking again.

"Eileen?"

"Aye?"

"I meant what I said. About courting you."

"I know."

"Good."

She poured another mug each. They stood there, awkwardly, for a while. Thomas suddenly couldn't stand it anymore. "Come on, I'll show you the city."

Eileen looked surprised. "Are we going out?"

"Aye, but not through the door. Come on." He took her hand and led her back through the apartment to his room. He opened the window wide and began to crawl through it. "Come on."

Thomas got outside and stood up, then held a hand out to Eileen.

She was staring at him, her mouth open. "You *are* insane."

"Aye," he agreed. "Now, come on."

Shaking her head, she followed his lead and stepped out of the window.

* * *

An hour or so later, Thomas was sprawled on his back on the shallow slope of the roof above his window. Below the window, the roof stretched out flat, with a line of windows on either side to light the rooms of those who lived there. Above his head the roof peaked, then sloped down the other side to the courtyard below. Eileen was lying with him, her legs out to the side, her body leaning over his, his arms clasped about her and their lips together in a very long, deep, unhurried kiss.

A loud whistle brought the kiss to an abrupt end. Eileen sat bolt upright and Thomas came with her. Henry, standing half-in half-out of Thomas's window, was smiling broadly. He leaned down and called into the apartment. "I was right! They're here!"

"Stop right there!" Thomas called, reaching to tuck in his shirt. "Have you got dinner?"

"Of course."

"Well, go get it and bring it out here. Are the other two there?"

"Yes."

"Tell them to join us. And bring my map, would you?"

Henry stood there, smiling at them.

"Well, go!"

"I will," said Henry. "And I'll take my time so you two can get straightened up for company."

He ducked back inside and Thomas and Eileen both followed his advice. It had not gone much further than kissing, fortunately. The strong, dark passion that had grabbed them both in Thomas's bedroom was still too fresh in their minds to allow for much more. Still, even kissing could leave one a bit rumpled, and they hurried to put themselves together. True to his word, Henry took his time, and from the sound of the voices inside, was making George and Benjamin take theirs. Thomas grabbed another quick kiss before Benjamin, George, and Henry made their way out onto the roof, bringing the results of their respective searches with them. Thomas attempted to appear nonchalant, and Eileen emulated him. Judging from the expressions all around—especially from George—they weren't fooling anybody.

"I'm hurt," Henry declared as he stepped out. "Here we were, out risking our necks, while you two..." He sighed.

"Very funny," said Thomas.

"Very," echoed George. His brows were together, and while he wasn't obviously angry, Thomas found something in his expression quite disconcerting.

"Don't look at me like that," Eileen said to her brother. "It was only kissing, and we weren't doing much of that."

"No more than an hour or so," said Henry.

"Shut up, you," Thomas put enough heat behind the words that Henry momentarily quieted.

"It's not like he's the first boy I've ever kissed," Eileen said, her eyes still on George.

"I know," George's expression hadn't changed. There was worry there, and disapproval mixed in with other emotions Thomas couldn't read. "It doesn't mean it's a good idea."

"Enough for now," Henry said, putting a large cloth sack down in the middle of them. "Dinner!"

"George," Thomas began, but George waved him off.

"Don't bother."

"It's not something I planned."

George didn't bother answering. He turned to Henry. "What did you buy for dinner?"

Henry had bought roast chicken, bread, fresh berries, and a jug of ale to wash it down. "Because you didn't say, 'no ale,'" said Henry before Thomas could protest.

They ate quickly. Thomas was very aware that George's expression did not change at all during the meal. Henry, who was pretending to be oblivious to it all, told them what he had found at the Academy. True to the bishop's words, there were now guards at every entrance, even the ones that were rarely used, like the narrow gate they'd snuck in and out of earlier that day.

"Wonderful," Thomas muttered. "Well, we guessed we'd have to go over the wall."

"This might make it easier," Benjamin said. He reached into the large bag that he and George had returned with and came up with a length of rope.

"Good thinking." Thomas spread out his map. "I think we'd be least likely to be seen if we went through the cemetery."

"Oh, of course," said George, his already dour expression souring even more.

Henry raised an eyebrow. "You don't like graveyards, then?"

Eileen answered before George could open his mouth. "He never has. Hates walking through them at night. Thinks the dead will rise up and get him."

George glared at his sister, and began to turn red.

"The dead don't walk," said Benjamin hastily, doing his best to sound reassuring. "The dead are with the High Father."

"Not dead professors, I'm certain," remarked Henry, earning a glare from both Benjamin and George.

"The cemetery is the only part that isn't in sight of a gate," Thomas said, attempting to steer the conversation back on course. "We should be able to get in without any guards spotting us."

Benjamin looked over the map. "It's a bit of a walk from the cemetery to Theology. How do we get there?"

"I hadn't thought of that," Thomas admitted. He looked at the map again. "What's the closest building?"

"The church," said Henry. "After that we're equidistant from the dormitory, the library, and the gymnasium."

"All of which will be locked," Benjamin said, "except the dormitory."

Thomas sat back on the roof. He took a sip from his ale, let the liquid roll around in his mouth while he thought about that. "All right, so we need to get from the cemetery to the dormitory—"

"The door to the baths is closest," put in Henry.

Thomas nodded and kept going, "—and then from the dormitory to Theology, then into the room with the witchcraft books, all without being spotted. Any suggestions?"

They were all silent. At last George spoke up. "There are too many of us. We can't sneak five people in. Someone will notice."

"What if some of us were already inside?" asked Eileen. "Henry needs to be inside anyway, to get the key. He can meet us at the cemetery, and Benjamin could be at the dormitory."

Henry nodded his approval. "Why is a girl as clever as yourself wasting her time with him?" he gestured to Thomas with a thumb.

"Keep your mind on business," Eileen snapped, "not on things that you can never have."

Henry attempted to look hurt. Benjamin laughed. George's expression stayed the same. Thomas waited for the moment to pass before asking, "What will be your excuse for being in the dormitory?"

"Michael Pasternac," Henry said promptly. "He's one of the wardens for the young ones' floor. He owes me money."

"Michael knows me, too," said Benjamin. "I can make sure that the door to the baths is open while Henry gets the keys."

Thomas thought the plan through. It was simple enough, which meant there was less that could go wrong. "I'd say that we're ready, then. Nothing to do but wait."

"Until when?" asked George

"I was thinking midnight."

Benjamin shook his head. "The Master of Keys does a turn around the grounds at midnight."

"After the first night bell," suggested Henry. "Most of the people around here will be inside and asleep by then."

"If you're not in by the second bell, we'll assume you're not coming," said Benjamin. "We'll meet back here in the morning."

"Right," Henry pushed himself to his feet. "I'm going to get a nap." He headed for the window, adding over his shoulder, "And I suggest that you lot do the same."

"I think I'll nap here," Thomas said.

Eileen, who was just getting up, looked at him and, with a twinkle in her eyes, said, "What a good idea. Me, too."

"Not likely," George rose, dwarfing his sister. "I'm not leaving you alone with him."

"Don't worry," said Henry, smiling at Thomas. "He does this with all his girls. Takes them on the roof, feeds them, shows them the sunset. They feel sure he won't do anything, what with all those windows, there." He pointed to the other side of the roof where a half-dozen windows, exactly like Thomas's in size and shape, were looking back at them.

"And this should make me feel better?" asked George.

"George!" Eileen snapped. "I am staying out here, with Thomas. Now go inside and pass out our cloaks so we'll have something to lie on."

George's expression turned mule-ish. Benjamin stepped between them. "Don't worry about Thomas. He'll behave himself," he fixed Thomas with a glare. "On his honour."

Thomas nodded. "If it will make George feel better. Yes. On my honour."

"It will be all right, George," Eileen said, her voice soft. Her big brother met her eyes, and she gently touched his arm. George bit his lip, then nodded. Eileen smiled suddenly, and mischief danced in her eyes. "If he tries anything, you can throw him off the roof."

The thought obviously cheered George up. He nodded. "All right," he said. He raised a warning finger at her. "But don't you go trying anything, either."

He and the other two clambered back inside, leaving Thomas and Eileen alone. Thomas was about to breath a sigh of relief when Eileen pinned him with a glare. "All right you, what other girls was he talking about?"

Fortunately, George tossed the cloaks out just then, and Thomas had time to formulate a reply while getting them.

Chapter 21

Four hours later, as the sun began to creep down, Thomas took Eileen to the peak of the roof to watch the sunset. They had slept, though probably not as much as the others had. Still, the kissing was quite refreshing in its own way. Clouds had come in over the course of the afternoon, though no rain had fallen. The evening sunlight burst through in shafts of red and gold, streaking across the buildings of the town, and making the stone walls shine with a brief, warm glow until the sun vanished beneath the horizon. It would be a dark night, Thomas realized; easier for creeping about without being seen. As long as it didn't rain, they would be fine.

Thomas kissed Eileen one more time and led her inside. They found George fleecing Henry and Benjamin at cards. George's expression when he saw them wasn't much different from the one he'd used earlier that day. It worried Thomas, who thought, quite rightly, that they had enough problems already. Still, Eileen ignored it, and Thomas followed her example. The card game broke up in favour of left-over chicken and ale. No one said much, except the occasional request for a jug or plate.

The food vanished quickly, and Benjamin and Henry left as soon as it did, to get into the Academy before the gates closed for the night. Neither took any weapons. Thomas wished they could, but any arms inside the Academy would draw questions, and if they were caught in the Theology building, Thomas knew that neither of them would draw against the professors. He watched them go and then settled in to wait.

Time crawled uncomfortably by. George was still looking grumpy, but wasn't saying anything. He paced about the apartment a while, until he noticed the broken hinges on one of the cupboards. He immediately started mending them, becoming absorbed in the task and pointedly ignoring Thomas. Eileen retreated to Thomas's room to read, taking several candles with her to light the dark little room. Thomas, his nerves going on edge as the time grew closer, wandered back and forth in the apartment and on the balconies outside.

The first bell of the night rang out. Eileen changed back into boy's clothes and Thomas put on his sword belt. George slung the bag of tools on his back and took up his stick. Both he and Eileen wore the knives they'd picked out from the smithy two rather long weeks ago. The three slipped the student robes over their clothes and headed out the back door and slowly down the pitch black stairs to the street below.

"All right," Thomas said when they reached the street. "Anyone you run into this time of night is either looking for a good time, offering a good time, or looking for someone to rob. So keep an eye out, and don't let anyone touch you."

"Right," agreed George, looking around. "Darker than the forest at night around here."

"It gets better ahead," Thomas pointed to a faint glow of light in front of them. "The major streets usually have some lighting. Mostly torches in front of the taverns."

"Better that than this," Eileen said, moving up beside him. "How long will it take us to get there?"

"It's a short walk if we take the straight road," said Thomas. "Tonight, though..."

They wandered through the city, passing occasional open inns and taverns with light and music and laughter coming from within. For the most part, though, the streets were dark, their residents having retired with the sun. Thomas had not brought a lantern for fear of drawing unwanted attention on them from others on the street or any of the bishop's guards who might be walking the bounds of the Academy. This left them in near-total darkness on the side streets. Several times they passed groups of revellers carrying torches or lanterns and laughing their way down the street. A group of students, drunk and noisy, went by in a rush of black robes and boisterous conversation. Off one street, four men lurked in the darkness of a short alleyway, stepping out when they saw the three friends. Thomas, guessing that they were being sized up for a robbery, drew his sword. The hiss of Thomas's blade being drawn from its scabbard stopped them cold, and when George stepped up beside Thomas, his stick at the ready, the men faded back into their alley. The three moved on, with

Thomas keeping an eye out behind until they were well away.

At last, they reached the street that ran along the Academy wall. The windows of the houses on the other side of the road, mostly occupied by students and tradesmen, were dark. The street itself was empty, and unlike the other thoroughfares, there were no inns or taverns to provide light. Thomas led them down the street at an easy, casual walk until they were opposite where he judged the cemetery to be. He took a careful look to make sure no one else was around and quickly led his friends across the street to the wall.

George put himself against the wall, facing out, and tossed Thomas the rope. Thomas took it and passed Eileen his sword. Stepping first into George's cupped hands, then high up to his shoulder, Thomas easily scaled to the top of the wall. He kept low, as much out of nervousness as in the hope it would make him harder to spot. He dropped as quietly as he could to the ground and then secured the rope to a tree with a pair of quick knots, before tossing the other end back over the wall.

Eileen came next, boosted by her brother. She straddled the wall, passing the sword and the bag of tools to Thomas, then slid off the wall into his waiting arms. A moment later George heaved himself up the rope, grunting as he pulled his bulk over the top of the wall and landed with surprising gentleness on the sod below. Thomas gathered the rope up, untied it, and put it back in the bag. George took the bag, and Thomas led them slowly and cautiously towards the gate. George attempted to move faster, but stubbed his toe on a gravestone for his efforts. He cursed long and with passion, but kept his voice to a whisper. Thomas waited until he was done, then led them forward again. Eventually they reached the gate, and pulled it open. It squeaked—not loudly, but enough to make all three of them jump. Thomas and Eileen immediately crouched down, but George slipped through the gate before doing the same.

"Are you all right?" Thomas whispered.

"Fine," snapped George. He stopped, took a deep breath. "I don't like graveyards."

"It's all right," said Thomas.

"And I'm not happy about you and Eileen, either."

Of all the times. Thomas managed to keep his voice to a whisper. "I noticed."

"Everyone noticed," whispered Eileen. "Just leave it be."

"Quiet you," growled George. "What were you two thinking?"

"George," Thomas began, but was cut off.

"Could your timing be any worse?"

"Could *yours*?" hissed Thomas. "This isn't the time or place to be talking about this!"

"I just want to say—"

"You've said it! Now come on."

George fell silent and the three moved quickly around the church. Thomas stopped them to scan the grounds. The Academy was dark; no lights shone from any of the buildings. The paths were empty and there was no movement but the occasional stirring of leaves as the night breezes slipped through the grounds. Thomas led his friends at a dead run across the open ground between the church and the dormitory.

Benjamin was lounging at the door to the baths and saw them coming. He opened the door and stood aside, his eyes scanning the grounds the whole time. The three slipped in and stopped, panting heavily in the dark. Benjamin quickly and quietly closed the door behind them and waited for them to recover.

"So far, so good," whispered Thomas, when he'd caught his breath. "Any troubles on your end?"

"Not a one," assured Benjamin. "How was the graveyard?"

"Dead quiet," said Thomas, earning a hard punch on his arm from Eileen.

Benjamin laughed, quick and whispered, then touched Thomas's arm. "Follow me."

Benjamin led them slowly through the baths, keeping everyone well away from the pools. Instead of going up into the dormitory proper, he led them through a thick oak door and down a steep, slippery set of stone stairs. At the bottom he paused, and a moment later the first of a pair of lanterns he'd obviously placed there flared into life. He handed one to Thomas and lit the second. "This is the heating room," he explained to George and Eileen. "It's connected to the storage rooms."

"Which are connected to the root cellar and the kitchen," Thomas added.

"And the kitchen entrance is closest to Theology," finished Benjamin. "Henry said he'd meet us there."

"Why don't we just go through the main floor?" asked Eileen.

"Door warden," said Benjamin. "Keeps the juniors from sneaking out. The hall to the kitchen goes right by him."

"This way," Thomas started across the room, "and keep the noise down. The furnaces down here carry sound all through the building."

Benjamin chuckled. "Remember when Graham had his tryst with that woman here, Thomas, three summers back? The entire building heard what he was doing."

"The entire building will hear us, if we're not quiet," warned Thomas. "Let's go."

Thomas led them forward, with Benjamin taking up the rear. The large room was filled with huge stone furnaces, black and squat and smelling of burnt wood and over-heated rock. The bath furnaces, with their tubs of water and pumps, were banked for the night, to be heated again in the morning. The other furnaces, with their great vents leading up into the ceiling, were for heating the air, and would not be brought to life again until the nights grew cold.

Thomas led the small troop across the room and through a large wooden door. The room beyond was filled with boxes and furniture of all kinds, most covered with a thick layer of dust. The narrow path left clear among the boxes and furniture wound its way through the room in a series of turns. Eventually they reached the next door. Thomas led them straight through the door to the kitchen cellars. Bins, casks, and shelves filled every available space, and lengths of cured meat and bags of vegetables hung from the ceiling. Squeaks and rustles at the first touch of the light let them know that they weren't the only nocturnal visitors, though none of them actually saw the mice that were certainly the culprits.

"Hey," called George, his voice low. "How come you know your way around under here?"

"Everyone does," Benjamin whispered. "It's practically a rite of passage to go creeping around down here in your first year."

"Here we are," said Thomas. "Come on."

A set of stairs took them a long way up, and the door at the top opened to the kitchens. Thomas blew out his lantern, and Benjamin did the same a moment later. The group was plunged into pitch darkness until Thomas pulled open the door, letting a thin crack of pale light seep in. He looked, found the room empty, and pulled the door wide. With a quick stride, Thomas led the group across the dark room filled with large tables for preparing food and equally large fireplaces for the cooking of it.

Halfway across, Benjamin hit his head on one of the pots that hung from the ceiling.

He doubled over, holding his head as the noise rang through the room. Everyone froze. Thomas listened, sure the door warden would appear at any moment demanding to know what they were doing. No sound or sign of movement came to him. At last, Thomas whispered, "Ben, are you all right?"

"Aye." Benjamin's tone voice was filled with more chagrin than pain. "Just stupid."

Thomas left that one alone. "Come on."

He led them across the rest of the kitchen through the pantry, to the outside door and slipped it open. There was no sign of anyone around, including Henry.

"Where is he?" muttered Benjamin. "He said he'd be here."

"Maybe something slowed him down," suggested Eileen.

"Aye, like getting caught," said Benjamin.

"We don't know that," Thomas snapped back, worry making the words harsher than he intended them. "We'll wait here until the third bell."

"And what if some junior sneaks in for a midnight snack?"

"Then we hide." Thomas felt his nerves riding higher again, and forced himself to calm down. "In fact, we should go outside so we don't have to worry about it."

"What about the Master of Keys?" Eileen asked.

"He carries a lantern," said Thomas. "We'll see him a mile off."

"Unlike me," Henry said from behind them.

The entire group spun in place, gasping.

"Why do you do that?" hissed Benjamin.

"It's fun."

"Well, stop it."

Thomas interrupted before Henry could reply. "Did you get the keys?"

"Yes, I did." He held up a large key-ring. There were at least twenty keys on it.

Thomas whistled quietly. "Any idea which is which?"

"Not in the slightest," Henry put the keys back under his robe.

"Wonderful. Come on."

The little group followed Thomas out into the night. He led them as fast as he could, trying to make as little sound as possible. There was no one about, and most of the ground they had to cover was grassy lawns. Still, the twenty yards or so to the College of Theology were some of the most nerve-wracking Thomas had ever traveled. By the time the five of them were pressed tightly against the wall of the Theology building, Thomas's heart was pounding loud enough, he was sure, to be heard at the main gates. Henry pulled the keys out of his cloak and started trying them on the door.

It took most of forever for Henry to find the right key, and Thomas could barely resist the urge to pull them out of Henry's hands and start trying them himself. Instead, he forced himself to keep his eyes on the grounds, searching for anyone that might spot them. His friends were only dim outlines in the darkness, holding as still as they could while they waited.

Something clicked, loudly.

"Yes!" Henry hissed and pushed the door open with a squeak that made Thomas wince. "Well, don't just sit there," whispered Henry, "Get inside!"

They did, Thomas waving his friends past until the last of them slipped through, then following after. Henry closed the door, fumbled the key into the lock, and with another loud *click*, sealed them in.

The hallway was dark, the nearest window too far off to give much light. Only the dimmest of outlines showed Thomas where his friends were standing.

"Right," said Henry "Now what?"

"Now we rely on Benjamin's memory," Thomas turned to the large shadow on his right and found an arm by feel. "Ready, Benjamin?"

"I am," said Benjamin from the other side of the hall, while George snorted.

Thomas shook his head. "I can't see a thing. Can we risk a light?"

"Not yet," said Benjamin. "There's windows at the ends of the hallways to let light in. Someone outside might see."

"Fine. We'll hold onto each other and follow you. Where are we going?"

"The basement, first, then there's a door that takes us to the vaults."

"Lead on."

There was some scuffling while everyone found each other and linked hands. Thomas ended up between Benjamin and George, and wondered who was hanging onto Eileen. Henry he guessed, and found himself feeling a twinge of jealousy. He put the thought away as ridiculous, given the circumstances.

"Everyone hanging on?" asked Benjamin.

A murmured assent passed through the group.

"Here we go." Benjamin led them at a slow, steady pace down the middle of the hallway. Thomas squinted through the dark, trying to make out possible obstacles, but only seeing dim shapes as they passed them. Benjamin kept them clear of any collisions, taking them half the length of the building to a large staircase. He found the banister, guided the others to it, and led them down. Their footsteps, as quiet as they tried to make them, echoed off the stone walls of the empty building. The dimness turned to pitch black as they descended and their pace slowed even further. There were several stumbles, and some quiet cursing as heels were trodden on and one person ran into another. Eventually, Benjamin whispered, "I'm on the floor."

"About time," muttered Henry. "Can we light the lamps, now?"

"Aye, it should be safe."

After a brief struggle with flints and oil-soaked wicks, the lamps were lit. The group found themselves staring down a very long, very dark hallway.

"Well, this is creepy," Eileen said, her voice shaking just a bit.

"Not as bad as the graveyard," muttered George.

"To you."

Thomas ignored the siblings and turned to Benjamin. "Do you know where the door is?"

Benjamin shook his head. "I only went there the once. It's down here someplace, though. A plain door leading to a flight of stairs down."

Thomas looked into the gaping darkness in front of him. "How far do the hallways go?"

"All the way around the building."

"Wonderful. What's the door to the vaults look like?"

"Rectangular, wood, iron handle," said Benjamin. "They don't label them, you know."

Thomas rolled his eyes. "Fine. You and Henry take that side—" he indicated to his left, "—George, Eileen, and I will take the right. First one who finds steps going down, say so."

Fortunately there were not many doors to be tried, despite the hall's length. Most led to storage rooms, though a set of four opened into small meditation chambers, each with a kneeling stool and a small window that would have let light in from outside, had it been day. Benjamin, discovering the first, covered his lantern and warned the others to do the same. They rounded the first corner and were half-way down the other side of the building when George pulled a door open and called, "Here!"

Benjamin came over and opened the lantern enough to see the stairs beyond the door. "I think this is it. Give me a moment."

He disappeared down the stairs and through a doorway below, leaving the others to wait nervously in the thin yellow light of Thomas's lantern. It was a short wait. Benjamin quickly reappeared with a smile on his face. "This is it."

"Right," said Henry. "Who's on look-out?"

Thomas, who hadn't thought of it, managed an "Uhh…" before Henry interrupted. "I thought so." He handed his lantern to George. "I'll be at the top of the stairs."

"Which set?" asked Thomas.

"The ones to the main floor," said Henry. "I won't see a thing down here."

"Can you find your way in the dark?" asked Benjamin.

"I can," said Henry. "Be quick, will you?"

Thomas watched him go, then let Ben lead them down the stairs.

The room below was large, with a door every ten feet and bleak grey stone walls. The thick, musty smell of old books filled the hall. Thomas surveyed the doors. "I don't suppose you remember which one it was, do you?"

Benjamin, standing in the middle of the room, swung his lantern in a slow circle to light them all. "No, but it's fairly obvious."

"How do you mean?"

"Thomas?" Eileen's voice had gone up an octave. "Here."

Thomas looked and his jaw dropped. Beside him, Benjamin nodded. "Aye, that would be it."

The double doorway was large, and carvings decorated all sides. Demons danced up the frame, and at the centre of the wide lintel was a carving of a young woman, rays of light shooting out of her eyes and flames coming from her hands. Above her, writing was inscribed into the wood. Thomas surveyed it all and whistled.

"Timothy said the Blessed Daughter was the goddess of magic," he said. "Looks like he was right."

"That is not the Blessed Daughter," Benjamin objected. "That is a representation of the evil caused by summoning unholy power from the Banished."

Thomas moved closer to the door. "Then why are the flames hurting the demons?" He pointed at the wall. "See, they're in pain here."

Benjamin frowned. "That's odd."

"How old is this carving?" asked Eileen.

"Don't know," said Benjamin. "But the room was built when the Academy was."

"Well, maybe it was here before the Church of the High Father declared all things magic to be sinful," Eileen suggested, moving closer to the door herself. "Maybe she's meant to be guarding the door."

"If she was considered to be the one who gave magic to mortals, it would make sense," agreed Thomas. "She's there to prevent the books from being used for witchery. What do you think, Benjamin?"

Benjamin shook his head, a troubled look on his face. "It doesn't make sense. If this is a representation of the Blessed Daughter as a giver of magic, why didn't the Church of the High Father have it destroyed when they declared magic evil?"

"Because the Church of the High Father doesn't own the Academy," said Thomas. "The king does, and they'd need permission from him to destroy one of the original carvings."

"So they changed the way the carving is interpreted?" asked Eileen.

Thomas nodded, then turned his attention to the rest of the door. The wood was solid, the handles brass, the hinges and lock iron. He looked to George. "Can you open it?"

"I think so," said George. "Pass me the light."

Benjamin, now looking very troubled indeed, handed George a lantern and got out of the way. The smith examined the hinges, grunting to himself. Thomas moved back beside Eileen to give George more room. He felt her hand fumble for his, then hold it tight. Her eyes kept going to the stairs, as if waiting for someone to appear and catch them all. Thomas knew exactly how she felt. At length she turned her attention to the writing above the door. "Thomas?"

"Aye?"

"Can you tell me what the writing says?"

Thomas examined it from where he stood. The script was very old fashioned, and while it was their own language, half the words were unfamiliar, and the spellings of the rest seemed to have been a matter of choice rather than custom. It took him a while to get through it, and when he did, he shuddered. "I'd rather not."

"Benjamin, can you hold the light and shine it here?" George asked. Benjamin took the lantern and held it up. George put down the bag of tools he'd been carrying and dug through it. "This should be easy enough. Just keep the light steady."

"Tell me what it says," Eileen said to Thomas. "I want to know."

"No, you don't."

"Just tell her," George ordered as he began prying at the hinges with a chisel. "She'll be asking for the rest of the night, if you don't."

Thomas sighed. "I warned you." He took a deep breath and began reading. "'Beyond these doors lies evil. Let none but the righteous pass, and all others receive the wrath and curse of the Giver of Magic. Let them be plagued with disease, pain, and sorrow to the miserable end of their days on this earth, and tormented to the end of eternity by all the Banished.'"

"Oh." Eileen's voice was very quiet. "How much longer, George?"

"Not much," George said. There was a grinding noise, and the hinge-pin pulled itself free and fell to the floor with a too-loud clank. Everyone froze in their place until the echoes died off. George stood up and began work on the next one. After a fairly short time that felt as long as of the rest Thomas's life, the second hinge-pin hit the floor. Thomas could see the door list slightly from its own weight.

"All right," George began prying the last hinge up. "Thomas, take the crowbar. Get it into the crack there." He gestured to the thin line between the door edge and the wall. "We'll need to get the door pried open this way, then we'll be able to slip in."

"Can we do it without breaking the lock?"

"I hope so."

Thomas did as he was told, and started to put his weight against it. George put out a hand. "Not yet. Wait until the hinge is gone."

Thomas nodded, watching George for a signal. Time dragged interminably on, broken only by the scraping of the chisel against the metal of the hinge-pin. The pin jumped free and fell to the floor with a metallic clatter. "Now," George grunted and Thomas put his weight against the bar, inching the door outward. As soon as there was space to get his fingers in between the door and the wall, George grabbed it and pulled hard. Thomas heard the wood creak in protest, but George kept on with a steady pressure. The last hinges popped free of each other and the bottom corner of the door hit the ground with a *clunk*!

Everyone froze, listening. There were no other sounds. George shifted his grip, manoeuvred the door out a bit further and then pulled back hard. There was a scrape and a crunch, and the door began swinging down towards Eileen. She let out a short, involuntary cry and dodged backward. Benjamin quickly grabbed the other edge of the door with his free hand and held it up. With an easy move, the two big men lifted the door away and leaned it against the wall. Thomas felt stuck in his place, afraid to look into the room, afraid what he wanted would not be there. It wasn't until George's hand landed on his shoulder that he shook the fear away.

"Right," Thomas muttered to himself. "Let's see." He raised his lantern and stepped into the small, windowless room.

It wasn't much wider than the double doors themselves, and was filled floor to ceiling, front to back, with books. They were all shapes and sizes and, from the writing on their spines, in a dozen languages. There was a chair and table in the middle of the room. They, too, were covered with books.

George stuck his head in and whistled. "How are you going to get through all of that?"

Thomas stared at the pile with horror. "I can't do this by myself. I'll never find anything."

"We can help," Eileen offered. "All of us."

"Not me," George backed out of the room. "I can barely read."

"Henry can read three languages," said Benjamin.

"Right," George headed for the stairs. "I'll go take watch and send Henry back. Call for me when you need the door closed up."

"It's going to take a long time, George," warned Thomas.

George nodded. "I know. Just get it done, then call me to put the door back in place." He clapped Thomas lightly on the shoulder, then turned and moved noiselessly up the stairs. He had no light, Thomas realized. He listened for the sounds of stumbling, but none came. Thomas turned to Eileen. "Can you read any other languages?"

"No. I can recognize them, but that's it."

Thomas nodded. "All right. We'll start with the books on the chair, then on the table. Sort them by language. Ben and I will start going through them." He looked to Benjamin. "We're looking for any references to one person stealing magic from another, and any references on how to stop them." Benjamin's very troubled look deepened, making Thomas worry for his friend. "You all right?"

"I don't know," said Benjamin, "I still don't like this, and the picture on the door... I never thought of it your way before."

"Think about it later," Thomas advised. "I need your help. We have until the fifth bell of night. Once it rings, we get the mess cleaned up, get the door on its hinges, and get out of here."

Benjamin nodded and Thomas stepped back into the room. The wavy light of the lantern seemed to be playing tricks, bringing flashes of colour to him out of the corner of his eyes. He shook them off and began skimming through the books on the table. The others set themselves to reading as best they could, sharing the books on the shelves among themselves.

A clatter of feet on the stairs made them all stop. The footsteps continued across the main room, and Henry appeared in the doorway.

"Could you be any louder?" demanded Benjamin.

"You told me not to sneak," Henry said with a shrug. He whistled at the sight of the books. "That's impressive."

Thomas explained what they were doing, and Henry joined in. Soon, piles of books grew all around them.

"How are we going to get these back in order?" Eileen asked.

"We don't," replied Thomas. "Just put them back on the shelves. By the time they find out they've been disturbed, we should be long gone."

"I hope so."

She turned back to her book, continuing to leaf through it. Thomas thought he saw a flash of blue light as she flipped the pages. He rubbed his eyes again and turned back to the piles of books on the table and floor. All the ones he'd looked at were about past laws concerning witchcraft, magic, and the nature of miracles. They were very thick and had nothing he could use. He sighed and picked up the next book. A flash of red caught the corner of his eye. He looked to see Eileen paging through another book.

An idea, stunningly obvious once he'd thought of it, leapt into his mind. "Eileen, what's that book?"

"Folk remedies," Eileen said. "Very strange, but nothing about witches, really."

"Pass it to me?"

She did. The cover simply said *Wisdom*. He paged through it, finding folk remedies and sayings, and, in the middle of the book, a single page containing a rhyme to drive away unwelcome guests.

The words glowed bright red.

He stared at it, stunned, for a long time. Finally, he took a deep breath and said, "Is it only me who notices that this page glows red?"

The rustling of pages being turned ceased. Henry, Benjamin, and Eileen turned slowly towards him. Each face had a matching look of disbelief and worry.

Chapter 22

Henry was the first to recover. "What?"

"The writing on the page is glowing red," said Thomas.

Benjamin leaned in. "No, it isn't."

"Yes, it is."

Henry looked. "No, it isn't."

"Well, it is to me!" Thomas flipped through the book. Another page leapt out at him, glowing bright blue. He held it up. "This one is glowing, too."

He looked closer at the page, then reached a tentative finger out and touched it. The coarse paper felt rough to his fingertips, and beyond that there was something… almost a vibration, but so faint Thomas could barely perceive it.

He realized no one had spoken and looked up from the page. His friends were all staring at him, faces wary. "I could use some help here."

"There are no colours," said Benjamin slowly, like he was speaking to a dog ready to attack at any moment. "Just the light of the lamp."

"There are colours for me," Thomas insisted. "And I'm not insane, so stop talking to me like that."

"All right," said Henry, stepping forward again. "Setting aside the idea that you are insane, what does the page say?"

"It's…" Thomas read down the page. "It's a spell for the calming of the mind in times of trouble."

"And the one that glowed red?"

Thomas flipped the pages back. "It's to drive off unwelcome guests."

"Any more?"

Thomas leafed through the rest of the book. Two more pages glowed blue, one more red. The blue were for finding direction and making flowers bloom. The red was for killing vermin. Thomas leapt to the conclusion. "Spells that do some sort of damage are red. Spells that help glow blue."

"All right," said Henry. "So what does that mean for us?"

Thomas put the book aside and looked at the stacks around them. "Has anyone figured out an order to this mess, yet?"

"There doesn't seem to be one," said Benjamin. "They probably just chucked them in as they found them."

Thomas thought about it, then put the book in his hand on the table. "Right. New plan. Henry, Ben, you two keep looking for references about stealing magic. Try for books written about witch-hunts, if you can locate any. They should have something."

"Oh, good," muttered Henry. "That should make for some lovely reading."

"And what are we going to do?" asked Eileen.

"Something much faster," Thomas said, "I hope."

In the next hour and a half, Thomas leafed through every book in the room, putting the ones that flashed red or blue on the table, and setting the rest back on the shelves. When he was finished he had a stack of forty or so books, waiting to be read. Henry and Benjamin, meantime, had found a dozen books on hunting witches.

Thomas set Eileen to helping the other two and started sorting through the pile of books on the table. All of them were hand-written—some in the practiced scripts of clerks or scribes, others in the messy scrawl of merchants or tradesmen. A half-dozen he set aside at once, unable to read the languages they were written in. The ones he could read varied from simple charms to nasty curses to prayers for divine guidance. In all cases, the spells and charms that helped glowed blue, and those that harmed glowed red.

What surprised him was that the books contained many other spells and charms, both for help or for harm, that didn't glow at all. He remembered Ailbe telling him that she'd never seen her magic working. He wondered how many others with some gift for magic had tried to seek out spells, only to find no magic in them. The search for real magic must have driven some of them mad.

Of course, the rational, logic-trained part of his brain reminded him, *you don't know if any of them actually work.*

Thomas ignored the thought. They had to work, because one of them had to have the key to stopping the bishop.

"Oh, ick," Eileen said suddenly, tossing aside the book she had been reading. A shiver ran through her. "That is disgusting."

"What is?"

"This witch-finder's method of discovering if a woman is a witch. He takes a large, cone-tipped rod—" She bit off the words. "It's vile."

"Do you want to give it a break?" asked Thomas.

She shook her head. "The sooner we get it over with, the sooner we get out. I just don't have to like it."

Thomas turned back to the stack of books in front of him and pulled another one into his lap. It was a small volume, possibly made to be someone's journal. There was no title on the cover, no author's name, not even a signature scribbled on the inside cover to say whose book it had been.

Every page in the book glowed.

Thomas flipped through the pages, scanning the titles of each one. The book was divided into sections. The first quarter glowed blue, the middle, red, and the last quarter blue again. There were charms to stop insects and charms to find lost things, curses that would make a man itchy or blind, and in the second half, spells to call wind or make water do one's bidding. There was nothing about stealing another's magic.

The fourth bell of the night struck.

Thomas started to put the book aside, knowing he was running out of time, then changed his mind and slipped the book into his shirt.

"Thomas!" Benjamin was scandalized. "What are you doing?"

"It all glows," Thomas explained. "The entire book." *I need to try them.* He didn't say it to Benjamin, knowing what his friend's reaction would be. "I need to look through it some more."

"Well, put it back. Someone will notice that it's gone!"

"They'll notice the crowbar marks on the door or the scrapes on the hinges long before that," Thomas argued. "Besides, it's not the only one we'll be taking, if we can find what we're—"

"Here!" said Henry and Eileen simultaneously.

"This one talks about witches transferring their powers to others!" said Eileen.

"This one describes spells that a witch can use to summon up more power from otherworldly sources!"

"We've got to get out!" hissed George from behind them, causing the entire group to jump and yelp. "Now! I saw lights outside the windows, and when I went to look, there were horsemen and soldiers on the Academy grounds."

"How many?" demanded Henry.

"I didn't stay to count. Lots."

"What are they doing?"

"The horsemen are riding up and down the grounds. The footmen are surrounding the dormitory and the gatehouse."

"The bishop," Thomas felt his heart sink. "They're looking for me."

"The bishop?" Henry was on his feet in outrage. "He can't do that. Only the king's men are allowed to enter the Academy."

"They'd need a royal writ to do this," Benjamin was equally outraged. "Are you sure it's the bishop's men?"

"Who else would it be?" demanded Thomas. "Who else would have a reason to charge in here at night?"

"There's going to be trouble over this," Henry vowed.

"And most of it for us if we get caught," said George. "Get out of there so I can close the door!"

The four tripped on the piles of books as they hurried out of the little room. Thomas grabbed the two books on witch-finding and brought them out with him. George and Benjamin grabbed the door and manoeuvred it back into place. George guided the bolt into place, then he and Benjamin, with Thomas levering the door from underneath, began the much more difficult job of putting the door back on its hinges. Wood creaked alarmingly, and at one point something splintered, causing George to swear under his breath. By sheer force the three managed to get the door back into its proper place and the hinges lined up.

"Right," said George, grabbing for the hinges. "Hold it there!"

Benjamin leaned against the door while George tried to put the bottom hinge-pin back into place. It wouldn't fit. George cursed again and grabbed a hammer from the bag. He banged the pin into place, every blow echoing through the room and making the entire group wince. It was the same with the second hinge, and the third. At last George called Benjamin to step away from the door and surveyed his handiwork. It stood firmly in place and, at a testing tug of the handle, seemed to be as solidly locked as it was before.

"Think anyone will notice?" asked Eileen.

"Not unless they're looking," said George. He grabbed up the bag of tools in one hand and his stick in the other, "and with all that's going on, I doubt that they will any time soon."

"I pray you're right," said Benjamin fervently. "Can we get out of here, now?"

They raced up the stairs, Benjamin in front with one lantern, Thomas taking up the rear with the other. Shadows jumped and danced around them as the lanterns swung. They charged through the basement hallway, round the corner and straight for the stairway. Henry called them to a stop and made them douse the lanterns. Thomas pushed to the front and went up alone. There was no movement in the hallway above, save shadows flickering from the yellow torchlight outside.

"Come on," Thomas called. "Quick!"

The others dashed up the stairs. Thomas didn't wait for them, but ran to the nearest window. There was no real light coming in, save for the torches of the horsemen riding past. He couldn't make out their livery.

"Come on!" hissed Benjamin, waving a now-doused lantern at Thomas.

Thomas grabbed at a hand, and the group formed a chain again, moving down the middle of the hallway towards the main door. The hall grew brighter when they turned a corner, light from torches outside giving a dim, flickering illumination to the hall.

They gathered at last around the main door. Henry tried one key after another until one matched the lock and clicked. He pulled the door open a bit and Thomas peered out. He could see the foot soldiers, gathered around the dormitories and the gatehouse. More soldiers on horseback were riding around the professors' homes. Thomas could hear the professors protesting, but no one was being allowed to leave.

"Well?" demanded Henry.

"They're everywhere. And they're wearing the bishop's livery."

"Wonderful."

"Can we stay here?" asked Eileen.

"I think we'll have to," said Thomas, still peering through the doorway. A group of a dozen soldiers had broken off from the others and were walking purposely down the main thoroughfare. There was a short, podgy man with them, dressed in a long night-robe. "Damn it!"

"What?" demanded four voices at once.

"They've got the Master of Keys. They're walking this way."

"They're going to search the buildings," said Benjamin.

"Good guess," snapped Henry. "We have to get out of here."

Thomas looked out the door to the buildings around them. "The graveyard's still the easiest way to get out."

"Can we get to the church?" asked Henry.

"Not directly," Thomas said. "Science is closest, but it's in the wrong direction." He checked the soldiers' progress, and saw them changing directions. Thomas jerked his head back inside and closed the door. "Lock it."

"What?"

"Lock it, quickly. They're coming here."

Henry fumbled with the keys, found the right one, and locked the door. The five retreated down the hallway. "How else can we get out of here?" Thomas asked, looking to Benjamin.

"There's a door that opens towards the library."

"Get us there."

Benjamin turned and led the group at a run down the hall and around a corner. The hallway here was small and dim, with no windows to let in the yellow torchlight from outside. Benjamin led them straight to the end of it. "Here."

Henry quickly stepped up, felt at the door until he found the keyhole. He put a key in the lock and clicked it open.

"Good guess," whispered Thomas.

"There's too few keys for every door to have its own," said Henry. "I guessed the one that opened the front probably opened the rest of them."

From behind them, they heard a door being roughly opened and the sounds of boots on the floor.

"Get outside," Henry hissed. "Fast!"

"What if they're waiting?" demanded George.

Henry opened the door and looked out. "They aren't. Now come on!"

They poured through the door and closed it behind them. Henry locked it immediately, and then turned to the others. "Now what?"

Thomas could see torchlight on either side of the building, but none of it was close. "The library."

"What?"

"It's the closest, and we can hide in there until they're done searching."

"How do you know they won't search in there?" whispered George.

"No one's allowed inside with a flame," Henry whispered back. "King's orders."

"And if they decide not to listen to the king?"

"They have to," said Benjamin. "The whole place is filled with dry paper. One spark and it will go up. And if that happens, there *will* be a riot."

"Pity there isn't one now," muttered Henry.

"We've got to go," said Thomas. He grabbed Eileen's hand. The torchlight was still distant, the ground between them and the library shrouded in darkness. "Run!"

They ran.

Thomas risked a look around them as soon as they were on open ground.

From the dormitories and the Masters' houses torches blazed in the hands of the bishop's men, but no one sounded an alarm. Those who might have been looking were probably blinded, Thomas guessed. A torch only threw light about fifty feet, and ruined the night-sight of anyone trying to look beyond that.

Thomas prayed the darkness and their black cloaks would be enough. He made himself run faster, Eileen's hand clutched in his own. The library grew closer and closer. The black of its walls and the yellow of torchlight reflected off its windows made it even more ominous and forbidding than usual.

Lights moved behind them, and for one horrible moment, Thomas was sure they were being pursued. A quick glance over his shoulder told him otherwise. The bishop's men were riding back and forth between the Masters' houses, but none were turning their way.

The library wall rushed towards him. He let go of Eileen's hand and used the wall as a brake, bouncing off it and letting himself fall to the ground. He lay flat, making himself as small as possible. Eileen dove down on the ground beside him, Benjamin and George joining them. Henry went straight for the door and began fumbling with keys. Benjamin put a hand on Thomas's shoulder. "Should we try for the graveyard?" he asked, gasping the words out.

"Maybe." The word had just left Thomas's mouth when a pair of horsemen galloped around the corner of the church, past the cemetery gate and towards them. "Or not. Hurry up, Henry!"

Henry looked over his shoulder, saw the riders. "No time!" he hissed, jumping off the stairs to the ground. "Everyone lie flat, and pull your hoods up, now!"

"They'll see us," protested Benjamin, starting to rise.

Henry grabbed him, shoving him back onto his belly beside the stairs. "No they won't! *Do it!*"

Thomas pulled Eileen close and pressed their bodies into the wall. George flattened himself on the other side of the steps from Henry and Benjamin. The riders were coming at a brisk trot, only thirty feet away. Thomas pressed his face into the ground, praying the bishop's men wouldn't notice the extra shadows along the wall.

The riders passed without slowing down.

"Stay down," hissed Henry, getting up himself and going to the door. Thomas watched as he shoved one key after another into the door. He could hear Henry muttering under his breath, but couldn't make out the words.

Probably just as well, Thomas thought. A dark corner of his mind began to wonder if there was even a key on the ring that matched the library, and if they should make a run for the graveyard.

Click.

"Thank the Four," breathed Henry as he pushed the door open. "Come on! Quick!"

They charged into the library as fast as they could. Henry came through last, pushed the door shut and locked it. The five stood there, gasping.

The dim light from the great windows cast down in grey and yellow upon the long tables and desks, the copying stations, and the floor to ceiling shelves of books. The wheeled ladders stationed along the walls to allow access to the top shelves cast strange, flickering shadows behind them as the light wavered past the windows. Even in the thin light of the torches outside, the library was impressive. George and Eileen, staring into the room, looked stunned.

"I didn't think there were this many books in one place," Eileen whispered.

"I didn't think there were this many in the world," returned George. He stepped away from the group, looking up at the high shelves and the hundreds of volumes of books. He shook his head, bemused. "I didn't think there was this much to write about."

"Neither did I," agreed Henry. "And sometimes I still don't."

"We should hide," said Benjamin.

"Not yet," Thomas headed for a window. "We need to see what's happening. There's windows on all sides here. We can keep a watch on them and see."

"If they come, we'll have plenty of time to hide," said Henry. "Everyone find a window and make yourself comfortable. It's going to be a long night."

George snorted. "It's already been a long night."

Thomas grunted his agreement and headed to a window. Through it, he could see the soldiers outside the dormitory. In the blaze of torchlight, he could make out bodies, but no faces. About a dozen or so boys, half-naked and shivering, stood on the lawn surrounded by guards. The rest were in a huddled group against one side of the building. Thomas guessed that there was some pretty strong resentment going on, but no one seemed to be voicing it in the face of sixty or so armed men. Orders were being shouted from one of the horsemen, though what they were Thomas couldn't really hear. A moment later, half the men left what they were doing and ran into the building.

"They're searching the dormitory," he guessed.

"How long will that take?" asked Benjamin.

"No idea," said Thomas. "They have to be out before dawn, though."

"How do you know?" asked George.

"Two reasons. First, when dawn comes, it's going to bring a lot of very angry, armed, older students. Second, they're after me."

"So?"

"So, if you were me, and you saw all of them inside the Academy, would you go anywhere near the place?"

Henry's voice drifted through the room. "I don't know, how dumb am I?"

"Ha-ha."

Thomas turned his attention back outside. The soldiers, made dim and wavy by the uneven glass, seemed to undulate into the buildings or back and forth on the lawn. Six of the horsemen began to ride the length of the Academy, as if hoping to flush Thomas out from the few bushes on the grounds. Another group rode back to the gates, blocking anyone from entering or leaving. Time crawled by.

"They're leaving Theology," said Benjamin, making them all jump.

"Do you think they'll come here next?" Eileen asked.

"With the way our luck is running…" Benjamin stared out the window. "They're still at the building… They seem to be arguing… They're moving this way!"

"Everyone head for the third floor!" snapped Henry. "Hide in the stacks!"

"Why the third?" asked Eileen. "What does it matter?"

"Third floor has the most books, and the least windows," said Henry. "Now, go!"

Henry led them to the nearest stairs at a run. They were nearly pitch black, and George and Eileen stumbled several times. Thomas took up the rear, making sure no one fell behind in the dark. The group practically tumbled out onto the third floor. The windows here were tiny, letting in almost no light. Giant shelves and stacks of books loomed at them on all sides.

"Eileen?" Thomas hissed.

"Aye?"

"Stay with me. Everyone else, scatter!"

He pulled Eileen between two shelves and behind him. In the intense gloom he could barely see the shapes of the others, looking for their own hiding places. There was some stumbling and a muttered curse, then all the shapes vanished into the stacks and the room filled with silence. Eileen was still holding Thomas's hand. He raised her hand to his lips, kissed it, and then let it go. He drew both of his blades, the hissing noise filling the silent room. A moment later, a small noise told him Eileen had pulled her knife out. Henry and Benjamin didn't have swords; they couldn't have gotten on the Academy grounds with them. Still, Thomas bet Henry had at least a knife on him. Benjamin, on the other hand, wouldn't have anything. George had his stick, and the crowbar he'd used to jimmy the door. It was not good odds if it came to a fight.

From three flights below, Thomas heard the faint, distinctive screech of hinges.

"Could they be in here?" a strange voice demanded.

"No. No students are allowed in here after dark."

Thomas recognized the second voice as the Master of Keys. From his tone, he was barely containing himself.

"They could have snuck in."

"No one," said the Master of Keys, "goes into this library after dark. There are too many books to risk an open flame."

"Look anyway."

Thomas heard a single boot hitting the floor.

"Halt!" There was steel in the Master's tone, and it obviously worked, because Thomas heard no more footfalls. "There will be no lights inside this building."

"We can't search without lights," protested a new voice.

"He's right," The first voice agreed. "Bring the light in—"

"You will not!" The voice of the Master of Keys was loud enough to fill the entire library and, Thomas was certain, most of the Academy compound. "You may have decided that it is within your purview to disturb the sleep of the entire Academy—without a writ from the king, I might add—"

"I don't answer to the king!"

"You will in this!" There was no uncertainty or room for argument in the Master's voice. "The library and all its contents belong to the king and you will not under any circumstances enter this building with a flame in your hand or he *will* have your heads!"

"And who is going to tell him?" There was an unpleasant edge in the man's tone.

The Master's tone was calm, cold, and much more menacing. "I am, and if I don't manage it, be assured that someone else will. The Masters are watching, and if a single light goes in this building you can be assured that there will be a hue and cry far greater than your men are capable of suppressing, and far greater consequences than you are prepared to deal with."

"Look—"

"*There will be no lights in the library! Do you understand?*"

The bishop himself, using all the magic he had at his disposal, could not have been more persuasive. There was a long silence down below, then the first voice muttered, "Right. Give me the torches, then spread out."

Boot steps rang through the hall below as men walked the length of the building. There was a pause, and after what was obviously an unspoken command, the footsteps split up. A moment later, Thomas could hear them echoing up the stairwells on either side of the library. Thomas crouched low to the ground, and felt Eileen doing the same behind him. No one made a sound.

The boot steps that had been moving up the stairs had begun to slow down. The tone of them changed as they stepped out onto the floor below. There were a few reluctant steps onto the floor itself followed immediately by a crash and muffled curses as someone ran into a table. The footsteps retreated, and someone called down, "We can't see anything."

"Look anyway," came the shouted reply. "Check the next floor!"

The footsteps resumed their journey, getting louder and louder until stopping, the final steps echoing through the third floor. Thomas forced himself to breathe as quietly as possible. No one else on the floor made a sound. The footsteps resumed, slow and cautious. Thomas sensed more than saw the men go by; black shapes against a near total darkness, crossing in front of his hiding place and moving further into the darkness. From the other direction, he could hear other boots on the floor, approaching. The wait as the soldiers crossed the huge room was interminable. At last, though, there was a grunt and a startled shout, followed by a round of relieved cursing as two soldiers realized they had bumped into each other.

"Well, I still can't see a bloody thing," said one soldier. "You?"

"Not a thing."

"What's happening up there?" shouted the voice from down below.

Another soldier in the room snorted, "Notice how he isn't up here."

"I already had," the second replied. "You want to go further in?"

"No."

"Me, either. I say the place is empty."

"Me, too." His voice grew suddenly loud. "There's no one here!"

There was a pause from far below, then, "Are you sure?"

"Aye."

"All right, then, get back here. There's other buildings to be searched. Come on."

The soldiers separated, crossing the floor just as slowly and cautiously as they had when they came in. It took forever. At last, the sounds of the footsteps changed, then began to recede as the soldiers found the stairwells and made their way down. Thomas waited, motionless and barely allowing himself to breathe. There were no other sounds in the darkness as the patter of boots on steps changed to the steady stride of men crossing a floor. A moment later, hinges creaked wildly and a door slammed shut.

On the third floor of the library, there was a mass exhalation.

"I thought we were dead," moaned Benjamin.

"We might still be," whispered Henry. "They might have left someone on watch."

"Stay here," whispered Thomas. "I'll go make sure they're gone."

He moved as silently as he could across the floor and down the stairs. It was a long, slow walk, and every time he made the slightest sound he froze, listening and dreading. At last he made it to the main floor. It was empty. The only movement was of the shadows, flickering from the torchlight outside. He heaved a sigh of relief, then ran back up the stairs to gather his friends.

"That was not good for my health," Benjamin declared as they headed down the stairs.

"Think how much worse it would have been if they'd caught us," said Henry.

"I don't think I will, thank you."

"So now what?" asked Eileen.

"Back to the windows, I'd say," suggested Benjamin.

"Aye," agreed Thomas, "but keep your heads down. That was too close."

"I thought we were dead when they reached our floor," said George, nervous energy pouring off of his voice. "I thought we were all going to hang."

"Don't worry," Henry replied as he headed for a window. "After they'd have gotten through questioning you, you wouldn't even feel the noose."

"You mean they'd torture us?" asked George, horror in his voice.

"Aye, but only until you confess."

"But what if you have nothing to confess?"

"Oh, you'd find something," said Henry, his voice grim. "After a few hours, everyone finds something."

George abruptly sat down on one of the benches.

"Shut up, Henry," said Thomas. He went over to George. "Don't worry," Thomas said, trying to sound confident. "They haven't caught us yet."

"They'd better not," George warned. "If I come home tortured and hanged, I'll never hear the end of it."

Thomas, relieved to hear the humour—forced though it was—in his friend's voice, clapped him on the shoulder, then went to find a window ledge.

Hours began to creep by again. The soldiers outside continued searching buildings while others patrolled the grounds. Inside, the five alternated watching, pacing, talking quietly, and cursing fate. Benjamin and Henry had a lengthy discussion on the nature of magic and witchcraft, which Thomas stopped when they started to get loud. Eileen sat with Thomas for a while, but neither had much to say. George sat in his window, silent and alone. Eileen gave Thomas a quick kiss, then went to sit with her brother. Thomas sat, wishing he could do something, until it occurred to him that there was one book that he could read without any light at all.

He pulled the spell book out of his robe, and opened it. The words glowed in the darkness. For a moment he tried to cover it, to keep the light from shining out, then remembered he was the only one who could see it. He shook his head, not quite believing what he was doing, and started reading.

The first section of the book was mostly charms; to keep one safe, to keep from getting lost, to help a plant grow. One even helped with pimples. The second section was much less pleasant. One spell would kill insects, the next would cause sores; one would sour milk, another would send frightening dreams. It was rather creepy and Thomas quickly turned to the third section.

Benjamin's voice interrupted his reading. "Has anyone else noticed how light it's getting?"

Thomas looked out the eastern window. The sky was turning from black to blue, and the first light of the morning was touching the clouds overhead.

"Any sign that they're leaving?" asked Henry.

Thomas craned his neck towards the dormitory. "I don't think... wait." He looked closer. "The soldiers are coming out of the dormitory."

"The riders are all coming in," said Benjamin from the other side. "I think they're headed for the gates."

"How about the students?" asked Henry, coming over to join Thomas.

"Some are being herded together," Thomas said, watching the bishop's troops round the students up and lead them towards the gates. The other students were following behind. Even over the distance and through the glass, Thomas could hear them shouting. "The rest are not too happy."

"Are all the troops going?"

"Aye, I think so."

"Thank the Four," Benjamin said fervently. "Can we leave now?"

"Aye." Thomas picked up the book and his sword. "But not through the cemetery. Everyone will see us if we head that way now."

"Then where?" asked George.

"Back the way we came. To Theology, then around and through the kitchen door."

"Everyone in the dormitory will see us," said Benjamin.

"Everyone in the dormitory will see us in the dormitory," corrected Henry. "Which is where students are supposed to be."

"We'd better run," Eileen pointed out the window to the lightening sky. "Dawn is coming on quickly."

"Then open the door, and let's run."

They trooped to the door. Henry found the right key and unlocked it, and the five slipped outside and into the thin light of the morning. The sun hadn't cleared the horizon yet, but the black shadows of the night were gone, replaced with pre-dawn grey. In the east, the first true colours were beginning to show through. It looked like it would be a very nice sunrise, but none of them took the time to watch. Henry locked the library door and they all took off at a run, charging for the Theology building. On one side, the voices of the students, loud and angry, were filling the air with talk of riot. From the other direction, quieter but equally strident, the Masters were arguing about what to do. Neither group saw or heard the five black-robed figures crossing the grounds.

They reached Theology unseen and ran around the building rather than going inside. They stopped at the final corner. Ahead of them, Thomas could see the kitchen door, a short dash away.

"The staff will be in the kitchens," said Benjamin.

"After all this?" Eileen asked, amazed. "How could they?"

"They live in the building," Henry explained. "The last time they didn't have breakfast on time was the day the dormitory caught fire. A little event like this won't even slow them down."

"Doesn't matter," said Thomas, taking off his sword and hiding it under his robe. "It's still our best way in."

"So what do we say to them?" asked Benjamin.

" 'Good morning,' " said Henry. "Now come on."

They charged across the lawns, found the kitchen door unlocked, and the staff at work inside. With nodded "good mornings" the five made their way through and out the other side. Several disapproving glares fell their way, and the head chef gave them several succinct words about going where they didn't belong and after such a night as well. Henry gave a short, eloquent apology, but none of them slowed down.

"All right," Thomas began as soon as they left the kitchen, "let's get the—"

He got no further when the sound of returning students filled the building. Voices shouted back and forth in outrage, and footsteps echoed through the hallways.

Henry cursed. "They'll be coming from everywhere."

"Just act like you were here all night," Thomas said. "Once we're through the baths, we can run."

They went through at a fast walk. Students hurried past. Others stood in clusters, arguing. The younger ones looked to be in shock, faces pale and occasionally smeared with tears. The older ones didn't seem any less shaken, but anger was the main emotion among them.

Thomas realized he was still wearing his rapier at the same time he saw that he wasn't the only one. Any student who owned a sword had it with him, the rules to the contrary having been obviously disregarded for the morning.

The five pushed through the crowd, nodding and making appropriate comments, but never stopping. A sharp turn and a short flight of stairs later, they were into the bathhouse.

The place was nearly full. Many of the students, it seemed, had decided to make up for their lack of sleep with a morning dip. Boys and young men were jumping in and out of the baths, scrubbing themselves at the basins, and hurling angry ideas back and forth. Some wanted to write letters to the king, others to march on the bishop's house. Thomas dodged through them, heading for the door to the courtyard and escape.

"Thomas!"

George's call brought Thomas to a stop. He turned and saw Eileen, stuck just inside the door of the bathhouse, with a dozen naked young men blocking her path and arguing vociferously. She was trying to get through, but no one was moving and several of them were turning to her demanding her opinion. She didn't answer any of them, and her face was working very hard to be the same colour as her hair.

Thomas turned back, and with George beside him, cleared a path to her and grabbed her arms. Several students protested at being shoved aside, but took one look at George and let the matter alone. Thomas and George pulled her the length of the hall and out into the courtyard. Henry and Benjamin were already there, waiting for them to catch up. The five dashed across the courtyard to the little path and the gate beyond. The guard Thomas had feared would be there was gone. He threw open the gate and led the others in a mad run down the road to the apartment block.

Chapter 23

The apartments were just coming to life, though no one was actually outside when Thomas and his friends ran into the courtyard. Voices carried past them from each floor as the five climbed the stairs and stumbled into the apartment. Henry pulled the balcony doors shut and put on the latch. Thomas was ready to collapse on the spot, and from the look of his friends, so were they.

"I do not," Benjamin gasped, "believe we got out of there."

"Neither do I," agreed Thomas. "I thought we were dead."

"I think your friend may be," said Henry, pointing.

George was sitting on the floor, head in his hands. Eileen knelt beside him. "Are you all right?"

George shook his head. Thomas came over. "Anything we can do?"

One of George's big hands reached out, wrapped itself into Thomas's shirt and pulled him in close. George raised his head and their eyes met. For a moment, Thomas was afraid. George's eyes narrowed, then his mouth widened into a big, relieved grin. "Aye," he said. "You can never make me do anything like that again, you twit." He let go of Thomas and pushed him back. "If our father heard about this, he'd kill us all. Twice."

"And that's before he finds out Thomas has been kissing his daughter," added Henry, stepping to the cupboards and pulling out a bottle of wine.

"You know just how to say the wrong thing, don't you?" Thomas realized he was grinning, too. Around the room, his friends all had similar expressions on their faces; relief and exhaustion and victory intermingling. Benjamin was swaying on his feet. Henry, pouring himself some wine, looked like death warmed over. George and Eileen were on the floor, leaning on one another.

All for me, Thomas realized. *They all risked themselves for me.*

"Thank you," Thomas said, "All of you."

Henry waved him off. "It was fun."

"It was not," objected Benjamin. "It was dangerous."

"And that's what makes it fun." Henry held up the bottle. "Everyone come and get some."

Henry filled the cups, and Thomas, rather than making everyone go to Henry, passed them around. They drank the wine down as Henry poured a second for himself. He quaffed it, then said, "We'd best get ready."

"Ready?" Benjamin repeated, incredulously. He put his cup down and headed for his room. "I am not getting ready for anything except bed. See you this evening."

"Don't bother," said Henry. "You won't get the chance."

Benjamin stopped to look at Henry. "Why not?"

A bell rang from the Academy, sharp and loud and pealing through the air. There was a moment of silence around them, then the sound of doors being thrown open and students racing down the stairs. Thomas led Eileen and George to the balcony. All around them, students were racing out of the building, most carrying swords.

"That's not the same bell as yesterday," said Eileen, watching the chaos below. "What is it?"

"Alarm," said Henry from inside. "I'm surprised they didn't ring it last night."

"The soldiers probably stopped them," said Thomas. He went back inside. "You two should get going. And wear your swords."

George looked confused. "You said swords aren't allowed in the Academy."

"They aren't, normally," said Henry, stepping onto the balcony as he put on an intricately tooled sword belt. The blade that hung off it was of much higher quality than the one Thomas wore, with an intricately engraved bell guard. He drew the blade half-way, then let it slide back in the sheath.

Behind him, Benjamin was buckling on his own sword belt which held his own, much plainer weapon.

"I thought you were studying to be a priest," Eileen said.

"I am," Benjamin tightened the buckle in the belt. "It was a gift from my father my first year here. When I realized I wanted to be a priest, I put it away." He drew it half-way, looking at the blade for rust. "I never expected to wear it again."

"We'll come back as soon as we can," promised Henry, "and tell you all the news."

He led Benjamin out the door and down the stairs. Thomas watched them go.

Beside him, Eileen said, "Now what do we do?"

"We sleep," said George, pushing himself to his feet. "Benjamin had the right idea."

"He did," agreed Eileen, stifling a yawn. "Though how we'll sleep through this racket," she gestured in the direction of the still-pealing alarm bells, "is beyond me."

"I'll manage it," promised George, heading for the bedroom. "See you two later."

"Are you going to sleep, too?" Eileen asked Thomas.

Thomas shook his head. "Not yet. You two get some sleep. I'll stay here for a while."

Eileen hesitated a moment, then followed her brother into the bedroom. Thomas stayed out on the balcony, listening to the alarm bell. It rang for most of an hour before it finally fell silent. Thomas listened for sounds of fighting, or arguing, or anything to indicate what was happening. There was nothing. He sighed. At least there hadn't been a riot.

He waited a while longer, then picked up his sword and belt, and crept quietly out the back door and down to the street. He took a long, circuitous route, keeping his eyes sharp for any sign of the bishop's men. There were none. Thomas got within sight of the Academy's gates, found them closed. It was the only time he had ever seen them shut during the day. It didn't bode well,

Thomas thought, but at least there was no sign of anyone fighting.

He turned away and walked to the market. He would get food for everyone. After that, he would start reading the books Henry and Eileen had found. Maybe there he could find some answers on how to deal with the bishop.

A yawn caught Thomas off-guard, bringing him to a halt as it worked its way through his body. He added a nap to the list of things he needed to do.

The market was bustling with early-morning shoppers; housewives come to collect the day's meal, servants picking up orders for their masters, tavern and restaurant owners bespeaking the best goods for their establishments. Thomas didn't take long to find a baker's stand, and he bought enough beef pies, tarts, and pastries to feed all five of them. He stopped at the fruit seller's next, then a wine stall. He bought some bottles of a substantially better wine than the one they'd been drinking. The price made him wince a bit, but his friends deserved a treat.

"Hear the news! Come hear the news!"

The loud voice and ringing bell called for everyone's attention. Thomas turned with the rest of the crowd to see a Crier, dressed in the bright colours of his profession, step up onto a small stool. Thomas, too tired to care, shouldered his purchases and was about to leave the market when he caught the words, "By order of the bishop!"

"Wanted for witchcraft and murder!" the Crier called. "Thomas Flarety! A fugitive from the town of Elmvale! Seen with a large man and a red-haired girl! Wanted by the church for witchcraft and murder!"

Thomas felt himself go pale. The Crier kept going, calling out descriptions of all three of them. It was all Thomas could do to keep from running. Instead, he turned slowly around and headed back towards the apartment. Behind him, the Crier repeated the message.

Thomas felt the hairs on the back of his neck rise. Someone, he was sure, would see him and grab him. He desperately wanted his back against a wall and his sword in his hand, even though he knew there was nothing in the world that would draw attention to him faster than that. He kept walking, not making eye contact with anyone, moving at the same pace as the rest of the crowd until he was clear of the market.

In the street Thomas let himself pick up the pace. He moved through the neighbourhood at a brisk walk, dodging other pedestrians and carts and carriages until he reached the apartment. He would have taken the stairs two at a time if he hadn't been weighted down with food. Thomas hustled up them as quickly as he could and into the apartment. It wasn't until the door was shut behind him and he had thrown the bolt that he felt some small measure of relief. He put the food down on the table and sank onto one of the chairs. Everything suddenly felt overwhelming again. He put his face into his hands, retreating into the darkness there.

"Thomas?"

He pulled his head up. Eileen was standing in the door, a blanket wrapped around her shoulders. She was still dressed in her shirt and breeches, though her feet were bare on the floor.

"Are you all right?" she asked. "Why are you wearing your sword?"

Thomas didn't answer either question. "I bought food."

Eileen frowned. "You shouldn't have gone out there."

"No, I shouldn't have," agreed Thomas, "but I needed to see what was happening at the Academy. And since I was out..." he gestured to the table and the food piled high on it. "Is George up?"

"No."

"Can you wake him?"

Eileen did, and while George wasn't happy at all about it, his mood lightened considerably when he spied the tarts on the table. Thomas's own appetite was gone, but he watched his friends dig into the food, only cautioning them to leave enough for Henry and Benjamin. Once they were full, he told them the news. Both went pale.

"So now we can't even walk in the streets?" George asked, though they all knew the answer already. "We can't even be seen?"

"Not during the day," said Thomas. "And not together."

"Then what do we do?" asked Eileen.

"We stay out of sight." Thomas reached out and squeezed her hand. "As long as no one sees us, we'll be all right."

"Everyone's already seen us," George rose to his feet and pacing. "The students in the dormitory, the students here, the meat seller—"

Thomas snorted. "Bernard wouldn't turn us in unless I insulted his cooking."

George didn't acknowledge the attempt at humour. "And everyone else?"

"The students won't say anything," Thomas assured him. "They hate the bishop right now."

"How about the ones they took away? If they're tortured..."

"They won't torture them," said Thomas, wondering if he was right even as the words left his mouth. "They're under the king's protection. They weren't even supposed to arrest them. They can't risk torture."

"They still might," George stopped pacing; he stood in the middle of the room, like a bear in a pit, wanting to run but finding no direction to go. "Maybe we should go away."

"And do what?" demanded Thomas. "Run until he catches us? We're better off here."

"But what if they *do* come here?" asked Eileen. "What then?"

"We can escape across the roof, if we have to."

"I don't like it," said George.

"Neither do I, but it's all we can do!" The look on George's face told Thomas his friend was ready to argue the point. Thomas forestalled him. "At least wait until Benjamin and Henry get back. We'll find out what's happened at the Academy and then make a decision. All right?"

George, his arms in front of his chest, brows low over his eyes, obviously didn't like that idea either. Still, he said, "All right."

"I think we should pack," Eileen said getting up from her chair, "so we can run if we need to."

Thomas nodded. "That's a good idea."

Eileen went into the bedroom and started packing clothes into her bag.

Thomas watched her through the door a moment, then turned back to George. The big man was staring at his hands.

"You all right?" Thomas asked.

George didn't look up. "I don't like it here."

"I know."

"The city is too big, and the Academy..." He shook his head. "This isn't a place for me."

"I know. I'm sorry."

George shook his head again. "Your friends seem all right, but half the time I don't know what they're talking about."

Thomas smiled. "Half the time, neither do they."

"You know what I mean."

"I do." Thomas punched his friend lightly in the shoulder. "It will be all right."

George sighed. "Eventually, I'm sure." He raised his head, looked his friend in the eye. "Are we going to go home again, Thomas? Ever?"

It was Thomas's turn to sigh. "I don't know."

"I thought as much." George pushed himself to his feet. "Might as well get packed, then."

Thomas joined him, and soon all three of their bags were packed and laid out in a corner of the room. With nothing else to do, George announced his intention of going back to sleep. He stayed in the common room, though, spreading himself out on a pile of pillows. Thomas and Eileen took over the bedroom and started going through the books. Eileen sat on the bed and read through the book of spells. Thomas sat at the desk, working his way through the books on the witch hunts.

They were a gruelling read; page after page of obscene acts and ideas, all attributed to witches and others who were declared to have "power beyond the natural order." There were long, detailed, gruesome descriptions of rituals involving the abuse and sacrifice of animals and people. Thomas skimmed through those as quickly as he could, then found himself reading with absolute horror the prescribed ways of testing witches and gaining confessions of them. He read a bit further, and then shoved the book away with a grunt of disgust.

"What is it?" Eileen asked, glancing up from the book of magic.

"Obscene," was Thomas's reply. "It's obscene and vile and disgusting."

"Well, don't bother sharing it with me," Eileen warned. "I'd like to sleep tonight."

"One of us should." Thomas took a couple of deep breaths to steady himself, "And since I'm not going to..." He opened the book and skimmed forward from the same point. Page upon page of the same stuff followed. It was all horrific and completely unhelpful. He reached the end of the chapter and stood up for a much-needed break. He stretched, feeling the muscles in his shoulders and back protest.

Eileen was still absorbed in the small book of spells that they had found. He leaned over her to look. "What do you think?"

Eileen shook her head. "I don't know. I mean, they say they're spells..."

"They all glow."

"So *you* say."

Thomas smiled. "Still think I'm insane?"

"Oh, aye," Eileen said, smiling back. "But I'd like to believe you."

Thomas nodded. "That's the problem. If I could *show* you..."

Eileen raised her head, her eyes meeting his. Their faces were within inches of each other and Thomas almost took the moment to steal a kiss, but Eileen's expression was serious, and her brow furrowed. She leaned back, setting the book down. Her tone was almost accusing when she said, "You want to try one."

Thomas set the idea of kissing her aside, and nodded. "Aye."

"You're not serious!"

"Why do you think I took it?" Thomas asked. He stood up, rubbing his face to drive away the tired he felt. "I can see magic. I can *feel* it. If I can *do* magic as well, maybe I can find a way to undo what the bishop has done."

"*If* you can make magic work," said Eileen.

Thomas nodded. "Aye."

"What if you can't?"

Then I'm insane. "Then I can't. But I've got to try."

Eileen took a long moment to think about it, then picked up the book again. "The first part is all little spells. You could try one of them, but most require ingredients." She flipped the pages. "Like this one. 'Spell to give one pleasant dreams and a restful sleep'. You need a candle, a pot of chamomile tea, and some violet petals to put under your pillow." She snorted, "With all that, I doubt you'd even need a spell. Same with a lot of them, though I haven't gotten to the nasty section, yet."

"Which ones don't need ingredients?"

Eileen paged through the book. "How's this: 'Spell to make lost objects found'?"

"I haven't lost anything."

"Oh. Well, 'Spell to calm the mind'?"

"How would you know it worked?"

"True." She paged some more. "Here, then. 'Spell to make light from darkness'."

"It's not dark."

"It will be if you close the shutters."

"True enough." Thomas reached up and closed the shutters tight, then pulled the tattered curtains across the window. Eileen handed Thomas the book, then got up and closed the door. The room wasn't truly dark, but it was considerably dimmed. Thomas, looking down at the book in his hand, was suddenly very nervous. The thought that he might succeed was nearly as frightening as the idea that he might not. Eileen sat back on the bed, watching him.

The spell was very clear. All one had to do was close one's eyes, and imagine a light appearing in one's outstretched hands. The imagining had to be thorough, the book cautioned. One had to be able to see the light completely; to feel the warmth from it, and to imagine exactly what effect it would have on the room. After that, one outstretched one's hand and placed the light there with one's mind.

"Seems simple enough." Thomas put down the book, sat on his chair and closed his eyes. He held out his hand and tried to concentrate. He couldn't. He rolled his shoulders to let out some of the tension, then tried again. He still couldn't concentrate. He opened his eyes. "I feel stupid."

"No one's here to see but me," Eileen pointed out.

"And scared," Thomas admitted. "I mean, if it works..."

"If it works," Eileen repeated slowly, her own nervousness coming out with the words, "it works. We'll worry about that if it happens. It's only a light, after all."

"So is a bonfire," Thomas muttered. Still, he closed his eyes again.

It's just another exercise, he told himself. *Just another meditation.*

Thomas realized he had no idea what sort of light he should call. Should the light be bright, dull, large, small? Should it be like the flame of a torch or the light of the sun? Should it fill the room or just his hand? The possibilities nearly overwhelmed him.

An image came suddenly to mind, bringing a catch to Thomas's throat. He embraced it. After all, it worked for Timothy.

He went deep into himself, working hard to make the image perfect: A ball, blue with swirls of white, glowing without burning, and floating gently above his hand. He raised his arm and opened his hand.

At first, his mind rebelled. Try as he might, he could not get the image to go from the abstract to the concrete. It was as if his mind sensed the task was impossible. He began to sweat from the effort, even though all he was doing was thinking. Nagging doubts crept into his mind, and a voice somewhere in the back of his head told him that Henry was right; that he was insane and all he was going to do was prove it.

Thomas pushed the voice and all the other thoughts away, focusing on the image of the ball and putting every ounce of will power he had into the effort. Suddenly, there was a single, clear image, more real than anything he had seen in his life.

Eileen gasped, and from the sounds of it, fell off the bed. Thomas opened his eyes.

There, floating above the palm of his hand, just as it had on Timothy's, was a small blue ball of light, shimmering and glowing, with streaks of white swirling inside it.

Thomas cried out in surprise, jumping away from the light and promptly falling to the floor. The ball of light winked out of existence.

"By the Father!" he gasped. "By all the Four!" He looked at Eileen. "Did you see that?"

"Aye," Eileen was also on the floor, her body pushed back against a wall. Her voice was filled equally with fear and wonder. "Aye, I did."

"It was real?"

"Aye."

"By the Four," Thomas whispered. "It worked!"

It was a long time before either of them moved or said anything else. Thomas was at once elated and terrified. When he managed to look at Eileen again, he could tell she was mostly feeling the latter. Thomas reached over to her and found her hand. She flinched away from him, not meeting his eyes.

"It's all right," Thomas said.

Eileen didn't look at him.

"I can do magic." He felt himself starting to grin like an idiot. "Real magic."

She nodded, and this time her eyes came up to meet his. She still looked scared, but a hint of a smile was coming to her lips as well. "Aye," she said, at last. "You can."

Chapter 24

Late in the afternoon, a wave of noise rolled into the courtyard. Thomas and Eileen rushed to the balcony, nearly tripping over George, who was coming groggily awake and struggling to his feet. He joined them on the balcony a few moments later. Together, they watched a wave of students flowing into the courtyard. Their voices were animated and angry, but their swords were sheathed and no one was injured. Most stopped in the courtyard, talking furiously amongst themselves.

Henry and Benjamin broke free from the crowd and charged up the stairs. Thomas could barely control his impatience when they mounted to top stair and gestured the three inside. Both students looked at once exhausted and triumphant.

"News!" Benjamin trumpeted as soon as all of them were inside and the door was closed. "The bishop's search was illegal! It was done without writ! The Master of Law and his faculty got all the students released this morning!"

"You should have heard the Principal's speech," Henry said, putting his sword down and taking up the wine. "He called us all together to voice his 'annoyance'. He's arming the gate guards, he's locking all other entrances, and he's denying the church collection rights until the bishop apologizes for the insult."

"What about the students?" asked Thomas. "Did they riot?"

"Surprisingly enough, no," Henry poured himself a rather full cup. "And now we know how the Master of Rhetoric got the job. I've never seen anyone talk so well so fast."

"It was impressive," said Benjamin. "He took over after the Principal and managed to get everyone's outrage out into the open without sending them off to riot. As of now, no students will attend any other church except the one on the grounds, and no Theology students will work in the bishop's house until he apologizes." He reached under his robe and drew out a letter, a blot of black wax stamped with the Academy's seal holding it shut. "We spent the rest of the day composing formal letters of protest to the king."

"He will be receiving a thousand of them, hand delivered, tomorrow morning," said Henry. "They're going to make a march of it. Every student will hand-deliver his letter to the castle, and they'll all walk by the bishop's house on the way."

"Though it may not do any good," Benjamin reached over and took the bottle from Henry, then snagged one of the cups from the table. "The students who served there said he was half-packed already. He'll be gone by tomorrow."

"Which is too bad," said Henry. "I was hoping to see his face." He drained his cup in a single, long drink, sighed happily, then turned to Thomas. "So, what have you been doing behind locked doors all day?"

"The door was open and her brother was in the next room," Thomas said firmly. "And what we were doing was research."

"Did you find out what the bishop is going to do?" asked Benjamin.

"No. We were sidetracked before that," said Thomas, smiling at Eileen.

Henry and George raised simultaneous eyebrows. Eileen smiled back. "And if you'll sit down, we'll show you what we've found."

"Can you feed us first?" asked Benjamin. "We've been working all day, unlike some."

"There's food in the cupboard," Thomas said. "The remains of lunch and some much better wine than what you're drinking."

"Fine." Benjamin emptied his glass and headed for the cupboard. "Wait until we're done, then show us."

"You'll want to see this first."

"Wrong," said Henry, following Benjamin.

A startled gasp from George made them both spin in place. Thomas was holding out his hand, the small, glowing ball of blue light floating just above his palm. The two students stared, mouths open, eyes wide. George's head was swivelling back and forth between the light and Thomas's face.

"It's all right," said Eileen, grinning. "It's just magic."

"Aye," George's eyes were huge, his voice barely a whisper. "Aye, it is." He leaned closer to Thomas's hand, squinting at the little ball of light. "It's just like the one Timothy did."

Thomas managed a nod, but didn't take his eyes from the ball of light.

"That can't be real," said Benjamin. He stepped around George and reached out to touch the ball of light. Thomas held very still, keeping his mind focused on the ball of light as Benjamin poked at it. His finger sank into the surface of the ball. Benjamin stumbled back, nearly falling. "Sweet Father, it is real!"

Thomas blinked and the ball of light vanished. Eileen clapped him on the back. "That's the longest you've made it last so far! And someone touched it!"

Henry was looking very pale. His mouth worked a couple of times before he managed to get out the words, "Well. You're not insane."

Thomas grinned. "I told you."

"You said you couldn't do spells," said Benjamin, stumbling back and finding a chair. He sank heavily into it. "You said so."

"I couldn't, then."

"And now you can?"

"Aye."

Benjamin's face was etched with fear and confusion. He rubbed hard at his face, as if the action might drive away what he'd seen. "I have to report you to the Master of Theology."

"What?" Thomas realized on the instant what he had done, "Ben, no. It isn't witchcraft."

"Then what is it?" demanded Benjamin. His face was pale and fear was bringing sweat to his brow. "That... *thing*. What was it?"

"Magic!" Thomas felt his desperation rising. He struggled to control his tone, to sound calm. "It's just magic."

"Just?" Benjamin's voice rose an octave on the word. "There's nothing 'just' about it!"

Benjamin started to rise. Thomas stepped in his way. "You can't, Ben."

"I have to!" Exhaustion and shock edged his voice. He was shaking where he stood. "It's my duty to report witchcraft, Thomas. I have to."

"But you don't know that it's witchcraft," protested Eileen, stepping up beside Thomas, "You don't know anything about it!"

Ben stayed where he was, swaying on his feet. Henry stepped forward. "Sit down, Ben," he said. When Benjamin didn't move, Henry laid a hand on one of his arms. "Ben, listen to me. All right? Not to Thomas, to me. Will you listen?"

Conflicting loyalties warred in Benjamin's face.

"Please," begged Thomas. "For our friendship. Please."

Benjamin bit his lip, then nodded. "All right, Henry. I'll listen to you."

"Good," Henry put gentle pressure on his arm, guiding him back to the chair. "Sit down, now."

Benjamin swayed in his place a moment longer, then allowed himself to be seated. Henry went to the table and got Benjamin's wine cup, pressing it into the bigger student's hand until Benjamin took it and drank some.

"Good," Henry repeated. "Now let me think." He rubbed at his face just as Benjamin had done a moment before, and Thomas remembered that neither of his friends had slept the night before.

Of course, Thomas realized, *neither have I.*

"All right," Henry paced the floor, still rubbing at his face and muttering to himself. Benjamin looked almost ready to rise again when Henry stopped pacing. "All right," he said again, nodding to himself. "It's a court; we're in court. Thomas, you stand accused of witchcraft—"

"This isn't a game—"Benjamin's protest stopped dead at Henry's suddenly raised hand.

Henry's words were slow, his tone steady. "Thomas is making little balls of light float in the air, Benjamin, and I'm trying to find out whether or not we hand him over to be hanged. I know this isn't a game!" He pointed a finger at Thomas. "Thomas Flarety, you stand accused of witchcraft. How plead you?"

There was fear in Henry's voice, as much as in Benjamin's, but there was a gleam of excitement in his eyes and Thomas knew that Henry was doing his best to give Thomas a chance to prove himself. Eileen, still standing beside Thomas, took his hand, squeezing it hard. Worry had drawn two lines across her forehead, and tightened the skin around her eyes.

Thomas raised her hand, kissed it, then gently guided her towards her brother. George took her arm and the two sat on the floor against the wall, leaving Thomas standing alone in the middle of the room. He turned back to Henry and Benjamin. "I plead my innocence."

Henry nodded "Right, then. Will you answer all my questions?"

"I will."

"Will you tell me only the truth?"

"On my soul."

"Not enough," interrupted Benjamin. "If your soul is already tainted—"

"On the souls of my mother and father, then," said Thomas. When Benjamin still looked doubtful, Thomas added, "On my oath as a student of the Academy."

"That will do." Henry turned to Benjamin. "Will that do?"

Benjamin looked fretful still, but nodded.

"All right, then," Henry took a chair and sat in it facing Thomas. "What you did—the ball of light. How did you do it?"

"Uh…" Thomas looked for a way to describe what he'd done. "I called it."

"From where?"

"I don't know," Thomas thought about it. "From inside, I suppose."

"But you couldn't do that before," protested Benjamin. "You said you couldn't."

"I couldn't," agreed Thomas.

"So how can you now?" asked Henry.

"I... I learned."

"From what?"

"From the...." Thomas realized at once where Henry was going, and his heart began to sink. "From the book."

Eileen caught the change in his tone. "What? What's the matter with the book?"

"A book can be a tool of the Banished," said Thomas, his eyes still on Henry, who was beginning to look grim. "Meant to ensnare the unwary."

"Aye," said Henry. "There is that."

"And you used it!" Benjamin practically shouted the words. He drove himself to his feet and advanced on Thomas. "You knew that if you used witchcraft I'd have to report you! You knew that you might be dooming your soul!"

Thomas held his ground. "Aye."

"And you did it anyway!" Benjamin was nearly on top of him. "Why? Why would you do that?"

"Because I had to know!" Thomas shouted back, weeks worth of anger and helplessness spilling out of him with the words. "I'm the only one who has been able to see anything! The only one who could hear anything! I've spent half a month wondering if I'm right or insane and now I know. I'm right!"

Benjamin grabbed Thomas's shirt, shaking him. "You've lost your soul!"

"No!" Thomas's hands closed over Benjamin's, stilling the bigger man. Thomas made himself speak quietly. "It came from inside me, Ben, not anywhere else. I made that ball of light appear. Not any evil power. Just me."

Benjamin let go of Thomas's shirt and stepped back, his hands falling to his sides. The anger drained from his face, and his voice was as quiet as Thomas's when he asked, "How do we know that?"

Thomas realized he had no answer to the question. Benjamin stayed where he was, staring at Thomas as silence filled the room.

"Got it!" Eileen slapped her hands on the floor and pushed herself to her feet. "I've got it!"

"You?" said Henry, sounding surprised.

"Aye, me. I knew all that time with the nuns would pay off." She turned to Benjamin. "Thomas claims that what he can do is a gift, right?"

Benjamin blinked, obviously not expecting to be answering questions. "He claimed his ability to see magic was a gift," he said, "but this is different."

"How?"

"He used a spell book," Benjamin explained. "Anyone can use a spell book."

Eileen smiled. "Can you?"

If her first questions had caught Benjamin off-guard, this one nearly knocked him over. After a moment's spluttering he managed, "I wouldn't."

"But can you?" Eileen persisted.

"Of course!" Thomas, picking up where she was going. "If anyone can use the spell book, then the power could come from anywhere. But if only those with the gift could use it..."

"Then the power comes from within," finished Henry. He smiled at Eileen. "Very well put."

"But how do we know that power doesn't come from the Banished?" demanded Benjamin.

"Because!"

It was George who said it, and the other four all turned in some surprise at the big smith. His brow was furrowed in concentration and he held up a large hand, one finger upraised while he thought. It was a long thought, and Thomas nearly went off his mind with impatience, but they waited, letting the man work through it. At last, George put down his hand and smiled. "Because."

"Because why?" demanded Benjamin.

"Because that which is within is given to us by the ones who created us," said George slowly. "the Banished didn't create anyone, and so can't give a person something that comes from within."

"Good!" Henry crossed the room and clapped a hand on George's shoulder. "Very good! You know, we might make a student of you yet."

George shuddered. "I hope not."

Thomas turned to Benjamin. "Well?"

Benjamin stood, silent, a puzzled frown on his face. He was obviously going over the argument in his mind. At last, he fixed Henry and Thomas with a glare. "Logic can be the tool of the Banished."

"False logic can be a tool of the Banished," both Henry and Thomas protested at once. They looked at each other in surprise then began to laugh, the sound breaking the tension in the room.

Benjamin rolled his eyes skyward. "The High Father save us from philosophers and law students."

"Does this mean you agree?" Thomas asked.

"Aye, I do," said Benjamin. "And the Four help us all."

Relief rolled over Thomas in a wave, and the smile broke free. "Thank you."

"Don't thank me yet," warned Benjamin. "We still have to test the theory."

"I already have," said Eileen. "Everything Thomas managed to do, I tried. I couldn't make any of it work."

"That's as may be," said Benjamin, "but I didn't see it."

"Fair enough," Thomas headed for his room. "I'll get the book and you can try it."

"Not me," said Benjamin, "I'll not be endangering my soul."

Eileen rolled her eyes. "I'll do it, all right?"

"And me," said Henry. "After all, there's no sense in only one of us endangering their soul."

"And me," added George. "I'd hate to be left out if it does work."

"All right, then, we'll all try it." Thomas got the book from his desk, and brought it out to the table. "Do you want to try the ball of light first, or would you prefer levitation?"

The eyes of George and the two students widened. "Levitation?"

* * *

Several more hours passed before the students got their supper. They passed the spell book around, all save Benjamin trying whatever they could, Thomas demonstrated the ball of light again, then levitation with a spoon, then the relaxation spell. Of course, no one could see the last one work, other than by the expression on Thomas's face. The others, without exception, could not do any of them.

The experiments also began to yield the extent of Thomas's gift, for try as he might, he could not make the ball of light any larger, or lift any items larger than a spoon off the table, and that would come rattling down the moment he stopped concentrating. He tried levitating a cup, but it only wobbled back and forth. Thomas could feel himself getting tired by then, and called an end to the experiments for the day. The others asked to see more, but Thomas shook his head.

"I can't. I'm exhausted."

"Exhausted?" Henry protested. "You haven't done anything."

"I've made the ball of light a half-dozen times and I lifted that spoon ten times. It's tiring."

"But it's just lifting a spoon."

"Without touching it," reminded Thomas. "Can you do it?"

"No."

"Then don't tell me how tiring it is."

That gave Henry pause. "Fair enough. How about the other ones, can you do any of them?"

"Most of them are complicated," said Eileen. "Some need ingredients, some require chanting. The one for healing a broken heart gives you a phrase which you have to chant for an hour, every evening, for a month."

"Probably to keep you distracted," suggested Henry.

"There's also spells that need you to be in certain places," Eileen opened up the spell book and paged through until she found the one she wanted. "Look at this one. 'To divine a man's whereabouts'."

Henry read it. "You need to be in a stone circle, facing moonrise."

"Well, we won't be trying that one," said Benjamin. "The nearest circle's a two day ride south from here." He took the book and opened it to a random page. "This one's 'For causing harm to those you hate'."

"Aye," Thomas took the book from him. "The entire second section's like that. The first section is spells of luck and charm, the second section is spells of harm."

"Are there only two sections?"

"Four," said Thomas. "But only two I can use." He held up the book for them to see. "The last two sections are titled 'Greater Magic'. It's all stuff you hear in the old legends, like calling a storm, or sending fire out of your hands. I can't do them."

"Why not?"

"Not enough strength," Thomas explained. "You need a lot of power to make those spells work."

"How do you know?" demanded Henry. "Have you tried any of them?"

Thomas nodded. "Aye."

"Which one?" demanded Benjamin

Thomas paged through the book. "This one. 'Spell to cause fog to rise from the earth'."

"Good thing it didn't work," said Benjamin. "Someone might have noticed a fog rolling into the city on the middle of a sunny afternoon."

"I did think of that." Thomas pointed to one of the lines on the page. "You control the spell by imagining the area you want the fog to fill. So I imagined my room."

"And?"

Thomas sighed. "Pass me a cup."

Henry raised an eyebrow and handed Thomas a cup. Thomas put it on the table and stared at it. The others waited quietly at first, but as more time passed, Henry began to fidget. Benjamin started to ask Thomas something, but Eileen shushed him. "Wait," she said. "Just a bit longer."

Thomas was sweating now, and his breathing was getting a bit ragged, but he kept his eyes on the glass. The others, at Eileen's prompting, did the same. A small curl of mist began to form inside the cup. It swirled, and some spilled out, but it vanished almost as soon as it touched the table. Thomas kept staring. The little cloud of mist stayed a bit longer then began to vanish. Thomas took a deep breath and sat back in his chair, completely exhausted. "There you go."

George took a big breath himself. "That's impressive."

"Aye," agreed Henry. "Though not as impressive as a roomful of fog."

"It's all I can do," Thomas explained. "And that nearly did me in."

"I can see." George gave his friend a good looking over. "I'd say you need something to eat."

"In fact," Benjamin said, "I think we all need something to eat."

There was general agreement to that, and for the next little while the students bustled about in the room, getting food and wine and ale to the table. Soon everyone was devouring beef pies, pastries, and fresh blueberries from the fruit stand. It wasn't until the food was gone that conversation resumed.

"Well," said Henry. "Now we know what the bishop is doing."

Benjamin stopped in the midst of taking a drink. "We do?"

"Aye. He's building his power by taking other people's magic."

Thomas nodded. "If each gift gives some magical talent, then putting the gifts together should increase a person's magical power."

"But why is yours so important?" asked George.

"My gift is spotting other people's," said Thomas. "Think how much easier that would be for him."

"The next question is, what will he do with it?" Henry took the book from Thomas and paged through the last section. "There's some very nasty things in here."

"But he's not that powerful," protested Thomas. "If he was, I never would have escaped from him the first time."

"Maybe he's looking to become that powerful," Henry turned some more pages, and then held the book open for the others to see. "'Spell to increase one's magic.' Did you see this?"

Thomas nodded. "Yes."

"But he doesn't have this book," George said. "He can't know that spell, can he?"

"He might have another one," said Benjamin. "He might have a worse one."

"Worse how?" asked Eileen. She suddenly straightened up and waved her hands to ward off any possible answer. "No, don't tell me, I'm already imagining it."

"Maybe you should use the spell, Thomas," suggested Henry.

"I thought about it," Thomas said. "Look what it requires."

Henry read it and whistled. "Four hours meditation, one hour facing each of the cardinal directions."

"On a night of a full moon," finished Thomas, "in a circle of standing stones, sitting in the centre of a circle made like the one in the book."

Henry put down the book for the others to see. The picture showed a pair of circles, one imbedded inside the other, with geometric shapes and knot-work designs connecting them.

"The drawing has to be begun just after sunset and finished by moonrise," said Thomas, "and the person who draws it has to stay in the centre of it, turning as instructed, in order to gain the power. Which isn't even permanent, I might add."

"How long does it last?" asked George.

"From one full moon to the next."

"Benjamin," horror filled Eileen's voice, "where did you say the nearest circle was?"

"Two days south, by horse."

"And where's the bishop's summer house?"

"Two days south, by—" Benjamin didn't finish.

Thomas felt very grim all of a sudden. "That's why he's going south."

"When's the next full moon?" asked Henry. "He can't do it before then."

"Two days," said George. "It starts two days from now, and will last three nights."

"And he's leaving the day after tomorrow," said Benjamin.

Henry looked thoughtful. "The timing's right."

Thomas's head sank to his hands. "Great. Just what we need."

"If that's what he's doing," said Eileen, putting a hand on Thomas's shoulder. "We don't know."

"No, we don't," agreed Benjamin. "He could just want a few days in the country." Thomas gave him a look and Benjamin amended that to, "Or he could be planning something else."

"Like what?" asked Thomas.

"I don't know. Did the books on the witch hunts say anything?"

Thomas shook his head. "I didn't get that far. When we found out that the magic actually worked, we got distracted."

"Not surprising," said Henry, dryly. "You should go through them. We saw references to raising power and transferring magical ability."

"I will," Thomas straightened up and stretched in his seat. "But I can't do it tonight. I'm not sure I can even stand up, right now"

"How do we catch him if he leaves town?" asked George. "Two days' ride is a long walk."

"We'll buy horses," Thomas said.

"And where are we going to get money for that?" demanded Henry.

"We have it," said Thomas, smiling at George. "I put it someplace very safe."

"So what do you want Henry and me to do?" asked Benjamin.

"Stay out of trouble. And see if the Criers are still talking about us."

"Criers?" asked Benjamin.

"There's a reward out for us," George said. "I'm surprised you didn't hear them."

"There's always Criers about," Henry replied. "I usually ignore them."

"Well, now they're crying about us. Criminals wanted by the church for acts of witchcraft and murder."

"Wonderful," Benjamin put his chin on one hand.

Thomas put his feet under himself, pushed up and managed to belie his earlier statement. He stood, wavering for a moment, and then caught his balance. "And now, I'm going to head for bed."

"It's only dinner time," protested George.

"I know. Wake me after first bell tomorrow."

Chapter 25

A rough hand shook Thomas into consciousness and for a moment he thought he was back in the loft at George and Eileen's house. His half-asleep brain despaired at having to make the journey to Hawksmouth all over. Then he was shaken again and remembered where he was. His room was still dark, the only light coming from the common room. Thomas blinked the sleep out of his eyes and muttered an imprecation at the silhouette leaning over him — Benjamin or George from the size.

"No time for that." It was Benjamin. "The bishop's soldiers are in the yard."

Thomas woke up, hard and fast. He tossed his blankets aside, punched George in the shoulder, and rolled to his feet. Benjamin was already gone. Thomas reached for the bed, found Eileen's leg and shook it. She kicked out at him in her sleep and tried to tunnel under the blankets. Thomas pulled them off the bed. She let out a yelp at the sudden cold and tucked herself into a ball. She was wearing one of George's shirts as a nightgown, and the length of her bare leg would have been a very fetching sight if Thomas had the time to enjoy the view. She sat up a moment later and glared at him. George, on the floor, was doing the same.

"Soldiers coming," said Thomas to their glares. "Get dressed."

He put on his own clothes as fast as he could, then knocked open the window shutters. The sky was only just beginning to turn from the deep black of night to the dark blue of pre-dawn. The night was clear, and the moon spread its light into the room.

From outside he could hear the soldiers and students yelling and the sounds of horses' hooves. A fight was brewing. The senior students were not pleased at having their sleep disturbed and were letting the bishop's men know about it in no uncertain terms. Thomas put the spell book and the two tomes on witch-hunting into his bag, then tossed his blanket in after. George and Eileen had both dressed, and were forcing on their boots. Eileen had thrown on a skirt, rather than attempting to struggle into boy's clothes. As Thomas watched, they got their boots on and started stuffing their blankets into their bags. Thomas was just about to order them out the window when Benjamin stepped into the room, a lamp in his hand casting flickering yellow light and shadows into the room.

"Hurry!" Benjamin hissed. "They're calling everyone out of their rooms!"

From the common room, a door slammed, making them all jump. Henry appeared in Thomas's doorway a moment later, fully dressed and sword on his hip. "The bishop's soldiers are out back, too."

"What now?" demanded George. "Do we fight?"

"No!" Thomas was emphatic. "If we fight them, we'll end up caught and hanged. We need to get away." He headed to the window. "Come on. Across the roof."

"We have to go downstairs," Henry said to Benjamin. "Get your sword."

"I shouldn't," argued Benjamin. "I'm supposed to be—"

"You don't have a choice," snapped Henry. "Listen!"

The soldiers' shouts were getting louder, but from all around them a greater shout was rising up. Demands for a writ and calls for the king's guards were coming from all around. Cries of "Go home!" were drowning out the sounds of the bishop's men.

"Sounds like a riot," said Thomas, who was surprised to find his voice shaking.

"Not yet," Henry's voice was hard and angry, "but it will be. Get your sword, Ben!"

Ben hesitated a moment longer, then ran. Thomas put down his bag. "Henry, look out there and see if you can see the bishop's familiar. Tall man, all dressed in black."

Henry left.

"What are you doing?" demanded George.

"I want to see what's happening."

"They'll recognize you if you go out there."

Thomas shook his head. "They won't. Not from the top balcony."

Henry came back. "No one like that down there."

"Good." Thomas went out to the balcony, Henry following. Students were standing on all the balconies and in the yard, shouting epithets at the bishop's guards. The soldiers were shouting back. It was only ugly words being exchanged at the moment, but Thomas could see bottles and pots in the hands of those on the upper floors, and students with swords, knives, and sticks standing in the doorways of their ground floor apartments. In the courtyard, some twenty of the bishop's guards were standing, while ten more sat on horseback. Long-shafted halberds were clutched in their hands, the steel of their axe blades and spear points glowing in the torchlight.

"They're outnumbered," said Henry. He leaned on the railing and looked over the crowd. The shadows cast by the torches below hollowed out his thin face, making it into a death mask. Suddenly, Thomas could see the soldier that the older student had been, sizing up a battlefield. Henry's tone was almost conversational. "They have no room to manoeuvre. And the horses will panic if people start throwing bottles down on them. Stupid to bring them in here."

"They must have known this was going to happen," said Thomas. "They should have brought more men."

"They did," Henry said. "There were about twenty more in the stairwell."

"There's about two hundred of us living here. Did they think they could get us to do what they wanted so easily?"

Henry shrugged. "It worked at the dormitory."

Thomas shook his head. "The dormitory is filled with boys who aren't allowed to carry weapons. They must have known this was different."

Henry straightened up, his eyes and Thomas's meeting. "Of course, if all they wanted was to keep everyone looking at the courtyard…" He turned back to the apartment. Thomas followed his gaze. George and Eileen were standing in the common room, looking scared. Benjamin was standing beside them, doing up his sword belt with shaking hands. Behind them, the back door stood, bolted but unblocked.

"It's a diversion!" yelled Henry. "Ben! Block the back door!" He drew his sword, running into the common room. "Run, Thomas!"

Benjamin took one startled look at the back door, then grabbed the table and shoved it hard against the door. Thomas ran for his room, George and Eileen hard on his heels. A loud crash came from the common room. Thomas risked a look back. The door was still shut, Benjamin bracing the table against it. There was another crash of bodies against the door, then pounding and a loud voice shouting, "Open this door, in the name of the bishop!"

"Get out!" yelled Henry, adding his weight to Benjamin's. "Now!"

Thomas grabbed up his bag and ran for the window. He jumped on the desk, helped Eileen up. "Come on! Quick!"

There was the sound of wood splintering in a nearby apartment, and a startled shout. Eileen went through the window, George right after her. Thomas came through and led them across the flat section of roof at a run. Beneath their feet they heard a scream, then the sound of two hundred voices raised in anger. Horses screamed, dozens of bottles smashed on the cobblestones, and steel clashed against steel.

Thomas desperately wanted to turn back, but knew it would only make the whole mess worse. He reached the northern peak of the roof, climbed up, then shimmied down the other side. He looked back and saw George and Eileen stopped at the top and staring at the sloped roof opposite them and the fifteen feet of space between the two.

"There's nothing there!" George hissed.

"Yes, there is," Thomas hissed back. He reached the edge and dropped his bag off it. There was a *thud* almost immediately. "Come on!"

They came. Eileen first, then George taking up the rear. Thomas pointed to the flat roof he had dropped his bag on, some ten feet below. "Keep your knees bent and try to fall quietly," Thomas said.

"Oh, no problem," George muttered. He dropped his bag, took a big breath, and launched himself off the roof. He hit hard, but managed to keep his balance and didn't seem to hurt himself. He got to his feet and held out his arms for Eileen. She tossed her own bag down, then jumped into her brother's waiting arms. Thomas took a deep breath himself and jumped. He hit and collapsed, letting his knees take the shock, then shoved himself to his feet. He grabbed his bag. "Come on!"

He led his friends across the flat to a place where the roof sloped steeply upward. Thomas pointed to a door set deep in the side of the roof. "That's the way in."

"What is this place?" asked Eileen.

"Another apartment block. They'll raise a cry if they see us, so move fast."

"Is the door open?"

Thomas tried the handle, and cursed. "No, it isn't."

"Does it open in or out?" asked George.

"In."

"Good." He stepped forward and rammed his shoulder against it. There was a splintering sound and the door flew open.

"Stay low," Thomas crouched and led the way into the low attic on the other side of the door. It was dusty and had beams running across it at the perfect height to brain somebody. Little of the pre-dawn light reached inside, and they had to move far more slowly than Thomas would have liked. Several times Thomas felt cobwebs brush his face as they moved towards the narrow, rickety stairs at the far end. The sounds of people moving about and talking came clearly through the wood beneath their feet. Thomas prayed it was just a reaction to the noise next door and led his friends in a dash down the staircase.

The hallway below was as dark as the attic above. Thomas ran down it, George and Eileen hard behind him, passing a dozen doors Thomas feared would spring open at any moment. He found the stairs at the far end. Thomas took them two at a time until they reached the ground floor and another hallway with double doors open to the street beyond. Thomas made them stop just before they reached the doors. He stepped to the doorway and peered gingerly around the corner. It opened on a different street from his own apartment, and there was no one in sight.

Thomas led his friends through the city streets at a run. Behind them, the clash of weapons and screams of horses and men ripped into the oncoming dawn. In the buildings around them, Thomas could see curtains being pulled back and lights being lit as people tried to see what was happening. A company of soldiers, dressed in the livery of the City Watch, hastened down the street.

Thomas and his friends flattened themselves against a wall and let them pass, then ran again once they were by.

They put a good number of blocks between themselves and the apartment, turning and twisting down half a dozen different side streets before Thomas allowed them to slow down. The sun had broken the horizon, spilling light into the streets and rousing the citizens. From houses all around came sounds of movement. Shutters opened in the buildings around them, as the city's residents began their day. Thomas picked an alley and led his two friends into it. They stood there, panting with exertion.

The Academy's alarm bell started ringing, the harsh tones carrying through the city. Thomas could still hear the sounds of the riot faint in the distance.

"Do you think it will spread?" Eileen asked, between gasps.

"Aye," said Thomas, "but not this way. The bishop's house is in the other direction. If it goes anywhere, it will go there."

Thomas, making certain there were no windows above him for someone to drop the contents of their chamber pot on his head, leaned against the wall. Eileen did the same, while George just squatted down on the ground, hunter-style. Outside the alley, the city was well awake and people were starting to come out of their houses. The three stayed where they were, dragging air into tired lungs and letting their hearts slow down.

A fair while later George rose to his feet. "So, now what?"

"We find a way to get a message to the others and tell them we're all right," said Thomas. He listened closely and found he could still hear the riot over the noise of the waking city around them. The Academy's bells were still ringing, the peals rising over the city and calling the students to action. "Then we get some horses and ride out of here as fast as we can."

"What about Henry and Benjamin?" Eileen asked. "Aren't we going back for them?"

The idea of leaving his friends behind sickened him, but Thomas knew there was no choice. "No. If we go back, we'll be arrested for witchcraft and they'll be arrested for harbouring a fugitive. If we stay away, they can claim that I was never there."

In the street beside the alley, neighbours were greeting one another and wondering at the noise. A few heads turned towards the three in the alley, but no one stopped what they were doing to stare, or called out an alarm. Still, Thomas started to feel nervous. "Let's get out of here. We'll find some breakfast, then a stable. They usually have boys who can run a message for you, if you pay them." A terrible thought crossed his mind. "You do have the money, don't you?"

George snorted. "I wasn't that scared."

Thomas found himself smiling in spite of his fear. "I should have known. Come on."

They put their bags back on their shoulders and stepped out of the alley. Thomas picked a direction and led them away. It took some time before they found themselves on a major street, and a long walk before they found a bakery. The Academy's bell kept ringing, and others were joining it. Thomas recognized them as the bells of the City Watch, and wondered how bad things were getting.

At the bakery, they bought buns and pastries and Thomas made inquiries, learning that there was a stable three blocks and a couple of turns away. They ate as they walked, all the while keeping nervous eyes out for any signs of the bishop's guards. Thomas walked with one hand on his sword, scanning the crowd around them for any sign of danger. When he met his friend's eyes he could see his own fears mirrored there.

More troops dressed in the city's livery went by, headed for the student quarter. Thomas stepped aside with the rest of the crowd, letting them pass, then continued leading the others towards the stable. George, who had spent half his life dealing with horses and horse-traders, listed off what they would need, and estimated a price. Thomas whistled when he heard it. The money they had would cover the cost twenty times over, but the amount was still a shock.

They found the stable quick enough and, under George's instructions, left him to go in alone. It was a long, long wait, and the bells kept ringing. Thomas paced back and forth, desperately nervous and anxious to get away.

"What is he doing in there?" he finally asked Eileen. "By the time we get the horses, we could have walked there."

"He's making a bargain," Eileen said.

"Well, I wish he'd hurry up."

"He'll be done as fast as he can," she snapped, "and he'll save you a lot of money."

Thomas just about snapped back at her, but managed to quash it. Instead, he went over to her. Eileen was pale, her eyes wild, and her short hair stuck out in all directions. She looked a terrible mess. "How are you doing?"

"Fine."

"You sure?"

"What do you want me to say?" Eileen demanded. "That I'm scared and I want to go home?"

"It's what I'm feeling," said Thomas, reaching out a hand for hers. "I was hoping someone else felt the same."

She slumped, collapsing in on herself like a weight was pressing her down. He stepped closer, putting his arm around her shoulder. She leaned her head against him.

"I'm sorry," he said.

"I'm frightened."

"I know," Thomas squeezed her gently. "Me, too."

He left his arm around her while they waited. At last, George emerged from the stables with three very good looking horses, complete with saddles, bridles, and saddle bags. There was also a boy with him, who Thomas guessed was to be the messenger.

George waved them over, looking very pleased with himself. "How do you like them?"

Thomas, though he didn't know horses too well, thought they looked good and said so. Eileen, on the other hand, practically crowed over hers, a brown mare with a white blaze on her head. "She's absolutely gorgeous," she took the bridle and petted the horse's nose. "Does she have a name?"

"Aye," said George. "Fred."

Eileen's eyebrows rose. "Fred?"

"Aye, Fred." George watched as Thomas took the bridle of the second horse, a black, shaggy looking stallion, with a proudly arched neck and a rather wicked gleam in its eye. "That one's Biter."

"Oh, wonderful," Thomas had an image of losing a pair of fingers on top of all else that had happened and made certain his hands were away from the horse's mouth. "How about yours?"

"Mine?"

"Well, it's the only one left."

George sighed. "Flower."

"Flower?" The horse in question was also a brown mare, but with no distinguishing markings whatsoever. "Why Flower?"

"She likes to eat them, apparently."

Thomas turned to the boy, who was fidgeting. "Are you going to be our messenger?"

"Aye, if you'll give me the message."

"The message is…" It took a while to put it together in a way that wouldn't incriminate either himself or his friends. "The message is that I've gone to the summer house and I want them to wait until I get back."

"And who are you?"

"They'll know. Got it?"

"You're at the summer house. Wait until you get back."

"Right. Now, you know the Academy?"

"Where all the layabouts are?"

George snorted, Eileen snickered, and Thomas let it pass. "Aye, that would be the place. There's an apartment nearby it, and my friends live there." He gave explicit directions, then handed the boy two coppers and promised that Henry would pay the same when he got the message. The boy dashed off and Thomas turned to his friends. "You both know how to ride, I take it?"

"Oh, aye," Eileen said. "Not any long trips, but half the time, people would leave their horses with Father and we'd ride them back." She handed George Fred's bridle and reached into her bag. "I'm going to put breeches on, if I'm to be riding all day. Otherwise I'll be chafed raw."

"Fair enough," Thomas agreed. She put them on under the skirt; a process which she managed without showing the slightest bit of skin. Thomas, despite all his other worries, found himself watching with amusement. When she was done, he turned to her brother. "How about you?"

"Same as her, not any long trips. You?"

"It's been a fair while," Thomas admitted. "My father taught me how to ride, but I haven't done it since I started the Academy."

"We'll all be stunningly sore by the end of the day, then," said George. He put a foot in the stirrup and pulled himself into the saddle. Eileen did the same. Thomas, the last up, managed a fairly competent mount, much to his own surprise. His happiness was short lived as his horse attempted to pick the direction they were going. Thomas got the beast under control and, turning it around to the other way, led his two friends out of the city at a walking pace.

The streets were lively now, and they had to be careful not to run anyone down as they guided the beasts through the crowd. The Academy bells were still ringing, and while many people commented on it, no one in the area seemed to know why. Thomas, glad neither the news nor the riot had spread this far, kept his friends moving.

They rode across the river on the great bridge, past the warehouses and taverns and shipyards, heading for the coast road. The cobblestones of the city streets ended abruptly, though the houses continued, looking less and less well-kept, until they were riding past the shanties of the city's poor. Men and women and children tried to sell them food or wine or animals, or cried for alms as they rode past. Thomas didn't slow down.

They left the last shanty behind and were soon surrounded by open farmland. Thomas kicked his horse to a canter, and the other two followed suit, leaving the ringing bells behind. The road led them south along the coast. Dozens of carts were headed into the city, farmers with loads of produce or animals. None took notice of them. Merchants sitting on much nicer carts also rode past, their wares covered with canvas sheets or crated in wood. Off the sides of the road, Thomas could see the men and women working in the fields, or readying boats to go out on the water. They rode past them all without slowing.

By late morning, they had left the crowded parts of the road behind, and were riding alone down the coast. Thomas had been keeping his eyes ahead, not wanting people to notice him watching for pursuit. Now, he risked a look behind. What he saw made him rein in his horse, the animal protesting at the abrupt stop. George and Eileen did the same, and turned in their saddles.

A plume of black smoke was rising into the sky over the city.

"What do you think it is?" asked Eileen.

"I don't know," Thomas felt a cold rage building inside him. "Nothing good."

For a moment he wondered how much smoke the Academy would make if it were on fire, then put the idea aside. The Academy had not been at the centre of the riot, and the students would not let anyone put it to the flame. He wondered about his apartment, and if his friends might be trapped in the blaze.

"They'll be all right," said George, who must have sensed Thomas's thoughts. "I'm sure."

I'm not, thought Thomas. Still, there was nothing he could do. "Come on. We've got a long way to go."

Chapter 26

They rode in silence through the morning. Thomas's thoughts were dark and best kept to himself. He had no idea what his companions were thinking, but neither of them ventured any conversation either.

Just after the sun passed noon, George spotted a fishing village with an inn. Part of Thomas didn't want to stop, but he was sore and tired and hungry and had no doubt his friends were feeling the same way. The horse beneath him was moving more slowly, and the other mounts were also showing signs of fatigue. Reluctantly, he let George lead them off the road to the inn.

A stable boy came out and greeted them, offering to water their horses. The three dismounted and Thomas discovered at once that he was much more sore than he had believed possible. The walk into the inn was painful and slow, and one glance at the hard wooden benches and chairs was nearly enough to make Thomas rebel. They eased themselves into the seats and accepted large bowls of fish stew and cups of ale. Conversation, which had been limited to groans before the food came, faded entirely. For the next little while, there was no sound save the occasional smack of lips or spoon rubbing against bowl. Too soon, however, the meal was finished. Tempting though it was to linger, Thomas rose to his feet instead, and led the group out of the inn.

"How much further are we riding today?" asked Eileen, rubbing her backside.

"Until it's dark," Thomas replied, watching her hand. Eileen realized what he was doing and stopped, sticking out her tongue. Thomas smiled back, reached over, and rubbed a hand up and down her back. Eileen groaned and leaned into it. He wrapped his other arm around her shoulders and kept going.

"That's nice," said Eileen. "But it's not the bit that really hurts."

"And don't even think of rubbing that," said George from behind them.

"Spoilsport," muttered Eileen, though not loud enough for her brother to hear.

Thomas smiled and let her go. To George, he said, "I wouldn't dare."

"Lying scholar," said George, though there was no real energy in it. He shook a finger at his sister, "And you, behave."

Eileen snorted. "This from you."

Thomas felt slightly relieved, listening to them. If George and Eileen could mock each other, then they weren't feeling too badly. It wasn't much, he knew, but at least *something* was normal.

"Never mind me," said George. "I'm your brother. It's my job to keep him from pawing you."

Eileen smiled at her brother. "A good thing you weren't on the roof yesterday, then."

George's eyebrows went up at that, but before he could say more, the stable boy came out with their horses. Eileen went immediately to her horse and mounted.

"We're too tired," said Thomas to George's glare. "Hit me later."

"Hey!" Eileen called from atop her horse. "Are you going to stand there all day, or will you be getting on your horses and riding?"

"We'll ride," said Thomas taking hold of his horse's saddle and pulling himself up with a loud groan. George smiled at the other's discomfort until it was his turn to do the same. After that, it was wincing all around as the three headed off down the road, moving at the same ground-eating canter that had so damaged them before.

The rest of the day passed slowly. Every step of the horses became a test of willpower. Even at a walk the movement of the horses pounded tender flesh, leaving all the riders to wince and groan and bear it as best they could. Once they left the fishing village behind they saw no sign of people along the road. To one side of the road, rough hills dotted with groves of twisted trees rolled over the landscape. On the other, the land sloped into pebble beaches and low cliffs leading to the sea.

Supper time came and went, and while they stopped to let the horses graze for a bit, there was nothing for the riders. They could only mount and keep going, watching the sun growing lower in the sky as they rode.

After another hour, George threw up his hands. "That's it," he announced. "I'm done."

He pulled his horse to a stop and, with a groan, stood in the stirrups. The rolling hills around them held only low, lush vegetation, and made it impossible to see a great distance in any direction, save out towards the sea. What trees they saw were distant and no less twisted than the rest they had seen. None of them would provide good shelter. George looked thoroughly disgruntled when he sat back down. "Unless anyone has any better ideas, I say that we call it a day and camp here."

"If we camp here," said Thomas, "we'll be seen by anyone that rides by."

"And who is going to ride by?" asked George, gesturing at the emptiness around them. "The bishop's guards?"

Eileen snorted. "The way our luck's been going? Yes."

"I'd just rather not be out in the open," said Thomas.

"We could hide," George suggested hopefully.

"We could. The horses can't," Thomas argued, though more than anything he wanted off the animal and onto the ground. "We could make ten more miles before dark."

"Aye, we could," Eileen agreed. "Come on, George, just a few more miles."

"All right," George sounded not at all happy, "but we're stopping at the first inn we find."

"Agreed."

Thomas put his heels into the horse's sides and led them down the road once again. The horses were tired, but still faster than the three friends could have managed on foot. The sound of hooves on the road filled their ears, broken only by the call of gulls and the noise of the surf. They rode five more miles up and down hills and through small copses of trees, one of which looked nearly comfortable enough to sleep in. Thomas thought long and hard about stopping there, but let it alone. Finally, they topped a rise and were greeted by the sight of another small fishing village on the edge of the sea, with a very large inn whose sign proclaimed it to be the Sea's Edge.

"Thank the Four," said George, eyes raised to the sky. "I thought we were going to be riding all night."

They kicked their heels into the horses' sides. The tired animals sped up without protest, sensing the stables ahead. The three galloped down the hill and over the final half-mile. They entered the inn yard just as the sun began to sink below the horizon.

A stable boy who'd been dozing on the stairs rose to his feet and held out his hands for the horses' reins. Thomas tried to dismount and discovered that the muscles that had been sore at lunch were now stiff and aching. Neither of his friends looked to be any better off. It took a long time for all three to get down, and many groans, curses, and complaints accompanied the act. At last, they handed over the reins and headed for the inn.

The inn was larger than most and much better appointed. Thomas guessed that the inn served as a stopping house for merchants and nobles who travelled to the town where the bishop kept his summer house. They opened the big oak door and stepped inside to the most welcome sight of all: each of the chairs inside, and even the benches, were all cushioned with fabric. They all breathed sighs of relief and headed for a corner table with four chairs around it.

A woman appeared only moments after they gratefully and gingerly seated themselves. With a smile on her face and good humour in her voice, she welcomed them, informed them that her name was Harriet, and offered them their choice among roast beef, chicken, potatoes, bread, cheese, apples, pudding, and ale. Without hesitation, Thomas told her to bring some of everything, and then asked about rooms.

"Well, there is the common room, of course," said Harriet, "and we have some private rooms available."

"Can we get private rooms?" Eileen asked Thomas. "Please? It's been a long time."

Thomas had been ready to suggest they share, but the look on Eileen's face was hard to resist. He turned to George.

George shrugged. "It would be nice to sleep alone." He smiled at his sister. "Get away from Eileen's snoring."

Eileen rolled her eyes, but refrained from stating the obvious. She turned back to Thomas. "Please?"

Thomas saw the plea in her eyes and caved. Eileen hadn't had a room to herself since they started the journey, and being stuck with him and George all the time couldn't be easy. Beside which, Thomas was also heartily tired of George's snoring. "All right. Three private rooms, it is."

"And a bath," added Eileen. "Not a stand-up one, but a proper one, if I can." Thomas and George exchanged a glance of amusement. She caught it. "It wouldn't do you two any harm, either, and it might get some of the aches out."

"Nothing like a hot bath for that, Miss," agreed Harriet.

"Anything that can loosen the muscles, I'm for," said Thomas. "Is it possible?"

"Oh, aye," Harriet nodded. "We've got a proper bathhouse behind the buildings. We get so many travelers, you see, and there's nothing like a bath to make time on the road seem better. We've got water to wash with if you just want to clean up, and proper tubs to soak in, if it's a long soaking that you need."

"It is," Eileen said, fervently. "With lots of hot water."

"It will be dark, though," Harriet warned.

"I'll bathe in the dark," said Eileen.

"Or we could get candles," suggested Thomas.

"We can have candles set out," agreed Harriet, "though it will cost some."

The need to mind his money—the result of four years of relative poverty—welled up in Thomas. He thrust it aside. *A lot of good a full purse will do if we're caught*, he thought. "Just add it into the price of the rooms. Three baths—"

"Three?" said George, shaking his head.

"It would do you good, too," said Eileen, sniffing the air around him.

"In the morning it will do me good. Tonight, it will drown me."

"Baths for two tonight, then," said Harriet. "And one for the morning."

"Umm…" Thomas turned to Eileen. "Is that all right with you?"

"Aye, it is," Eileen's tone was somewhat less sure. "I mean, we can take turns."

"Oh, there's plenty of room," said Harriet. "You can both go at once."

Thomas watched the blush go up Eileen's face, felt it rising in his own. George saved both of them from having to say anything. "I'll not be having them bathing together." He declared. "We have enough troubles."

"Troubles?" Harriet looked from Thomas to George, then back to Eileen. "Isn't he your brother?"

"Nay, the great lug here is my brother."

"And the great lug will have this one's ears if he does anything untoward," George growled, tossing a glare at Thomas for good measure.

Harriet laughed. "Not to worry. The baths have curtains between them. You'll be quite private."

"That will do for me," Thomas said. "Will it do for you?"

"Aye," Eileen said, relieved. "It will." She looked at her brother. "Will it do for you, or are you going to stand guard?"

"I'm too tired to stand guard," growled George. He glared at Thomas. "Just behave yourselves."

"Right." Harriet smiled at the three. "I'll get the water heating as soon as dinner's on the table."

"We'll need a good breakfast in the morning as well," said Thomas. "Can you put it together with the price of the room?"

"I will," Harriet promised. "I'll give you the tally with the first course."

"Thank you."

She went away, and conversation lagged among them. They were all too exhausted to talk, and no one had anything new to say. Harriet came back a moment later with the first course of bread and cheese and told them the cost of it all. It was rather impressive, and Thomas would have argued the price had he not been so tired. Instead, he let George pay her, and the three dug into the food. They devoured the first course at once, and ate the rest as quickly as it appeared. The food was probably excellent, but all three were eating too fast to comment. For his part, Thomas hardly tasted it. It wasn't until the last plate was cleared that anyone had anything to say other than a request for the passing of a plate or the pitcher of ale.

"I meant to ask," said George, "did you have a plan when we rode out of the city?"

"Same as before," Thomas said. "Find out what the bishop's up to. Stop him. Benjamin said he was heading south, so there's got to be something there."

"How are we going to stop him?" Eileen asked. "I mean, if he's got all his guards ..."

"I don't know," Thomas rubbed at his face, trying to scrub away some of the exhaustion. "I'll read the books and try to figure out something."

"Too bad we can't read his books," said Eileen.

That gave Thomas pause, and a blazingly obvious solution. He shook his head. *I should have thought of it sooner.* "I'll steal his books."

"What?" George's mouth stayed hanging open at the end of the word.

"It makes sense," said Thomas. "He has to have books. I can't think that pulling a person's—" he caught himself, then leaned close and lowered his voice. "I can't think of what he does as being his gift. He had to have learned it somewhere." He leaned back in his chair and thought about it. "If we steal his books, it might stop him. Or at least let us know what he's doing."

"And all we have to do is get past his guards," George pointed out. A huge yawn took him. "The thought alone makes me tired."

"Excuse me," Harriet came to the table. "We've got water heated and fires going under the tubs, if you're ready."

"I'm for bed, then," said George, rising slowly. "I'll see you in the morning."

Harriet first showed them where their rooms were, then led Thomas and Eileen out the back of the inn. They walked stiffly behind Harriet across a small court to the bathhouse.

It was a low-slung affair, with a gently sloping roof and thick stone walls with narrow windows just below the roof-line. Inside, a good sized stone hearth stood against one wall, with a fire crackling within and a great kettle sitting on top, steaming. There were a half-dozen large stone baths against the outer walls, each easily big enough to seat two comfortably, and quite deep. Two of them, side-by-side, were full of steaming water. Washtubs were on the floor beside them, with buckets of water—also steaming—for rinsing, and stands with towels and soap. Candles were set into niches in the walls, and long swathes of thin fabric hung from rods on the ceiling, separating the baths.

"I set them up together so you can chat while you're washing," said Harriet.

"If we can manage conversation," Thomas looked to Eileen. "Which one do you want?"

Eileen pointed. "The one by the fire. It will stay warm the longest."

Harriet smiled. "The baths are heated underneath so they'll stay warm, no matter how far from the fire you are. Now, if you'll excuse me…" She turned and headed back for the inn, leaving them alone. Neither moved for a time.

"Well," said Thomas at last, "after you."

"Right," Eileen hesitated a moment longer then headed to the far bath. At the curtain, she stopped to look back. "You won't peek, will you?"

Thomas shook his head. "On my word."

"Good." She stepped into the bath alcove and pulled the curtains. A moment later she stuck her head back out. "Well, don't just stand there."

Thomas headed for the other bath. He tossed his bag on the floor, and started going through it for fresh clothes. The brown breeches and white shirt were in the best condition, and he hung them over the rail away from Eileen's tub. From the other side of the curtain, he heard clothes hitting the floor, and a moment later, the splash of water being poured over a body, followed by a groan of pleasure.

"Oh," the words came out of Eileen in a moan, "this is heavenly."

In his mind, Thomas could see Eileen standing in the washtub as the water flowed down her. The image shook him on several levels. He forced it aside, stripped his clothes off, and stepped into his own washtub. He picked up the large dipper and poured water down his own body. He groaned himself as the hot water rolled down his flesh. He did it a second time, then a third, revelling in the feeling.

"You're right," he called to Eileen.

"I was," corrected Eileen, a shiver running through her voice. "It's great while you're pouring, but now all I can think about is getting in that bath!"

Thomas, feeling goose-pimples rising over his body, understood exactly what she was talking about. He picked up the soap and washcloth and began to lather. The day's sweat—from running, from riding, from fear—sloughed from his body. It was wonderful.

"You know," Eileen said, "This is the first time I've bathed with anyone that wasn't family."

"We're not exactly bathing *with* each other," said Thomas as he scrubbed at the dirt.

"You know what I mean."

"Aye," Thomas grinned. "No peeking, now."

Eileen snorted. "You wish."

Thomas did, indeed, wish, but kept that to himself. Instead, he finished soaping up. From the other side, he heard the splashes as Eileen rinsed the soap away, and set himself to doing the same. The water sluiced away the suds and the last of the road dirt, leaving him clean at last. The cool air ran lightly over his body, raising the goose-pimples again. From the other side of the curtain, he heard wet footsteps, then a loud splash. Eileen had gone into the bath. He waited until he heard the second splash of her surfacing, then called, "How is it?"

Eileen's tone was something close to rapture. "Wonderful!"

Thomas stepped carefully out of his washtub. The flagstones were cold and hard beneath his feet as he crossed the floor to the big bath. The outside of it was stone, and rough against his body as he pushed up onto the edge of the bath and swung his legs over. The moment the water closed over him, he forgot everything else. He hadn't been in a proper bath since the smithy, two weeks ago. Even then, it hadn't been a large one. For the first time in months, he could completely submerge in hot water. He lay underneath as long as he could, then let himself emerge, spluttering and shaking the water from his face.

"Good, isn't it?" Eileen called from the other side.

"Aye," Thomas let himself stretch out. "These baths are huge."

"Big enough for two." There was a pause, then Eileen added a rather embarrassed, "That wasn't meant as an invitation."

Too bad. Thomas quashed the thought at once. "I guessed."

He slid back into the water and floated, letting the heat pull the ache from his muscles and bones. There was no sound from Eileen's side of the room, and Thomas guessed her to be doing the same. He closed his eyes, and let himself lie suspended. Every part of his body started to relax.

Water closed over his head and went up his nose. He came up spluttering. George had been right. There was a good chance he could fall asleep if he let himself relax too much. Still, the water was far too nice for him to leave just yet.

"Thomas?" Eileen's voice had an uncertain note to it.

Thomas sat up in the water. "Yes?"

"What if you can't stop the bishop?"

Thomas had spent most of the day working very hard on not thinking about that. "I don't know."

"Can't you just..." Eileen fell silent for a moment. "Do you have to try?"

"I do," Thomas looked at the curtain between them, wishing he could be holding her hand. "He's hurt my family. He took my father's gift. He killed others to get theirs. He hurt my friends and started a riot just to get to me." He thought a moment, and added, "He hurt you."

"I know," Eileen's voice was muffled, and Thomas realized she was crying. "I just..." she stopped, her breath hitched, then she started again. "You're the first boy who's really been interested in me and I don't want you to get killed."

Thomas had nothing to say to that.

"Thomas?" Eileen's voice was pleading. "Thomas, say something."

Thomas couldn't promise he wouldn't die, and that knowledge shook him more than anything else. In truth, he hadn't thought about the possibility of getting killed, all jokes about Eileen's father aside. He'd been too busy dwelling on his problems and planning how to deal with them to let the idea of death be more than a vague shape, lurking in the back of his head.

He didn't want to think about it now, either, he realized, and turned the topic away instead. "I can't believe that I'm the first boy who's been interested in you."

"You're the first one who offered to court me and visit my parents, instead of just trying to feel me up in a haystack." Her voice was muffled again, as if she was scrubbing at her face. "And even if it doesn't mean anything to you, it means something to me." There was silence for a moment, then, "Does it mean something to you?"

"It does." Thomas's voice caught in his throat, and it took a moment before he could finish. "It means a great deal to me."

"Then please don't die."

Thomas searched for a way to answer. At last, he pushed himself upward, reaching for the curtain. He found an opening and put his hand through. "Can you see my hand?"

"Aye."

"Can you reach it?"

There was silence then a swirl of water. Small, wet fingers entwined with his. He grasped them as tightly as he could. "I'll do my best to stay alive," he promised. "And I'll do my best to make it so we can all go home again. All right?"

She squeezed his hand back. "All right."

"Good." He squeezed again then let her go. "I need to get out before I drown. Do you want to stay a while longer?"

"No, I'll come with you."

Thomas levered himself out of the high tub and onto the ground. He grabbed his towel and rubbed himself briskly, trying to dry off before the cool of the evening sent his skin into goose bumps again. From the other side, he heard Eileen coming out of the tub, and her gasp as her feet hit the cool stones of the floor. There was some rustling, then she said. "Cover up, Thomas."

"What?" Thomas turned to the curtain and saw Eileen's hand reaching through and grasping one of the panels. He had just enough time to wrap the towel around his waist before she opened the curtain. She was wrapped in her own towel, the long cloth tight around her frame. Her shoulders and arms and a good deal of her legs were bare. Thomas tied his own towel tight about his waist, tried to find some words.

Eileen crossed the floor, wrapped her arms about him and pulled her body tight to his. She leaned up and kissed him on the mouth. Surprise kept him from responding at once, but she kept kissing him until his arms went about her, and he started kissing back. The bare skin of her arms and legs was warm and wet against his own. His arms rested gently on her back, feeling the skin of her shoulders and the thin cloth that separated the rest of her body from his. Her mouth against his was soft and gentle and insistent. His whole body responded to her.

After a far too short time, Eileen pulled back. There were still tears in her eyes, though she was smiling. "That's for saying what you said," she wiped at her face. "And also a reason for you to stay alive."

She let him go. Thomas remained where he was, speechless, watching her walk back to her own side of the curtain. She smiled back at him over her shoulder. "Now hurry up before they think we've drowned."

She pulled the curtain shut and Thomas stood, bemused, a moment longer before turning away to finish drying off.

Chapter 27

Eileen met him outside the curtains and the two walked hand in hand out the door. Thomas found himself grinning like an idiot. Eileen was in the same state, and for a moment they just stood, smiling at each other until Eileen began giggling. Thomas took her hand, kissed it, then leaned in and kissed her on the mouth.

When he pulled back, she smiled. "Looking for more reasons to stay alive?"

"I have you," said Thomas without thinking. "There's no reason better."

Eileen blushed. "Now there's a line."

Thomas smiled again. "I rather liked it myself." He kissed her once more. "And it's true."

For a reply, she squeezed his hand tightly.

They were half-way across the inn yard when Eileen stopped. "Listen."

Thomas listened. Somewhere in the distance, something was rumbling. He peered out into the night, but couldn't see anything. The lights of the inn lit only the yard, leaving the area beyond in darkness. The sound grew louder, and Eileen cocked her head, trying to figure out where it was coming from. "What is that?"

Thomas was about to say he didn't know when he spotted a wavering band of yellow light just over the horizon. The rumbling separated itself into dozens of individual thumps coming hard and fast together. "Horses," said Thomas. "A lot of them, coming down the road."

He grabbed Eileen's hand and pulled her back around the side of the bathhouse. The corner away from the inn gave them a clear view of the courtyard and the road to the north. Peeking around it, they watched as the light over the horizon grew brighter then crested the hill: a dozen torches, perhaps fifteen, carried by fast-moving riders in a disciplined formation. They came closer and Thomas could make out twenty riders, half carrying torches. In the midst of them was a large coach drawn by six horses. Two torches lit it from atop the driver's seat. Thomas's breath caught as he recognized the soldiers' livery.

The riders slowed to a walk outside of the inn yard, and a sick feeling grew in the pit of Thomas's stomach.

"He's coming here," he whispered. His heart sank. He pulled the rapier and dagger out, knowing the gesture was futile as he did it.

Eileen freed her own knife. "What about George?" she whispered. "He's inside."

"We can't get there before they reach the yard," Thomas whispered back. "We have to stay here."

They watched as the riders turned into the yard. Their leader, clad in black as always, started shouting for someone to come out. Two stable boys emerged, and Harriet followed after. Randolf rode forward, sneering down at them.

"We need fresh horses for the coach, food and drink," Randolf said without preamble. "Get them and bring them here."

"Your pardon," Harriet said, her tone polite and firm. "We only keep fresh horses for the king's riders and the mail."

"This is the bishop's personal carriage," Randolf's voice was cold and hard. "You will get the horses, and you will hook them up. Now."

Harriet didn't move or change her tone. "With respect to the bishop, the horses are for the king's riders and the mail. Not for anyone else."

Randolf leaned forward in his saddle and without warning or change of expression, punched her hard in the face. She stumbled back and fell. Randolf pulled out his sword and pointed it at the stable boys. "You," he said to the smaller of them. "We need food and drink for twenty hungry men, plus the bishop and his drivers. Get it, or I'll have my men burn this building to the ground. You," he turned to the other one, "I want those horses off the bishop's coach, and I want fresh ones put on now or I will cut your eyes out."

The stable boys stood, frozen in place. Randolf rode slowly towards them, and the youngest one broke and ran for the inn. The second, finding himself alone, did the only thing he could and began to unhook the bishop's horses from their harness. Thomas felt a vague hint of hope in spite of what he'd just seen. "They aren't staying,"

"It doesn't look like it." Eileen whispered back. She peered around the corner at the inn, then at the riders and the carriage. "I think I can get back inside."

"How?"

"There's no one near the back door, and they can't see it from where they're standing."

Thomas saw she was right. "What are you going to do?"

"Find George and wake him up," Eileen said. "He needs to know what is happening."

"You don't even know what room he's in."

"I'll check all three." She put her bag down beside him. "Keep an eye on them."

"I will. Be careful."

She kissed him on the mouth for a reply, then slipped quietly back the way they'd come. Thomas kept his eyes on the bishop's guards, but none of them saw her. The stable boy that had gone inside came out with a basket of food. He handed it to the bishop's familiar.

"Is that it?" Randolf demanded.

"No, sir," the stable boy said, shaking. "There's more coming. That's just the first."

The second boy took the first pair of horses from their traces and led them to the stable. Thomas, feeling nervous and helpless, waited and watched. Harriet slowly pulled herself upright on her knees, then to her feet. The familiar watched as she rose, then rode to her and grabbed her by the hair. She cried out in pain. He pulled her against the side of his horse.

"I want the troop fed and watered by the time the horses are changed,"

Randolf said. He ran his hand down from her hair to her neck, then closed it tight and squeezed. "If they are not, I'll drag you with us behind my horse then let each man have you at his first available convenience." He shoved her away. "Now, hurry up."

She stumbled into the inn, holding her face and weeping. A short eternity later, two men emerged from the inn and began to help with the horses. Several others began bringing out baskets of food. The soldiers tore into the meal, shoving the food down their throats and tossing the baskets aside.

Harriet came back with a larger basket and held it out to Randolf. "For the bishop."

Randolf dismounted and took the basket. Harriet stepped back, trembling, as soon as it left her hands. Randolf opened the basket and inspected the contents, then carried the basket to the carriage and knocked at the door. It opened and Randolf passed the basket inside. Thomas tried to see in, but the door obscured his view. Randolf stepped away, hands empty, and closed the door.

By now, the last of the horses were free of their traces and headed for the barn. The bishop's men had all dismounted, attending to their horses or their own bodily needs. The torches had been planted in the earth, forming a wide circle of fire in the dirt of the inn yard. Men and women from the inn came back and forth, bringing food and drink, or carrying away empty plates and cups. Thomas, tired of crouching, allowed himself to sink to a sitting position and lay down the weapons that he had been clutching. His hands were sore and cramped from his too-tight grip. He rubbed them together and kept watching. So far, no one in the bishop's train had made a move toward the inn, and Thomas prayed it would stay that way.

Footsteps, moving fast and quiet behind him, caught his attention. He grabbed up both the weapons and twisted, nearly impaling George and Eileen. The two ground themselves to a stop and jumped back. George had brought his bag, and was obviously ready to run. Thomas put the weapons down, and couldn't help but snort at the sight of the luggage.

"What?" George whispered.

"Nothing," Thomas whispered back, shaking his head. "It's just that we're probably the first ones to try to sneak out *after* they've paid."

George snorted back, but kept it quiet. "What's happening out there?"

"They're changing the bishop's horses."

"So he's not staying?"

"I don't think so, but that doesn't mean they're not going to go inside."

"That's what I thought," Eileen said. "There's no sign we were there, now."

"Unless someone asks after us," George pointed out.

"Then let's hope they don't," said Thomas.

George peeked around the corner. "They're bringing horses out."

Eileen and Thomas joined him. Eileen surreptitiously put her hand on one of Thomas's, and though he was still holding his dagger in it, he unwrapped two fingers from the grip to grasp hers. The stable boy and two men from the inn brought six fresh horses out of the barn. The boy, obviously the most practiced at the task, harnessed the horses with quick, angry motions. His loathing for the bishop's familiar was plain on his face, but he kept his mouth shut and did what he was told.

Randolf had remounted his horse and watched the boy with contempt.

Thomas touched George's shoulder, then Eileen's, and pointed. The inn door was open, and at least a half-dozen men stood there, watching. Thomas thought he spotted weapons in their hands, but no one was making any moves. To attack the bishop's men was to invite certain death, if not in the combat itself, then in the investigation that would follow. Even so, there was enough anger radiating off the men in the inn door that, had any of the bishop's men tried to come in, a fight would almost certainly have ensued.

The bishop's men must have sensed it. Despite Randolf's casual brutality, there were no hostile moves on anyone's part. By the time the last horse was tied in place, all the men were mounted and ready to go.

Harriet, who had been quietly serving the food and collecting the baskets, stepped forward. Randolf looked down his nose at her, his disdain clear on his face. Harriet stood her ground. "All this costs money."

"So it does," Randolf sounded amused.

"Are you going to pay for it?"

Randolf sneered down at her. "Call it your tithe to the High Father."

He turned in his saddle and barked an order to his men. Torches, once more in hands, flickered and waved wildly as the men turned their horses and, with quick jabs of their heels into their beasts' flanks, moved out. The bishop's driver slapped the backs of the horses with his reins and called out a command, turning them and sending them out of the yard. Thomas felt Eileen's hand squeezing his as the first riders left, and squeezed back. George pushed himself off the wall and picked up his bag. "We need to get back inside."

"What's the rush?" asked Eileen.

"No one will be very impressed with us if they thought we were sneaking out at the sight of trouble."

"Not to mention that they might start asking *why* we were sneaking out," added Thomas, letting go of Eileen's hand and sheathing his weapons. He picked up his own bag, then captured her hand for the walk back in. "I would hate for them to think there might be a reward out for us."

George raised an eyebrow at the hand-holding, but only said, "Given what just happened, I don't think anyone's going to be turning you in to the bishop's men tonight."

"Maybe not," agreed Thomas, "but it can't hurt to be safe."

They crossed the inn yard quickly and, making certain that no one was looking, crept up to their rooms. George led the way, showing them up the stairs to a hallway which ran the length of the building. They had been given three rooms in a row, and George had claimed the one closest to the stairs—the better to reach bath and breakfast in the morning. He opened the door and revealed a rather small space, perhaps ten feet long and six wide, with the bed taking up most of it. Still there was room at the end for a table with a pitcher and basin, and a chair in which one could sit and overlook the yard. George pointed at the view. "If I'd seen them I would have run out to warn you. I was dead asleep until Eileen came in and woke me by dripping on my face."

"It wasn't intentional," Eileen protested. "It fell on you while I was shaking you."

"A likely story that I'm too stiff and tired to argue about," George replied. "How were the baths, by the way?"

"Oh... fine," Eileen turned away, a blush spreading over her face.

Thomas, remembering the feel of her skin against his, found himself smiling. He quashed it before George saw. "Fine. Just fine." He stepped away from the door, into the dark of the hallway so George couldn't see his face. "Which room do you want?"

"I'll take the one in the middle," Eileen said.

"Aye. Well, then." He nearly leaned in to kiss Eileen again, but her brother was watching with eyebrows raised. "Good night, all."

Thomas headed for the farthest room. He heard Eileen say good-night to her brother and follow behind him. George's door closed. Thomas stopped at Eileen's door and waited for her to catch up. When she did, he caught her hand up in his and kissed it again. She let him, and then leaned in close to kiss him on the lips. It was a short kiss, ending with Eileen giggling. "I thought you were going to burst when George asked about the baths."

"Me?" Thomas shook his head. "You were going red as a beet."

Eileen giggled some more and kissed him again. "Good night, Thomas."

He kissed her once more, then stepped back. "Good night, Eileen."

She waved at him and closed the door. Thomas went to his own room and was not at all surprised to find, once he had lit the lamp, that it was the same size and shape as the ones beside it. Still, the bed was made up and the room was clean and warm. He set the lamp on the table and stripped, hanging his clothes over the footboard. Relief and happiness had taken the place of the fear that had held him while the bishop was in the inn yard.

Thomas blew out the lamp and quickly put himself under the blankets. The bed was firm and comfortable and after the day's ride and the bath and the evening's scare, Thomas found himself actually tired. He settled himself in and let his mind drift back to Eileen and the baths.

For the first time in a fair while, he fell immediately asleep.

Chapter 28

A loud rapid knock and the words, "Get up, you slug!" nearly made Thomas fall out of his bed, convinced he was going to have to run off in the middle of the night again. Instead, the early morning sun was shining in through the window, filling the room with pleasant golden light and nearly blinding Thomas's freshly opened eyes.

"What is it?" Thomas asked, struggling to his feet and grabbing for his breeches. "What's the matter?"

"Matter?" said George from the other side of the door. "There's no matter. It's time to get up."

Thomas squinted out the window, then back to the door. "It's just after dawn."

"Aye, and since I'm up, you get to be up, too."

Thomas groaned, pulled the breeches up, and stumbled the foot and a half distance to the door. His body, though nowhere near as sore as it had been the night before, was still suffused with a dull ache. He struggled with the latch a moment, then pulled open the door, ready to berate George for waking him. One look, however, made him hold his tongue. Whatever else had happened, the time Thomas had spent immersed in hot water had certainly done some good. George was bent over, and supporting himself on the door frame. Thomas leaned himself on the other side of the frame and said, "Why are you waking me?"

"I'm going for a bath."

"I took mine last night, thank you."

George smiled crookedly. "I know. I wanted to see if it did you any good."

Thomas rolled his eyes. "You woke me up for that?"

"Aye," said George. "That, and you wanted to be at the bishop's summer house today."

"We're half-way there."

"And yesterday we started just after dawn."

He was annoyingly right, Thomas realized. "I hate you."

George snorted with laughter. "You should have seen Eileen's face."

"I'm sure it was hilarious. Come back when you're done in the bath." He closed the door unceremoniously. He contemplated crawling back into bed, but gave it up. They did have to get moving if they were going to reach the bishop's summer house by nightfall. He stumbled to the washstand to rinse his face off. The water was cold, as morning water always was. He splashed it on his face to wake himself up, then held his head over the basin and poured some through his hair, gasping all the while. Eyes closed, he felt around for the towel, came up with it, and started briskly rubbing his head. He felt something close to human when he straightened up and opened his eyes.

Out of his window, past the inn yard, the hills were green, and beyond them, the sea was calm and clear. Both were covered with a thin, light mist that the morning sun would soon burn off. All in all, it was shaping up to be a very nice day.

Pity I'm going to have to spend it on a horse.

A knock at the door, much more tentative than the previous one, brought him out of his reverie.

"Hello?"

"It's me." Eileen's voice was soft and very welcome.

Thomas scrubbed at his hair some more. "It's unlocked."

Eileen came in quickly, smiling at the sight of him. She closed the door behind her and sat on the bed, tucking her legs under her. "Did you sleep well?"

"Aye," Thomas put down the towel and ran his hands through his hair to get the tangles out. "For the first time in ages."

"Good." She looked pointedly at his bare chest. "Are you planning on putting on a shirt?"

"I was, yes."

"Well, hurry up. I won't be seen sitting on the bed of a half-dressed man."

Thomas leaned over her. "How about kissing one?"

She smiled, leaned up, let her lips meet his briefly. "No more until you're dressed."

Thomas pulled on his shirt and settled himself down beside her on the bed. "Better?"

"Much," said Eileen.

"Good." Thomas leaned in. This kiss was much longer, and much more satisfying. He sat back, smiling at her. "Now all I have to do is get your brother's approval."

"Good luck with that." Eileen snickered. "He'll be harder to please than Da, and Da will have our ears."

"That he will," said Thomas wincing at the thought. "And no doubt George will have the rest of me."

"Not all of you, I hope," Eileen moved her face closer to his. "I kind of like the lips."

"Me, too," Thomas leaned in himself until their lips were almost touching. "Not to mention the rest of it."

"You haven't *seen* the rest of it," Eileen teased.

"Not yet," agreed Thomas. "But I have high hopes."

Eileen pushed him away. "Oh, do you?" She pushed him again. Thomas caught her hands and pulled her in as he fell back on the bed. She yelped, falling over herself into his lap. She attempted to tickle him, succeeded, and nearly got thrown off as Thomas squirmed. She regained her balance and pounced. In moments, she had him flat on his back and was sitting astride him. "Surrender?"

"Aye, I surrender."

"Good." She leaned down close to him. "Kiss me."

He did, thoroughly, and she returned it with equal attention. They broke the clinch eventually, and Eileen snuggled herself down on his chest. For a time they stayed there, watching the light play on the hills as the sun rose higher. Thomas could see the last of the mist burning off from the ground. George, he guessed, would be on his way at any time. He said as much to Eileen, who pouted and muttered something unkind about her brother. Still, she pushed herself off Thomas's chest with a sigh and got off the bed. Thomas pulled himself to his feet and finished dressing. Hand in hand, the two went down to breakfast.

The common room was full with early rising travellers, and abuzz with the previous night's events. There was an ugly, angry undercurrent to the discussions around the tables.

"Shouldn't act like that," one merchant was saying. "Not fitting..."

"And hitting Harriet like that..."

"Not right..."

"What's the hurry anyway?"

"Probably wasn't even the bishop," said a fat man at a table in the corner. "No bishop should act like that."

Thomas and Eileen said nothing as they made their way to a table. A serving girl spotted them and two mugs of hot tea arrived moments after they sat down.

"Not happy in here," muttered Thomas.

"Aye," agreed Eileen, her voice as low as his. "We should go soon."

"As soon as George gets here," Thomas promised. "We get breakfast and we go."

George arrived before they were half-way done with their tea. His hair was wet, his skin shiny, and his clothes were a fresh brown pair of trousers and a green shirt that made him look like a grass-covered hill. He was moving much more easily, and almost smiling until he saw their interlaced fingers. Worry and disapproval replaced the smile as he sat down. Thomas waited for him to say something. Instead, George looked away.

"Oh, get that look off your face," said Eileen, sounding more worried than exasperated. "We're holding hands, is all."

"Aye," George's expression didn't change and Harriet arrived before anyone could say anything further. She put down a mug of tea for George and raised a pot to refill Thomas's and Eileen's mugs. She looked exhausted. Dark circles surrounded the eye that wasn't swollen shut. A bruise covered the entire side of her face.

"Now don't look so concerned." There was enough asperity in her tone to make the words an order, rather than a suggestion. She put George's tea on the table. "I've had worse when there's been fights in here, thank you very much."

Thomas, who had been on the verge of asking if she was all right, forbore. "You dealt with them well enough."

"I've seen their like before." Harriet dismissed the bishop's entire revenue with a wave of the hand and a casual tone, though her posture still radiated anger. "Bullies, they were, and a right mean lot, too. But they're gone now and good riddance. You'll be wanting your breakfast, will you?"

"Aye," said Thomas. "And could we have our horses saddled? We'd like to get going as soon as we're done."

"I'll send the boy out to do it straight away," Harriet promised. "And I'll have your breakfast before you as soon as I've done that."

She left, and Thomas half-expected George to take up where he left off, but his friend didn't say anything, just drank his tea and stared at his hands.

"Are we doing the rest of the trip today, then?" Eileen asked Thomas, ignoring both George's expression and silence.

Thomas nodded. "Aye. Whatever... the *man*—" he emphasized the word to make it clear they weren't to mention names—"has planned, he must be in a hurry."

"A good thing he was," Eileen muttered, keeping her voice quiet to keep it from carrying. "If he'd stopped here, we'd be waking up in a field somewhere, wondering what we were going to eat."

"And how to get there without horses," agreed Thomas.

Harriet came back with three large plates of bacon, eggs, and fried potatoes accompanied by a loaf of bread and a small pail of butter, all balanced expertly on her arms. All conversation stopped as the food was brought, and didn't resume until the plates were nearly empty. Thomas had known he was hungry, but hadn't realized how hungry until he was wiping the last bit of egg from his plate with the last bit of bread and washed it down with the last of his tea.

"So," said Eileen once she'd cleaned the last from her own plate. "What do we do if he gets done whatever it is he's doing before we get there?"

"I don't know," said Thomas. "But I don't think he'll manage anything tonight. Not after travelling all day and night."

"Let's hope not." Eileen started to drink the last of her tea, then put the mug down. "Thomas," there was new worry in her voice, "what if he isn't there?

What if he just kept going and is going to do something else?"

"Then I keep following him," said Thomas. "Until I can find a way to stop him."

He looked at the empty mug and plate in front of him for a moment, wishing he could eat the whole meal again, just to delay having to get back on the horse. Instead, he pushed his chair back and stood up. "Come on. Let's go."

* * *

The road stayed close to the sea, sometimes running in view of it, sometimes winding around a hill and putting it just out of sight. The tangy smell of water and seaweed filled their lungs like mist with every breath. A stiff breeze blew in off the ocean, but the sky stayed clear. The sea birds called harshly to one another, filling in the silence between the three. George was still looking worried, and still not saying anything. Thomas took a couple of tries at conversation with Eileen, but it felt stilted. Soon, though, the pains of riding were back in full force and any desire for conversation faded. All the aching muscles that the bath had put to rest were awake once again. Aside from the occasional groan, and the odd creak of leather, none of the three said a thing.

Just after noon, Eileen spotted a fishing village. There was no inn, but one of the women there offered to sell them dried fish to eat. Lacking other alternatives, they bought it and sat on a hillock near the road to eat. The meal was short, silent, and not very good. Thomas had his own down as fast as possible, then was on his feet. "We should get going again."

"Already?" George protested. "We just sat down."

"And now we get back up," Thomas held out his hand to Eileen. She put the last bite of her lunch in her mouth and grabbed his hand, using it to pull herself to her feet and land in his arms. Thomas let her stay there, wrapping his around her and hugging her tight. George watched the two of them a moment, then rose and headed for his horse, wearing the same expression he'd had on at the inn.

"George!"

George stopped at Thomas's call, but didn't turn back.

Thomas gently let go of Eileen and walked towards his friend. "George, just say it."

George didn't move. "What's to say?"

"Whatever you didn't get a chance to say in the graveyard," said Thomas. "Whatever you wanted to say this morning."

George shrugged. "Nothing to say."

He started walking again. Thomas grabbed his sleeve and pulled. George stopped, more out of surprise than anything else, and looked down at Thomas's hand on his arm.

"George, please."

George raised his head, and Thomas saw pain and worry etched deep into his friend's eyes. "What is there to say?" asked George, his voice quiet. "That it's a bad idea? That I disapprove? It's not like you're going to listen." He shoved his chin in the direction of his sister. "It's not like *she* is going to listen."

Thomas found himself momentarily at a loss for words. After a moment, he tried, "I wouldn't hurt her, George."

"Aye?" George turned all the way around, squaring off with his friend. "And if you die? Did you think about that?"

Thomas nodded, remembering his words to Eileen in the bath. "Aye."

"She doesn't need to be hurt like that," said George, his voice still quiet though the fear in it was plain enough. "You should have left her alone."

The truth of the words made Thomas's throat close up. An image of Eileen mourning for him blossomed in his mind, and shook him to his core.

"George," Eileen stepped forward and put her hand on her brother's arm. "I thought about it, too. I mean, when we first... When we started it was just... it was letting go. It was something breaking free, some way to get rid of all the fear and the anger and everything else."

Eileen's eyes went to Thomas, her need for understanding clear in her face. Thomas remembered the hard, dark passion that had gripped them, and the torrent of feelings it had unleashed. He nodded.

Eileen smiled back, the expression hopeful and brittle at once. "After that, when the bishop's soldiers were raiding the apartments, I started thinking about dying, too. And how I shouldn't hang onto Thomas when he might..."

Eileen trailed off, looking at the ground. The sound of the sea rolling to the shore and the wind rustling the grass swirled in the silence that came between the three of them.

"I'd rather have this," said Eileen at last, still looking at the grass beneath her feet. "Even if this is all that I get, I'd rather have this."

The wind and the sea were the only sounds for a long time.

"I thought you'd say something like that," said George. He sighed. "I've been thinking about dying since the night you were stabbed. About all of us dying, or me and Thomas dying and leaving you alone." He put a large hand on his sister's shoulder. "I don't want you dying. And I don't want you hurting any worse than you already are."

"I don't want to get hurt either." Eileen stepped closer to her brother, tilted her head to look into his eyes. "But George, can I have this? Even if it's just this and just for now. Can I have this and can you give it your blessing?"

George looked at his sister a moment, then reached forward and engulfed her in an embrace. "I thought about us leaving, too," said George, the words coming out in a rush. "You and I going someplace else and being safe, but then Thomas would be left all alone and we still wouldn't be able to go home." He raised his eyes to Thomas, and now tears were flowing. "I want to go home, Thomas. I want all of us to go home."

Thomas found his throat closing up again. He reached up and put a hand on George's shoulder and managed to say, "We will."

"Aye," said Eileen, her voice half-muffled in her brother's chest. "We all will."

George squeezed her again and for a long time, "Aye. We all will."

Thomas stepped back, letting the siblings have their moment together. After a time George looked up again. "We have to go home," he said, managing a shaky grin. "I want to see the look on Da's face when you tell him that you want to court his daughter."

Eileen looked up from her brother's chest. "Does this mean we get your blessing?"

George nodded. "Aye. If you two want to court, for what it's worth, I'll give my blessing."

"It's worth a great deal," said Thomas, feeling suddenly light, as if George's words had made a great weight drop away from him. "Thank you."

Eileen's eyes were shining. She squeezed her brother again. "Thank you."

George held her tightly for a time, then growled and pushed her off, muttering something about clinging girls and wiping at his eyes with a sleeve. Eileen stuck out her tongue at George even as she took Thomas's hand. George ignored her and headed for his horse. "Come on," he said. "Are we going to be here all day?"

Thomas, grinning, led Eileen to her horse. She hugged him tight, squeezing hard.

"Haven't you two had enough?" called George.

Eileen looked pointedly at him over her shoulder. "I thought you gave your blessing."

"Aye," said George. "But that doesn't mean I'm going to be quiet about it."

Eileen stuck out her tongue again, then mounted her horse. Thomas mounted his own and the three headed down the road.

* * *

The afternoon passed like the morning. The sore muscles felt worse with each passing mile, and what conversation there was died out soon enough as each focused on just staying on their horses and keeping moving. The hills around them went from mainly grass to more heavily wooded as the afternoon ran on, blocking the view of the sea.

The road moved inland for a time then looped back towards the sea as the sun descended slowly from its high place. The shadows started to grow long, and the sun was just getting ready to touch the highest of the hills when the three, coming around a bend in the road, found themselves facing farmlands and, in the distance, a town.

"Is this it?" Eileen asked.

"I think so," Thomas said, "and if we can get clear of the trees we can see it."

"Thank the Four," said George with great feeling. "At least now we can get off the horses for a while."

"Not yet," Thomas stood in his stirrups, looking over the town. "First we need to find out where the bishop's house is, and then we need to find the standing stones."

"And how do we go about doing that without getting his attention?" asked George. "As soon as we start poking about, someone's going to talk. We may as well go to the inn and announce ourselves as fish bait."

"How about up there?" Eileen suggested, pointing to a particularly tall hill about a half-mile away. "We could see everything, I'll bet."

"How will we know from looking which house is the bishop's?" George asked.

"It'll be the biggest," Thomas replied. "It's a good idea. Come on."

Thomas kicked his horse into a quick canter and they rode towards the hill. It was steep, but the woods weren't heavy and the horses made it up easily enough. They reached the top, found a cleared bit of land, and saw the town and sea stretched out below them.

Seaview was almost as large as Lakewood, and had a proper harbour and a high stone tower looking off to the sea. The houses were huddled close to one another, the better to face the cold winds that would come off the sea in the winter. Beyond the village edge, fields stretched in all directions, creating a plain where there had once been forest. Other fields, cut into the woods themselves, stretched further from the village; small houses teetered on the edge of the fields, half in, half out of the forests; and sheep and cattle grazed in the open places in the woods.

The bishop's house stood in the midst of the open fields, the ground before it sloping gently away to give a view of the sea. A low stone wall enclosed not only the house itself, but also stables and a chapel. The land around had been stripped and tilled, and was green from the first shoots breaking through the soil. Thomas whistled. "Nice place."

"We'll never get close," said George, dismay on his face. "There's no way to sneak up on it."

"There!" said Eileen

Both men turned to look at her, then to follow the line of her arm. Some distance away, mostly covered in trees, were the tops of a pair of stones. Thomas squinted at them, and saw several others as well. "Good eyes."

"Thank you." She flashed a smile at him. "How far away do you think it is?"

"A mile, maybe more," Thomas said. "We should get going now if we're going to get there before dark."

"We'll need food," said George, "if we're going to spend the night in the woods."

Thomas's belly announced its agreement with that statement even as his mind began to worry over the logistics of getting a meal. "We can't go into town."

"There's farms," said George. "We can get something from them."

They let their horses pick their way back down the hill and through the woods until they found the road, then skirted wide around the town. They found a farm and bought themselves enough cheese and bread and sausages to get them through the night and breakfast the next morning. Finding the stone circle, however, was far more difficult.

There was no direct road to the circle, and the paths they thought headed the right way meandered along with no particular direction. Several times they were startled along the way by sudden noises, and once by movement on the side of the road. In all cases the culprits were sheep, leading to much chagrin among the party.

It was near dark when they found a little path that was going in the right direction. There was no sign it had been used recently, and certainly not by a large party of riders.

"Maybe they aren't on their way, yet," Eileen suggested.

"Maybe they took a different road," said George, ducking a branch. "A straight one."

"I don't think there is a straight one," said Thomas, ducking the same branch.

"I hope there isn't," said Eileen. "I'd hate to find him already there, doing whatever he has planned."

Me, too, thought Thomas, wondering how he would stop the man if the bishop was already calling power.

"There!" said George.

The stone was taller than George and Benjamin would have been, stacked on each other, wider than Eileen was tall and twice as thick through as George was wide across the shoulders. What stone they could see was deep grey. The rest was crusted with moss and lichen, or hidden under the surrounding plant life. It split the path in two, sending it off in either direction. Thomas dismounted and, handing his reins to George, stepped close to examine it.

"See anything?" asked the smith.

"A big rock." Thomas leaned closer. He could almost make out writing, or perhaps some kind of drawing on the stone itself, but time had worn the pattern down to near invisibility. He ran his hand over it, feeling the cuts in the stone, long since smoothed by wind and rain.

"Then I guess I can do magic, too," said George, "because I'm seeing the same thing."

Thomas ignored George and stepped around the stone. The actual circle was some fifty feet beyond, surrounded by wood. There was no sign of anyone. Thomas felt a moment's relief. "This way. Lead the horses."

Eileen and George dismounted and followed Thomas to the edge of the circle. There was a clear area near one side of the circle, too small to be called a clearing, but large enough to make camp. They tied the horses, and Thomas led them between the big stones and into the circle itself.

The trees and undergrowth had taken over the entire area, making footing treacherous. The stones were the same as the first they had encountered, and spaced equidistant from each other. The evening light cast long, deep shadows from the trees and the rocks themselves, covering everything they touched with a thin layer of darkness.

Thomas paced the circumference of the circle as best he could, tripping on roots and old deadfalls. There was no sign of anything magical that he could see, just the huge, ancient rocks, and the forest that had grown up around them. He walked between two of the stones to where he estimated the middle of the circle was. Thomas found a wide disk of stone there, set deep into the earth and covered with plants and debris. Thomas squatted down and ran his fingers over it. There was a hole in the middle of the stone, which looked to go all the way through to the earth beneath. He squinted at it until his eyes hurt, then at the rest of the circle. He couldn't see anything magical about any of it.

"Find anything?" asked Eileen.

Thomas rubbed his eyes and looked up. George and Eileen were sitting on a fallen log, waiting for him. He picked himself up and dusted the dirt and leaves from his body. "Only a rock with a hole in the middle of it."

"Probably where whoever built this place drained the blood from their victims," put in George.

"Ha-ha," Eileen said, hitting him. "Thank you for making it that much more creepy out here."

"I think it's just used to mark the center of the circle," offered Thomas.

Eileen stood up from the fallen log. "It's starting to get really dark. Are we going to camp here?"

"I don't know." Thomas made his way carefully to his friends. "There's nothing magical here."

"And no sign of the bishop," said George.

"Aye, well, there is that, isn't there." Thomas took another look around the circle. "I thought certainly this would be the place. This is where the book said to go."

"To increase your powers," Eileen said. "Maybe that's not what he wants."

"Or he has a different book." Thomas shrugged. "I don't know. Let's get a camp set up and a fire started."

"A fire?" George repeated. "Do you think that's wise? What if he comes?"

"I doubt he will. This place is hard enough to get to during the day. If he was going to do something here, he would have shown up by now."

"Besides," Eileen pointed at the stones and the long, dark shadows they cast across the forest floor. "I want a fire."

Thomas had little more to say, and kept silent as they set up camp for the night. George dug a deep pit to hide the fire from any watching eyes, while Thomas and Eileen found deadwood to feed it. When it was finished, Thomas sat, searching through the stolen witch hunt books as the last light of day began to fade. As it became too dark to read, he closed them with a thud and sat back with a sigh.

"Anything?" asked Eileen.

"Nothing," said Thomas. "I found the bits on sharing power, but they all assume the witches are working together. There's nothing about stealing magic from anyone else, and nothing about stone circles, either, except in the spell book." Thomas picked up the little book again, and paged through it until he found the spell. It glowed, blue and bright to his eyes, though he knew no one else could see it. "I don't understand it, though. If the circle itself isn't magical, why do you need to be here? Why won't the spell work in your kitchen, or the stables?"

"Maybe the spell attracts the magic to the circle," suggested George as he tore at some bread. "The way a cheese on a hook attracts fish."

Thomas snorted at the image. "I don't think it's quite the same thing, but you're probably close."

"Maybe the spell draws the magic in," Eileen suggested. "Like a lodestone. And maybe being in the circle is what makes the magic grow stronger."

"I don't know." Thomas stared down at the book, then looked back at the circle.

Eileen straightened up suddenly. "You want to try it."

Thomas took a big breath before replying. "Aye."

Chapter 29

George stopped in mid-bite. "Are you crazy? You don't know what might happen if you do that."

" 'Spell to increase one's power,' " said Thomas, quoting the title. "It increases your power."

"How?" demanded George. "What happens to your power? How does it increase?"

"It doesn't say," said Thomas. "It just gives the instructions."

"And you want to try it anyway?"

"Aye. I need all the power I can get to face down the bishop."

"If it *works*," warned George. "What if it causes you to turn to ash instead?"

"It won't do that," said Eileen.

George raised his eyebrows at his sister. "And how are you so sure?"

"Well, the person who wrote it down probably did it."

"So?"

"So if he did it, how could he have turned to ash?"

George's eyebrows came down, and his eyes narrowed. He struggled with it for a moment, then doubtfully suggested, "Maybe he wrote it down first?"

Eileen smiled at her brother. "And why would he do that if he didn't know it worked?"

George sighed. "You've been spending too much time with him. You're starting to sound the same."

"What are you going to do?" Eileen asked Thomas.

Thomas looked at the book in his hands. "I don't know."

"Well, you'd better make up your mind fast." She pointed to the horizon, where the last of the light was fading. "Didn't the spell say you had to start the circle after sundown and finish before moonrise?"

"Aye."

"Well, then?"

Eileen and George both waited. Thomas tried to think about the reasons not to do it, but curiosity, as always, got the better of him. Thomas picked himself up, "I'll need a light."

Eileen stood up. "George can make a fire in the middle of the circle."

"You're daft," said George.

"Aye," agreed Thomas. "Will you help?"

George sighed, and put down his food. "Aye."

Thomas went through the spell again, reading the words by their own glow as the sunlight faded. "All right, I'll need the fire and something to draw with. I have to make two circles, one inside the other, and write a bunch of symbols inside them. I also need your walking stick, George."

"My stick?"

"Aye, I need to make a compass."

George, puzzled, handed over the stick, and turned his attention to charring the ends of a dozen small twigs. Thomas stepped into the stone circle, the thin light of the flames and the last fading daylight making the ground hard to see and making safe footing even harder to find. He stumbled his way forward until he found the stone disk in the centre. He ran his hand over it until he found the hole in the middle, then jammed George's stick into it. "I need some string."

"Here," Eileen began unlacing her bodice, "use this."

By the time she had the bodice unlaced and the strings out, Thomas had scraped the leaves and moss and dirt away from the surface of the stone disk, and had put the book down in the middle. George had a dozen twigs charred and another, large branch in full flame. He led Eileen into the circle, both moving carefully amidst the undergrowth. Eileen gave Thomas the laces. He measured the distance he needed as best he could, tied one end of the laces loosely around the stick and made a loop in the other.

George handed him the charred twigs. "Use these. I'll get the fire going."

Thomas pulled the lacings tight to what he hoped was the correct length for the outer circle. He made a loop at the end of it, then put in the first of the twigs and began to draw. The going was slow and painstaking, and he used up six twigs by the time the first circle was drawn.

George had the new fire going a few feet away from the stone disk. Eileen was searching through the underbrush for more twigs to char. Thomas adjusted the length of the lacings and drew the inner circle. Once it was done, he pulled George's stick free from the hole, tossed Eileen her laces and George his stick, then took off his sword-belt and handed it to Eileen as well. Thomas looked up into the night sky.

"What are you doing?" asked George.

"Finding north," said Thomas. He turned in a slow circle clockwise from where the sun had set until he spotted the pinpoint of light that was the northern star. "I knew that astronomy class would come in handy."

He marked the point on the inner circle and picked up the spell book. The inscriptions that needed to run between the circles were intricate and formed symbols Thomas hadn't seen before. Drawing them was slow going, and the little twigs seemed to break as fast as Eileen and George could make them. Thomas glanced skyward, worried he wasn't going to finish on time. The moon hadn't risen yet, though, and he turned back to the symbols. He kept working, painstakingly reproducing the diagrams, symbols and numbers from the little book. At the end of an hour, his fingers were numb and his knees ached from kneeling on the stone, but he was finished. He straightened, feeling his back complain.

"That," said George, "is impressive."

"Academy training." Thomas stood and rubbed feeling back into his legs. "In your second year, they make you copy old manuscripts that are falling apart to keep them from being lost. You aren't allowed to make mistakes."

"Well, you didn't make any here," said Eileen. "Now what?"

"At moonrise, I have to sit and meditate into the north for an hour. Then east, then south, then west."

"How are you going to know when an hour has passed?" asked George.

Thomas gestured at the sky. "The position of the moon and guesswork. Unless you have a better idea."

George thought about it. "Nope."

"Should we stay in the circle?" asked Eileen. "Or will that wreck it?"

"I don't know. Best to stay outside, I guess."

"All right." She leaned in and kissed him, careful not to touch the circles on the ground. "We'll be at the other fire. Call us if you need anything."

"I will." Thomas sat himself down in the center of the circle, watching his friends climb over the fallen branches and underbrush. The light of his little fire didn't carry far, and George and Eileen faded to dark silhouettes in a few steps, and then vanished entirely into the darkness between the fires. It wasn't until they were next to their campfire that Thomas could see them again. The light from the pit fire was barely enough to allow Thomas to make out their faces. He waved at them, then turned to the north, and worked on getting as comfortable as possible. Sitting cross-legged seemed to be his best bet, though he wished he had a cushion. Still, he did the best he could, and read the instructions one last time:

> *Sit quietly, back straight. Breathe deeply in the nose and out the mouth. Focus your mind on the magic and stare directly ahead. Once you have achieved the vision, change your focus to drawing the magic inside yourself.*

What *achieving the vision* was, Thomas had no idea, but the moon was starting to rise. He took a quick, last look at his friends, then, sitting cross-legged and keeping his back straight, began to breathe. In through his nose, out through his mouth. His thoughts danced in different directions, from breakfast that morning to Eileen to worries about the bishop to wondering how his mother was doing. He closed his eyes and tried to focus. Again and again he turned his mind from other paths, back to the images of magic that had come to him the last few months. He remembered the white glow from Ailbe's hands as she healed Eileen's cut. He remembered the change in the bishop's voice as he commanded John Flarety and the stunning, tiny beauty of the ball of light that both he and Timothy had summoned.

When he opened his eyes again, the night was glowing with lines of power.

Thomas had no idea what they were. There were stories of roads, invisible to the mortal eye, that carried magic and power. What he saw before him, though, bore no resemblance to a road, save that they stretched across the land. They were made of light that rose out of the earth itself to almost twice the height of a man, and he was sitting at the crossing of two of them. The light flowed around him, rushing past in a blur of brilliant blue-white. Thomas risked a glimpse to the side, and found that he could see through the light and beyond the edges of the stone ring, where George and Eileen huddled by their fire watching him. Thomas turned his face back to the north, facing once more into the lines of power.

When you have achieved the vision... He turned his mind inward again, though this time he kept his eyes open. Following the instructions, he willed the magic to enter into his body, to fill him. A strange vibration touched his body, as if something huge was humming against him. Around him, the stones of the circle began to glow.

Thomas remembered his astronomy lessons as best he could, and used them to make the moon his timepiece. He was aware of the cold stone underneath his legs, the light of the fire beside him and the one beside George and Eileen, and above all, the vibrations against his skin. He focused his mind on the magic, on drawing it into his body, until he guessed the first hour to be done.

He turned to face the east. The humming sank through his skin to become a steady vibration in his belly. It was a bizarre feeling. It began to spread, taking itself downward into his legs and feet, then up to fill his chest cavity. It reached his shoulders, moved down his arms like molasses pouring down a hill. It had reached his elbows when the position of the moon told him he was at the end of the second hour. He turned to the south and caught a glimpse of his friends, still awake, sitting by the fire and waiting for him.

He was, he realized, neither tired nor sore from his two hours of sitting. Instead, he was feeling alive in every pore. The vibrations continued to move through his body, down to his hands and the tips of his fingers. They began spreading upward from his shoulders, into his neck and his head. The vibration grew deeper, sinking through muscle and bone. All his senses were sharper now. The feel of his skin against his clothes was almost unbearable. He could smell the forest around him with every inhalation; the mould and leaves and animals and plants each had a distinct smell. Every whisper of wind through the trees became a shout, every creak of a branch a scream. The world was as bright as day to his eyes. Every leaf, twig, and blade of grass was sharp and clear to his sight.

There was movement around him, now; pale wisps, like shadows left behind after their owners had gone. He wondered at them, but kept himself focused on the magic. Blurred figures, twisted bits of movement and darkness without substance, flitted past him. None of them touched him. They moved around the circle; pale imitations of those who had danced and held rituals there in the centuries past.

The moon showed Thomas the beginning of the fourth hour, and he turned to face west, the final direction. The vibration that filled his body had taken on a deeper rhythm, slowing to the pace of a giant heartbeat and shaking him to his very core. He could almost see his muscles jumping in response to it, could feel his bones trembling back and forth in time with it, could sense his organs following the beat of it. The shapes in the circle became more frantic in their movements, flitting past him in a pattern that he couldn't see or understand.

He suddenly wondered if he was still sane. Part of him insisted there was no way for any of it to be real, that he was sitting alone on a cold chunk of rock, in the middle of the night, slowly going mad. Thomas set the thoughts aside. What he was seeing, what he was feeling, was far too real to be dismissed as fantasy. A nasty part of his mind pointed out that all lunatics probably felt just the same. He pushed the thought away and continued to sit in his place. There was no pain, no stiffness, no discomfort. The shapes danced around him, and inside he felt the deep, beating pulse of the world's heart.

Thomas looked up to the moon again, and was surprised to see that it was the end of the fourth hour. He switched his gaze down to the book before him. The instructions to end the spell were prosaic and anti-climactic. He closed his eyes, breathed deep, and visualized the power inside of him; willing it to calm itself, to settle within his body, and to be at his command. Then he rose to his feet and, with a single motion of one booted foot, broke both charcoal circles and stepped out.

He was stunned at how bright everything was.

Everything alive glowed, filling the world with energy and light. The grass was edged with a thin covering of deep, green light. The trees glowed green and white gold, their radiance large and spreading out into the night. Thomas stared at it all in amazement. Even the great, grey stones of the circle radiated light, though theirs was a rich, deep purple that pulsed as Thomas stared at them. Thomas picked up the spell book and walked to the edge of the stone circle. He put his hands against one of the stones, feeling the beating of the earth's heart deep inside the rock.

The glow from the lines of power dominated the night. The shadows were still now, save for those that flickered in the small remaining light of George and Eileen's campfire. He could see the energy that radiated from the wood, glowing with a light beyond that of the flames. He shook his head, bemused, and made his way to the fire.

Eileen and George were side by side at the fire, deep asleep. Both were glowing. The light seemed to shine from inside them, radiating through their skin and clothes. Eileen was a vibrant light blue, mixed with white and silver and flecks of green. George was darker blue with bits of red and brown flowing and melding in and out of the other colours. For a long time he watched their lights, moving and pulsing with their breaths. He wondered what they would look like in motion.

Fatigue, which had been sitting to one side and waiting for his attention to be distracted, suddenly overwhelmed him. He lay down far enough from his friends that he could watch both of them for as long as he remained awake. He wondered, as sleep overtook him, what his own light looked like.

* * *

Waking up was much less painful than Thomas thought it would be. The aches and pains of the riding had vanished in the night, and he had no stiffness from his long hours on the rock. He opened his eyes and saw his friends sitting across the fire-pit from him, talking quietly. He stared at them a while, blinking. "Where did the light go?"

Eileen jumped to her feet as Thomas started to sit up. "You're awake!" She jumped over the fire pit and knelt beside him. "What do you mean about the light? You're not blind, are you?"

"Not that light." Thomas finished sitting up and looked closely at Eileen. It took him a moment to see it, but her light was still there, nearly invisible in the sunlight. Eileen watched him warily. Thomas smiled, took her hand and kissed it. "How long have I been sleeping?"

"It's noon," George said. "Eileen wouldn't let me wake you."

"Good," It was the second decent sleep he'd had in weeks, Thomas realized. "Is there anything left to eat?"

"Well, that's a good sign," George got up and headed to the saddle bags. "I'll get the food."

"Did it work?" Eileen asked.

Thomas, feeling the vibrations of the earth inside his body, smiled. "Aye. It did."

"Can you show me?"

"After I've eaten. I'm starving."

"Hush!" said George, suddenly. "Quiet."

Both Thomas and Eileen turned to George, who had a finger against his lips. "Listen."

The birds and insects had gone silent. Thomas looked around for his rapier and found it sheathed on the ground beside him. Eileen rose to her feet, making no sound.

The silence was shattered by the sound of a branch breaking. Thomas rose to his feet. George stepped silently back beside them.

"There's nowhere to take the horses," George said, shifting the grip on his stick. "The undergrowth is too thick beyond here. They can't get through."

Wonderful. "How many are coming?"

"I can't tell, yet. Be quiet."

Thomas did, standing stock-still beside Eileen and waiting. In the distance, he could hear the sound of horses, unhappy at riding such a path, and the cajoling voices of their riders. The latter was a shock to him. George, listening grimly, said, "All right, they've dismounted."

"What do we do?" whispered Eileen.

"Nothing," said Thomas, sounding almost as surprised as he felt.

"Nothing?" repeated George. "They're almost on top of us."

"Aye," said Thomas. "And we'll probably need more lunch."

George and Eileen looked at him in shock, then turned back to the forest as they heard the first sound of feet crunching through the underbrush. A moment later, the first of the arrivals pushed through to the edge of the clearing and stopped dead.

"Well, by the Four, it's you," said Benjamin. He turned and called back. "I told you they'd be here."

Eileen and George heaved huge sighs of relief as Thomas, who'd recognized their voices, stepped forward to greet Benjamin. Henry joined Benjamin in the clearing, leading two horses. The five came together in a flurry of hand-shakes and back-slaps. Thomas found he could see the glow of each student's inner light, faint and silver-blue in the sunlight. Henry produced a full wineskin and passed it around while Benjamin reached into a bag he'd brought and pulled out enough food to feed them all and anyone who should be passing by. Soon all five were seated on the ground, with each side demanding to know the other's story.

Thomas finally shouted them all down. "We'll tell everything that's gone on with us, I swear, just let us know what happened after we ran out."

"We heard sounds of fighting," Eileen said. "And saw soldiers running toward the building."

"There was fighting," agreed Benjamin, his face and voice both grim.

"They shouldn't have tried to break in," said Henry. "While we were trying to keep the bishop's men out of our apartment, one of our neighbours started screaming that the bishop's men were killing him."

"Were they?" asked George.

"He was certainly in bad shape when we got there," Henry's voice was calm and cold, though Thomas could sense an undercurrent of anger. He could also see it, flickering red around Henry's head. "He'd been stabbed through the leg and was screaming like a pig getting cut up alive. That's what set off the riot."

"It was an awful mess." said Benjamin. "The students heard the screams and someone shouted 'Attack!' Half of the students started throwing bottles and pots and anything else they could at the soldiers, while the other half raced up to help us. The soldiers tried to put up a fight, but they were outnumbered and their horses were panicking."

Thomas closed his eyes, imagining the scene. Softly he asked, "How many dead?"

"Amazingly, no one," Henry sounded honestly surprised. "Say whatever else you like, but the bishop keeps his troops sharp. They managed to pull together an orderly retreat."

"With fifteen of theirs wounded and the same on our side," added Benjamin. "It wasn't very pretty at all."

"The City Guard mustn't have been very impressed."

"The guard had nothing to do with it," Henry scoffed. "They let the bishop's men go past, then scattered when they saw all of us."

"You went after them?" Eileen sounded appalled.

"Aye, we did," said Henry, a wide wolf's grin growing on his face. "I sent ten to rouse the Academy, and the rest of us followed them back to the bishop's house. The students in other buildings and the dormitories joined us as we went. By the time we'd reached the house, there were close to five hundred of us."

Eileen shuddered at the thought. "What happened?"

Henry's grin grew wider and more unpleasant. "We lodged a protest."

"How?" asked Thomas, dreading the answer.

"With cobblestones, mostly. Also with bottles, sticks, several torches and a cart full of cow dung."

"I'll never be able to go back again," Thomas moaned, his head falling into his hands. "I'll be hanged the moment I arrive."

"You weren't in the riot," reminded Benjamin.

"No, just the cause of it."

"We kept the bishop holed up there for hours," continued Henry. "He finally came charging out in his carriage just after noon. Ten horsemen in front and ten more behind with swords out and ready. They rode straight out into the crowd at a full gallop. Nearly ran us down."

"Any more hurt?"

"Aye, though hurt was the worst of it. He and his men were too busy getting away to think about doing a proper job."

"Fortunately for us," Benjamin put in.

"Aye, it was," said Henry. "With the bishop himself gone, the rest of his soldiers beat a retreat and the students sacked his house, and a right proper job they did of it, too. Not a window left unbroken, not a stick of furniture unsmashed. They were torching it when we rode off."

Already guessing the answer, Thomas asked, "Where did you get the horses?"

Henry shrugged. "The bishop had stables. We thought it best to follow him, in case he caught up to you."

Eileen's jaw dropped. "You stole the bishop's horses?"

"Borrowed," corrected Benjamin. "We'll take them back."

"No we won't," argued Henry. "Spoils of war."

"Oh, by the Four." Thomas let himself fall backwards to the ground. "Is there any good news?"

Henry thought about it. "No, actually, there isn't."

Thomas covered his face with his hands, and let out his breath with a long and dramatic sigh. He was actually feeling much better than he had since they'd left. His friends were unhurt and no one had died in the riot. As for the bishop's house burning down, he was finding it very hard to feel at all sorry about it.

"I take it the bishop didn't come here?" asked Henry.

"The town, yes," said Eileen. "At least, we think so. Here, no."

"Too bad. So what happened to you three?"

Thomas sat up, and took turns with George and Eileen to relate all that had happened. When Thomas described the spell he had performed, Henry looked at once dubious, impressed, and horrified. Benjamin just looked horrified. Thomas, at Henry's insistence, went into great detail. As soon as he'd finished, Henry got up and went to examine the remains of the circles that Thomas had drawn on the ground. He came back suitably impressed and said so.

It was George, though, who asked the question. "Did it work?"

"You mean you don't know?" demanded Benjamin.

"They don't know," corrected Thomas. "They were asleep by the time I finished, and I was asleep until you lot arrived."

"You slept until noon?"

"It takes a lot out of you."

"But did it work?" asked Henry.

"Aye. It worked."

"How do you know?"

"Well, for a start, you're glowing now."

"What?"

"All of you. You're glowing." Thomas smiled at the stunned look on everyone's faces. "I can barely see it in the daylight, but it's there. Every living thing is glowing with magic."

"Everything?" asked Benjamin. There was a deeply disturbed look on his face.

"It's all right," Henry said, smiling wickedly. "Everyone knows that the world's a magical place."

"But… but the High Father created the world," protested Benjamin.

"Aye, he did," agreed Thomas.

"Magic comes from the Blessed Daughter!" protested Benjamin. "How can it be in everything?"

That stopped Thomas. "I hadn't thought of that." He took a moment to think about it there, and came up with a possibility. "Well, if the High Father created all things, then he would have been the one to put magic in all things. Maybe what the Daughter did was give some people the ability to use the magic within."

"Like the Rebel Son gave man tools and fire," suggested Eileen.

"I suppose," Benjamin looked unconvinced. "Can you really see magic in everything?"

"Everything," said Thomas. "It's in all of you and in the horses and the grass and the trees and lines of it circle the earth"

"Lines of magic?" George's head swivelled on his shoulders, his eyes scanning the woods. "Where?"

"Over there," Thomas pointed back into the circle. He could barely see them himself, now, only a faint haze in the air. "At night, they're beautiful."

"Are they?"

"Aye." Thomas's voice grew softer. "And so is the light around you, my friend. You and Henry and Benjamin and Eileen and all living things. It's stunning."

"You sound like you've had a revelation," said Benjamin.

"I guess I have."

"Has it brought you closer to the Four?" Benjamin asked, hopefully.

Thomas snorted. "Leave it to the Theology student to ask that."

"Has it?"

Thomas saw how serious Benjamin was. Still, he had to shake his head. "I don't know. There's a bit too much going on right now to think about that."

"I suppose," Benjamin sounded disappointed.

"How about the spells?" Henry asked. "Can you do any of them any better?"

"I should think so. It feels like I could, but I haven't tried."

"Well, try now."

Thomas picked up the little book and began scanning it. "Anything in particular?"

"Nothing so big as to get us noticed," warned Eileen.

Thomas paged through the book. One spell caught his eye. There were no ingredients needed, nor any chanting. It was in fact, very simple. Still, he guessed his friends wouldn't like it too much. He smiled at them. "How about I call lightning?"

"Lightning?" Eileen was horrified. "Do the words *forest fire, loud noise* and *too much attention* mean anything to you? You might as well put a sign up!"

"All right," Thomas said, chuckling. He read through the spell again and promised himself he'd try it when he had a chance, just to see what it was like. "All right. How about..." he paged through the spell book, "levitation. I'll try levitation."

"And what will you levitate?" asked Henry. "I don't think anyone brought any spoons."

"Oh, ha-ha." Thomas looked around the little clearing. His eyes settled on a rock, easily twice his own size. He pointed. "How about that?"

"That?" George's eyebrows climbed high on his head. "You could barely lift a spoon three days ago."

"That was then." Thomas turned his attention to the rock, and found that he could feel its shape and size with his mind. It wasn't one of the large, grey stones from the circle, but a chunk of local granite, half-buried by time under the forest floor. He extended the energy out from within himself towards the boulder and visualized it rising into the air. The pulse of the earth, quiet since he'd woken up, began to beat strongly through him. Energy gathered itself together in his body, and for a moment he could almost feel the rock as if he was lifting it in his own hands. The world filled with a white light that gathered itself in his chest, then raced out towards the rock.

It leapt thirty feet straight up and hovered. Everyone yelped in surprise and scrambled back. Thomas held his concentration, and the boulder stayed up. A moment later he began to feel the weight of it, pressing on his mind. The effort to keep it where it was grew greater and greater. He needed to let it down. He tried to lower it back down to the earth, and realized he had no idea how. The thought broke his concentration.

The boulder wavered in the air then came crashing down. The rock bounced several times, gouging deep scars into the earth. It came to rest only a few feet from Thomas's boots. He stared at it, aware that the only sound was his own ragged breathing. His friends had all frozen in place when the boulder had stopped moving, and were all staring at him.

"Well," Thomas tried to sound less frightened than he was, "I guess it worked."

"Aye, I'd say so," said Eileen, weakly.

"Very well, in fact," agreed Henry with a slight tremor in his voice. "Right up to the end there."

"Aye." Thomas felt the sudden urge to sit down and realized he already was.

"You're pale," said Benjamin, his voice as shaky as Henry's.

"I feel pale." In fact, Thomas felt dizzy and weak, as though part of his blood supply had been tossed away with the rock.

"Of course you do," said Eileen. "You could barely lift a spoon three days ago. This…"

"That," said Benjamin, nodding to the boulder, "weighs at least a ton. Maybe two."

"That much?" Henry sounded half-impressed, half-scared.

"Stonemason," said Benjamin, tapping his chest, "remember? A ton at least. Probably two."

Thomas felt the world beginning to spin. He closed his eyes. "It certainly felt it."

Henry looked thoughtful for a moment. "For every action, a reaction, right?"

Thomas felt tremors starting through his body. "And this is the reaction for the action of using magic?" He shook his head, trying to clear it. "Wonderful. Some help this will be."

"Maybe you need to pace yourself," suggested Eileen. "Until you're used to it."

"Maybe." Thomas opened his eyes and forced them to focus on his friends. They were all still keeping well away from him. "Do you think you could come back over here now?"

There was a rather sheepish movement as the group edged themselves back to the positions they'd scrambled from moments before.

"Sorry," Eileen said, sitting beside him and taking his hand.

"It's all right," Thomas squeezed her hand, using the gesture to try to anchor himself against the spinning world. It didn't work. "I'd run away myself, if I could."

"All right, then." George mustered himself together. "What do we do now?"

"Well," said Thomas "I think another nap might be in order."

"That bad?" Worry filled George's face. "You just woke up."

"Aye, and now I think I should go back to sleep."

"Try eating instead," suggested Benjamin, holding out an apple. "You might just need something inside you."

"We just had lunch," Thomas's world spun again, and he had to close his eyes until it slowed. When he opened them again, Eileen was helping him lie back on the grass. She was biting her lip, and her eyes were filled with concern. Thomas smiled at her, tried to say something reassuring, but the world slid to the left and she, and everything else, went away for a while.

Chapter 30

It was night when Thomas opened his eyes, and the world was alive in colours. The trees overhead, the brush around him, and every blade of grass was shining deep green. The horses gleamed gold and red and the magical lines of power glowed their bright blue and white. He turned his head, and saw the light blue, yellow, and white light that surrounded Eileen. She was watching him, but it took her a moment to realize he was looking back. When she did, she blinked rapidly, leaned in, and put a little smile on her face. "Hello," she said in a gentle, quiet voice.

"Hello, yourself," Thomas replied. He pushed himself up on one elbow and took in the rest of the clearing. The others were sitting around in various states of repose. Henry was even playing chess with George, leaving Thomas to wonder when Henry had found the time to pack a board. He turned back to Eileen. "How long was I asleep?"

"The sun just set," Eileen replied. "We've been waiting all day for you."

"You should have woken me."

Eileen bit her lip and turned her head away. "Benjamin thought that would be a bad idea."

"And I'm sure he's an expert," Thomas muttered, pushing himself into a sitting position. "Well, I'm awake now."

"Aye, you are. How do you feel?"

"Starving," Thomas said with certainty.

"Well, food we have," Eileen assured him. "I'll get it."

"I can go."

"No." Eileen's voice was suddenly sharp. "I mean, you keep resting."

She got up and headed towards a pair of bags sitting under a tree, wiping at her face as she did. Thomas watched her go, saw the others ask quietly if he was awake. She nodded and hurried back to Thomas with a basket in hand. Thomas hadn't seen it before and guessed that someone had made a trip into the town. It certainly explained the chessboard. Then Eileen was back beside him and putting the basket down where he could reach it. He reached out, but captured one of her hands instead.

"Hey," he said, gently. "What's the matter?"

"Nothing." She wiped angrily at her eyes with her free hand and turned away. Thomas pulled her back.

"Nothing doesn't make anyone cry." He leaned close and took her other hand as well. "What is it?"

"You."

"Me?"

"Aye, you." She took a deep breath, then pulled one of her hands free and struck him hard in the chest. "Don't you ever do that again, you hear me?"

"Ow! Do what?"

"Do what you did!" She was crying now, and hitting him on every second word. "I've been sitting here for hours! I didn't know if you were going to wake up! You could have died!"

"You should have shaken me!" Thomas protested, trying to ward off the blows.

"We did!" She hit him again. "We shook you and yelled at you! If you didn't wake up soon I was going to start kicking you!"

"All right! All right!" Thomas made a quick grab, caught her shoulders and pulled her in close, smothering her fists against his body. "It's all right. I'm awake now."

"We couldn't wake you up," she cried into his chest. Her arms relaxed, then went around his waist. "Don't you ever do that again."

"I won't," Thomas promised. "I swear, I won't."

"She does speak for the rest of us," Benjamin said from his spot on the other side of the fire.

"Aye, she does," agreed George. "Though she said it better."

"Could you really not wake me up?"

"No, we could not," said Benjamin. "We were about ready to go looking for a healer, or a physician."

"But we couldn't tell anyone what was wrong with you, could we?" said Henry.

"Nay, I suppose not."

"But you're all right, now," asked George, "aren't you?"

"Aye, I think so," Thomas squeezed Eileen again then gently pushed her back so he could see her face. "Are you better, now?"

Eileen wiped her eyes and nose, sniffed a couple of times. "Aye."

"Good."

"Do I look a fright?"

The question brought a smile to Thomas's face. "No, you look beautiful."

"No she doesn't," declared George. "She always looks terrible after she cries."

"Shut up, you," Eileen said, wiping away more tears. "I'm fine."

"Good," Thomas took her hand again. "Because I am really, really hungry."

She gave him another hit, though not as hard as the others, and handed him an apple. He dug his teeth into it without a second thought, and was stunned at how good it tasted. It was much better than any apple he'd eaten before. He wondered if that was due to the magic, or just that he hadn't eaten anything since lunch. He moved closer to the fire, and the others joined in for an impromptu late supper. Soon, all the food was gone and Thomas was feeling much better than he had since the night before.

So. Now what?

Thomas looked around the fire and saw the glow of the magic emanating from each of his friends. Inside him, he could feel the beating of the world's heart, slow, deep, steady. Thomas knew all he had to do was reach for it and the magic would rise, more powerful than anything else.

If I'm going to face him, now is the time. "Well, are we ready, then?"

"Ready for what?" asked Benjamin. "What are we going to do?"

"The same as before."

"Run around aimlessly through the country, searching madly for answers?" suggested Henry.

"Exactly," Thomas grinned and got to his feet. "Though you left out wailing like banshees."

"Well, we mustn't forget that," Henry said. "But what, exactly, are we doing?"

"Going after the bishop," Thomas headed for his horse, "and stopping him."

"Stopping him from what?" asked George. "He's not casting spells in the stone circle."

"Well, he's certainly doing something down here." Thomas began saddling the animal. He was feeling remarkably good, though he wasn't about to test his luck by casting a spell. "And even if he's not, he still took the magic from my father and Timothy and Ailbe and the Four know how many others. We need to stop him."

"At this time of night?" protested Benjamin.

"Night's the best time of night for scouting," said Henry, getting to his own feet.

"And stealing," said Thomas, getting Henry and Benjamin's total attention with the words.

"Stealing what?" asked Henry.

"Books."

"Again?" protested Benjamin.

Thomas nodded. "The bishop has to have some books with spells in them. It's the only way he could learn to do everything he does. If we steal them, we can figure out what he's up to, and we can stop him."

"The bishop lost most everything in the riot," said Benjamin. "How do you know he managed to take them with him?"

"Think about it," said Thomas. "What's the most important thing to him right now?"

"Killing you?"

Thomas threw a sour glance at Henry for the suggestion. "No. But thank you for thinking of it."

"The magic," said Eileen. "He wants to take the magic."

"Aye." Thomas finished tightening the last strap on his saddle. "And if the books give him the spells he needs to do that, he wouldn't have left them behind. They were probably in the carriage with him."

"In which case they'll be at his house," said Henry. "Under his pillow, probably. Surrounded by twenty guards."

Thomas nodded. "Aye, that would be about right."

"And you're just going to waltz in and steal them, then?"

Thomas felt his lips pull back in a grin like the one Henry had worn when describing the riot. "Aye. You coming?"

Henry grinned back and got to his feet. "Aye."

George and Eileen stood up a moment later, followed by a much more hesitant Benjamin. The five packed up their food and gear, and Eileen went behind one of the stones to change into breeches and a shirt. Henry made them wait until the moon was well on its way across the sky before setting out. Thomas, best able to see, led them single file down the path towards the little town. Thomas let his horse pick their pace on the path. He wished he could urge the animal to go faster, but forced himself to remember that just because he could see in the dark now didn't mean that his horse could.

They rode out of the forest and followed the road through the village. There was no sign of anyone awake. Even the village inn had closed its doors for the night. They rode as silently as they could through the town and towards the bishop's house. Thomas scanned the open ground, looking for a place to hide the horses. He spotted a copse of trees in the middle of the fields. They were much farther away than Thomas would have liked, but he couldn't see any other cover.

Light flared ahead of them. A dozen men with torches were streaming from the bishop's house into his yard. Thomas pulled his horse up short, hissing, "Stop!"

His friends were already stopping. Beneath the yellow light of the torches Thomas could see the deep red light that glowed from within each of the bishop's guards. The academic portion of his brain wondered if the light revealed the men's true nature, or just showed their intent. The rest of him, however, wanted to get off the road and into hiding before the men spotted them. Hissing, "Come on!" to his friends, he turned his horse and charged for the stand of trees. His friends were right behind him, all of them galloping desperately—and blindly, Thomas realized—across the fields, trusting him to get them to safety.

He jumped off the horse as soon as he reached the copse, and led the animal deep into the little wood. His friends did the same. They tied their horses to branches and went back to the edge of the stand of trees, weapons drawn and ready.

"What do you see?" Henry demanded.

"Nothing," said Thomas. "The barn's in the way."

Shouted commands, audible but not intelligible, floated through the air, accompanied by the sounds of many horses protesting being woken.

"Are they getting ready to leave?" asked Benjamin.

"I think so," said Henry. "Sounds like it, anyway."

"Is that good or bad?" asked Eileen.

Henry shrugged, the motion nearly invisible in the dark. "Depends where they're going. If they come here, it's bad. Anywhere else is good."

Thomas kept his eyes on the road, waiting to see some sign of Bishop Malloy. Time dragged itself out. At last, there was movement from the yard, and the soldiers rode out and down the road. There were fourteen all told, all of them carrying torches. There was no sign of the bishop or his familiar.

"Fourteen," Henry mused. "That leaves six inside."

"At least," said Thomas. "He might have had some here before."

"It still makes the odds better than they were." Henry said. "This is as good a place to leave the horses as any. We can walk from here, and keep the barn between us and the house."

"What if we need to get away in a hurry?" asked George.

"Then Benjamin can bring the horses to us," said Henry.

"Me?" Benjamin was startled.

"You," said Henry. "You're big enough to control the horses, and if we went in and got caught, you'd be duty-bound to answer all his questions. Also, you can't move quietly to save your life."

Benjamin glared at Henry a moment—a move whose effectiveness was probably completely lost in the darkness—and sounded both unhappy and relieved when he said, "I'd argue but you're right. I'll wait here."

Thomas watched until the riders' torches were only pin-pricks of light in the distance, then led his friends out of the copse of trees and into the fields. The ground was still newly seeded, with only blades of grass and furrows to hide in. Thomas felt terribly exposed in the bright light of the full moon and angled their path to keep the barn between them and the house. They moved at a crouching run, hands clutching weapons, feet making almost no noise against the dirt and sprouting plants.

It felt like forever before they reached the low wall that edged the bishop's property and crouched behind it. Thomas waited, listening. He heard nothing. He leaned up and peered over top of the wall, scanning what he could see of the grounds.

"All right," Thomas breathed. "There's no one in sight. I'll go over the wall and look around the corner of the barn. If I don't see anything, I'll wave you forward."

"No you won't," whispered Henry. "If they see you, we're all in trouble. I'll go."

"I can see better."

"It's across a yard in a full moon," Henry said. "I can see well enough. Wait here."

Thomas wanted to protest, but Henry was already over the wall and moving fast and silent to the barn. Thomas cursed to himself and kept his eyes out for anyone that might be coming around the other corner. No one did. Henry took enough time to thoroughly inspect the yard before waving the others forward. George reached him first, Eileen and Thomas close behind.

"All right," Henry whispered. "There's no lights on in the house, which doesn't mean that there'll be nobody awake. Suggestions?"

"The doors will be locked," said Thomas. "If he's in there."

"So we find a window."

"What if none are open?" asked George.

Henry grinned. "Then we set fire to the stables. That will get his attention."

"And bring the rest of his men charging back here at full speed," Thomas said. "You can see a fire like that for miles."

"You have another suggestion?"

Thomas thought about it, but couldn't come up with anything.

"Right," said George, before Henry could say anything else. "My turn."

George left the shelter of the barn wall and moved quickly across the yard. He passed through the shadow of the chapel and reached the house in absolute silence, disappearing around the side as the three watched.

Thomas kept his eyes roving over the yard, watching for any signs of life. There were none, but the house itself exuded a faint glow. It wasn't the bright light that surrounded people, or the deep green of the forest. It was as if long years of use had left their impression on the building, giving it a life of its own. Thomas turned his eyes towards the stone chapel, and saw light coming from there as well. It was faint, but what he could see glowed red. Thomas wished that he knew enough to interpret the colours.

Henry touched his shoulder. Thomas looked. George was standing at the far side of the house, waving at them to come forward. Thomas left his thoughts behind and followed Henry and Eileen across the yard. George, a finger across his lips, pointed with his other hand to an open window on the second floor, some fifteen feet above the ground. Thomas made sure no one else was in the yard, then dared to whisper, "How are we going to get in there?"

"Like the wall of the Academy," said George.

"I should do it," volunteered Eileen. "I'm lighter."

Henry shook his head. "Not tall enough. I'll do it."

"I'll do it," countered Thomas, taking off his sword belt. "I'm lighter."

He handed Henry his sword and stepped into George's cupped hands, then up onto his friend's shoulders. He was still a good three feet away from the window, and even with his arms outstretched couldn't reach the sill. He started to curse under his breath and was readying himself to come back down when he felt George's hands wrap themselves around his heels. He realized what George was planning to do just as the big man straightened his arms, lifting Thomas high into the air. Thomas grabbed at the window as much for his balance as anything else. He levered himself up and got a leg over the sill as quietly as he could. There was no one inside, fortunately. Below, Henry hissed to get Thomas's attention and then tossed up his sword. Thomas caught it and slipped inside.

He was in a servants' room; narrow and plain, with beds for six. All had blankets on them, and saddlebags hung off the footboards. The soldiers, Thomas guessed. He waved his friends to the front of the house and crossed the room. The door squeaked as it opened, making Thomas wince. A quick peek showed nothing but empty hallway. He went down it as quietly as he could. He passed several other rooms, but there was neither sound nor sight of anyone.

He found the stairs and went quickly down them, ending up in the kitchen. He moved on, through a dining room and a parlour. He couldn't see the front door anywhere. Thomas took a moment to wish the bishop had chosen a less ostentatious dwelling, then moved on. A door led to a hallway that moved at right angles from where he thought he wanted to go. He followed it anyway, guessing rightly that it would lead to another. That one was wide and clean and went in a straight line towards the foyer and front door. He went as fast as he could, passing several closed doors and a set of wide, carpeted stairs before reaching the entrance-way.

He drew back the bolts on the door, opened it a crack, and peered into the night. The yard was empty. He looked to the side of the house, spotted George, and waved him forward. The big man came in quickly, the other two following close behind.

"This place is huge," Thomas whispered, locking the door behind them. "There's no way we're going to search it all."

"So where would he keep his books?" asked Henry, his voice just as quiet.

"His bedroom," guessed Eileen.

"Or his study," said Thomas.

"Bedroom and study would both be upstairs," Henry said.

"Then it's upstairs we go," said Thomas. "Follow me, and no more talking."

He led them back down the hallway, to the wide, carpeted stairs. Up they went, moving as quietly as they could and wincing at every squeak of the stairs or sound of their boots. Nothing in the house moved save themselves. Thomas could feel his heart pounding with every step up. All it would take was one guard at the top of the stairs to shout the alarm and give them away.

There was no one. At the top of the stairs a long, straight hallway stretched out to either side, going the width of the building and lit only by the moonlight that spilled through the window at either end. Thomas, his vision still better than the others', could make out nothing more than dim shapes. He breathed a sigh of relief. There was no life in the hallway save himself and his friends.

George stepped up beside Thomas, touching him on the shoulder. Thomas watched his friend mime opening doors, then pointing to one side of the hall. Thomas understood and nodded. George tapped Henry on his shoulder and led him to one side of the hallway. Thomas and Eileen took the other. Thomas went down the length of the hallway, listening at each door first, then opening them and looking in. Every time he reached for the handle on the door he wondered if he was going to end up facing the bishop, and what he could do if he did.

All Thomas found were empty rooms.

He growled in silent frustration and waited for George to join them. George shook his head and shrugged. Annoyed, Thomas retraced his steps and started down the other part of the hall.

Halfway down, George found another, much shorter, hallway leading to a large, ornate door. Thomas tried it, found it unlocked. He silently thanked the Four and opened it. On the other side was a sumptuous sitting room, filled with what looked to be well-appointed furnishings, though the dark made it difficult to see for certain. There was a set of large double doors on one wall, and a smaller, single door on the other. Thomas pointed George and Henry to the smaller door and led Eileen to the other.

Thomas put his ears against the doors and listened intently. He heard nothing. These doors, too, were unlocked. Holding his breath, he opened the door a crack and listened again. Silence. He opened it further and peeked in. The room was huge, the bed in the middle was hung with heavy curtains, all closed. The moonlight streaming through the window gave everything a silvery hue, and turned all the colours in the room to shades of grey.

Thomas looked behind him. George and Henry had opened the other door and were going inside. Thomas gestured at Eileen to stay where she was, then stepped into the room. Nothing within caught his eye; no life energy or magic glowed. His eyes were drawn to the thick, heavy curtains that surrounded the bed. It would be, he was certain, the worst of all possible outcomes if the bishop was sleeping on the other side of them.

Thomas drew his sword and began to advance on the bed. Behind him came a sharp intake of breath as Eileen realized what he was doing.

The room, large enough in truth, grew larger in Thomas's mind, and crossing to the bed took forever. Every step he took on the thickly carpeted floor was silent, and still he was certain that on that bed, behind the curtain, the bishop was sitting, waiting for him to pull back one of the panels. The thought of being in that man's hands again nearly stopped him in his tracks, but he put the fear aside and kept moving. At last, he was touching the curtains. Gently he ran his hands along them, searching for an edge to one of the panels. His fingers stumbled on an opening in the fabric. He was holding his breath, he realized, but didn't dare exhale until he knew for certain. With a sudden move, he pulled the curtain back.

The bed was empty.

The air left Thomas in a rush. *Of course the bishop isn't home. If he'd been home, his guards would be all around the house, and Randolf would be sleeping at his feet.* The bed was still made up, as if no one had ever been there. Thomas cursed softly and thoroughly and turned back to Eileen. "He's not here. No one's here."

"What do we do?" she asked.

"Search everything."

"Should we be careful?" asked Eileen, "I mean, should we make it so he doesn't notice he's been searched?"

"I don't think we can," said Thomas, turning his attention back to the bed. "Just try not to make too much noise."

Thomas searched under the bed, under the pillows and blankets, and even under the mattress. There was nothing. He swore again and turned his attention to the stands on either side of the bed. They were both locked, but yielded easily enough to the tip of his dagger. One held papers, none of which had any magical properties as far as Thomas could see. The other was empty.

Eileen had covered half the room by the time he'd finished. Thomas joined her and together they went through the rest. Nothing turned up.

"Do you think he has it in a secret panel?" asked Eileen.

"I doubt it," Thomas said. "I think the books are wherever he is."

"And where do you think that is?"

"I don't know." Thomas took one last, disgusted look around the room. "Let's get out of here."

George and Henry were still in the other room. It was, as Thomas had thought, the bishop's office. The two had gone through every drawer in the desk, had opened all the cabinets and had even taken the pictures off the walls in case there was something behind them. Thomas shook his head at the mess. "Well, he's certainly going to know we've been here."

"There's no sign of anything," Henry said. "The papers we could read are all about land purchases and tithe collection. There's nothing in the cabinets except liquor and books and more bloody papers on the same thing."

"Books?"

"Aye," George said, pointing. "Have a look. Maybe you can see something."

"Maybe," agreed Thomas. "In the mean time, straighten this place up as best you can. With luck he won't notice anything immediately."

"Where is he, anyway?" asked Henry.

"I don't know."

Thomas went through the books. They were ledgers. He went through every one, just to be certain. By the time he finished with the last, the other three had straightened the room into some semblance of order.

"Now what?" whispered Eileen, sitting down on the edge of the desk.

"We get out of here," said George. "There's no saying he won't be back any moment."

"He's probably got them with him," Thomas felt anger and disappointment welling up inside of him. "Come on. We'll get back to Benjamin and figure out something."

Down the hallway they went, then down the stairs to the first floor. Their footfalls, silent on the carpets above, echoed on the hardwood floor. Thomas, now certain the house was empty, didn't bother slowing down or trying to be quiet. He led his friends to the door, opened it a crack, and peered out. The yard was empty. He opened the door wide and looked around.

"Look," Thomas gestured Henry forward and pointed up the road. "They're coming back."

Chapter 31

The others crowded around the door and peered out. A dozen torches, shining like red fireflies, swarmed up the road.

"They won't see us," said Henry. "They're too far away." He looked again. "But they're riding fast. We need to move."

Thomas led them out of the house, moving fast and and quiet and cursing the bishop with every step. *Where is the man?*

The yard was empty, and there was no sign of anyone alive. The chapel was still glowing red to his eyes, and another paler light flickered at the windows.

Candlelight.

Thomas stopped dead and was nearly knocked over by Henry, who was hard on his heels. "The chapel!"

"Get moving!" snapped Henry. "They're coming!"

"But the bishop's in the chapel!" protested Thomas.

"It's too late!" Henry grabbed his collar and started to drag him. "Get out of here before you get us all caught!"

The words were just out of his mouth when one of the riders sounded a horn, then sounded it again. On the second sounding, someone in the stables cursed and called for someone else to bestir his lazy self.

"Run!" hissed Henry. "Now!"

The stable doors were flung open, and a half-dozen rough-looking stable hands stepped out. Both groups froze, staring at the other.

"RUN!" shouted Henry, drawing his rapier and dagger. Thomas did the same and George lifted his thick walking stick. The stable hands moved to block them, shouting, "Help! Thieves! Help!"

The torches coming up the road burst into a whirl of flame and sparks as the riders pushed their horses to a gallop. Thomas and his friends tried to go around the stable hands, but the men blocked them. Henry and Thomas swung their rapiers to drive them back, but couldn't clear a path.

The doors of the chapel swung open and torchlight flickered yellow over the yard. A half-dozen soldiers spilled out. Randolf, wearing his customary black and with his rapier in hand, was leading them. He spotted Thomas and grinned.

The bishop stepped into the doorway. "Who dares—" His eyes widened when he recognized Thomas. "Capture them!" He shouted. "Catch them all! Alive! Now!"

There was no time to think. George let out a bellow and charged the stable hands, swinging his stick with furious accuracy. The swordsmen charged in and Henry and Thomas faced off against them. Blades clashed, flickering yellow in the torchlight. Henry deftly ran one of his opponents through the thigh and shoved him against another. Thomas fought his way forward, dodging the soldiers' blades and cutting open one man with his own.

"Leave that one! He's mine!"

Thomas turned and Randolf was upon him.

Thomas's world was instantly reduced to the flashing steel before him. The man was incredible. Thomas was nearly skewered a half a dozen times and he backed away as he fought, looking for an escape. He could see the four remaining guardsmen surrounding Henry, driving him back towards the stable wall. George was fighting furiously against the stable hands, and three of their number lay bleeding on the ground. Thomas couldn't see Eileen, and the riders were now charging towards the yard.

Randolf stayed on him, driving him backwards. Thomas parried and thrust as best he could with both his blades, but the other man was far quicker. A cold panic gripped Thomas's belly. He wasn't going to win. He redoubled his efforts and got driven back again.

A piece of horse dung flew past Thomas's shoulder and directly into Randolf's face. The man stumbled back. Eileen, standing behind Thomas, lobbed another one, catching him in the face again.

"Come on!" she screamed, shoving Thomas towards the stables. Thomas ran with her towards the wall, cutting open the ribs of one of Henry's opponents on the way and thrusting into one of George's from behind.

"Run!" shouted Thomas, but his words were drowned in the thunder of hooves as the rest of the bishop's guard charged in. The four ran for the wall but the riders blocked them, forcing them back against the side of the stable. Thomas shoved Eileen behind him, and the three men faced outward, weapons forming a bristling guard.

In the field beyond the wall, Thomas glimpsed streaks of blue-white light and red-brown; Benjamin, riding hard towards them with the other horses in tow. Then the riders surrounded them, blocking off the view. The bishop's men looked tired and grim in the torchlight.

Across four of the saddles, small bodies lay firmly bound. Children, Thomas realized, perhaps twelve years old and not moving. Thomas hardly had time to wonder why they were there when Randolf, still wiping horse-dung from his face, snapped an order. Two men pulled the children off the horses and towards the house.

"I told you we should have set the barn on fire," said Henry, voice shaking with energy and anger. His eyes darted to either side, seeking a way out. "Ideas?"

"Benjamin is out there," muttered Thomas.

"And if he's smart he'll stay put," Henry lowered his voice to match Thomas's.

Thomas shook his head. "I saw him. He's riding this way."

"Damn fool."

"Put down your weapons." The bishop's voice carried across the yard. "Put them down and I will guarantee you a fair trial."

No one in the small circle moved. Thomas could see the fear in George and Eileen's faces, and the grim determination in Henry's.

The circle of horses shifted, and the bishop stepped forward. His eyes were on Thomas. "Surrender," he said. "And I'll let your friends live."

The bishop glowed deep red and black to Thomas's eyes.

Thomas had not thought it was possible for black to glow, but Bishop Malloy radiated a darkness that was deeper than the night around him and strong enough to absorb the light of any who happened to be standing close enough. There was victory in the bishop's voice and a cold, hard glitter in his eye. Thomas looked into his eyes, and knew as soon as they dropped their weapons, his friends would be killed.

Hatred blazed up in Thomas, white hot and impotent against the blades levelled on them. They were badly outnumbered, by soldiers whose friends they had wounded or killed. Any fight was going to go very badly for them. From the smile on the bishop's face, Thomas could see the man knew it. They were going to die.

Unless...

He dropped both his blades to the ground behind him and stepped forward.

"Thomas!" Eileen yelled, horrified.

She tried to grab at him, but George held her back. Thomas kept walking, spreading his arms at his sides, his hands open. The bishop gestured and two guards on foot stepped forward to meet him. Thomas closed his eyes, wrapping his thoughts around the coiled energy inside his body and the simple spell he hadn't been able to try that afternoon.

He opened his eyes, and lightning spewed from his hands.

The world turned brilliant white and crashed with thunder. The guards about to touch him were flung away. Four horses tumbled to the ground, taking the burnt remains of their riders with them. Two other riders toppled off their mounts. The animals panicked; bucking, rearing, and bolting. Thomas raised his hands and another wave of lightning sprayed out. More men died. Bolts crashed into the stables and house and chapel. Wood exploded outward and the buildings lit up with sudden flame. The stable with its thatched roof blazed instantly into an inferno. From inside the house and chapel, there was a red, smouldering glow. Thomas turned, looking for the bishop. He spotted the man, stumbling away, leaning against his familiar's shoulder.

Thomas tried to call the lightning again, but the power wasn't answering. He took a ragged breath, and then turned to his friends. "*RUN!*"

His friends, still half-deaf and reeling from the force of the blast, stared blankly at him. He yelled again and they caught on, stumbling towards the low wall. Henry reached it first, and stayed to help Eileen over before going himself. Thomas tried to chase after them and felt the strength fail in his legs. "George!"

George saw Thomas lose his balance and ran back. A stable hand stumbled in front of him. George knocked the man down with a fist and caught Thomas just as his knees hit the ground.

"I can't walk," gasped Thomas.

George tossed Thomas over his shoulder like a fresh-killed deer, then bent down and scooped up the rapier and dagger from the ground.

"Come on, George!" shouted Eileen.

George ran across the yard. Thomas hung on hard as he jolted on his friend's shoulder. They reached the fence and George vaulted it, Thomas on his shoulder, without slowing down. In the field, Benjamin was struggling to hang onto the frantic horses. Henry, first there, grabbed two sets of reins and held them while Eileen mounted. George caught up and threw Thomas over the back of his horse. Thomas righted himself and took the reins.

"Are you all right?" Eileen demanded, riding up beside him.

"Yes," Thomas gasped. The weakness wasn't as bad as it had been before, and he could feel some of the strength coming back to his legs. Thomas wondered if it was actually easier to call lightning than throw a boulder, or if he was just getting used to it.

"Hey!" George shouted. Thomas caught the grips of his weapons as George thrust them towards him. Thomas sheathed the weapons and looked back to the bishop's yard. The bishop's stable was truly on fire now, and the house was beginning to catch as well. The men in the yard had dragged themselves into some semblance of order. Two of the surviving stable hands were readying themselves to charge into the barn. The soldiers were starting a bucket brigade. Thomas spotted Randolf, staggering as he dragged his master towards the chapel.

"We've got to get out of here!" shouted George as he mounted. "Now!"

Thomas, weary in every bone of his body, wished with all his heart he could agree. "You go. I've got to get to the chapel."

"Don't be insane!" Eileen snapped. "You can't go in there!"

"The books are in there," Thomas said, wheeling his horse around.

"You don't know that!"

Thomas charged towards the low stone wall. The horse tried to shy away but Thomas kept it on course. It jumped, clearing the fence with room to spare. Thomas drove the animal across the yard, ignoring the shouting and stumbling bodies around him. Randolf saw Thomas riding directly at them. He shoved the bishop's semi-conscious form to one side and jumped the other way. Thomas ducked his head low and charged into the chapel.

The back of the building was empty; standing room for worshippers of the lower classes. Near the front, boxed seats were set on either side of a central aisle. Above him, flames licked one corner of the roof and were spreading to the support beams. Smoke was starting to roll across the ceiling. His horse shied and Thomas had to fight to keep the beast moving forward. There was a large metal box sitting in the middle of the floor before the altar. He pulled the horse to a stop and tried to dismount, nearly falling as the animal spooked and reared beneath him. Thomas got his feet under him and held tight to the reins as he stumbled towards the box. It was unlocked, with only a thick bolt holding it shut. Thomas pulled the bolt and threw the lid open. Three large, thick books lay inside. Thomas began to pull them out and realized he wouldn't be able to hold one, let alone three while riding. He'd have to get them into his saddle bags. He grabbed for his horse, hoping the books would fit.

Someone in the doorway yelled.

Thomas turned. Randolf was charging at him. Thomas threw one of the books at him and backed away, letting his horse go and, pulling his blades out. The horse spooked, backing itself into a corner and turning one way and another, its nostrils flaring. The familiar ducked the flying book, and attacked. Thomas was far slower than he should have been, and could barely keep the other man off. The black-clothed man kept attacking, cut after cut, thrust after thrust, driving Thomas back as fast as he could. Thomas put a pair of the boxed seats between himself and his opponent and kept backing away. The other man thrust over them, point seeking heart and eyes. Several times the blade nearly pierced Thomas's flesh. The smoke was growing thicker, and Thomas was sure that the entire roof was about to catch fire.

Hooves clattered against the chapel floor. George, bellowing a cry that shook the rafters, ducked through the door and charged. Randolf dodged as George's thick walking stick swung at his head. George pulled the reins to turn the horse, but Randolf was quicker, stepping in and driving his blade, hard and deep, into George's side. George let out a cry and grabbed the blade in his hand, holding it tight. Thomas, stepped forward and thrust his own weapon into the black-clad man's throat, then ripped it viciously free with a twist of his wrist. Randolf dropped, dying, to the ground, pulling his sword from George's flesh as he fell. George cried out and clutched his side.

"George!"

"Don't just stand there!" George snarled, hand pressed tight to the bloody wound in his side. "Get the books!"

Thomas ran to his horse and grabbed for the reins. It took him several tries to get a grip as the horse, now on the edge of panic, darted back and forth against the wall. George rode over, using his own horse to block the beast's motion while Thomas tried to calm it down. The animal didn't stop moving, but was hemmed in enough that Thomas could force two of the books into his saddlebags. The last book he shoved into George's saddlebag, then he tried to mount. The horse wouldn't hold still, and Thomas, his legs beginning to buckle again, barely managed to grab hold and gain a seat. George waited for Thomas to mount then both headed for the door. George all the while gripping his bleeding side and cursing through clenched teeth. The bishop was standing, dazed, in the doorway.

"Go!" Thomas shouted. "Ride him down!"

George whipped his animal into motion. The horse, already skittish from the smells of smoke and blood, leapt forward. Thomas followed hard after. The bishop must have regained some of his senses, for he stumbled out of the way. The two animals burst out of the church and into the yard. Henry, Eileen, and Benjamin were still in the field, waiting. Thomas and George drove their animals across the yard and over the fence to meet them.

"Back to the circle!" Thomas shouted. "They won't be looking for us for a while." He turned to George. He could see deep red spreading, not only from George's wound, but through the light that surrounded his friend. He suddenly felt very afraid. "Can you ride?"

"Aye," the big man said through gritted teeth. "Just get us out of here."

They ran, hooves pounding across the field, then down the road. From the town, Thomas could see torches being lit and people stumbling out into the streets. The five charged through, scattering the people and nearly running several down. They left the main road and followed another, then turned off onto the path towards the stones. The forest swallowed them, forcing the horses to slow to a walk as the moonlight vanished behind the thick leaves above. Thomas, his vision bright with the greens of the living forest, led them onward until they found the lone standing rock, and the stone circle beyond.

As soon as they reached the clearing, Thomas was off his horse, ignoring the weakness in his own body as he raced to George. The others stared at him until he shouted, "George is hurt!"

All three were off their mounts at once, and rushed to help. The big man slid to the ground, almost crushing Thomas. Benjamin and Henry raced to either side and hauled him up.

"Put him against a tree," Thomas said. "We don't know if he's been pierced through the lung."

"I don't think so," George growled. "By the Four, it hurts, though."

The two men put him down against the nearest tree, and tried to staunch the flow of blood. It oozed from the wound, despite their best efforts. Thomas was terrified George would bleed to death. He pulled the spell book out from under his shirt and paged through it for a healing spell. He was light-headed and dizzy with fatigue from the magic he had performed, and sickened to his soul by all the killing.

Eileen wrapped blankets around her brother. "Anything?"

"I'm looking," said Thomas, flipping one page after another.

"Hurry!" she was crying, now. "Please!"

"I'm trying!"

"I'll get a fire going," said Henry to Benjamin. "We need to keep him warm."

Eileen took George's hand and squeezed it tight. Benjamin worked on the wound, adding more cloth and doing his best to keep George conscious and upright. Henry gathered together wood and dumped it into the fire-pit. Thomas went through the rest of the book and found nothing.

He swore ferociously and hurled it at the ground. "It's useless!"

He turned towards the horses and the world spun around him with the sudden movement. He stumbled forward, lost his balance and fell. The world faded to grey, then cleared.

"Thomas?" Eileen was desperate now.

Thomas tried to rise. His legs refused to move, and the darkness was getting ready to overwhelm him. "I can't walk," he said, trying to get to his feet. "Get the books from the saddle bags! Mine and George's!"

Eileen ran for the horses, pulling the books free and practically throwing them at Thomas. He opened the first and began skimming through it. Behind him, the fire sparked into being, Henry gently nurturing its small flame.

Eileen grabbed one of the books and thrust it at Henry. "Look through it!" she snapped. "Find a spell of healing!"

Eileen took the last book and slammed it to the ground beside the fire. She knelt above it and peered close to read the words by the dim light of the new flames. "Stay awake!" she shouted at Thomas.

"I will," Thomas promised, though he was not at all sure he could. The world kept spinning at random times, and more than once everything went black. He forced himself to stay conscious, to keep looking.

The spell book in his hands was very thick, but only had two dozen or so spells, and only half of them actually glowed with magic. He skimmed through the ones that did. Each spell was written out in the greatest possible detail, taking up a dozen or more pages. The first two summoned insects, the ones after summoned different types of birds and animals. One summoned fish. Three of the last four were for summoning the Banished, but they didn't glow with any magic at all. The academic part of Thomas's mind that wasn't desperate to save George wondered if there were any theological implications to that. Thomas didn't bother to think about it, and paged quickly through to the last spell, hoping it would be for healing.

The last spell in the book was for summoning power, and like the three before it, the ink lay dead on the page, devoid of an signs of magic. Thomas was about to toss the book aside, when the word *sacrifice* caught his eye. He began scanning the page, horrified as he read the opening details of the ritual.

"Is it there, Thomas?" Eileen demanded from her place at the fire.

"No." Thomas pushed the book away. "It's not in there, but there's something else—"

"Who cares?" demanded Eileen. "Find something to help George! Hurry!"

"Here!" called Henry. "A spell for healing!"

Thank the Four, Thomas tried to force himself to his feet, but found that he could only crawl. He moved as fast as he could, reaching the fire and taking the book from Henry. "You hear that, George? Just hold on!"

"I hear." There was an eerie calm in George's tone, "Hurry, will you?"

"I am, I swear." Thomas read through the spell as quickly as he could then read it a second time. "All right. Henry, hold the book. Eileen, help me get to him."

Eileen grabbed Thomas and hauled him over. Thomas pulled the bandage away, making George hiss in pain, and placed his hands directly on the wound. Henry held up the book. Thomas read the spell once more then began chanting a series of five words. Each word was important, the book said. Each was specific and had to be said a specific way. He chanted them over and over again. Nothing happened. He turned his attention away from the book, taking the words from memory and focusing all his attention on George's body. The man's inner light was fading. Thomas was terrified. He couldn't let George die.

He took a deep breath, letting the words come out on the exhalation and focused on the wound. He did it again, and again, and again.

When white light came from his hands, he nearly started to cry.

He kept the chant up, kept concentrating on healing George's body. He could feel energy moving through his body and into George. George's light began to glow brighter. His breathing became deep and slow. Thomas kept up the chanting until George reached down and captured both of Thomas's hands in one of his own.

"Thomas," George said softly. "Look."

Thomas followed George's eyes down, saw that where the gaping hole had been in the man's side, there was only a small scar.

"You healed me, Thomas," George was smiling. "You healed me."

"Oh." Thomas sat back onto his heels. "Good."

The world turned black and somewhere in the very great distance he felt his body hitting the ground. After that, there was nothing.

Chapter 32

"Get up! Thomas, GET UP!"

It sounded like Eileen, but very far away.

"Get up. Now!"

People keep saying that to me.

Someone slapped him, hard and stinging. *"GET UP!"*

Eileen's voice was suddenly much closer. Thomas's eyes snapped open just in time for Eileen to hit him again. His head rocked to the side. He brought his hands up to protect his face.

"I'm up, I'm up!" Thomas blinked until his eyes focused. The night was much darker than when they had left the bishop's house. The moon had set, leaving only the stars to cast what little light they gave down on them all. Thomas shook his head, rubbing his face to clear away the effects of the slaps. "I'm up. Why are you hitting me?"

"Get on your feet." Eileen pulled him into a sitting position. "They're coming and you have to get up."

Thomas put his feet under him. However long he had been unconscious, it had helped. His limbs no longer felt like they weighed a hundred pounds each. He no longer felt in danger of passing out with every motion. Still, he didn't really feel awake. He forced himself to stand and looked around. He was inside the stone circle, with his friends crouched in the underbrush around him, waiting. George and Benjamin were closest, on either side of the rock slab that he had been lying on. Henry was crouching a short distance away. "Why are we in the circle?"

"It's the best place," said Henry. "There's no way they can bring the horses in here."

"They?" Thomas saw no one. "The bishop?"

"His men. George took watch after you passed out. He spotted them coming through the woods. Can you call lightning again?"

"I don't know." Thomas closed his eyes, looked inside himself and found the power, still there and still as strong as ever. He reached for it and nearly blacked out. Eileen caught him, holding him up. "I can't," said Thomas. "I'll pass out before I can do any good."

"Wonderful." Henry turned away, peering out into the darkness. "I hate night fighting."

Thomas reached for his sword-belt and realized he wasn't wearing it. Eileen pointed. His weapons were on the ground next to where he'd been lying. He picked the sword and dagger up and unsheathed them both. "It's not night for me," Thomas said. "I can still see in the dark."

"Good."

"Listen," hissed George.

It was the sound of hooves, drumming on the earth that made up the trail, and of branches being snapped back as the riders pushed through the forest.

"How many?" asked Thomas.

"All of them that are still alive," whispered George. "A dozen at least."

"All right," Henry kept his voice pitched low. "Spread out in a line. Find a place to hide. No one moves until I do. Scream as you attack. Try to kill at least one before they have time to react." He turned to Benjamin. "Can you do this?"

Thomas looked at the sword in Benjamin's hand. It seemed awkward there, and Benjamin stared at the blade as if he had never held it before. "I don't know."

"Try," said Henry, his voice hard. "Right, spread out."

Thomas took a deep breath, hoping the extra air would steady him. His friends crouched low in the brush, save for Eileen, who stayed beside him. He saw her expression, and reached for her hand. She crouched down with him.

"I'm sorry," Thomas whispered. "I truly am."

"Me, too." Eileen suddenly hugged him tightly, squeezing him with all her strength. He squeezed back just as hard, his blades making an awkward cross behind her back. The noise from the horses was getting louder, closer. Thomas released her.

"Stay out of sight," he whispered. "With luck, they won't even notice you."

"But you and George—"

"Will fight better knowing that you're safe. Please," he added when she hesitated. "Let us do this. All right?"

"Aye."

"Have your knife out. If one tries to grab you, stab for his face or cut at his throat."

She swallowed convulsively. "I will." Tears started flowing down her face, and Thomas felt his own answering. "Oh, Thomas."

"Shush!" He took her in his arms again, pulling her down behind the cover of the tree and kissed her desperately. She kissed back, her body arching hard against his. He held her as long as he dared, then let her go. She slid back into the bushes, still in sight to Thomas, but not to anyone else.

The flicker of yellow torchlight lit the night. The soldiers entered the little clearing beyond the circle. Half stayed on their horses, scanning the trees while the others tore the camp apart. Every bag and saddle bag was torn open. Every article of clothing was torn apart. The basket of food was scattered to the ground.

Thomas realized immediately what they were looking for. He turned to Eileen. She pointed behind them, to a clump of underbrush just below the edge of the center stone. All the books were wedged there, both his and the bishop's.

"Search the area," ordered one soldier. He was burly and dressed slightly better than the others. "Fifty yard sweep in a circle around me. Look for freshly turned earth. They must have hidden them somewhere."

The mounted soldiers got off their horses to join in the line of men that was starting to stretch into the woods.

"What if they have the books with them?" asked one soldier.

"Then we flush them out and take them."

"What if he does that trick first?" demanded another.

"Kill him when you see him," was the answer, "and he won't get a chance."

The soldiers disappeared into the woods at the far side of the clearing. The light of their torches marking off the path of their slow circle. Thomas watched them for a moment then looked back at the books. Moving almost without sound, he picked one up and opened it. Eileen gestured at him to stay hidden. He shook his head, waving her back into the bush. She sank back, and he turned his attention to the books.

The first had the healing spell, but nothing else of use.

The second book he opened was the book of summoning. The glance he'd had at the book before told him which ritual the bishop was intending to enact that night, and the fury he didn't have the time to feel before began to rise inside him He closed the book and set it aside, knowing that what he wanted wasn't there.

The third book had the spell he wanted.

Eileen hissed. The sound of bodies moving through the wood had grown louder. Within the green glow of the trees he could see the red lights of the soldiers, moving slowly through the brush. His friends, he knew, couldn't see anything but the occasional glimpse of torchlight in the pitch black of pre-dawn.

There was still time. He turned his attention back to the book, memorizing every word, putting the spell into his mind as solidly as possible. It was a simple spell, and Thomas had no doubt he would remember it.

Bushes shook nearby. The light of torches had grown stronger, almost illuminating the thick brush of the circle. The first soldier was nearly at the circle's edge. He gently set the book down and took up his blades again. Beside him, Eileen crouched lower, trying to blend into the bush. His friends were still, weapons clenched tightly in their hands. Benjamin's lips were moving in a silent prayer.

The soldiers advanced through the gaps between the stones, moving slowly and carefully. It was impossible for Thomas to believe that he and his friends had not been seen, even though the soldiers only had the light of their torches.

The soldiers were almost on top of them when Henry impaled one on the tip of his rapier.

"Kill them all!" Henry screamed. "ATTACK!"

Thomas, George, and Benjamin rose up screaming. The heavy thud of wood meeting flesh told Thomas that George had taken one. He had no time to think about it. He thrust his own blade into the closest soldier. The man cried out in surprise and pain. Thomas twisted the blade out and went after the next man. The soldier in front of Benjamin stumbled back but kept his feet. Three dead in the first moments of the fight.

The torch-light flickered madly as the soldiers returned the attack. They were well-trained, and now that the initial shock was gone, their greater numbers were turning into a great advantage. Fighting began to condense into little knots of action as the remaining soldiers attempted to surround the friends. The underbrush hampered their movements. Blades clashed and men shouted in rage and pain.

"Now," screamed Henry. "Call the lightning now!"

All the soldiers stumbled back, looking wildly for lightning. Henry and Thomas used the moment to attack. Two more soldiers fell. George and the man he had been fighting both jumped back and ended up staring at each other.

Benjamin made a queer grunting noise and fell to his knees, clutching at his stomach. George, still free of his opponent, charged over, bellowing like a bull and swinging his stick for all it was worth. Another man dropped. Benjamin, behind him, struggled to get to his feet, one hand holding his stomach. The man that had been fighting George charged in again.

Blades flashed back and forth, steel flashing yellow in the torch-light and clashing hard against other steel. They were still outnumbered. Thomas and Henry pressed their attacks, but couldn't do more than hold their own. George, driven back by two attackers, lost his balance and went down in a tangle of brush. One of the soldiers stepped in to finish him off.

Eileen screamed and charged, ducking low and burying her knife in the man's leg. He yelled in pain and shoved hard against her, sending her sprawling. His companion stepped forward and drove his boot into her face. She hit the ground like a broken doll. The second man kicked her again and the first raised his sword above his head.

Benjamin tackled the man, knocking them both to the ground. The other soldier stabbed down at the big student as George rose to his feet. The big smith out a terrible cry and swung hard, knocking the man flying. George raised his own boot and stomped down hard. The man Benjamin had tackled didn't get up.

Neither did Benjamin.

Thomas dodged and parried furiously against his two attackers until one soldier left an opening. Thomas thrust forward, burying his blade in the man's body. It stuck. The man collapsed, pulling Thomas off balance. His companion took advantage of the moment to slash hard. Thomas attempted to parry with the dagger, but didn't quite succeed. The force of the blow and the cut made his dagger hand go numb. The weapon dropped from nerveless fingers. Thomas pulled hard on his rapier, freeing it just in time to parry the man's second cut and hack into the man's neck. The soldier fell.

Thomas, with no other opponent in reach, ran to help Henry. The young noble was fighting hard against the two remaining soldiers. Thomas stepped forward, cut the legs out from one soldier and buried his point into the man. The last soldier died on Henry's sword.

Thomas turned looking for others. The soldiers' commander was retreating across the clearing with George stalking him like a bear on a doe. The commander swung his sword back and forth, trying to keep George at bay. George kept advancing. The soldier's courage broke and he fled for his horse. He had almost mounted when George caught him. The sound of the blow that killed the man reverberated through the clearing.

The silence, after the noise of battle, was overwhelming. Torches, dropped by the soldiers, guttered on the ground, their flickering light made the shadows dance over the bodies. The wounded moaned on the ground. Thomas could see the inner lights of those still living. Some were stained deep red, others fading slowly into darkness.

Henry came towards him, bleeding from half a dozen places. "Are you all right?" the young noble asked.

"I think so. You?"

"Aye."

Thomas looked around the circle again. "Where's Eileen?"

"I don't know," Henry peered around them. "Where's Benjamin?"

"I don't know."

George stumbled over. "Where's Eileen?"

"I don't know," said Thomas. "I'm looking."

Thomas stumbled back, casting around the ground for the place she'd fallen. He caught sight of her shirt, shiny with blood. "Here!"

George ran over, pushing Thomas aside and gently picking up his sister. He cradled her in his arms. She moaned at the movement.

"How is she?" asked Thomas.

"Her nose is wrecked," said George, crying. "Her face is cut."

"I can see that," snapped Thomas. "How's her skull?"

George ran his hands over it. "All right, I think."

From behind them, Henry started to swear slowly, despairingly. Thomas went over.

Benjamin's body was still entangled with the man he had tackled to save Eileen. There was a gaping wound between his ribs where the other soldier's thrust had ended his life. Henry cursed again, then knelt down and closed his friend's eyes. Thomas felt part of his own life flowing out of him as he looked at his friend's body. A dozen moments flashed into his head; arguments over theology and nights in the tavern and quiet moments of study and reflection. Tears started to well up into his eyes even as he realized he didn't have time for them.

Thomas stumbled away from Benjamin's body towards the books. He picked them up and found the one he needed. It had blood on the cover. He nearly threw up, but forced back the gorge. He went over to George and Eileen.

George raised his eyes from his sister as Thomas came close. "Can you help her?"

"Not now," Thomas said. "I can't reach the magic, now, and we have to get Bishop Malloy."

"Not tonight," Henry's voice was cold and distant. "We aren't in any shape to face anyone. We need to get better." He still stared down at Benjamin's body. "Then we can kill him. Slowly."

Thomas felt his own grief beginning to well up and he forced it ruthlessly down. "It can't wait."

"Why not?" Henry demanded, still looking at Benjamin's body. "The bishop has no men left. What can he do?"

"He's sacrificing children."

The silence that greeted that statement was as large as the star-filled void above them.

Henry took his eyes off of Benjamin and put them on Thomas. Thomas handed him the book, opening it to the spell. The young noble took it in one hand, skimmed the first page in the light of the fallen soldier's torches, then dropped it to the blood-soaked ground. "Bastard."

"What does he want with children?" asked George, cradling his sister closer.

"He's using them to build his power," said Thomas. "The spell is supposed to bring the caster great magic. The power of life that flows in his victims' blood is supposed to be drawn into the caster as the blood empties from their bodies."

"Why?" demanded Henry. "Why didn't he just come here?"

"Because this," Thomas waved a hand at the stones, "gives temporary power. The blood spell is supposed to be permanent."

"Bastard."

"Aye." Thomas shook his head. "And the worst thing is, it doesn't even work."

"It doesn't?" echoed George. "Then why is he doing it?"

"Because he can't tell which spells work and which don't," said Thomas. "I can."

"How are we going to stop him?" George asked, wiping at his face with a free hand. "Eileen's still unconscious. Benjamin..." He glanced at the man's body, then away. "Henry and I are practically in pieces and so are you."

"Me?" Thomas remembered that his left arm had felt numb and looked down at it. The pain that had been hiding behind shock started to race down to the tips of his fingers. Blood was oozing from a deep cut across his arm, just below his shoulder. Thomas tried to flex his hand, and the movement brought a rush of pain. He had half a dozen other, smaller cuts as well. Thomas realized he had no idea where they came from. "I guess I am."

"How long before he kills the children?" Henry asked.

"Just before sunrise." Thomas looked up at the sky and guessed, "Maybe an hour, if that."

Henry got up. "Then let's hope he's still at his house."

Thomas shook his head. "He won't be. The book said that the ritual must take place in a place of great death and carrion. I doubt his house will do."

"It might after tonight," said George.

"Not enough," said Thomas. "Great death and carrion means a battlefield."

"Benjamin said there was a battlefield around here," Henry looked again at his fallen friend. "Maybe the bishop built his house on it."

"Or the chapel," said Thomas. "He had the books in the chapel. Maybe it's built on the battlefield."

"As good a place to start as any," Henry knelt beside Benjamin and put his hand on his friend's brow. "We'll be back for you."

Thomas felt the grief rise up again, and for a moment it nearly overwhelmed him. He pushed it aside and started making his way out of the circle. "What do we do about Eileen?" asked George, not budging. He was still cradling her in his arms. "We can't leave her here."

"Then take me with you." Eileen's voice was small and strained. All three young men turned to look at her. Thomas fell to his knees beside her, taking her hand. She blinked at him. "Did we win?"

Thomas, seeing the blood smeared on Eileen's face, and the way her nose was crooked, felt tears coming again. He forced them away, forced himself not to think about his injuries or George and Henry's wounds or Benjamin's body. "Aye. We won."

"Fat lot of help I was," Eileen said bitterly, trying to hold the front and back of her head at once.

"You kept one from killing me," said George, petting her arm. "That's help enough."

"I suppose."

"Come on," Thomas pushed himself to his feet, ignoring the weariness and light-headedness that the motion brought. "We have to get going."

"I heard," Eileen muttered. She reached up an arm and got hold of George's shirt. "Help me to sit up. And get me a sword, this time."

George did, moving her slowly and gently. She was bleeding from the back of her head as well, Thomas realized. "How's your skull?"

"Hurts," Eileen ran her hands over the bloody hair on the back of her head. "But still intact, I think."

"I'll heal you as soon as we take care of the bishop," Thomas promised.

"Heal Benjamin, too," she whispered. "Saw him go down."

Thomas had no answer to that. Henry came close, handing a soldier's sword to George. George hefted it in one hand, his walking stick in the other. Henry gave Eileen Benjamin's rapier.

Eileen took it and then realized what it was. Tears welled up in her eyes. "Oh, no."

"Keep it," said Henry, his voice as tightly controlled as Thomas was trying to make his own. "He has no use for it."

Thomas exhausted and numb, forced himself to head for the horses. "Come on. Let's finish this."

* * *

They were a motley looking group by the time they got going. Strips of shirts and skirts served as bandages, and all four wore them. Blood—theirs and the soldiers'—stained their clothes. The smell made the horses skittish, and the lack of rest and a hard night's riding made them listless. Thomas was pretty sure he knew how the animals felt, but kicked his beast hard anyway and managed to get something of a trot out of it. The eastern sky was beginning to lighten.

The others followed in his wake, forcing their own tired horses as fast as they could. They broke free of the forest and rode toward the town. The place was dark once more. Those who had gone to fight the fire had returned to their beds, leaving the streets empty and silent. The four passed through the town like ghosts in the grey pre-dawn light.

The bishop's yard was a mess. Spilled water from the well had turned the dirt to mud. The stables were a mouldering ruin of jutting timbers and supports. Two stable hands, survivors from the earlier battle, were wearily tossing buckets of water on the few remaining hot spots. The house had sustained some minor damage, but the chapel was in much worse shape. The roof was half gone, and Thomas could see the light of flames, still flickering from within.

It took him a moment to realize that it wasn't a fire running uncontrolled, but the flames of torches. He kicked his horse harder, and charged into the yard. The two stable hands turned and ran at the sight of the four riders, blades drawn and clothes spattered with blood. Thomas didn't bother with them. From within the chapel he could hear someone chanting, and other younger voices, high and muffled, screaming in panic. He pulled the beast to a stop and dismounted, the others following. The doors were locked.

"George!"

George tested the doors once, then took a step backwards and kicked them with all his strength. They burst open, bolts flying off in either direction. Thomas stepped in, his friends right behind.

The front of the church had been changed. The altar had been pushed aside, the fixings cast into a corner. The entire place smelled of blood now, and the floor where the bishop was standing was awash in it. His chanting grew louder and faster, his eyes blazing as he stared at Thomas and his friends, but he didn't move. He had a thick-bladed knife in one hand. On the floor, Thomas could see the children, tied, gagged, and blindfolded. One wasn't moving, and his blood was oozing over the bishop's feet.

Thomas and his friends charged.

The bishop held out a hand, spoke a word Thomas didn't understand, and fire flew out from his fingertips to strike at them. Thomas ducked low and the flames passed over. George's shirt caught fire. He howled, dropping his sword and using his big hands to slap the flames out.

A second word flew from the bishop's mouth, and this time lightning speared out, catching Thomas and Henry both in the center of the chest and sending them crashing back. Thomas landed hard on his back. Henry, trying to dive out of the way, was slammed back into the boxed seats. The bishop was not nearly as strong as Thomas, and the spell only burned and knocked the wind out of them.

Eileen, untouched by the attacks, charged forward. She yelled, loud and long and full of rage, and swung Benjamin's rapier at the bishop. The bishop jumped back and spoke a word. Fire erupted again, directly in Eileen's face. The yell became a scream and she dove to one side, frantically covering her flesh and slapping at her hair to douse the flames.

The bishop raised his hand again, opened his mouth to speak. George, still on fire, threw his walking stick, hard. The thick knob on the end collided with the bishop's skull.

The man reeled backwards, tripped on one of the children and fell, his arms sprawled out to either side. Thomas shoved himself back to his feet and charged. The bishop was half-way back up when Thomas drove the heel of his boot into the man's face. Bishop Malloy sprawled back. Thomas slashed out with the rapier, cutting deep into the man's wrist. The bishop's dagger rolled out from his suddenly useless fingers. Thomas cast his sword away and jumped on the man's chest. The bishop tried to grab for him and Thomas drove the pommel of his own dagger into the man's forehead with a resounding *crack*. The bishop's head snapped back, bouncing off the floor.

Thomas reached inside himself for the power that he knew was there. It didn't want to come. He made it come anyway, forcing it out from a place deep inside. Suddenly it was all-encompassing. The world shifted and it was all Thomas could do to stay conscious as the power buzzed through his body. His rage kept the darkness back. He placed his hand onto the bishop's chest.

"Give it to me," Thomas enunciated clearly. "Give it to me, now!"

The bishop, hardly conscious, still realized what Thomas was doing and started to struggle desperately. Thomas smashed him again with the dagger pommel. The bishop's head lolled sideways. "Give it to me!"

The bishop moaned and tried to fight, but had no real strength. Thomas now felt what he was pulling, felt the bishop's magic in his hand. He pulled harder, calling out all his power to do it. "You will give it to me, NOW!"

There was a feeling of tearing, and the magic, ripped from the bishop's body, flowed into his own. Thomas's exhaustion faded at once. The bishop had been collecting for a long time, Thomas realized. He sat there, astride the man's chest, feeling the power flowing through him.

"They're mine," the bishop said, his words slurred. "They'll always be mine."

"No, they won't," Thomas pushed himself to his feet, stumbling back from the bishop. He found his sword and picked it up. "I'm sending them back."

"They won't go." The bishop rolled over, pushing himself to his knees. Thomas watched him try to get up and fail. The man started crawling towards the boxed seats, slipping on the blood on the floor. "The magics follow the path they came from," the bishop slurred. "If you let them go, they come back to me." He reached the boxed seats, leaving bloody handprints on them as he pulled himself to his feet. "They will always come back to me." He sneered at Thomas. "And I will have yours, after the High Father's court gets through with you. I will pull it from your broken body before they hang you, and all your power will be mine."

Thomas looked down. The children lay practically at his feet. Three of them were staring, horrified, tears streaming down their faces and sobs coming out from between tight-clenched lips. The fourth lay still, her head mercifully turned away.

"Where did you get the children?" asked Thomas.

"Orphanage." The bishop let go of the seat box and wobbled. He grabbed it again. "Five miles from the town. It is run by followers of the High Father. I sent word when I arrived in town that we would have need of them, and that we might call unexpectedly."

Thomas looked at the body of the child on the floor. "Did you tell them why?"

"Of course not," Bishop Malloy sneered. "They would not understand."

"The spell you were doing," said Thomas, still looking at the child's body. "It doesn't work."

"What?" For a moment, the bishop's voice faltered. It grew strong again almost at once. "You're lying."

Thomas shook his head. "I can see magic, and there's no magic in that spell. It doesn't give any power."

"You're lying," hissed the bishop. "I had power. You took it! It was raising power!"

Thomas turned away from the three terrified, squirming children and the one who lay so still, to look at his friends. Eileen was cradling her burnt face in her arms, George kneeling beside her, his chest black and blistered. Henry was on his feet again, unsteady and blinking hard, as if he couldn't quite see. Thomas took them all in, then turned back to the bishop. Bishop Malloy was leaning against the boxes, struggling to make his way to the door. Thomas stepped lightly behind him. "Your Grace?"

The bishop turned, saw the weapon, and laughed, the sound bitter and angry. "Do you know what they'll do to you if you kill me?"

Thomas dropped forward into a full lunge, putting the weight of his body into the thrust. The bishop stood, eyes staring, mouth wide, until Thomas twisted the blade free. He remained standing, staring, a moment longer, then collapsed to the ground, dead.

Thomas stood there for a time and then turned to Henry. Thomas gestured at the three children—one boy, two girls—who were still alive, crying and squirming in their bonds. "We need to cut them free,"

"I will," promised Henry.

Thomas walked past his friends and out the door. He stopped on the chapel stairs and looked to the east. The sun was just breaking the horizon, casting rays of gold over the landscape. Inside him, he could feel the magic of many different spirits. There was power in him, now; power to wield all the magic that was in his book, without fear of falling unconscious.

Thomas watched the sun creep slowly up into the morning sky, and wondered what his family was doing.

It took only a thought to release the magic.

Most of the small magics flew out of his body, back to their owners. Some—from the ones the bishop had killed, Thomas guessed—stayed and merged into his own magic. He felt the joining inside, felt himself becoming more than he was before.

Timothy's magic was inside him.

The thought made Thomas smile just as he realized that, without all the small magics inside him, he wasn't going to remain standing very long.

He managed to sit himself down and lean against the wall of the chapel before he, very predictably, passed into unconsciousness.

Epilogue

It took over a month to get home.

Thomas, George, Henry and Eileen were arrested and gaoled that morning, charged with the deaths of the bishop and his men. That afternoon, the surviving children told their story. By evening, the four friends were out of the gaol and given rooms at the inn to await the High Father's inquisitors and the king's sheriffs.

They buried Benjamin the next day, in the Seaview cemetery, and spent the night grieving.

Thomas took the time before meeting the authorities (whoever they were going to be) to heal his friends, taking away the worst of their injuries and burns. The four also worked out their story, sticking as close to the truth as they could without mentioning Thomas's magic. The inquisitors and the sheriffs arrived on the same day, and the arguments began. The right to arrest them was hotly contested between church and state. Both wanted them, though neither side was certain what they could be charged with. In the end, the state won more by numbers than legal right. The four were escorted back to the city and to the king's Judgment. Henry sent word ahead to the Academy, and they were greeted by the head of the School of Law and his entire faculty.

After a week in a courtroom filled with much argument and debate, all the charges from Seaview were put aside. The four, it was decided, were heroes who fought bravely against great odds to try to save the four children. The manner of the bishop's death was left alone in light of the acts he had been practicing, which were abhorrent in the eyes of both the law and the church. George, Eileen and Henry were set free at once and Thomas was put in the cells under the School of Law to await news on the charges from Elmvale.

Thomas spent two weeks in the Academy gaol, waiting. The cells had been built for those students who broke the Academy rules or the king's law. No one was in them save Thomas. They were clean and well maintained, and the food he received was the same as the students ate in the dormitories. The gaolers, students themselves, gave him books to read. He wasn't allowed visitors. He spent the time thinking; about his family, about his friends, about Benjamin, and about the men he had killed.

He grieved for them all, letting the tears run down his face and sobbing into the darkness of the night as he lay awake on the small, hard bed.

Thomas saw the full moon rise from through the tiny window of his cell, and felt the great power he had borrowed at the stone circle fade away. He stared out of the window, watching the inner lights of the world fade away and knowing he would probably never see them again.

They didn't fade entirely.

The magics still inside him, from Timothy and from however many others the bishop had killed, were enough to let him see. The lights were dim but still there; faint, glimmering images of life in the darkness.

He sat on his bed, held out his hand, and called the ball of light. It glowed a strong, pale blue-white in the darkness of the cell. He thought of Timothy again, and smiled though tears flowed down his face.

In the middle of the second week, a messenger arrived from Elmvale. Ailbe had recanted her story. She was now saying that the bishop's familiar had killed Shamus. It took three more days of argument and debate, but in the end all charges were dropped and Thomas was granted his freedom.

When he stepped out into the open air he found Henry waiting for him. He looked around, and Henry smiled. "They're outside the gate. Given the trouble we've been in, I thought that sneaking them in wouldn't be that good an idea."

"True." Thomas and Henry walked down the wide path to the main gate. Students passing by immediately started whispering to one another. Thomas watched them, then raised an eyebrow to Henry. Henry shrugged. "You're famous," he said. "Though notorious might be a better word." He leaned in and lowered his voice, "Is the magic still there?"

"Some," said Thomas. "It's faded, but it's there." The thought led him back to the standing stones, and the fight there. "Henry, have you told Benjamin's parents?"

"I wrote them," said Henry. "They came and cleaned out his room. They let

Eileen keep the sword."

"Good." The thought of Benjamin's parents having to clean out their son's room freshened Thomas's own grief. He felt his eyes welling up, and wiped at them as the front gate came into sight.

Eileen was standing on the other side of the gate.

Thomas took off at a run, leaving Henry behind and dashing over the last dozen yards. Eileen, under the eyes of the guards, barely managed to keep herself from doing the same. She practically danced in place until Thomas rushed through the gates and wrapped his arms around her. She squeezed him tight, tears from her eyes wetting his cheeks. He squeezed back just as hard and turned his face to hers. They kissed, mouths hard against one another in shared passion and joy.

Behind him, Thomas heard Henry saying, "Aren't you going to do anything about that?"

George laughed. "They'd both have my ears if I did."

Thomas ignored them and went on kissing Eileen. He would have happily kept at it for the whole day, but yells and catcalls started coming from the Academy. Breaking away from the kiss, he saw a dozen or more students whistling and applauding. Eileen began giggling. Releasing her from his arms, he took one of her hands, and turned to face her brother. George's eyebrows were raised high.

"So, let you out did they?" George said, grinning. "Too bad."

Thomas stepped forward and embraced his friend. George returned it, hard enough to make Thomas's ribs creak. Thomas released his friend and stepped back. Eileen immediately caught his hand again.

"Well," said Henry. "Now what?"

"Now, we go to the Broken Quill," said Thomas. "We eat, we drink, and we celebrate me no longer being in gaol."

"And after that?" asked Eileen.

Thomas smiled and squeezed her hand, knowing exactly what she was thinking. "After that, we go home."

* * *

A week and a half later, the road turned down a hill, the forest gave way, and they were home.

It was evening when they reached the town common. The sun was heading past the horizon, its light catching the edge of the buildings and lending a gentle glow to everything it touched. The people were closing up their shops or having one last gab with their neighbours before heading home for the night.

Thomas pulled his horse to a stop and watched them for a moment, then turned to his friends. Thomas had treated them all to new clothes before they left the city, and they all were wearing them. George still had the soldier's sword at his side, though in a new scabbard, and Eileen wore Benjamin's rapier. Thomas grinned at them, sure they all looked outlandish.

"Home," George sounded immensely happy. "At last."

"Aye," agreed Thomas. He was nervous, he realized. "At last."

Eileen caught his tone and cocked her head at him. "What's the matter with you?"

"Nothing," Thomas said. "I'm just..."

"Afraid your father's still angry?" guessed George.

Thomas nodded. "Aye."

"He'll be glad you're back, now that all's done," Eileen said. "I'm sure of it."

Thomas wasn't. "I hope so."

Eileen pulled her horse beside Thomas's, leaned in and kissed him on the mouth. Thomas returned it while her brother gave his usual moan of disgust. Eileen straightened and smiled. "I'm sure of it."

"Thomas Flarety!"

The three turned in their saddles. Bluster was coming out of the inn and straight towards them. Thomas pulled his reins, turning his horse around to face the Reeve, and kicked the beast into motion. The two met half-way, and the Reeve looked up at Thomas disapprovingly. "As I recall, I told you not to go anywhere."

"Aye," said Thomas, smiling, "you did."

"And you saw fit to ignore me."

Thomas shrugged. "I wasn't guilty."

"Then you should have stayed to prove it."

"And there were these men trying to kill me."

"So I heard." Bluster shook his head. "You have a knack for getting into trouble, Thomas. I had to spread word through the county. The Academy even sent a messenger to see if it was true."

"I know."

"A lucky thing that woman came to her senses," said Bluster. "You could have been at the end of a rope."

"That's what they told me in the gaol."

Bluster glared at him, and Thomas smiled back. "Is Ailbe all right?"

"She wasn't until a few weeks ago. Some sort of shock, made her insane for a while. The smith's wife took her in, cared for her until she regained her senses."

"Is she still here?" Eileen asked, riding up. "At our house?"

The Reeve gave Eileen and her brother a withering look. "And here's the other trouble makers. Aye, she's at your place."

"We've got to go see her," Eileen declared. She tugged at Thomas's sleeve. "Will you come?"

"I'll be by," Thomas promised. "Maybe tomorrow, if all goes well."

Eileen grabbed his sleeve and pulled him closer. "It *will* go well," she said. "I'm sure it will."

They kissed again, long and slow. From below Thomas heard the Reeve saying, "How long has this been going on?"

"Far too long," said George, woefully.

They broke apart and Thomas gave a last squeeze to Eileen's hand. "I'll see you tomorrow."

"There's always a place under our roof," George said, riding to Thomas's other side. "Always."

Thomas held out his hand and George took it. Thomas gripped it hard. "Thank you."

George gripped back, then released Thomas and turned to his sister. "Time to tell our parents what you've been doing with the merchant's son."

"I haven't been doing anything," Eileen said, tossing back her hair. "Except the obvious."

Thomas, knowing the words were not quite true, grinned at her. She smiled back.

"Aye?" George looked from one to the other. "Well, if you get home first, you might even make them believe that."

Eileen's jaw dropped, and she started to turn bright red. "You wouldn't dare!"

George grinned. "See you!"

"You wouldn't!" Her words were futile, for George had already turned his beast and was heading to their house at top speed. Eileen threw a quick glance back at Thomas.

"It's all right," he said, laughing. "Go! Go!"

She pushed her heels into her own horse and drove the animal after her brother. Thomas watched them go, smiling to himself. At last, he turned back to Bluster. "Is my mother still at the convent?"

"Nay. About five weeks ago your father went up and started apologizing. After three weeks of it she came home."

"Good."

The older man nodded. "Well, I'll be off then." He turned his piercing gaze on Thomas once more. "Get going, lad. He misses you."

Thomas nodded and nudged the horse gently with his heels. He rode through the village, past the buildings and people he'd known all his life. Several waved hello, then turned and started whispering to others. He'd be the centre of the town gossip for a month to come, at least.

The sun was nearly down and in the near twilight, Thomas took a good look at the village and its inhabitants. It was dark enough for him to see each person's inner light. They no longer blazed like torches in his sight, but glimmered faintly in white and blue and green and brown; the colours of the earth and sky.

Thomas rode out of the village and to his father's house. The light of candles burning in the front window cast a glow out onto the yard. Thomas reined his horse in, tied it to the gate and stepped up the path.

At least my clothes are much better this time, he thought. *Pity I'm still wearing the sword.*

He reached the door and raised a hand to knock. After a long hesitation, he let it drop to the handle instead. It swung open and he stepped into the front hall. There was no one in sight. Three more steps took him to the parlour door. His father, mother, and brother were sitting together, talking quietly. His mother spotted him first, and whatever words she was about to say died on her lips. His father and brother turned, following her gaze to Thomas.

Thomas wanted to speak, but the words stuck in his throat. His mother and brother were rooted in their places, not saying anything either. Thomas watched his mother's eyes dart back and forth between her husband and her youngest son. After a pause that felt like an hour, John Flarety pulled himself to his feet and stepped forward to meet his son.

"So." John opened his mouth to say more but stopped. He tried again, stopped again. He looked his son up and down. "So," he repeated. "New clothes."

Thomas nodded, his mouth dry. "I bought them before I left the city."

"They're good." The silence that followed was awkward, painful, and far too long for Thomas. John spoke again. "Still wearing the sword I see."

"Aye."

Neither moved, but the space between them grew immense. Thomas began to feel that the distance would never be crossed. Thomas's brother was not looking at all happy and Madeleine Flarety started to open her mouth to speak, when John stepped forward and embraced his son. "Oh, lad, I'm so sorry."

Thomas was stunned stiff at first, then relaxed and hugged his father back. "It's all right, now."

"No, it's not." John held his son a while longer, then stepped back enough to look into Thomas's eyes. "I treated you badly. You and your mother and your brother. I don't know why…"

"I do," Thomas said. "And I'll tell you all about it."

"You do?" John smiled at his son. "I'm glad, because I don't." He gripped Thomas's shoulders, hard. "I will make this up to you, Thomas. I'm not sure how, but I will make it up to you. *I promise.*"

On the last words, his father's voice changed, becoming like fresh, warm honey. Thomas smiled, feeling his father's magic wash over him. He could see John Flarety's inner light shining brighter as he spoke the words. He looked to his mother and his brother, saw their own lights shimmering, brighter than the dim glow of the candles.

His father embraced him again, and his mother and brother came forward to join them. They held tightly for a long time. Thomas felt tears of relief and joy welling into his eyes. He let them flow.

"Right, then," John Flarety stepped back and wiped his own eyes. "I'll bet you're hungry. We'll get some food put together for you at once, then you can tell us everything that happened. Unless you have some news that can't wait until we've fed you?"

Thomas thought about that, "Well, I'm courting the smith's daughter."

"What?" His mother was shocked. "When did that happen?"

"About three months ago."

"And you didn't tell us?"

"I haven't told anyone. I've been busy."

"I'm sure you have." Thomas winced at her tone, and guessed that the explanations were going to take most of the night.

John Flarety intervened, laughing. "Come, we'll get him food first, and then he can tell us."

"All right," his mother still looked sternly at her younger son. "But you will tell us everything."

"Aye, I will," Thomas lied, knowing of some things he would definitely keep to himself.

"Good." John Flarety smiled at his son. "Come, then." He turned and led them towards the kitchen. "And do take that sword off in the house."

Thomas, feeling much better than he had in months, did what he was told.